c.1
Fie
Amo

14.99

THE CHOCOLATE LADY

Other books by Joseph Amamoo:

The New Ghana
Constitution Proposals for Post-coup Africa
The Ghanaian Revolution

THE CHOCOLATE LADY

by Joseph G. Amamoo

To Merrill School library
with best wishes to staff
and pupils.
Joseph Amamoo
Feb. 18, 1997.

Jafint Co., Publishers,
24 Hamilton Road, Dollis Hill,
London NW10 1NY U.K.

First published in 1993 by
Jafint Company,
24 Hamilton Road, Dollis Hill,
London NW10 1NY, England

C.1 1997
14.99

© Joseph G. Amamoo 1993
ISBN: 0-9522365-0-8

Printed in Finland by WSOY

Typeset and designed by: Culross & Sproston Ltd
6/7 Glebe Road, London E8 4BD, England

Dedicated with love to Breid, an outstanding Wife, Mother and Human Being

Chapter 1

The weather had been very bad in the past fortnight and particularly tonight, it was atrocious. Raining fiercely, with the usual tropical thunderstorms, and lightning, the Colonel could not sleep easily. He had been tossing in bed frequently thus constantly disturbing the peaceful slumber of his mistress, Sophia Fumey. Colonel Kofi Johnson was no ordinary Colonel in APPAPA, capital of the African State of BASSA. For only a week before this unnerving, sleepless night, he had once again been informed by the local Military Promotion Board that his long expected promotion to Brigadier had not been passed.

As he tried to sleep, but could not, he got up and put on the bedside light. "Sophia, I can't sleep at all. I don't know what's happening. I simpply don't feel good inside me, although I am not sick," he said half-heartedly. He fingered his moustache deliberately, and appeared for a few moments to be lost in thought.

"You know, although we've been friends, good friends for three years, it is only today I feel easy to tell you this - if the bastards keep playing monkey tricks with my promotion, as they have been doing, I will soon teach them a little lesson, his voice growing angrier as he went on. He paused.

"What do you really mean, Kofi?", Sophia meekly asked, rather annoyed that her sleep had been so unpleasantly inter-rupted. For although the Colonel and her were now almost man and wife, at least to his aide-de-camp, he only came to spend the night with her on Tuesdays. It was well known to her that Colonel Johnson's infrequent nocturnal visits were not due to any special demands of his work, but to the very active sexual life which he led in APPAPA, outside the barracks.

Still, she had never had a full explanation from Kofi, much as she persisted about his rather odd, irregular visits. As before,

1

she went on "Kofi, I don't wish to both you, but may I know why you visit me only on Tuesday?" She stopped for effect. Then she continued "You told me from the beginning that your mariage was, for all practical purposes, finished, yet I see less and less of you as time passes on".

Kofi smiled. It was a rather sad smile. After a long pause, he stroked his whiskers again, and then said "Darling Sophia, I will shortly, one of these days, tell you the whole truth, the real truth. At the moment my whole mind is confused, and of late, I feel as if two major, opposing forces are at war inside me. The truth is very simple, but rather unpleasant, but I promise, dear, I shal tell you. Don't worry". It was about three o'clock in the morning.

A few of the nocturnal, tropical birds were beginning to stir themselves for the day ahead. Hidden in the luxuriant trees and bushes around Sophia's two bedroomed, detached blue-painted bungalow in the Madina area of APPAPA, these sweet little birds, with their lovely, angelic tunes, felt far freer than the Colonel and his mistress.

"Chirp", "Chirp", "Chirp", the birds went on. Inside the chest of the Colonel his heart-beat, although regular was very forceful. There he lay in all his glory. A dark-brown African male of about 5ft 8ins, with jet black, close cropped, back swept hair, and a flourishing moustache. He was beginning to be chubby, but not yet fat. His general physique was very good and he was in robust health. His tight biceps and strong thighs showed that indeed his health was good.

At 40, Colonel Kofi Johnson, was beginning to feel that life was passing by. It is true that he was of very humble background from APANDI in BASSA, but subsequently after attending the local Roman Catholic School in his home town of KOKOPU, had later attended the MANTOW College, where he had later worked as a tutor. There, and throughout his life, his main interests had been women, booze and cigaretes in that order.

It was general disillusionment with life, coupled with a lack of progress at the MANTOW College which had finally decided him to join the BASSA Army. And up till now he had been a promising solider. Rising from the ranks, among whom his womanising, boozing and chain-smoking made him a popular figure, Kofi Johnson, had, "Thank God," he would often say, won a scholarship to the famous British Miliary Academy of Sandhurst. His record there was not exemplary. But it was not mediocre either. English friends and colleagues who knew him at Sandhurst remember him as always impeccably turned out, as an officer and a gentleman. Much as he enjoyed his period at Sandhurst, he had found it not fully satisfying. Kofi did not have much money to entertain. He also found the moral climate in Sandhurst rather stifling. As such, at every possible opportunity or leave, he quickly made a dash by train to London. There in the Borough of Hackney, among some of his old BASSAIN friends, he could indulge in all his passions to his full satisfaction. No wonder African conetmporaries of his at Sandhurst often noticed a marked change in him after a return from his London jaunts.

But on this fateful early morning, as he tried to kill the sleepless hours ahead of him, by reflecting over his past achievements in life, his disappointments and failures, he pondered over why once again the Promotion Board had blocked his promotion. To him the progress which had been made by his fellow officers was completely unjustified.

Whether the Colonel was aware of it or not, is not clear. But it must have dawned on him that his pursuit of women instead of military excellence, was the root-cause of his problems. In fact, at the last promotion exercise, which he was now fretting over, he had nearly got his expected leap forward, but for the President of the Board, by name Brigadier Kwame Battah. After a fierce discussion of Colonel Johnson's case, the board had split five to five against his promotion, Brigadier Kwame Battah, had, after briefly recounting some of the immoral activities of Kofi Johnson, used his casting vote to scupper the promotion of Kofi.

A few minutes later, as the meeting broke up in smiles, and professed cordiality, the Brigadier called a close colleague on the board aside. Remonstrating and whispering, he told him "That

3

stupid bugger was scheming to have sex with my wife. Look at it. Is that right, Colonel? I've fixed him up"!

Not knowing how to react to yet another story of Kofi's sexual escapades, Colonel Peter Sampson, just listened intently and nodded non-committantly. This was not the first time he had heard stories of sexual misbehaviour against Col. Johnson. He mused to himself that the alleged Johnson/Battah saga would probably not be the last that he would come to hear about Kofi.

The officers, with their promotion assignment over, retired to the near by officers' mess in MANDALAY camp for drinks. It was a modestly large concrete building, consisting mainly of a large hall, a restaurant, a bar and a library. It was a historic place. For a number of military coups had been conceived in the portals of this very place. Decorating the walls of the main hall were various regimental flags, trophies and plaques. Some of these commemorated the outstanding service of the BASSAIN Army, and its predecessor, the BASSAIN regiment, in historic battles in Ethiopia, India and Burma.

Meanwhile, Kofi Johnson continued to fret in his sleep. "You see, darling, these people at not being fair at all to me. Last two years, on some bogus grounds they refused to promote me. From my contacts on the board, I understand they talked a lot of nonsense about me being a chaser of women, drinking too much, smoking too much. They could find nothing, nothing at all against my career as a soldier". He stopped for a few split seconds. Sophia continued to listen to him patiently.

"This year too the damned idiots have done the same thing again. No sense of shame. No sense of fairness at all in their tones!" Sophia tried to coax him to go back to sleep, but he was too excited and angry to do so. Suddenly Kofi cooled down, and turning off his bedside lamp, closed his eyes to sleep.

But he could not sleep. So he got up, spruced himself and put on his mufti dress. It was about four o'clock in the morning. He kissed his mistress goodbye, and drove back to his office in camp. The orderlies and guards on duty were rather surprised to see him clock in so early, but then they were all used to the irregular hours of work of their affable, superior officer.

4

For a number of years, especially since he became a captain, Kofi had always kept a spare set of uniforms in his closet at his office. As such, he changed into his officer's uniform, sat in his chair for a few minutes, then decided to telephone his lonely wife at their home.

It was about 4.30 am and mrs Kofi Johnson was asleep. Throughout their ten year marriage, Margaret had got used to her husband's frequent acts of unfaithfulness. Many a time she had thought of leaving her husband. But again and again she had been persuaded by her parents, expecially her mother, to soldier on.

Margaret was an attractive, African woman of about thirty-two. Her face was rather round, with strong features, and her vital statistics were impressive. She knew herself that indeed if she left Kofi she would not be single for too long. But the old BASSAIN traditions and taboos among her people especially the APANDIS made it difficult to seek a divorce.

As a matter of fact she was having a lovely dream, when her husband's telephone call woke her. And in the dream, she was a bride getting married to a young, oil rich Italian businessman of about forty-five years.

"Hello, darling, I fear due to a rather hush-hush operation yesterday I've been out of the office for the whole day. I've just come in, and will be in about 5 pm. OK? Everything alright?", Kofi asked. Although he was not in love with his wife, he felt as an officer to maintain a certain modicum of civilised behaviour towards his wife. He was particularly attached to his three sons, who were then ten, eight and five.

Being rather used to her husband's brusque way of talking to her, Margaret felt that there was no point asking her husband too many questions. She knew that it would be the same old story of lies, lies and bigger lies. So she resumed her interrupted sleep, lying half awake and half asleep till about 6 o'clock when her maid came to knock, to announce her reporting for duty.

The early tropical birds, whose tuneful songs always open the day's activities for Africans were once again stirring themselves up.

5

Back in his office at MANDALAY camp Co. Kofi Johnson sat morose and moody at his desk. It was about 8.30 am. His batman brought him a cup of coffee. As usual, it was black, without sugar. As he sadly sipped it, he kept saying to himself, "Why, why, why?" "What in hell is happening?" He thought and thought but seemed to be getting nowhere. As he looked through the office windows, he could see the gardeners mowing the lawns, whilst the soldiers on duty, apart from the sentry-officer, stood or walked about languidly.

Kofi was continuing his self-analysis, and reflecting on his future calmly and quietly, when his messenger brought in his mail. Among them was one specific and important letter. It was from the Military Secretary at the camp, Col. Peter Kumi and the news was not good. It confirmed in writing the rumours which he had heard before and over which he had anguished with his mistress. It began in the way in which such letters of unwelcome news usually begin "Dear Col. Johnson, I regret to inform you that ...." He felt there was no point to read the rest. After all, he had sensed the contents even before the letter was written. Just as Kofi was thinking about what to do with the letter, whether to place it in his private, personal file, or fold it and put it in his wallet-pocket, the special red telephone rang. He nearly shouted, "What again?", but he controlled himself.

No less a person than the Commander of the Southern Brigade was on the phone. And Kofi knew that his boss, Brigadier Stephen Boateng, popularly known in the Army, by friend and foe alike, as 'Big Steve', was a fair-minded man. He was forty-five years old, married with two grown-up daughters and a son of fifteen.. Educated first at the BASSAIN Military Academy in APPAPA and later at Sandhurst in England, he was the old, British-trained type of officer - honest, straightforward and dedicated to his profession. He had no political interests whatsoever.

On the phone, he asked Kofi to see him at 12.30 for lunch if he was free. The Brigadier was ever such a polite gentleman, that often his colleagues chided him that he was in the wrong job. They felt he would make a brilliant television evangelist of

6

the American brand.

For the next hour or so, before his appointment with his superior, Kofi tried to think about what the Brigadier wanted him for. Could it be more woman trouble? He simply could not concentrate. He simply could not tell or guess what was in store for him in his confrontation with the Brigadier.

Musing over all the possibilities and probabilities ahead of him, he got out of his office and walked to the car park. As the solidiers nearby saluted obsequiously with broad smiles on their faces, he boarded his car. He drove the mile or so to the Brigadier's office and announced himself to the Brigadier's Secretary. It was a Tuesday and the time was 12.20 pm. The weather was clear and humid. It was a hot day, even by tropical weather standards.

Kofi was announced in. He smartly saluted the Brigadier, who beckoned him to a chair.Kofi, with all the many years of soldiering behind him, still felt rather nervous. The Brigadier, sensing the unease of his visitor went straight to the point. It was exactly 12.30 noon. "Kofi, I am so happy that you could come. Very good. For I wish to discuss some rather important matter with you" he said. The Colonel put on a bland, non-committal smile, as he really was not sure of what was coming.

The Brigadier went on "Needless to say, I am sorry to hear of your recent set back. I meant the promotion exercise". He paused. Kofi was boiling inside, but saw the need to control himself and let the Commander do as much of the talking as possible. He feared that he might say the wrong word at the wrong time.

Stephen continued, "I felt like inviting you here this afternoon to talk with you frankly about your future. Despite this major set-back, to you, I wanted to assure you that you are a highly-esteemed officer" "Thank you Brigadier", "I know that you are upset, but Kofi you should not be unduly depressed. These misfortunes, as the saying goes, are really blessings in disguise. As a confirmed believer in God, I am convinced that even misfortunes have a purpose in our lives".

Brigadier Stephen Boateng was well known among his

7

fellow officers, both low and high, as a good living, decent, fair minded, God-fearing officer. He was a happily married man, who was always distressed by the numerous rumours about the philanderings of Kofi. However, he had always maintained that there was some good in Kofi and he felt it his duty to help to bring it out.

"Whilst I cannot interfere in any way with the decision of the Promotion Board about you, I wish you, Kofi, to know that it's not all lost".

"That sounds encouraging, Sir", remarked Kofi. "But quite frankly , Sir, I feel so unfairly treated once again by the Army that sometimes I've wondered whether to call it a day. After all, Sir, if you are in my position ...." he was going on when Stephen mildly interrupted him.

"Colonel, remember you are an officer. Remember, these difficulties are all part of life!". He stopped and asked Kofi a question. "Kofi, are you ready to consider an offer which I have for you?" "Sir, I should be glad to do so. Naturally, the nature of the offer would also have to be taken into account", he replied, his voice becoming firmer as his confidence grew. For he was almost at the point where he really could not care less, whether the offer was an attractive one or not.

Finally, after a few seconds' hesitation, which felt like endless minutes to the Colonel, the Brigadier came out with his offer.

"Well, Kofi, last week the Chairman of the Joint Chiefs of Staff referred to me an invitation which he had received from his opposite number in the West Indies Armed Forces. It was a request to recommend to them an officer, not below the rank of Lieutenant-Colonel, to head a military commission into a mutiny in their army a month ago. I've thought carefully on this matter, and have decided to recommend you for the position". Before he could go any further, the Colonel, with a big, broad smile on the face, said, "Smashing, Sir, this is too good to be true". The Brigadier got up, straightened himself, and said, "Well, Colonel, I think we better go for lunch. Eh?" The Brigadier's official driver was called and the two officers left for the officers' mess. The menu for the day was very attractive. Over a mouthwatering dish of peanut beef stew, rice and ladies fingers, washed down with a glass of beer, the two officers concluded their discussion on Kofi's future.

"So I take it, Kofi, that I can put your name forward now to the Chief". remarked Stephen before they left the mess. The large smile on Kofi's face said everything. "Brigadier, I really feel very grateful to you. This has been the best news I've received for many years". He paused for a few split seconds to ensure that his mentor was happy with what he was saying. Believing that he was saying the right things at the right time, he went on "And, Sir, whilst on this matter, I wish to assure you that all the rumours about me being a raving womaniser, chain-smoker, frequently drunk, are simply not true..Well, not completely true. They are enormously exaggerated". All that his listener did was to put on a small, laconic smile. "And anyway, Sir, is it not odd and ironic, that those who are busily waging a smear-campaign against me in the camp, have personal records which are as disgusting as mine, if not worse! What about the alleged rape last week of the sixteen year old nanny from the north, by that Brigadier? What about the case of the Naval Commander who still has not accounted for the $20,000 U.S dollars that the Italian businessman was rumoured to have paid to his London account. Chief, I know a lot, far more than my detractors think or suspect and if they push me to it, I shall certainly go down the gutter with all of them".

The driver continued to drive, and soon they were back at Stephen's office. Kofi once again thanked his host, and went towards his own car. He went in, started the engine, and began to drive back to his office, smiling all the way.

As soon as he reached his office he sat at his desk and said a few prayers. Then he rang his wife. "Maggie, something good has happened. Great news. I am going to be appointed Head of a Military Tribunal in Jamaica soon. The official announcement is to be made any day from now. Yes, we're going abroad soon. You see, I always told you the series of bad luck on me will not be forever. This is the beginning of better days to come".

He could hear his wife's exclamantions of happiness and excitment at the other end of the phone. "Thank God, thank God, praise be his Name. Our enemies have been shamed!" She kept on saying until Kofi put down the phone, with a fond goodbye kiss.

As soon as he had put down the phone's receiver, he rang his mistress, Sophia. He was anxious to break the good news to her. But she was not in. After the phone had rung for a couple of minutes without any response, Kofi put the receiver down.

Chapter 2

It had been raining very heavily. It was Monday night, and Kofi could not sleep well. He tossed from side to side. At about 5 o'clock in the morning, he got up. "I feel strongly Maggie that something is going to happen today. I don't know what, but I know something is going to happen, so pray for me". His wife listened dutifully, with a blank look on her face. She did not know what to say. "Darling, I am sure that nothing worse can happen now", Maggie told him. After all that our enemies have done, what more can they do again, these dirty bastards. I leave them in the Almighty's hands and one day all their dirty evil tricks will be exposed to the full glare of daylight". Not being a man for big breakfasts, Kofi took his usual morning cup of black coffee, and a slice of brown bread, with a spread of margarine. He kissed his wife goodbye, and drove to his office. He was at his dek at 8.30 prompt.

As soon as he had settled into his morning routine, a despatch rider from Headquarters arrived with a note for him marked "Urgent". Kofi tried to calm his nerves as he opened it. It was an order to report to the headquarters immediately upon receipt of the note. He walked to his car, and could see a few yards from him the motor-rider whizzing back to headquarters on his motor-cycle.

Arriving at the military headquarters Kofi put out his last cigarette and reported his arrival to the aide-de-camp of the Chairman of Joint Chiefs of Staff, General Raul Manu. A tall, stiff, ram-rod gentleman of 55, the General was a no-nonsense officer of about twelve stones, and height of 5ft. 10 ins. Greying nicely on both sides of his head, smooth shaven and with a sharp piercing look in his eyes, he was a man who could easily be taken to be in his late forties, certainly not more than fifty.

A strict Muslim, he loathed drinking, smoking and adultery.

He was a family man with two married daughters, and was happily looking forward to becoming a grand-father within the next couple of months.

He had seen active service with his troops in the turbulent days of the Congo, before it became Zaire. The General was a strict disciplinarian, but if anything at all, he exacted higher professional and moral standards of himself than of his officers. General Manu had trained originally as an engineer before joining the army, where his rise to his current position had been swift, uneventful and well deserved.

On at least a couple of occasions he had called Kofi into his office for what he always called "a friendly conversation" and at each opportunity, he had expressed to him his unease about some of the rumours which he had been hearing about his extra-mural, non-military activities. Consequently, when the Colonel was ushered in by the General's A.D.C, 30 year old Major Ibrahim Mohammed, Kofi did not know what to expect. Was it going to be another lecture on ethics? Was it another trouble again? He simply was not sure.

"Ah, Kofi, nice to see you again. How are the boys? You look very fit!" Before Kofi could express his thanks to the general, he continued, "Sit down, young man, really good to see you. I've some news for you. By the way, how's Maggie?"

"Pretty well, Sir," Kofi replied as he sat down on the comfortable three-seater settee a few feet from his Chairman's desk.

"You know, I'm not one for beating about the bush, so let's get straight to the point. I have recommended you to the Jamaican Armed Forces, as the President of the Military Tribunal which is to investigate the recent bloody, but short-lived mutiny in their army. And a telex arrived a couple of hours ago, accepting and confirming your appointment. This is really good news for us all especially for the Southern Brigade. I felt it was only right and proper to inform you first before the official announcement is made during the one o'clock news!" General Manu smiled, and paused for a few seconds. Those brief seconds loosened Kofi's tongue, and he told his boss, "I am really honoured and delighted with this appointment, and I shall do

12

everything within my power to live up to your expectations. I am certain that .....", but before he could finish Manu mildly interjected, "Well, Kofi, this important new assignment carries with it enormous responsibilities, for yourself, the officer-corps, your family, friends and relatives, and our dear country. Please don't let me down".

You will be paid whilst there in foreign exchange, namely, US dollars, plus general allowances, the provision of a chauffeur driven staff car, secretarial staff, batman, and an A.D.C. In addition, free first-class accommodation and other necessaries will be provided for you and your wife during the period of the commission. Already my officer - on - duty, Ibrahim has contacted the airlines for a provisional booking for you and your wife to leave in a fortnight's time. I hope that's sufficient notice, Colonel. If not, please convey my apologies to Maggie.

The General got up, signalling to Kofi, in his usual mild, gentlemanly way that the interview was over.

"Thank you, General. I am deeply touched", Kofi said, as he smartly saluted. He turned towards the exit door. As he did so, Paul told him "expect the announcement on today's one o'clock news. Goodbye and goodluck.

The Colonel drove back to his office, with the excitement and enthusiasm of a born again Christian. He felt that at long last, providence was beginning to forgive his proven shortcomings and smile on him. He was very pleased with himself. Although, truthfully, he would have preferred to go to Jamaica alone, in the circumstances, after a series of knocks and buffettings by life, he felt that the deal he had was not bad at all.

He reflected on the lovely Jamaican beaches, the new privileges and foreign money that were now all coming within his grasp. He even reflected on the possibility of giving up smoking, drinking and bonking. Kofi felt that if it was true that every dog has its day, then indeed his had arrived. Arriving at his office, he tried to compose himself. Having done so, he telephoned his wife the good news.

"Maggie, darling, how're things?. Everything is OK now. I've just returned from the office of the Chairman. He has officially confirmed my appointment to Jamaica", Kofi told her emotionally. "Try and tune into the one o'clock news and hear it for yourself". "Praise be, praise be", she remarked, "at last our prayers have been answered. God is on our side. I'm too excited". The time was about 11.15 in the morning. Her eyes were transfixed on the clock in their sitting-room, as she looked at it, and listened to her husband. For she had always felt that if only the catalogue of career mishaps to Kofi were to end, he would become a changed person, more family-minded and more settled. She was of the firm belief, which she often expressed to her parents in confidence, that her husband's rather unhappy situation to date was the result of his troubles and not the other way round.

Many a time, in her quieter, reflective moments, she had intoned, "Poor Kofi, he's never had any break. No break at all. Why? Why? Whilst his fellow officers kept marching forward, my Kofi kept marching time. Why?. The telephone conversation, although brief, was a pleasant one, unlike quite a few other calls from her husband's office during their period of marriage. Finishing the telephone talk, she busied herself with the usual household chores - ordering the 18 year old maid here and there, supervising the gardener and the cook.

Whilst she did all these things, her mind was on one think - the one o'clock news. For she had always believed as an article of faith, that once Kofi made a break-through his thick shell of misfortunes, there would be no end to his success. Indeed, on occasions she even saw him as a future Chief of the Army. She felt that her husband would be a far better head of the army, or preferably the combined services, than any past or present incumbents. And towards this end she always prayed, as a good Catholic, saying as many Holy Mary's as possible, at every convenient, private moment. Kofi was only a nominal Roman Catholic, but not his wife. She took her religion seriously and had brought up their children appropriately.

Back at his office, after phoning his wife, Kofi rang a few close relatives and friends with the good news. He tried to restrict the number of those who were to receive advance information, so as to maximise the emotional impact of the news. He also phoned his mistress Sophia Fumey. Lucky for him, she was in, although just about to leave for her weekly shopping. "Sophia, darling, I've made it. I've done it", he said excitedly. Whilst she was beginning to fathom it out, Kofi continued. "I've been appointed to be the President of the Military Tribunal in Jamaica, to investigate the recent army mutiny. The Chairman has just told me personally, and you will hear the official announcement on the one o'clock radio and T.V news!" Sophia remarked "You mean, you've got a big job overseas? simply great, fabulous!"

"Sorry, darling, I've got to go now", the Colonel went on, before she could say more. "I will see you tomorrow, but shall ring in the morning to confirm; about 9 o'clock okay?. Bye-bye, love", he ended.

And until one o'clock, although Kofi tried to go through his normal routine, his mind was engaged elsewhere naturally. At the appointed time, he put on the news with much attention and anticipation. The weather, although hot, was not too hot. It was rather humid, otherwise it was fine.

The first news items did not interest him much. They dealt with famine and floods in part of Africa. Just as his patience was getting exhausted, the news-reader announced: 'It is officially reported from the office of the Chairman of the Joint Chiefs of Staff this morning that Colonel Kofi Johnson, deputy Commander, Southern Brigade, has been appointed President of a Military Commission to enquire into the causes of the recent army mutiny in Jamaica. He is expected to leave for his new assignment within a fortnight'. It was the last item on the day's one o'clock news broadcast.

Kofi put off the radio. He sat relaxed in his chair, expecting his telephone to start ringing. And he was not disappointed. The congratulatory calls began to pour in. Ironically the first one came from Brigadier Kwame Battah, who as President of the Military Promotion board, had, only a few weeks ago been very instrumental in blocking his promotion .

"Kofi, I'm so pleased with the news. It's really super. Con-

15

gratulations", said the Brigadier on the phone. As he listened to the complimentary words from Kwame, the Colonel was fuming inside. He knew and felt that the Brigadier did not believe a word of what he was uttering. However, Kofi controlled himself, and could only utter mildly, "Thank you, Sir, I am touched by your kind words". The Brigadier having said goodbye, ended his conversation.

The next call came from his mistress, who had failed earlier to get through, as had been many others, anxious to wish him well, and solicit foreign gifts, items and money from him.

"Darling, the news is so good, I've started my packing plans already. It's terrific. When are we leaving?" Sophia confidently asked. Kofi paused for a few seconds and then said "Hmm, Sophia, its not as simple as that. The boss told me that there are specific conditions attached to the tour. It would be for about twelve months and I am to go with Maggie".

"What, what do you mean, Kofi?" she queried, her voice rising with temper. "Are you suggesting that I cannot come along. Why?" she asked brusquely.

"Darling, I'm expecting other calls, and it will take too long to tell you the whole thing on the phone. After all, my phone may be tapped, and it is unwise to go into long details now, okay? When I see you I shall explain everything. Right?" Before he could finish, Sophia had hung up in exasperation and anger.

Apart from telephone calls, a few of Kofi's office colleagues came personally to offer their congratulations. They were not doing all this for only altruistic reasons. They knew from past experience that such foreign assignments were invariably a harbinger of bigger and greater news of advancement and promotion.

After he had talked with his wife, Maggie, whose was among the last telephone calls to get through, Colonel Kofi Johnson, not hearing from his old parents in Kokopu, decided to telephone them himself. Although the distance between APPAPA and Kokopu was less than two hundred miles, because of the ancient telephone equipment being used, the call had to be routed through three different telephone operators.

16

"Hello, hello:, Kofi shouted at his end when he got the call through to his parents. Sadly for him, after all the waiting and yelling on the phone, he ws told by the operator that the telephone in his parents' house was out of order. He therefore left a message with the operator, which he had done before in similar circumstances. The telephonist was to pay a messenger a few pence to go to his parents' house to tell them to phone him from a public call box or a neighbour's telephone which was working, that evening.

He was exasperated with the country's telephone system, about which he had frequently complained. He mused, "All this nonsense must stop one day. Millions of pounds are paid to install a national telephone network, and what do we get, a state of shambles, frequent breakdowns and crossed lines. Sometimes I wonder whether the whiteman should have stayed. At least the phones were working, and there was some discipline in the public service. Now the big shots are only interested in big deals for themselves, and salting away money in secret, Swiss bank accounts. Nobody cares anymore!"

Methodically and patiently, Kofi went through some of his files, in preparation for his departure. Here and there he made some wry comments. However, he felt an obligation to make positive, progressive comments that would assist the future careers of those under him. He thought it prudent to keep to himself what he really thought about some of his superior officers.

By the time Kofi returned home at 2.30 pm a special, lovely lunch was awaiting him. "Darling, this is a special day, welcome home" his wife said, with wide open arms, as Kofi got out of his car.

"We are really going to celebrate in a good way, before leaving", Kofi remarked proudly. "In celebration of the excellent news today, I've ensured, darling, that your favourite kebab is available. It was not easy getting it on very short notice, due to the constant meat shortages", Maggie said, smilingly.

They sat down to lunch, consisting of lobster soup, yam and kebab, a bowl of stewed tomatoes, garden eggs and mushrooms.

The dessert was fresh pineapples and ice cream. The drink was Kofi's favourite beer. For maggie it was orange-juice with ice.

Just before starting on the first course of the meal, a military staff car pulled in at Kofi's front entrance. It was the car of Colonel Johnson's immediate superior, Brigadier Stephen Boateng. Unknown to Kofi, his wife had, on hearing the good news on the radio, quickly rang the Brigadier and invited him to join them for lunch. "Who's coming in, Maggie?" he asked his wife, "Please look and tell me."

Putting on as innocent a face as possible, Maggie looked through one of the dining room windows and shouted, "It's Steve!" Not being sure of which of his friends, Kofi enquired "Stephen who?"

"I mean the Brigadier", she replied. By this time, the visitor had got out of his car and was walking towards Kofi's door. Briskly sprucing himself and walking quickly to the door, Kofi remarked loudly "Welcome, and welcome again, Brigadier. This is both a surprise and an honour".

And standing before his friend, with a bottle of expensive champagne in his left hand, was the Brigadier. His visit, expected or unexpected, was an extra pleasure to a very nice, good day for Kofi. Accompanying him was his beautiful wife, Ruth. It was only as the lunch went on, with Maggie playing the perfect hostess, and the family's steward hovering round the visitors solicitingly, that Kofi began to realise that Maggie, in her usual shrewd way, ever mindful of her husband's best interest, had invited his boss to lunch, to surprise him. A few informal toasts were drunk to the health and welfare of both families in a most relaxed atmosphere.

Finally, Stephen said. "We hope and trust that your mission succeeds and brings to you both all that we all desire".

"Hear, hear", Maggie said.

"Well, we must go now", the Brigadier remarked as he stood up.

They walked towards their car.

Ruth called Maggie aside, and whispered, "Tell Kofi to watch Brigadier Battah. He nearly ruined the whole thing", Maggie

18

nodded.

"Bye, bye, hope to see you soon", Kofi told the departing visitors, as they went into their car. They waved finally to them as the car sped off. "You know, darling, what Ruth told me? It just confirms all my past fears", Maggie was telling her husband.

"She said that that bad, foolish man, Kwame Battah, who's after your blood, nearly killed off this appointment to Jamaica. So for heaven's sake, until we leave, try, darling, and avoid him as much as you can. He's still dangerous!".

Kofi listened carefully, nodded and frowned. He was really simmering inside. "One day I shall teach this fucking bastard a major lesson. It will be the sum total of all the trouble which he's seen fit to give me. You wait!".

As they talked over the surprise visit of their friends, its planning and its execution, the maid and the batman kept busy doing the clearing of the table and continuing with the household chores still uncompleted.

Suddenly the phone rang. Before Maggie could take the receiver, Kofi had got it already. On the line was his mistress, Sophia Fumey, trying to disguise her voice.

"Ah, darling. I rang to talk for a few minutes about the exciting news. I hope you will be in tonight", she said.

"Yes,yes; please tell him I will be in at about 8 pm. Sorry, I've visitors with me now and I have to leave. Bye, bye", he concluded.

His wife was by this time in the kitchen. Kofi told her "It was one of the military intelligence boys enquiring about something. No problem, love".

The rest of the afternoon was spent by Kofi playing some High Life' records. After about an hour or so Maggie joined her husband to listen to the music.

When the record "Love me till Death" reached its crescendo, the pair could not resist it anymore. They got up and danced to their hearts' content. They did so with much affection, if not love. They danced as in a trance, ruminating over the number of years of bad luck which they had jointly gone through till now.

19

"Maggie, you're right. Now our turn is coming and I am sure that after Jamaica there will be even better news and assignments", he said.

Smiling approvingly, Maggie remarked, "The future is bright, very bright. One day ...." she stopped suddenly,

Both stopped dancing as the record came to an end. They sat down. Kofi got up and made a few local telephone calls to some friends. He then rang his old dad and had a little chat with him. The old man also called his wife to come and talk to their dear son.

"Kofi, dear. I heard the fantastic news from uncle Kojo. He sends his love and congratulations to you", she said in their local language. "Be sure to come home to see us before leaving", she ended.

"Certainly, mother", I'm not leaving wihout seeing you both. How's Anuti Esi? I hope she's better now", Kofi concluded.

The conversation although brief, had brought such joy and happiness to Kofi's parents. For, as he was their only son, and the eldest of five grown up children, they tended to look up to Kofi as the leader of the family.

Whilst Kofi was busy on the phone, his dear selfless wife was equally busy, organising the cutting of the lawn. The frequent tropical rains made it difficult to maintain the garden in the front of their house, and the lawn at the back, as neat, tidy and pretty as Maggie would like. Many a time, her confrontations with the gardener had been rather unpleasant. She was in her own way a perfectionist. The high turnover among the gardeners was an indication of the different standards demanded by Maggie as employer, and those provided by the gardeners as employees.

At 7.00 pm prompt, Kofi Johnson called his wife and said, "Maggie, I've got to go out shortly. You remember the phone call from military intelligence that I told you about? Well I have to go there for an hour or so, to sort out one or two matters. If anybody important rings, darling, please say I am out and will be in later, about 10.30 pm. Okay?".

He got himself ready and put on his local Bassain clothes, in

20

the toga-like fashion, as the ancient Roman senators did. He got into his car, after kissing Maggie.

"See you shortly, darling", Kofi was telling her. "Bye, bye, Kofi dear", she said.

He drove straight from the house to the military intelligence head-office in Mandalay camp. The officer-on-duty, Captain Issah Bujari, was an old friend of Kofi's. Indeed, he liked the Colonel very much, and owed much of his rapid promotion to the good offices of the Colonel.

"Issah", called Kofi as he saw him at desk.

"Yes, Sir". He saluted.

With a twinkle in his left eye, Kofi told the thirty-year old military intelligence officer, "Issah, you're an old friend of mine, so I can confide in you. In case my wife rings kindly tell her that I'm in, but cannot be disturbed as I am in conference. You understand?". He paused, and then continued "and should the C.O or any superior officer ring, please, Issah, use your discretion to handle the call diplomatically. Okay?".

"Yes, Sir, understood!", replied the Captain, as he saluted the Colonel goodbye. Before boarding his car, Kofi made a solidarity sign with his left thumb, which although silent, spoke a lot.

Kofi drove straight to his mistress's house. Waiting for him, in a gorgeous light blue frock with sequins on the bosom, was Sophia Fumey, full of smiles, and radiating warmth and happiness.

"At long last, darling. Welcome, darling, so happy to see you. You're really a gent", she said.

The welcome was a fullsome one. It included a table set for two, with some of Kofi's best loved dishes, chicken curry with fried rice, mushroom, sweet and sour pork, with yam, and an array of spices and condiments, including onions, red pepper and mango chutney.

Although not keen for another big meal, Kofi felt that he must not disappoint Sophia, especially considering the trouble she had gone to get everything right.

"This is most delicious, Sophia. You've surpassed yourself

today. Great".

She just smiled fondly and watched him eat. She ate also, but not with much gusto. She appeared to have something on her mind. Towards the end of the meal, at the dessert stage, when Kofi's emotional defences were down, she fired her first shots.

"Darling, I'm still not clear about what you said about me not going with you. Why?" she asked. Before a reply was forthcoming she continued, "I think this is all a play to get me out of the way. Why can she go and not I. Why, why?", she asked emotionally.

"I've done my best to solve this problem, Sophia, but it has not been at all easy. You know the Chairman is a devout Muslim, and simply would not countenance such a suggestion if even I had the courage to broach it". "Darling, you know already my enemies at the camp say all sorts of things about me, and would only love for me to make a fool of myself. Please, try and understand, darling".

"Quite honestly, Kofi, I don't believe all this crap. Do you want me to come or not? If it's the question of the fare or accommodation expenses, I can easily pay for myself. I understand apartments are fairly reasonable to rent in Jamaica and the return fair is only about 600 US dollars".

Kofi said nothing. "Where there is a will, there's a way, the saying goes. You either want me there or not. I will pay to be with you".

"Sophia, please understand. It's not the money at all. Damnit, what's money".

"Then, what is it? Tired of me already".

"Don't talk nonsense, darling. You know how much you mean to me. Please, try and understand. It's not at all easy", Kofi interrupted.

They were walking towards the bedroom as they talked. They sat on the bed, and talked a few minutes further on the same theme. "Sophia, darling, don't worry, we will find a way to solve this nasty problem", Kofi told her as he put out the bedside lamp on his side.

Sophia did the same.

"How's it, love?", Sophia was asking him, as she caressed his body, from his hairy chest downwards.

"As always, prima!", replied Kofi confidently. "Then an encore, like that supreme Wednesday, darling", she said.

"Hmm, darling. I really love you, but I must be going now".

The truth of the matter was that as a result of years of promiscuity, Kofi's sexual powers were beginning to flag. This annoyed him very much as he was proud of his macho image as a sexually active man. He himself knew better. So did Sophia. Over the past few years since she had come to know Kofi, his sexual potency had been diminishing with the years. The barracks image of him, therefore, as a man with insatiable sexual appetite, could not be corroborated by his actual performance in bed.

Although he was keen to prove to Sophia that his erotic powers were as great as before, he knew that he could not accept the invitation.

Suddenly, waxing eloquent, he said, "Sophia, you know, the spirit is willing, but the flesh is weak. Anyway, love, time is against me. I've to show my face at military intelligence again before dashing home".

"I see", said Sophia, very frustrated, but trying to hide her feelings.

Kofi had already begun to dress and get ready to go. Sophia slipped to the bathroom adjoining her bedroom and after a couple of minutes freshing herself up, returned. Meanwhile, Kofi was ready to go.

But the old issue would not die away. "So what's the position. Am I going or not going, darling. Yes or No?", she asked in a sharp voice.

"Yes, you're going, love. Good?"

"Delighted. I am so relieved. You've set my mind at rest darling. I was so worried that....", Kofi interrupted before she could finish. It was beginning to rain. The time was 10.15 pm. Kofi felt that it would be wise to leave immediately, in case the rain got heavier.

"Sophia, trust me. You leave it to me. I will do my best to work out the difficulties. Okay?", she nodded half heartedly.

Next she was kissing Kofi passionately. He walked towards his old, light blue Volvo saloon car.

"Bye, bye, darling", she said, as she waved. Kofi drove away, back to the military intelligence office. He walked straight to the office of his friend, Captain Issah Bukari.

"Captain, any calls for me?", he asked him. Issah stood up, with his hands resting on his desk. His pose was half formal, half informal.

"No, Sir, none at all", he replied.

"Good, very good", said Kofi.

Lifting the telephone receiver, Kofi telephoned his wife.

"Hello, darling, how are the children?", he asked her. "Sorry for the delay. I am on my way, be home within ten minutes or so. Bye, bye", he concluded.

Maggie did not feel it was worth asking him about the alleged night assignment with military intelligence. From past experience she felt she would only get a load of lies, abuse or silence.

"Goodbye, Issah. Many thanks", Kofi told his young friend before leaving.

"You're welcome, Sir. Goodnight", he replied, as he stood up.

Kofi went into his car, and belted away through the rain, which was getting heavier. Indeed, the rumblings of one or two thunders produced interference on his radio, as he tried to tune into the BBC World Service. This annoyed him a lot. For he made it a point to listen to the BBC Overseas Service, in case he heard something of interest not broadcast by the local radio.

"Oh, at last, Kofi, you're home", remarked his wife, as she stood at the door to welcome him.

"Terrible weather, raining heavily", he said, as the walked towards her.

"I've been very busy since I left the military intelligence office with Issah, that fine young Captain you met last week. Terribly sorry it took so long", he ended.

"What about your usual night-cap, darling?".

"Not tonight, darling Maggie, I feel so tired. I'm going to bed straight away, after a quick wash".

He slipped to the bathroom, had a refreshing shower, and then went to bed. He slept like a log, completely oblivious to his wife's wakefulness and restlessness.

Chapter 3

"Let's do it next week, just before we leave", said Kofi.

"Well, darling, I could not agree with you more. Once we've got it out of the way, then we can concentrate on other family problems. You know, the children's welfare, the bank standing orders, the monthly mortgage payments and the rest".

"Hmm", Kofi grunted approvingly. "Yes indeed. Also, we have to ensure that our little poultry farm will be well-looked after, by those lazy bones. By the way, darling, how many fowls are still left, following that disaster?" he enquired.

"I think about two hundred. Let me check", Maggie remarked.

Then she shouted, "Steward, ask Abongo how many birds are still alive. Quick", she ordered impatiently. For, left to herself, Maggie would like to sack Abongo, the farm-hand, and batman. She felt they were too lazy, and did not earn their keep and should be sacked.

The couple then turned their attention to the final arrangements about their farewell party. "Let's go all out, dear", said Maggie.

Kofi chuckled, but said nothing. After a pregnant pause, he continued, "I nearly forgot the D.M.I, (the Director of Military Intelligence), Col. Samuel Boham, you know how supportive a friend he's been, darling".

"Yes, true", she said, nodding. "But darling, what do we do if Col. Kumi wants to bring his beautiful girlfriend, instead of his wife? You know they are not getting on too well together, darling" she asked.

Before Kofi could reply, she answered her own question.

"We will have to put our foot down and tell him politely, but firmly, that no girlfriends are welcome, especially as the Chief will be here. Agreed?"

Kofi was not too happy about her decision, and his feelings mildly showed in his face. For as his wife talked, he was trying to solve an emotional problem. He could cancel the farewell party his mistress was also planning for him or get her invited indirectly and surreptitiously as a girl-friend of a colleague of his. For after all, due to clever strategic planning, and juggling of dates and appointments, he had been able to keep Sophia Fumey's existence from his wife's knowledge. However, as he listened to Maggie, it became too apparent to him that any question of Sophia being at their farewell party, clandestinely or otherwise, was out!.

They continued with the discussion of their guest list.

"Darling, already we have reached fourteen and I've not mentioned my friends yet".

"Well, darling, go ahead", said Kofi.

"I wish to invite my 'gynae' man and his wife, the midwife, my aunt Berth, and that lady-lawyer at Attorney-General's office, I told you about the other day". Not wanting to overload the list, she stopped mentioning more names. "So, Maggie, you've in mind five lovely women", Kofi interrupted. "Ah, I nearly forgot the bank-manager. You remember how helpful he was over that cheque that nearly created a storm. Also we should not forget the Chief of the Military Hospital, you never know when we may need him again".

"So, what's the total now?" Maggie asked. They went through the list together again, and found that they had a total of twenty so far.

"What do we do with the last three?" Maggie asked.

"Hmm, I think you should suggest two more names, and I the other, agreed?", Kofi enquired.

"Yes, lovely. Let's see", she said, stopped for a few seconds and then stated, "I feel that the Catholic padre, and the Inspector of Police at Cantonments should come. I was going to invite my father and mother, but when I talked to them last they were not keen on a long train journey. And with the roads being what they have been, both of them have vowed not to travel to APPAPA by car, until the sizes and number of gaping pot-holes

27

have reduced a lot", Kofi told her.

"Well, dear, let's leave the single vacancy unfilled. After all, the camp being what it is I'm certain that as soon as news of the party gets around, there will be a couple of gate-crashers, that's if we are lucky, and heaven help us if we unlucky, then you are talking of ten or so friendly, but unwelcome and uninvited guests".

The question of the guest list settled, Kofi felt that he should use part of that Tuesday to check on the final arrangements for their trip. He made a number of telephone calls to friends and relatives, and checked with the protocol section whether the travel and visa arrangements were all in order. Indeed, they were, for there were only ten days or so left.

However, one problem kept gnawing on Kofi's mind, Sophia's insistence on going to Jamaica with or without him.

Suddenly he said, "Maggie I must go to my office to collect one or two items. It's true that I've signed off, but I feel it necessary to go and be sure everything is nice, neat and tidy. Do go ahead and get everything okay in your usual efficient, superb way for next Monday. I've seen to the booze already", he said.

Then he quickly kissed her, and drove straight not to his office, but to the bungalow of his close friend Capt. Issah Bukari, who he knew was off-duty that day.

As he entered the compound of the Captain he hooted his car horn twice, which set the bush dog barking wildly as it ran towards the car.

It was about 1 pm when the Colonel reached the Captain's modest two-bedroomed bungalow. Although the house was not, naturally, as well furnished as that of Kofi, Issah's house and it's furnishings, for a young bachelor Captain were not bad at all.

With all his macho image at the camp, Kofi was uneasy with dogs. Not without reason. On Christmas day two years before then, he and his wife had been invited to lunch at the house of an American diplomat then living at the Airport area. The tall, lovely American hostess came to the gate to welcome them, followed by her big, fierce-looking Alsatian dog. Whilst the American welcomed them and Maggie patted the dog on the head, the dog had for some unknown reason gone for Kofi's clothes around the groin, and nearly did serious damage to his penis. Certainly part of his thigh was bitten, with the result that the much-looked for lunch did not materialise.

The American very embarrassed and angry with her dog, pushed him away, whilst Kofi and his wife hurriedly returned to their car and headed straight for the Military Hospital which was about two miles away.

"Was the dog wearing an inoculation tag?" the doctor on duty asked. Before the angry Kofi could reply the doctor who was a BASSAIN continued, "Colonel don't worry at all. The Americans are very fussy and very particular about their dogs. I'm sure he has been inoculated properly and is certainly not carrying the rabies virus. Don't worry; you're OK." he said.

Maggie looked on anxiously. "In any case, if the dog dies within seven days after the bite, then as rule of thumb, it must be carrying the virus, and we would then have to start you on a course of anti-rabies, anti-tetanus injections in your abdomen for seven days to nip in the bud the incubation period of the infection. If, God willing, it does not die within seven days, then it means the dog is OK. as I think it is, and you would not have to worry about any injections;" the doctor reassured them both. He then gave Kofi a few antibiotics, to be taken over a period of ten days against a possible non-rabid infection from the dog's teeth. Duly assured that everything would be alright, Kofi and Maggie went home and telephoned the American lady and her husband about Kofi's state.

For the next seven days, every morning at about 9 o'clock Kofi would telephone for the good or bad news; "Good morning, Mrs O'Brien, how's our friend" he would ask.

"Real good, alive and kicking, Colonel", she would reply sweetly.

Naturally, after the seventh positive reply to the same question, Kofi had sighed with relief, vowing never to have anything to do with dogs - tame, mild or otherwise.

Thus his insistence on waiting in his car until the Captain came to escort him made a bit of sense, although Issah felt that

Kofi was carrying caution to the extreme.

The two officers sat down. Isaah had in fact just finished his lunch and was thinking of taking a brief siesta, as it is custom generally in the tropics.

"Colonel, all I have is beer. I am sorry, no wine, champagne or anything fancy", he said apologetically.

"Thank you, Issah, but nothing at all. I mean nothing alcoholic. Today I've become a strict muslim like you. Coke will do, if there's any. If not don't bother;" Kofi told him. They both smiled.

As Issah's batman was off duty, Issah himself went to the kitchen and got two large glasses of coca-cola, with lots of ice.

The day was really hot even by tropical standards. It was also very humid, the sort of day that drains you easily and makes one short-tempered.

As they sat down, the Captain wondered what on earth had suddenly brought the Colonel scurrying to his little bungalow without the usual telephone warning or appointment. He did not have to wait for long. For Kofi was itching to unburden his soul to him.

After a sip of the cold drink, he said, "Issah, I am in trouble, really big mix-up, and I've come to you as a good friend to help me. What you do for me will never be forgotten and I shall ever be grateful to you. Please help, Issah", he murmured.

Issah was at his wits end with what was worrying his friend.

"My friend, you know too well, that I am leaving shortly for this assignment in Jamaica.

"Yes and really fantastic it is," Issah said. "Again congratulations, Sir," he repeated.

"Issah, what's happening is that my girl-friend, Sophia, insists on coming along. I've talked and talked to her about the problem, but she would not see reason. I have been so exhausted by this confrontation with her that, for peace of mind, I've promised her that she can come. But as you can see that is out of the question.

"Completely, Colonel, it would be sheer suicide career-wise, if she went, and a scandal broke out there involving you and her, and possibly your wife". "I agree, Issah. The situation is bad, really bad, and that's why I've come to you for help. After all, you're a brilliant intelligent officer, with already an excellent record for quick thinking and resourcefulness. Issah, I know you can help me", Kofi remarked nervously.

"Well, I will try. I will do my best", Issah stated, nodding.

"I've a simple plan for action my friend. I've already promised her and simply cannot get out of it, but as a result of the recent troubles in Jamaica, the government there is very security-conscious. And I want you to go on a delicate mission for me".

"Interesting, Kofi, I'm listening", the Captain said.

"I want you, please, to go by the next available plane to Pagos, where the Jamaica Embassy in Africa is. Sophia has already applied there for a visa. You're to go and see the First Secretary, who is also responsible for visa matters, and explain to him the position, man-to-man, begging him to delay the visa application as much as possible, enter into a long-drawn out correspondence with her, and eventually reject it on security grounds, saying that following the recent troubles in Jamaica, visas are no longer issued to tourists and visitors. In short, please tell him to apply any tactics or stratagem that he may find appropriate". He stopped.

"Issah, can I trust you with this mission? I'm sure you are the right man". As he said so, he pulled out of his wallet a bundle of US ten-dollar bills, and gave him a hundred dollars.

"This is for the fare and expenses", he said as he gave it to Issah.

"But Colonel, the time, how?" the Captain enquired, rather worried.

"Issah, luckily there is a plane leaving for PAGOS at 2.15 pm. If you agree to leave now, in mufti, as a matter of priority, you should be at the airport before 2 pm. The flight from APPAPA to PAGOS is only 45 minutes, and let's say another hour or so by taxi from the airport to the embassy. So you can be there, all things being well, between 4.30 pm and 5 pm. From my intelligence report, the embassy stays open on Tuesdays till 6.30 pm.

31

So barring any unforeseen activity, you should be there before the embassy closes. In anycase, as soon as you leave, I will telephone the gentleman, Major Brian Cox, at the Embassy, give him a brief outline of your mission, and inform him that you will be there by 5.30 pm or thereabout. OK, Issah?"

"Okay, Colonel", his friend replied to Kofi.

Hurriedly, Issah got ready, and as he did so, Kofi said, "You can return by the 8 o'clock plane. So by 9 pm you should be back in APPAPA for a well deserved supper".

"As a matter of fact, I had wanted to give you a brief, personal note to him. But since the episode of the diplomatic bag that got lost on the plane I've not been at all keen putting delicate missions on paper, especially a very controversial and dubious one like this", Kofi said, his voice sounding less strained than when he began to brief Issah on his mission.

The two of them quickly drove in Kofi's car to the airport, with Issah carrying nothing but a small brief-case, with a pair of pyjamas, toothbrush and toothpaste, a towel and face-cloth, and his shaving set. With the unpredictability of the flights he was taking no chances.

Arriving at the airport at 2 pm Issah had barely enough time to pay his fare in the local currency, show passport and I.D. card, and board the plane, after a quick vigorous handshake with his mentor. As the plane took off, Kofi Johnson sighed with relief. He went straight to the nearest public telephone kiosk and telephoned Major Cox as agreed.

The telephone rang at his desk in Pagos. It was 1 pm Pagos time, and the Major had just returned to his office after a really good lunch. He was in a rather relaxed mood.

"Major Cox, here", he said as he took the receiver.

"Major, sorry to bother you, this is Colonel Kofi Johnson, I am speaking from APPAPA".

"Hello, Colonel, what a pleasant surprise, when are you leaving for the Islands?"

"Next week, and I am looking forward to it very much and so is my wife. When I return, I would like you to come to us to swap stories, impressions and ideas".

"Jolly good idea, marvellous".

"Meanwhile, Brian, I've rather a delicate problem and a close friend of mine, Captain Issah Bukari is on the way, by air, to come and seek your help. He should be there before 5.30 latest", Kofi remarked.

"Good, look forward to seeing him, Kofi. Any idea of the problem?"

"Well, Brian, you know in our work the phone is the last thing to trust.... I've sent him on an urgent, delicate, family mission, that I trust you, as a fellow man, would understand", Kofi went on.

"In other words, Kofi you are keeping me in suspense for the next couple of hours until your emissary arrives. Is that it?" asked Major Cox.

"Yes, but do try and resolve this matter, I count on you", Kofi concluded.

He immediately dashed back to the house from the airport, stopping at a shop on his way to buy more drinks. He was very pleased with himself, and had in his mind a mental picture of his faithful friend arriving at PAGOS airport, clearing customs and heading, through PAGOS traffic towards the Jamaican Embassy on KROLI Island. He had pleasant visions of his friend being welcomed by Major Cox, serving him drinks, and then listening raptly to his mission. He even imagined a successful conclusion to Issah's assignment and his safe return to APPAPA.

He pulled himself together. Then he called the maid to serve him cold beer. The maid told him; "Master, madam is gone to see Aunti Berth, and said I tell you ring the padre".

"Is that all?" Kofi asked.

"Yes, master", she replied.

As he slowly sipped his beer, Kofi could not but reflect on the emotional mess in which he had got himself, and how, bit by bit, painstakingly, he was trying to extricate himself.

It was now about 4 pm, and by his calculations, Issah should be in a taxi on his way towards his ultimate destination.

The phone rang. At first he was not keen to take up the receiver. For it was too early to expect any call from Issah. As agreed, his friend was to ring him from PAGOS air port following the completion of his mission. The telephone kept on ringing. With great reluctance he took the receiver.

"Hello, can I help you, who?" the voice at the other end sounded rather odd, it sounded neither male or female.

"Who's it?" he asked again.

The voice became clearer.

"Oh, darling it's me. Surprise!".

"What a pleasant surprise indeed, darling. Nice to hear your voice again. How are things, love?

"Okay, darling. I wanted to let you know that I wrote to the Jamaican Embassy in PAGOS for the visa application form. I hear from a friend that formerly they used to issue the visas from London, but now since the recent upheaval there visitors have to get the visas from their country of origin or residence. Is that so, darling?" she asked.

" Sophia, I fear so. It's a big nuisance".

"What about yours darling?"

"You know, love, because of my assignment I've been issued with a diplomatic passport, and the visas for us were arranged by the Jamaican Armed Forces themselves, so there has been no problem at all.

"But what about mine, me?" Sophia Fumey asked him.

"Don't worry, you get the forms first, fill them as requested. Everything will be fine. If they ask for references, which I doubt, you may mention your uncle, the businessman, and me. If any difficulties, love, do let me know", he said softly and soothingly.

"Thank you, my dear. You're so sweet, so kind", she went on wanting to talk more, as she guessed correctly that the mistress of the house was not in.

Normally, Kofi would have loved to talk more with Sophia, but not this time. Although, the expected call from Issah was a couple of hours yet, Kofi wanted the telephone line as clear as possible.

So as firmly and kindly as possible he told her, "Sophia, dear, I must go now. I've to see to an urgent note from the C.O. okay, bye, bye, darling".

He sat back in a pensive mood, wondering how his emissary was doing. Well, there was no need for Kofi worrying. For just as he was talking with Sophia, Issah's assignment was progressing satisfactorily. As planned, he got through the Customs and Excise, and Immigration smoothly and swiftly, as he discreetly showed his military identification card. As planned he took a taxi to the embassy, meandering his way through the notorious Pagos traffic, crowded with cars, lorries and military trucks. There were a couple of corpses lying on the roadside, as he taxied along; but Issah was too pre-occupied to bother looking at them.

Issah knew how useful a successful outcome of his mission would be not only to the Colonel, but to himself. It was a matter of the Colonel being eternally in his debt, or his being in a matrimonial quagmire, with possibly disastrous consequences.

At about 5 pm. the taxi stopped in front of the Jamaican Embassy. Capt. Issah Bukari, quickly got out, paid the fair with a good tip, which brought a bright smile on the face of the cab-driver, then dashed to the embassy door. He rang the bell, announced himself through the entry-phone, and was let in.

The receptionist was a young woman of about twenty-five, asked him to fill in a visitor's form. He diplomatically refused to do so, telling the receptionist that it would be alright if he did not, and that Major Cox was expecting him. He persuaded the woman to announce his arrival directly to the Major, without the necessity of the form being filled.

With much reluctance she did so, and was instructed to send him up.

"Come in, Captain, how nice to see you. This is very good timing. How was your flight. No turbulence, I trust?"

"No, Sir, it was smooth and uneventful".

"Well, I've been expecting you during the last hour or so, and it's good you're here. Shall we go straight to the matter. By the way, Captain what shall you have, beer or something stronger?", he smilingly asked him.

"Sir, a glass of cold orange juice or even water will do".

"Well, orange then. I'm having a cold, cold beer".

As they sipped their respective drinks, Issah started,

"Major, I've been asked by the Colonel to put before you a rather delicate request", He stopped for a couple seconds, to judge the effect of his opening salvo.

Then he continued, "It's in connection with his official invitation to Jamaica, about which I'm sure you know. Well, this visit, to which he's looking forward immensely, has landed him in a matrimonial mess.

"How ?", the Major enquired, rather puzzled, "Headquarters in KINGSTON, have arranged every thing, accommodation, visa, transport, secretarial support, the whole works. He's getting full V.I.P. treatment".

"Sir, the problem is simply that a girl-friend of the Colonel insists on going to Jamaica, with or without him. Her decision has completely unsettled my boss, and he has asked me to come and plead with you, on his behalf, as a fellow officer, not to issue a visa under any circumstances, whatsoever". Issah went on, sounding more serious. "The Colonel suggests that as you are the only embassy in Africa where she can get a visa, if you refuse her, she would not pursue it too vigorously, as she might not be too keen to fly to London to try her luck, with the possibility of another failure".

"I bet. The Colonel is indeed in a mess", he chuckled.

"What's the woman's name, by the way?" he enquired

"Sophia fumey", he replied nervously.

"Ah, the name rings a bell. Sophia what?"

"Fumey, Sir".

For a brief moment both men were silent in the Major's modestly-furnished office. Then Cox said, "You know, it is only a few days ago that I received her application form, duly filled-in, and signed, with two passport photos. I don't think it's been dealt with yet. Let me see".

He called for the file dealing with fresh visa applications. It was quickly brought in by his secretary.

"Captain, amuse yourself with this official album, whilst I go through this", he said, as he handed a voluminous photo album to his visitor. For the next ten minutes or so, he studied the contents of the file. Then he looked straight at his guest, and remarked,

"Well Captain, I've just been studying her application for a visa, which apparently came in a few days a go. There's a lot of work to be done on it anyway. Please, tell the Colonel not to worry. Everything will be fine. I shall deal with the matter as he requested. No problem at all. After all, who knows, one day I might need him. That's life", he reflected.

Isaah sighed with relief as he listened to the Major. He felt inside him that his journey had not been futile. He knew the Colonel would ever be grateful to him for the success of his mission.

"Do give my warmest regards to him, and please, repeat that he's not to worry. It was nice talking with you", he said as both men stood up.

"Goodbye, and safe flight", the Major said as he showed his visitor to the door.

"Goodbye, Sir, and thank you very much", Issah told him as he neared the door.

Finally, with a wink in his left eye, Major Cox said, "I hope he enjoys his stay in Jamaica. Cheers", and with that he shook Issah's hand, and quietly shut his door.

The time was about 6 pm. The weather was beginning to be cool and less humid. Captain Issah Bukari looked at his watch. Elated and excited inside, but keeping an outward calm exterior, he walked for a few yards, then hailed a taxi. The taxi stopped, but when he told the driver that he wanted to go to the airport, the driver simple shot away without a word.

He walked a further few yards, and then stopped another taxi, again no luck. The driver was not interested in the long, slow, protracted journey to the airport. Issah was becoming frustrated. He could not understand why with so many taxis in Pagos, he could not easily get a taxi.

Not used to giving up easily, he kept on walking. Then he looked back, and saw a taxi driving towards him. He stopped it, and before he had uttered a word, he jumped in.

"Where to?" the driver asked rather brusquely.

"Independence Airport. Please hurry, I'm late".

"Big man, I'm no going airport, with all the "go-slow" at this time, no worth it".

Issah smiled diplomatically. He slipped a dollar note into the driver's shirt pocket. The driver smiled broadly, and shot ahead, driving like mad. On the way, Issah, with his mission accomplished, had time to look at the two corpses which he had seen on his way from the airport. The bodies were still there. One of them had a crowd of about twenty people around it, gesticulating and arguing.

"Driver, why are these bodies lying about?" he enquired.

"They thief, and people kill them. No nonsense. This be simple matter".

"But why, my friend, people don't arrest them and hand them over to the police?", the rather upset Captain asked.

"Man, you've time for the that, eh?"

For the next few minutes Issah said nothing. The driver went into long details about numerous burglaries in Pagos, describing in morbid detail a recent armed burglary in Pagos in which the victims, two Lebanese businessmen had been hacked to death. They stopped talking for a few split seconds, then the driver added, "If I have power, I go get their balls cut out before they face the firing squad. Don't agree?"

"No, I don't", replied Issah sharply.

"What you woman?" the driver asked Issah, equally sharply.

Issah did not reply. For the rest of the journey, both driver and passenger kept silent. Soon they had arrived at the airport, and quickly getting out of the car, Issah paid the fare on the meter. No tip. The look on the taxi driver's face was lethal.

Inside the airport building, Issah went straight to the nearest telephone kiosk, and telephoned his mentor. His first effort to get through to Kofi's house was a failure. The line was engaged. The second was also a failure. The APPAPA lines were all busy. His third attempt was a success.

But all the time Issah was talking with Major Cox, and after that, whilst travelling to the airport, Colonel Kofi Johnson was having a hard time of nerves, fidgeting and worrying. His whole mind was on the expected telephone call. As such, when eventually his phone rang, he jumped and rushed towards it with alacrity.

"Hello, this is Kofi Johnson", He uttered.

"Colonel, I've done it", Issah shouted on the phone, as the line was not clear at all.

"Colonel, it's me. I've fixed it", he repeated.

"Good, really great. Where are you now, brother?"

"I am at the airport, Sir. I shall be catching the 8 pm. plane, and should be arriving about 8 pm local time. See you soon, Colonel", Issah remarked happily.

"Great, brother, great, I will be there. See you soon. Many thanks, excellent. Goodbye for now". Kofi said, as he put the telephone receiver down. He was now a relaxed man, no longer chain-smoking or worried. He walked to one of the windows and looked ahead aimlessly. He was a relieved man.

"Maggie, dear, I am going to the M.I. office for a thing or two I should not be more than an hour at most", he told his long-suffering wife.

"Darling, do you really have to go. Why not rest?, she asked. "Whatever it is surely it can wait. After all, when you are not here from next week, can't they do without you? They must leave you alone a bit", she remarked sadly.

"Maggie, dear, don't worry. I shall be back in a jiffy", and as he said so, he kissed her quickly and walked briskly to his car.

As he started to drive away it began to drizzle. The clouds were beginning to gather. He drove straight to the airport, parked his car under some Nim trees, and walked to the arrival lounge of the airport.

Isaah's clearance through Customs, Immigration and Security were quick and smooth. And as his return-tickets were all in order, he was directed to the airport departure lounge. He waited there for about fifteen minutes, when his flight was called, and with the inner satisfaction which emanates from success and happiness, he boarded the plane back to APPAPA.

With his mission a complete success, Issah was looking forward to a smooth flight back. Indeed, the flight was quite uneventful for the first twenty minutes of its forty-five minute journey. But suddenly, the "fasten-your seat belts" sign came on. The pilot then confirmed it orally.

"We are having a bit of turbulence, and expect it to be so far the next few minutes. But there's nothing to worry about. We're still on schedule to reach APPAPA, in twenty five minutes time. Thank you".

Having flown frequently Issah had got to know that whenever the pilot announced that there's nothing to worry about, what he really meant, in as pleasant and comforting a way as possible was that the flight was experiencing one problem or another and that the flight crew are rather worried. Consequently, to calm his nerves, Issah started reciting quietly to himself passages from the KORAN. He was praying hard inside, but externally continued to keep an affable, confident manner, befitting an officer, albeit in mufti.

The plane continued its flight, lightly buffeted left and right by the heavy clouds. Sometimes it felt as if the clouds were really shaking the plane menacingly. Just when some of the more nervous passengers were beginning to exhibit panic symptoms, the pilot announced, "Ladies and Gentlemen, you may unfasten your seat belts now and relax. The turbulence is over. Thank you for your co-operation".

Together all the passengers burst into harmonious clapping, with broad smiles all over their faces. The plane continued on its journey, and shortly, after the little aerial difficulty had been overcome, began its descent to its destination. The relief which was felt by all on board when the aircraft landed, five minutes behind schedule, was visible to all the friends and relatives at the arrival lounge who had gone to the airport to meet people dear to them.

And among them was Colonel Kofi Johnson in mufti. "Hi, Issah, great to see you back. Let's go and talk", he uttered as Issah came out of the arrival lounge door. He hugged him, and walked briskly to a quiet corner of the hall.

"How did it go, man?", he asked.

"Wonderful, absolutely terrific. He was very co-operative and very friendly".

"So he agreed?"

"Yes, absolutely positive", he replied.

"You are sure, Issah, that he was just not being diplomatic. You sure he means business?" he asked anxiously.

"I am super positive. He sounded really serious and genuine. It's all okay, Colonel", Issah remarked.

The two of them walked to Kofi's car, chatting animatedly as they went along. They drove to Issah's house. As son as they arrived there they quickly walked to Issah's sitting room.

"May I use your phone, Issah?".

"Certainly, go ahead".

First Kofi rang his wife, Maggie. "Darling, I am okay and will be home soon, expect me within the next fifteen or twenty minutes. Okay, see you soon", he said quickly.

"Alright darling, but frankly you've been away too long. Why?".

"Don't worry, Mag. I will explain everything when I come. Cheers, darling", he said as he replaced the receiver.

He relaxed quietly for a couple of minutes or so, and rang again.

"Is that Sophia?" he asked, "your voice appears changed. What's wrong darling", he enquired sounding as serious as he could in the serio-comic circumstances.

"Well, darling I still have not heard from the Embassy about my visa. And I am getting rather worried. After all, you are leaving next week, and then what do I do?", she asked him.

"I've told you darling not to fret over this matter. You know these official things take sometime. I will see what I can do about it before leaving. Anyway I see you, darling, tomorrow 6 pm. Are you free, Sophia?"

"Yes, darling. I will be waiting for you, as always". Sophia replied.

After these two phone calls, Kofi repeated his profuse thanks and appreciation to Issah, ending "One day Captain, I will show my deep gratitude to you for what you have done for me".

"You're welcome, Colonel. It was a pleasure to serve you. Your wish is my command anytime. After all what are friends for but to help each other as necessary", Issah commented nicely.

The two officers shook hands. The Colonel patted the Captain on the back, and after waving him goodbye sped off. He drove straight home, smiling quietly to himself all along. He felt inside him that he had killed two birds, or possibly three, with one stone.

Kofi reached home contented, a relaxed man. The nervousness and fidgeting of the past earlier hours were now all a thing of the past. He was particularly effusive with praises for his wife.

"Ah, my dear Maggie, darling, what can I do without you. Eh?" he asked as she welcomed him home. "Nice to see you back. The children and I have been busy packing and getting things ready. Everything is all set for the party next Wednesday, love. The only news since you left is that the batman came and informed me that the farm-labourer's second wife had a baby yesterday. A boy", she went on.

Kofi enthusiastically welcomed the news. In fact, he was over excited about the news, which made Maggie remark. "What's come on you, darling? The way you're behaving, one would think you're the father".

"Merely delighted for the poor woman. It's her only son, and with four daughters under her belt, she had been anxiously praying and looking forward to the birth of a son. Now she will be so happy. Very happy indeed".

"I am so happy for her, but not all that much. How on earth is she, or are they going to look after these plenty children. How, simply how?"

"Don't worry, darling, 'God will provide', they say and believe. The fact that there are no maternity benefit payments or benefits, or social security payments from the state, does not worry them at all". The rest of the evening Kofi and Maggie spent reminiscing over the past, joking here and there with their children more than they usually do. The children were delighted to see their father in such a jovial mood, which as far as they could remember was more the exception than the rule.

At about 10 pm. Maggie having given her daily instruction to the maid and batman for the following day, retired to bed. Kofi stayed behind for an hour or so, listening to modern jazz music on his newly-acquired stereo music system, tapping his feet to the music as he went along. He retired to bed, pleased and happy with himself.

Maggie was putting out her bedside lamp when he went into the bedroom. He undressed and kissing and caressing Maggie, suddenly fell deeply asleep. It was about 6.30 in the morning when he got up, rather surprised that Maggie had been up already, with a cup of coffee in her hands standing near him.

The whole day was spent inconsequentially, with Maggie giving her usual, routine household instructions to her staff, while Kofi pottered round the house, going through some old papers, tearing some of them, and making a few telephone calls. He also confirmed with a neighbour about the arrangements which Maggie had made with them about their looking after their children during their absence. As Kofi's sabbatical leave had already begun, and as they were scheduled to leave the following Saturday for Jamaica, Kofi's excuses for leaving home were rather diminishing.

Casually, he told Maggie, "Darling, we're leaving on Saturday, and I must say you have organised tomorrow's party very well, with your usual efficiency and excellence. However, despite the generous allowance in dollars which we will be receiving whilst there, I think it's important that, we go there with maximum foreign exchange ourselves".

"Certainly".

"Good. Well, I did some deal with a Lebanese business man a few months ago, and he promised to pay me in dollars. He's not given it to me yet. So I am going to see him right away, before it's too late".

"What do you think of it, Maggie?"

"A jolly good idea. Go for it Kofi, dear, these businessmen are a tricky lot".

His latest assignment having received the blessing of Maggie, Kofi set out to achieve his undeclared objective. After a quick kiss on the cheek for his wife, he drove out waving to her, as she stood at the door. It was about 4.30 pm. when he left the house. The weather was beginning to get cool, as it usually does before 6 pm. The sky was clear and bright. With nothing on his mind but his mission, Kofi Johnson drove in the direction of Madina, stopping on the way to buy oranges and pineapples from the fruit-sellers on the side of the road.

At precisely 5 pm he parked his car in front of Sophia's house. There at the door, in a lovely, light green dress, was Sophia, beaming a most enticing smile of welcome. They hugged each other as he entered the door. They kissed madly, then settled on the three-seater settee. On the table before them were cans of cold lager beer, and a bowl of peanuts and stuffed olives.

"You made it, dear, so nice and great to see you again, darling. Oh, how I miss you, dear. What can I do without you?"

Kofi smiled, and said "You know, Sophia, how dear you're to me. You're part of me, and I trust, I am of you, Eh?"

They sat close, very close to each other, and sipped the cold beer, which Kofi frankly preferred to champagne. As they held their hands, and continued slowly to drink and talk generally, Kofi knew all along what was on her mind. Sooner or later, the problem had to be faced, and he was prepared emotionally for it.

"Kofi, quite frankly I am getting very worried about my visa application. I've not heard from the embassy yet. My ticket and everything are okay. I can't understand it, darling".

"Sophia, I've told you often enough that these official matters take a bit of time. Especially in the case of Jamaica, following their recent troubles, I will not be surprised at all that all applications are delayed by red-tape and officialdom. But don't worry, everything will be alright, I am hundred percent certain".

"You sure, darling?" she asked.

"Positive. It will be okay, no need to worry".

So reassured, she got up and walked to the kitchen. She returned with a large, silver-coated tray on which were two large plates of food. A firm believer in the old saying that the way to a man's heart is through his stomach, Sophia had been busy in the afternoon preparing one of Kofi's favourite dishes, boiled yam and beef stew, with green vegetables, tomatoes and mush-

44

rooms.

Although Kofi had firmly told her not to provide any meal, as there would not be much time for it, and although he was scheduled to eat his usual supper upon return home, he could not resist what had been put before him. As he looked at the meal, he reflected on the time factor. For the more time spent eating, meant less time for screwing. On the other hand, he felt equally strongly about the need to eat well, in order to get in abundance the calories needed for the sexual assignment ahead.

He deliberately, enjoyed every morsel. Sophia also appeared to relish the meal, although she talked more than Kofi. The meal over, and washed down with the last glass of cold beer, Kofi looked quickly at his watch, then began to caress her, starting from the ears, through the bosom and downwards. The adrenaline was flowing freely in both of them. The pituitary gland also was working at full speed. As their heart-beats increased in tempo and speed, Kofi got up, and winking to Sophia, walked hand-in-hand with her to the bedroom.

She undressed slowly and patiently. Kofi had already undressed, and was lying on the bed, ready for action. She put on some nice sexy record, and lay on the bed. Kofi caressed and fondled her further. They came closer to each other, and just when Kofi felt ready to go, and perform his manly duty, of which he was rather notorious in the barracks, his over-excited penis just went limp and dead. Suddenly the high voltage behind it had dropped to zero.

Sophia was furious and boiling inside. Kofi felt humiliated, angry and exasperated, with nobody but himself. He lay on the bed, quickly cursing himself.

"What's a man's use if he cannot impress his mistress. What's the world, my world coming to?" he quietly asked himself.

Sophia, like a good mistress, was more concerned to satisfy him, than herself. With a woman's intuition and realising the crisis that had suddenly developed said, "Darling, don't worry, just rest a bit and try again. It will be alright".

Kofi said nothing, as he lay on the bed in a sad, dejected state.

It took a lot of hard work on Sophia's part, massaging him, carousing him, kissing him, and doing everything possible within her power, before Kofi's sexual engine could be restarted, albeit faintly and slowly. It had taken her a full twenty minutes of sustained effort before Kofi achieved any worthwhile results.

"I love you, dear, forever", he said esctatically.

"So do I", she uttered lovingly.

Throughout the episode of Kofi's sexual anti-climax, Sophia had been very understanding. It had not come as a complete surprise to her. For she had noticed, with growing despair, that during the past three years that she had known Kofi intimately, his sexual powers had been rapidly diminishing. Many a time she had thought of telling him to consult a doctor, but on reflection had decided to keep her despair to herself.

After a deep sleep of about an hour by Kofi, during which time, she only slept lightly, she woke him up.

"Kofi, get up. It's getting to seven".

"What, darling?", he asked, eyes half-opened.

"It's about seven o'clock, so you better get up, unless, you're staying tonight".

"Hmm", Kofi sighed, as he gathered his thoughts together and realised that he should by then be at home, instead of being in Sophia's house.

"You mean, darling, it's almost seven?"

"Yes, Sir", she uttered slowly.

He jumped out of the bed, got himself together, and rushing to put his clothes on, put on his trousers without his pants. Sophia amusingly pointed out this to him.

"Eh, what are you doing, not putting your pants on?"

"Sophia, I'm late, very late. Forget it", he said as he quickly shoved the pants into his left hand trouser pocket.

"I must be going now, Sophia. I will ring you tomorrow evening. Cheers, darling, and take care", he remarked, and rushed towards his car.

As she waved to him, he sped away. En route home, he stopped at a public telephone kiosk and telephoned his wife.

"I'm on my way. Mag. Everything is alright. I had a long

46

discussion with that rogue. I will tell you more when I see you in five or ten minutes time. Sorry I'm so late".

Maggie said nothing. She was too angry to say anything.

Soon Kofi was home. Walking towards the door, he shouted affectionately, "Hello Maggie, I'm back". Maggie heard him, but made no remark. Kofi went in and said, "Darling I'm in, sorry for the delay".

"Where have you been all this time, Eh? and what have you been doing? You said you would be away for only a few minutes, and look at the time now. Look", she said furiously. She paused for a moment, and then continued, "You're supposed to be on leave. You're supposed to be getting ready for our departure not to mention tomorrow's party and you're always disappearing. Why, why?"

Kofi mumbled incoherently, and as his wife walked towards the kitchen shouting "I'm fed up. This is intolerable, it's despicable", Kofi remarked "I've been at the home of the Lebanese businessman trying to pry my money from him".

"I simply don't believe it, Kofi".

"It's true. In fact, I wanted it straight in cash, but after a long argument he undertook to send it to my London bank at the end of the month", he said unconvincingly.

"Quite frankly I do not believe this yarn, and please, may I know who is this so-called Lebanese businessman, Eh?", she demanded.

"I don't mind telling you, Maggie, but we each firmly promised not to tell our wives, for as you know news travels fast in the barracks, but believe me it's true. You'll see it when the money is in, Maggie".

"Well, Kofi, there's no point in going on and on. I simply cannot buy this story. Please, for heaven's sake, try and stay at home", she stated.

Her husband walked away casually to the sitting room, put on the television and began to watch it, dozing intermittently in the process.

Later on Maggie went to the kitchen and prepared a snack for Kofi considering that her husband had had a beautiful lunch, the snack was more than a meal. She placed a wooden, smartly-polished tray before him. Kofi was not keen to eat. He was almost on the point of saying that he was not at all hungry, when he suddenly told her, "I'm really looking forward to this. I feel rather famished". And as he began to eat, he added, "And as always, your high culinary skills are more than evident. What can I do without my Maggie?"

She smiled, and got up to put off the television.

The rest of the evening was spent discussing things generally, going over the following day's list of guests, and finalising their plans following their departure. Eventually, at about 11 pm Maggie and Kofi, after giving some pep talk to their children, retired to bed. No sooner had his head retired to bed than Kofi was completely lost to the conscious world, happily dreaming away. And as more often than not, Maggie spent the next fifteen or so minutes reading papers, a novel, a part of the Bible.

Chapter 4

This Wednesday was the day for the farewell party for Maggie and her husband. The morning and afternoon were spent putting finishing touches to all the arrangements. Everything needing polishing had been beautifully polished. The house was spotlessly tidy, ship-shape Bristol fashion. With military precision, Maggie had supervised all the arrangements, and the preparation of the dishes. In fact, all that that Kofi did was to ensure that there were enough drinks and fruit juices and soft drinks there to keep spirits high for about five hours.

At 7.30 pm the guests began to arrive. First to arrive was the Chairman, Joint Chiefs of Staff himself, General Manu in immaculate dark, lounge suit, white shirt, and smart black shoes, with gold buckles. Accompanying him was his gorgeous wife, Mrs Grace Manu, in a dashing, Northern-style, Muslim dress. It was white in colour, with strips of blue intricately woven into it, in a way and manner, that highlighted the attractive bust of its wearer.

Couple by couple they came in, to receive the same warm hugs from Maggie and Kofi. Indeed, all the invitees were present punctually, a rather unusual event in Africa. Their times of arrival, their clothes, their deportment, were all a confirmation of the fact that they were happily there to join Kofi and Maggie to enjoy themselves, and send them off on their mission to Jamaica.

After the padre had said prayers, the guests and their hosts tucked into the meal, elaborately laid out before them, the earlier drinks having already warmed their hearts and loosened their tongues a bit. Maggie had really surpassed herself. She felt that this was a chance, not too often come by, to impress the Chairman and his wife, especially. The first course was light garden-eggs soup, containing boiled snails. This was followed by a fish dish-steamed fish, with boiled potatoes, and a sprinkle of lettuce. The main course was beef-stew, served with boiled rice, fried yam and ladies fingers. There was an assortment of condiments on the large dining-table, covered with spotlessly-white table cloth, with cloth napkins to match.

As a good hostess, Maggie had ensured that there was ample non-alcoholic drinks at the tables, as the Chairman and his wife, and a few other guests were strict Muslims. No pork was in sight, obviously. For the non-Muslims, as the meal went on their champagne glasses were plentifully filled up. The dessert of chocolate mousse and coffee completed Maggie's handiwork, and what a fantastic success it was. The broad smiles on the faces of the guests, the look of utter satisfaction in their eyes said it all. It had indeed been a most enjoyable evening.

Then came the speeches. That of the padre, a happily-married man, with five children, was as expected. It dwelt heavily on morality, especially sexual morality, interspersing his after dinner speech with a few, apt quotations from the Holy Book.

The President of the Military Promotions Board, Brigadier Kwame Battah, a secret enemy of Kofi, stood up to say his piece.

"We've in Kofi Johnson, a first-class military officer of impeccable credentials and achievements. Both here at camp and during his stint in the Congo, now Zaire, he has shown the professionalism and dedication to duty which is an example to many officers", he waxed on eloquently.

"Hear, hear. Well said", many of the guests commented, interrupting him. Brigadier Battah, looking around him with complete self-satisfaction, continued.

"I speak not only for myself, but for my wife when I say that we are convinced and certain that the future holds a lot in store for this fine couple". Battah so concluded, amid vigorous clapping, as he sat down. Although the other speakers were listened to intently, the guests were all awaiting the words of wisdom from the Chairman, who by coming to the dinner-party had added his enormous prestige, rank and influence to both guests and their hosts. But General Raul Manu, a real officer and a gentleman, was a man of few words. He believed more in action than in a plethora of words. He stood up to speak.

"Friends, I wish first of all to thank Maggie for the sumptuous dinner which she has provided us. I am certain that she has applied to this exercise the same enthusiasm and dedication that she shows in her charity work for the disabled and the mentally-handicapped. She has been an asset to the wives of the officer corps, and I am certain that Kofi will go very far with such a woman behind him. After all, isn't there a saying that behind every successful man is a good woman. And we are happy that both of them are going together to Jamaica, on a mission that should bring credit not only to themselves but to the whole armed forces."

"For BASSA to have been invited to choose a president for this commission of enquiry, is an achievement to our dear country and her armed forces. For Kofi to have been selected for this important assignment is a credit to himself and his wife".

"More, more. Hear, hear. Good talk", his audience interrupted. He paused for calm, then continued, "In choosing Kofi to go to Jamaica, my senior colleagues and I took so many factors into account. We, metaphorically, looked at Kofi, from head to toe, warts and all. We considered his achievements, general record and shortcomings, everything. But in all this assessment I was mindful of the famous statement by Professor Hans Kuhn, Professor of Theology, Tubbingen University, in Germany, that, and here, I quote, if you permit me 'Nobody is perfect, except God'.

Turning towards Kofi and Maggie, he remarked, "You go with the best wishes of all your friends and colleagues in MANDALAY Camp. We wish you bon voyage, and hope that you come back soon, after a successful completion of your mission".

And lifting his glass, he stated, "And now, ladies and gentlemen, please, join me in toasting Kofi and Maggie, our new ambassadors to Jamaica". He sat down among much cheering and clapping.

The sultry evening continued with much dancing and funmaking. Everybody seemed to be enjoying himself. Then suddenly the telephone rang, and before Maggie could reach the phone, her husband had got hold of it already.

Although Kofi pulled the telephone cord so that he could speak in private in the corridor much as he tried to speak in whispers, he could still be overheard by some of his guests.

"No, no, impossible, please", he went on and on. The conversation went on for a few minutes, about two or three minutes in all. And when Kofi returned to his guests, he was ever so apologetic.

"Sorry, friends, just a little difficulty that I had to see to. Hope you are enjoying yourself", he said with a big smile on his face, which he hoped would conceal the internal turmoil that was going on inside him. For whether the guests who heard part of the telephone conversation from Kofi's end, understood the full meaning of it or not, Kofi himself was badly shaken. Why?.

Well, having just returned from a telephone call which included the bombshell that Sophia was planning on one pretext or another, to call at the house, at the height of merry-making, was not the sort of news that anyone in Kofi's situation at that time would welcome. And he knew that Sophia was if anything, a very determined woman. Consequently, although he joined his wife in enlivening the party as much as possible, it was evident to the discerning at the party, that Kofi, for the rest of the night, was not completely himself.

Still the show must go on, and indeed it went on till about 3.30 in the morning. When the guests began to depart Maggie was completely and utterly exhausted. With the maid, batman and other household staff entirely whacked, it would be no exaggeration to state that they were all rather pleased to see the backs of the guests.

Maggie, despite her flagging energies, supervised efficiently the clearing of the mess, to the utter annoyance of her household staff, who were exhausted, and could not avoid whispering under their breaths some fulsome, uncomplimentary language against their boss.

Meanwhile, Kofi more emotionally, than physically exhausted, had quietly slipped to the bedroom, had undressed and gone to bed. He had gone to bed a rather worried man. And with all his macho image among his colleagues, was fast a sleep within a matter of a few minutes. By the time Maggie joined him in bed he was far gone.

The V.I.P. lounge at the International Airport was full of military officers and their wives. Some of the officers were in uniform, other not. It was a bright morning. Everyone present was in good spirits. They were at the airport to see off Colonel Kofi Johnson and his wife, Maggie, on their official trip to KINGSTON, JAMAICA. Going round shaking hands, hugging and kissing, were the couple, beaming friendly smiles on their happy faces. Just before the final call for the plane was announced, Kofi slipped to a near-by telephone and tried unsuccessfully to telephone. Within a couple of minutes he had rejoined their well-wishers.

As Kofi was giving a final pep talk to his children, one of the minor airport security officials, came and told him that he was wanted outside.

"Who's it?" he whispered to the messenger.

"I don't know her name, Sir".

Kofi thought for a moment, and said "Go and tell him that the plane is about to leave, and I have to go for security check-up now", he remarked quietly to the messenger. He then turned round, and with a final hand-shake to his best friend, Issah Bukari, he and Maggie began to walk to the electronic security check-point in the departure section of the airport. He walked away sighing with relief that there had been no untoward event at the final departure hours of their journey. For Kofi had very good reason in not wanting to see Sophia before leaving. Only the previous day, he had firmly promised her, before and after sexual intercourse with her, that he would without fail, give her a personal note to send to the Jamaican Embassy in PAGOS, about her visa application, if she had not received it already by then.

As he had failed to do so, and knowing Sophia's temper, he felt that any confrontation of her at that time, at the airport would produce only disastrous results. He thought it best not, to tempt fate too much. After all, he mused to himself, the best strategy sometimes is calculated retreat.

Fully settled in their seats, Maggie and Kofi smiled at each other, as they enjoyed the flight. For Maggie, it was her first flight since their return from London, where they had got married twelve years ago. For her husband, this was also his first, civilian flight for years, if the military flights to the Congo and neighbouring African states, were excluded. In anycase, for both of them the six and a quarter hours flight from APPAPA to J.F. Kennedy Airport in New York, via Darkar in Senegal, was their first North Atlantic crossing.

The meal on the plane was good, and the service by the American cabin crew was faultless. Indeed, the flight was uneventful except that about an hour before landing, the aircraft got into a bit of turbulence. Kofi was sleeping when the sign 'Fasten your seats belts', came on. Maggie was not, woke him and he put his safety belt on. Despite the assurances of the Captain that the turbulence was nothing to worry about and no threat whatsoever to safety, Maggie was very nervous and worried.

"Kofi, what's happening? the wing of the plane on this side is shaking badly".

Kofi stretched his neck to have a look, and then remarked "Oh, this is nothing, Mag. It's just the heavy clouds beating on the wings. Soon it will be okay". The flight continued bumping for a few minutes, then it was all clear lovely skies again. Looking down through one of the windows of the plane on her side, the clouds looked like huge, vast expanses of white, light blue blankets or cottonwool. It was a most majestic sight.

Maggie could not stop admiring this aspect of nature, which, although lovely and beautiful, yet could pose, such a threat to the plane and its passengers. Arriving at J.F.K. airport, Kofi and Maggie quickly caught a connecting flight to Kingston, Jamaica. The changes of planes had not been as laborious and time consuming as they had feared. Everything went smoothly.

The second leg of their flight was equally uneventful but for a minor episode. An hour after they had taken off from J.K.F.

airport an African looking man of about thirty, with swarthy features suddenly walked from the rear of the plane to the front, and then shouted,

"Hands up all you bastards. I am in charge now. We're flying to Cuba. This is the P.T.S speaking", he muttered as he held a small automatic revolver in his left hand, with his finger on the trigger.

For less than a split second, there was complete quiet in the plane. Then he continued, "I've a powerful grenade attached to my balls, and any move by any of you, and I will let go". He paused then said, excitedly, "I am ready to die. I mean business, I ....", but he did not finish his sentence, for just at that moment, the Captain announced, "This is your Captain speaking. We've been hi-jacked. Please, do whatever the gentleman asks you to do. I repeat, obey his instructions".

As the Captain was speaking, an aircraft security man in the front section of the aircraft, who was dressed as an ordinary passenger, suddenly got up in a flash, and grabbed the gun, in a matter of a second or two from the gun-man. With the aid of another disguised security man from the rear end of the plane, and assisted by the male cabin crew, they tied the man's arms and feet, and there and then, pulled down his trousers. It was then that they found that it was only an ordinary tennis ball that was attached to his balls. Furthermore, as they gagged, blind-folded, and plugged the ear-holes of the criminal, the crew discovered that the gun was only a toy gun. Still this psycho-path, with his toy gun and tennis ball, had caused enough tension and havoc on the plane to the two-hundred and five passengers. For a matter of a couple of minutes, he had created a nightmarish hell for them that they will always remember for the rest of their lives. After the Captain and his crew had successfully dealt with this patently dangerous episode, the Captain announced, "This is your Captain speaking. My crew and I are very sorry about what's just happened. We thank you all for your co-operation. You may unfasten your seat belts and relax. I've asked the cabin crew to serve champagne all round to celebrate. Thank you".

As the air stewardesses went round with the drinks, smiling sweetly, trying to hide their own inner fear and nervousness, Maggie asked Kofi,

"Who are the P.T.S.? Are they connected with the Middle East or Africa?"

"Quite truthfully, Mag, I simply do not know. I've never heard of them. It may be a completely new terrorist group", he said with a meaningful sigh.

For the rest of the flight there was animated talk and discussion on the plane. Everyone was asking everyone how it was that the criminal had been able to smuggle the toy gun and the pseudo-grenade attached his balls without the airport security at the point of departure in J.F.K. detecting it. Listening to all the lively discussions among the relieved and happy passengers, Kofi remarked to Maggie, "Quite frankly, darling, I find this puzzling. If even the electronic detector failed to detect the gun and the ball, how could the security men who conducted, or should conduct, a thorough body search have failed to notice that the man's balls were oversize, eh? This's a mystery to me".

Maggie, who had not fully recovered from the shocking experience, merely remarked, almost in a whisper, "Thank God, it's all over. Hallelujah, God's name be blessed".

Finally, as the plane touched ground on landing, all the passengers, in unison started to clap. The aircraft taxied to its bay, and eventually, the engines stopped whirring. The 'fasten seat belt' sign was still on. The Captain and Co-pilot came out of the cock-pit and standing in front of the passengers, the Captain, said,

"Once again, on behalf of Foxton Airlines, my crew and myself, I wish to thank you all for your assistance and co-operation. We hope that we will have the pleasure of meeting you again on our flights. Goodbye". Both pilots doffed their caps and smiled. One of the passengers, a blond Irish woman of about sixty years who was a first-class passenger, got up suddenly and began,

"I am certain I speak for us all in expressing to you, Captain and your crew our heartfelt thanks for the miraculous way and

56

manner that you handled this unforgettable episode. We owe you our lives and we thank you very, very much. We certainly will be flying with you next time round, after this superb display of cool efficiency. Once again, Sir, thank you all", she concluded. As she sat down, the passengers could see a Police van and a military jeep approach the plane. Both vehicles stopped close to the aircraft. The door of the aircraft was opened. Meanwhile, most of the passengers, practically all of them, were literally throwing money towards the two security men, who sat on either side of the criminal. US Dollar bills, pounds sterling and other currencies in various large denominations were being showered on the security men by the grateful passengers, as they watched the man taken away by two police officers, and an army sergeant, followed by security men. Next, the safety belts were unfastened, and the passengers began to get off the plane, one by one, starting with the first-class passengers.

The Police van and the military jeep sped away, with sirens on the police van blaring. As Kofi and Maggie stepped on the tarmac, they had one look, one final look at the aircraft, before walking towards a party of four Jamaican officials who had come to welcome them. Among the four was an Army Colonel in uniform. After the preliminary exchange of greetings, the welcoming party took care of their guests, passports and luggage, and drove them to their bungalow. This was to be their official residence during their period of stay. It was a standard, two-bedroom bungalow, with tasteful furniture and fittings. The chandeliers from the ceiling in the bedrooms, lounge and dining room, were of pure Czech crystal, with an intricate 10-arm design. Without question, the bungalow was better furnished than their own in APPAPA. And the household staff of a maid, gardener, batman, were properly attired awaiting their new bosses. In addition, Kofi was given a driver, which service he had lacked in his own country.

The Jamaican officials, having settled in their guests, and introduced them to the staff, welcomed them to their new home and left. But before doing so, the most senior of the four gentlemen said, "Colonel Johnson I don't at all envy you your new assignment. It's a very delicate job, that you've been called to do, but we are certain our government has got the right man for the right job".

"Well, I'll do my best, Sir", Kofi said, with Maggie next to him.

"Colonel, we hope you and madam have a quiet rest for today, and if it's all right by you, tomorrow morning at eleven your driver will take you to the Attorney-General for formal briefing. He's such a charming man", so said the senior civil servant.

"No problem at all. We'll be ready at eleven. And once again our thanks to you all for all your effort on our behalf. We already feel at home here. It's so lovely", Kofi remarked.

"My husband and I will love this place, which is going to be a home from home. You obviously, Sir, did not leave anything to chance", she stated.

There were polite handshakes all round, before the senior civil servant and his three colleagues left.

As soon as they had left, Kofi and Maggie sat on the settee in the sitting-room, and really began to unwind.

"Maggie, is it not smashing? These Jamaicans know how to do things proper. Look at the ceiling, look at the kitchen. Smashing".

"Great, absolutely perfect. You'll have to find a way, darling, to prolong the enquiry beyond the agreed twelve months, Okay? After all, I've not had a really good holiday for years. You know that".

Stretching himself, Kofi said, "Let's call the people in. I am dying for a drink after all that we've been through, don't you think so?".

"Good, let's go", she said. They both got up, tired as they were with jet-lag and the nerve-racking torment on the aircraft, and walked to the staff quarters, which was quite close to the building. They walked back to the bungalow with their new staff. Then Kofi said,

"As you know I'm Colonel Johnson from BASSA. My wife and I will be here for somewhile, and we expect you to do your work as responsible adults that you are. We don't expect any trouble,

58

and hope that you'll enjoy serving us. Madam will be here most of the time, and you should always be at her service. You'll find her a very nice person to work with. Any questions?", he asked.

"No, Sir", the tallest of the four answered.

"What's your name?", Kofi asked.

"John, Sir",

"John what?", Kofi enquired.

"John Booker, Sir, but everybody call me John".

Maggie enquired, "And what's yours?", she asked the maid.

"Madam, I'm called Ruth, Ruth Morgan".

"And you?" Maggie asked of the rest,

"I am Clifford Trench, gardener".

"And I am, Madam, James Gordon, the batman".

"My name is Jacob Evans, the driver".

"So, I see. Nice, biblical names, Eh?"

"What do you have, John, to drink?"

"Madam, we've plenty whisky, rum, brandy, wine, champagne, sherry", he recited enthusiastically, until Maggie cut him short.

"We'll settle for two large cups of coffee and toasted sandwiches".

"Good, I've big roast chicken ready in the fridge".

"By the way who normally does the cooking?", Maggie asked them.

John talked first. "Madam, sometimes I cook, sometimes Ruth is doing".

Maggie dismissed her new staff to their rooms, except for John who went to the kitchen to get ready the sandwiches and coffee.

As they walked away, Kofi remarked to his wife, "Darling, we've to watch it or else we'll go back with a weight problem. I am bad enough now. Don't forget to remind me all the time about the smoking. I am determined to stop completely before we return".

"I shall try, Kofi, but I am so fed up with your stopping and re-starting that I really doubt whether you wish to stop at all. You saw at the airport all the anti-smoking posters, didn't you?"

59

Kofi just looked at her and smiled. As they were waiting for John's coffee and sandwiches, the telephone in the sitting room rang. It was from the Chief of Jamaican Defence Force, Major-General Tim Jones.

"Welcome, welcome to Kingston, Colonel. How was the flight. How're you and Mrs Johnson settling in?" the General enquired in a very friendly tone.

"Thank you, General. We're delighted to be here, and the flight, well, it was smooth, but not too smooth. I think you've heard about the attempted highjack of the plane".

"Yes, yes. I heard something briefly about it on the radio. How dreadful. This sort of thing is getting too much. I think it's high time these people were taught a lesson. You must be exhausted after this long flight. See you tomorrow. After your briefing with the A.G., and you've had some rest, my wife and I would love to have both of you for dinner at 7 pm at our home".

"You're so kind, Sir. We will love to come". Kofi told him.

"Don't worry, my car will call at your residence at 6.45pm. Right?".

"We look forward very much to it, Sir", Kofi said as he put the telephone receiver down.

The obsequious John had quickly got the sandwiches and coffee ready and brought them before his new master and his wife. As they tucked into the sandwiches, John who returned to the kitchen, opened the kitchen door just wide enough to peer through the corner of his eye at his new bosses eating what he had prepared for them.

The sandwiches were indeed good and delicious, and were an excellent advertisement of John's culinary skill. Having done justice to the snack, both Maggie and Kofi, looked round their new home, did a bit of unpacking, and then went to bed. It was about half-past five. They slept soundly and deeply. After all, they had been travelling almost twelve hours, crossing two time zones in the process.

At about 11.00 pm, John and his colleagues, seeing no sign of their bosses, decided after urgent consultation among themselves to leave them a note and go to bed.

The question was, who was to write the note?. Further consultations took place, and it was agreed that Ruth was to write the note, with the text agreed by all. As such, the note was a joint effort in all respects. It read, "Master, we go to bed together 11 pm. Morning call 7. Goodnight, Sir, John, Clifford, Jacob, James, Ruth".

At about one in the morning, Kofi got up to go to the bathroom. Returning to the bedroom, his eyes caught sight of the note. He stopped and read it, and then went back to sleep. The cool tropical breeze blew in through their windows, and with the gentle rumbling of the sea a more ideal scene and atmosphere for a long sleep could not be imagined or asked for.

With the morning birds singing, as they always do in the tropics, at about six in the morning, Maggie and Kofi gradually woke up. For a few split seconds, whilst the mind was still unfocused and rather unclear, they thought that they were at home in BASSA. A knock at the door soon put them right. Indeed, it was about seven in the morning, and Ruth, the maid, was bringing them their morning tea.

Grudgingly they got their tired bones out of bed, got themselves presentable and let the maid with the tea in.

"Good morning, Madam. Nice day", said Ruth hesitatingly.

Kofi and Maggie, responded appropriately and took the tea.

At 10.30 in a lovely, cool morning, following their arrival in Jamaica, Kofi was driven alone to meet the Attorney-General. He felt that it would be more correct to go alone on this first, formal meeting, and perhaps take Maggie to subsequent informal, social gatherings. Maggie said goodbye to him, and concentrated on familiarising herself with her new, temporary home and the servants.

"How nice to see you, Colonel. Really great. Did you come alone? You should have brought along your wife. We're very informal here", the tall smart-looking Attorney-General said. Although he was fifty, apart from the touches of grey on the sides of his head, he could easily be taken for forty or even thirty-five. He was thin, and unlike some of his colleagues, had not developed yet middle age spread. He was clean shaven, and well turned out in a dark blue, stripped business suit.

Stephen Baldwin was a good, decent minded, lawyer's lawyer. He had taken on the job only after much persuasion from the President, as he was doing so well at the Bar. Indeed, his salary as A.G. was only a quarter of what he was earning in private practice. He had felt that taking on the job was his modest contribution to his country's development and welfare. He was a lovable person, in all respects.

"By the way, how was your flight? I understand that you had some awful experience. These hijackers are really becoming a menace. Do sit there, Sir", he said in as friendly a way as possible.

"My department is at your service, should you need any assistance whatsoever. This mutiny, some call it an attempted coup, has given us a hell of trouble. It's really shaken the foundations of this quiet, peace-loving island, and we hope that this enquiry, headed by your eminent self, with all your experience, will assist us to get to the bottom of it all, and also that suggestions would be made about the prevention of a similar disaster", the A.G went on, as his secretary brought in coffee for two.

Like a good visitor, keen to learn, Kofi did all the listening, whilst his host did all, or practically all, the talking.

Between drinking their coffee, the Attorney-General, said, "Our little island has gone through hell. It's been most awful, and if you can get to the bottom of the whole dastardly business, Jamaica would owe you a lot, Colonel".

"Well, Mr Baldwin, I'll do my best. I am grateful for all that is being done to make my work as manageable as possible. You all have been so co-operative so far. I trust that it will continue".

"Certainly, no question about that. I understand you're having dinner with the Chief tonight. He's such a marvellous, good man. What we would have done without him, I simply don't know".

"I've heard so much about him, and my wife and I are looking forward very much to meeting him tonight", Kofi interposed.

For the next few minutes, the conversation continued pleasantly, dwelling on the weather, the vital statistics of the country and her people.

"Well, Colonel, I think I should not keep you any further. It's been so nice talking with you and I am certain that you will enjoy your stay and assignment in our struggling country. See you soon", the urbane, Attorney-General remarked, as he saw his guest off to the door.

Kofi went into his car, and was driven to his new home.

"Hello, darling, you're back. How was it?"

"It was a most fruitful and illuminating meeting. A most charming man, this attorney general. The cream of Kingston society. I learnt a lot, Maggie. How was your day?"

"Pretty good, darling. I've been sorting things out, and trying to pick a few words of the local lingo. A lovely lunch is ready cooked by John, under my watchful, eye. It tastes delicious".

"Hmm", he sighed, then asked for a glass of cold white wine. This was quickly brought in by the maid, on Maggie's order.

The couple enjoyed their first Kingston lunch, then had a short siesta, and then began to continue the sorting out of their luggage.

"These things, Kofi, cannot be rushed. Let's take our time, and do things properly. After all we are supposed to be here for the next twelve months or so. Eh?"

Later in the evening, Kofi and Maggie were driven to the home of the Major-General Tim Jones, the Chief of the Jamaican Defence Force.

"Ah, my dear Colonel, you're most welcome. Come in, right in", the General remarked to Kofi and Maggie. Both the General and his wife were appropriately dressed for the evening. His wife was in a stunning dark dress, with a modest slit on both sides. She wore three rows of cultured pearls, with earrings to match. Her marriage ring had a brilliant, diamond piece, which was neither big nor small, but was certainly impressive. Although now a mature woman of about forty-five, Elizabeth Jones had the beauty still of a film star.

Her husband, Major-General Tim Jones was an affable, jovial army boss, who could easily be mistaken for an ambassador from a wealthy Third World country. For the evening, he was in a dark blue suit with a spotlessly white shirt, with a light grey tie, supported by an appropriate breast-pocket handkerchief.

After preliminary drinks and light social banter, the guests and their hosts were served a four-course dinner, by two white-uniformed household staff, wearing matching white gloves.

"Colonel, please feel free to call in at anytime. Our home is your second home, and for your dear wife also, for your stay here", enthused the Army Chief. "I'm sure after the Colonel and his wife have got used to life here on our little island, they would not want to go back. I've an exciting full programme for Maggie", said his wife as she turned with a sweet smile to her.

Not only did the guests enjoy the meal, but equally lovely and magnificent was the company of their hosts. After the meal, they relaxed over glasses of champagne, and finally coffee. They talked about their children, their families and their various experiences in the army. Elizabeth Jones was the perfect hostess, and was at great pains to ensure that her guests thoroughly enjoyed themselves.

"You know, Kofi, your colleagues in BASSA, are really lucky to have been spared this sort of army indiscipline. It completely and utterly disorganises the army, undermines authority, and once the seed of military indiscipline is sown it is very difficult, to uproot it. Don't you think?" he asked.

"Precisely", Kofi replied briefly.

The General continued, "The rogues and criminals are in custody, and we are waiting for your report before dealing with them. We must punish them severely and appropriately, as an example, to others who may be nurturing similar ideas", he said and paused.

"General, my wife and I are already beginning to love this place. You've been so kind, and we hope that our work will be to your expectations".

"But I advise that you take the first week easy, both of you, familiarising yourselves with our country, and its problems. You must go easy, and break in gradually", Tim Jones advised his guests.

After more social talk and exchange of ideas and news on family customs and life styles in BASSA and Jamaica, and the existence in Jamaica of certain pure names of BASSAIN origin, the evening ended as it had begun, relaxed, charming and friendly.

As they were being driven to their new home, Maggie said, "Kofi I've something to tell you.- I've a strong feeling that .....", before she could finish, Kofi discreetly pointing to the driver, requested her by coded signals to stop talking or change the subject. "I've so enjoyed the evening that I am still thinking about their kindness and generosity. We'll talk when we reach home, Mag O.K?"

"Yes. Agreed". And for the rest of their return home they just looked through the car windows at the night lights of Kingston. At 12.30 in the night, they reached their new home, dismissed the household staff, and went to bed.

Unknown to Kofi, the very hour that he was talking with the Attorney-General of Jamaica, something was happening in APPAPA, which would have upset him immensely. For at that very time, Sophia was in the air, en route to the Jamaican Embassy in PAGOS, to enquire about the delay about her visa application. Sophia was a determined woman, bent on going to Jamaica, under her own steam, financially and otherwise.

Although she had no previous appointment with the consul, the ever-so polite, Major Brian Cox, on being told by her secretary of Sophia's presence, let her in.

"I am Major Cox, the Consul, Madam, can I help you?"

"Yes, Sir, sorry to bother you, but I applied for a visa for Jamaica sometime ago and I've not heard anything at all. I'm worried".

"Your name again Madam?"

"Sophia Fumey, from APPAPA".

Major Cox listened impassively, and asked, "When did you apply for the visa?"

"About two weeks ago or more, with the fee, passport photos and all".

"I see. Let me check".

Major Cox called his secretary in, and asked for the current file dealing with the most recent visa applications. After the file had been brought to him, he studied it or appeared to be studying for a few minutes, then said, "I see. Indeed Madam your application has been received and processed, but due to the recent troubles back home, it has been referred there, with others. Sorry about this, but you know bureaucracy. These things take a bit of time".

"But I've to leave shortly. I really cannot understand this. What about my going to London or Kingston itself and getting the visa there. That should be simple enough".

"Indeed, Miss Fumey, but I'm afraid under our new regulations, strictly enforced without exceptions, all visa applications from whatever source, must be referred to head-office back home. I'm really sorry about this but cannot help. I wish I could"

She eyed him solicitously and pleadingly.

"Please, Major, please, can't you help? You know, perhaps one day I may be able to help you in some way".

The Major looked at her soothingly and said, "So? Very interesting. Miss Fumey. How?"

"Well, few people know that Colonel Johnson, who has gone to Jamaica for the military enquiry is a very close friend of mine. I can assure you he listens to me".

"That's most fascinating. You know well the Colonel. What a small world. Yes, indeed, I notice he's one of the referees on your application. Good", he remarked, as he peered at her visa application file again.

As they were talking, his secretary came in and sought permission to leave. This was quickly granted. The conversation between the Major and Sophia went on about ways and means of resolving the problem at hand. They talked and talked, with the dialogue getting more intimate with time.

It all happened so imperceptibly and naturally. Sophia without realising it was being drawn closer and closer to the Major. He looked round to be sure that the doors were properly secured and the answerphone was on.

Next thing was that both of them were on the floor, with the

Major giving a methodical screw to Sophia. She was wildly enjoying it, as much as he was. Furthermore, whether her orgasm was pretended or not, she felt that the pre-ejaculation talk of Brian Cox was clear evidence that the visa problem was solved.

"Don't worry, Sophia, the impossible will be made possible. To hell with red-tape and officialdom".

"Thank you, Major, thank you very much", she said as they both rested on the floor, the Major more exhausted than the civilian.

"So I take it, Major, that I should expect the visa very, very soon".

"Certainly. First thing tomorrow, I'll send a telex to Kingston, about this and other matters. You can trust me. So give me a ring in a fortnight's time or so, by which time everything should be all right".

She dressed herself, powdered her face, applied a bit of lipstick and said goodbye to him, with an affectionate hug and a kiss on the cheek. Cox took her in his car, and drove her to the airport to catch the last but one plane to APPAPA.

Sophia felt that she had accomplished her mission. She felt elated that with or without the promised assistance of Kofi, she was going to get the necessary visa in order to be in Jamaica. She returned to her home, rather exhausted, but satisfied with herself. Sophia did not, as yet, have any grounds at all whatsoever to think that her visa application delays were in anyway to do with the very person that she was planning to visit.

After bidding goodbye to Sophia at the airport, Cox drove as quickly as possible to his house on ITOYE Island, where his long-suffering wife, had been anxiously waiting for him.

"Sorry, dear for being so late. I had to wait for a telex from home about some visa applications".

"You look exhausted, dear. Had a bad day?"

"Yes indeed, a very bad, tiring day with lots of work and the usual, numerous unscheduled calls and visitors. Sometimes they can be so exasperating". Brian said, as he relaxed on his favourite chair, musing over the emotional triangle that had been created by Kofi for himself and Sophia.

Chatting with his wife over his supper, he said, "I've not heard from Colonel Johnson yet. I hope that he and his wife are beginning to settle in. Wish them luck".

"So do I. How long, dear are they staying?", she enquired.

"I understand about six to twelve months or a bit longer. A lot of work is involved".

Following supper, the rest of the evening was spent watching television and seeing to some old family correspondence which needed attention.

For the next week or so, Brian Cox refused to have any sexual relations with his wife. The refrain was, always the same, "Very tired today, darling, tomorrow", and he would pass into a blissful slumber. But Brian was worried by a guilty conscience, and also about the possibility, however remote, that he had contracted a sexually-transmitted disease of one type or another. The days of involuntary abstinence had nothing at all to do with his ardour for his wife. On the contrary he had unwittingly put himself in the position where the best way to demonstrate his affection for her was not to have sexual relations with her, at least for sometime in the future.

Chapter 5

The bright Monday was the perfect setting for the opening day of the Commission of Enquiry, under the Presidency of Colonel Kofi Johnson of the BASSA Armed Forces. It had been convened to enquire into the causes of the mutiny in the Jamaica Army, in the previous six months, and the subsequent disturbances that followed, and to make appropriate recommendations to the Government of Jamaica, as might be found necessary. Assisting the President, apart from the secretarial staff, were two other officers, both Colonels. One was Colonel Frank Hopkins, Director of the legal services Directorate of the Armed Forces, and the other was Colonel Timothy Haig, the Directorate of Military Intelligence. Both officers, in their late forties, had been in the services for over twenty years.

Originally it was not intended to include the D.M.I. on the enquiry, but after much in-camera discussion by his peers and the civilian government, the latter had reluctantly agreed to his inclusion. Poor Tim Haig, had, for some obscure reason been under a cloud since the troubles. He was suspected by the civilian administration of being, indirectly responsible for the troubles, and at worst guilty of gross professional negligence. He was accused, of course, behind his back of having failed to foretell the mutiny.

Of course, he had stoutly defended himself and eventually won his position on the commission. He was actually aware of the fuss which had accompanied or preceded his appointment. Frank Hopkins' appointment, on the other, had been welcomed by all and sundry. He was a simple, straight forward lawyer, who happened to be in uniform. The Commission's Secretary, was a long-serving, senior civil-servant, and like all his peers in that profession, often had a wry, indecipherable smile on his bland face. Like many of them he was ever anxious to please his political masters at any particular time, and had become adept at hiding his own political or personal feelings.

At 10.00 am sharp, to the shouts of "Order", "Silence", "Silence", the three-man commission, preceded by a Military Police Sergeant, and the Secretary of the Commission, walked solemnly into the Arindel Hall, where the enquiry was to be held. It had been given a face-lift, and seating provision had been made for about five hundred members of the public.

Flanking the secretary were two audio-secretaries, with their equipment ready to go. Before the President, were three microphones. And to his right, mid-way between the spectators and the panel was the public prosecutor, no less a person than the Attorney-General. Opposite the Attorney General, was the dock with a chair in it, for the convenience of the infirm. The whole hall was full of excited, curious people, awaiting the unravelling of the account. At last, many felt the opportunity was coming for the truth, the whole truth probably, to come out.

On the previous Friday afternoon the members of the commission and the secretary had been sworn into office, and taken oaths of secrecy, by the Chief Justice of the Island. That ceremony had been duly reported in the press, without much public reaction or visible notice. What the public looked forward to were the actual proceedings and not the preliminaries, and this Monday was the day. The press gallery was full, with both local and foreign pressmen. For the story of how the mutiny or coup attempt nearly succeeded had attracted considerable external interest, especially in the neighbouring islands and the United States of America. Interest in the latter nation was particularly caused by the rumours that there was a communist dimension to the troubles.

The hall was buzzing with excitement, when the secretary of the enquiry got up.

"Ladies and gentlemen, it's my pleasant duty to introduce the members of the panel. The president is Colonel Kofi Johnson of the BASSA Armed Forces", he paused as the Colonel took a polite bow. "On his right is Colonel Timothy Haig, the Director of Military Intelligence, and on his left is Colonel Frank Hopkins,

Director of the Legal Services Directorate. On the left is the Attorney-General, Mr. Stephen Baldwin", as he mentioned their names the gentlemen bowed slightly to the public, looking as sombre as possible.

"Finally, I am the Enquiry's Secretary. The terms of reference are "to enquire in to the causes of the military events of last May, review the subsequent military-civilian events, and make appropriate recommendations", he concluded and sat down.

There was complete silence in the hall, except for the gentle whirring of the huge ceiling fan in the hall.

"The commission is now in session", remarked Colonel Johnson. The time was about 10:30. Briskly the Attorney-general got up, straightened his tie, and began, "Mr. president, Members of the commission, ladies and gentlemen, this is a momentous day in the history of this country. For today, we are set on a public search for the truth, the truth concerning the events of 5th May, in which tragically seventeen soldiers and three civilians lost their lives. We come to this enquiry with no preconceived ideas or suspicions. We start with an open mind, uncluttered with any prejudices or fixed ideas or positions. Indeed, our job here is to assist in the process of eliciting and elucidating the truth, for we are convinced, beyond any shadow of doubt, that with the facts, the true facts of the tragic episode established, by the principle of 'Res Ipsor Loquitur', the appropriate conclusions and inferences can be drawn. That a fledgling island democracy, tentatively trying to find its way in the maze of international trade and finance, with a freshly-elected, civilian democratic government, should be the victim of an irrational, futile attack from a group of self-styled liberators, should give much food for thought for all our people. For the events in question, although originating from a tiny section of the army, had ramifications and deleterious results not only in the Armed Forces, but outside". He paused and sipped a glass of water, and then fired on.

"Evidence will be led to establish conclusively before this enquiry that the military personnel currently in custody, had by a diabolical and ruthless plan, ingenious for its strategic simplicity, attempted to cause disaffection, chaos and confusion in

71

a section of the army, as part of a programme of eventually taking over the Armed Forces, and subsequently the civilian administration. And part of their scheming machination was a complete eradication of the whole officer-cops, above the rank of captain, by direct murder.

Ample evidence, Sir, shall be put before the august panel to show that by no stretch of the imagination, by no reasonable explanation of the chain of events on that sad day, could they be interpreted as being coincidental. Stage by stage, a story will unfold of a web of deceit, violence and chicanery of a type and extent never before known in our dear country. And as the mountain of evidence, poco-a poco, yields its secrets, one thing, inter alia, becomes as plain as the sky, namely, the existence of a sinister, albeit clever mastermind, with long satanic arms, behind the whole diabolical attack on the free people of Jamaica and their Armed Forces. It is our duty in the name of the people of this country, and their sons and daughters of today, and yet to be born, to expose completely the brains and hands behind the tragic May events. And in the process, the state will endeavour to show that the persons who are appearing before you were, at best willing agents and voluntary participants in these tragic and unnecessary deaths of 15th May, or at worst the real hands and brains of the operations, clothed in the loyal uniform externally of the Jamaican Armed forces, but internally and physically, were living embodiments of communism, treason, unbridled and baseless ambition, consummate and shameless disloyalty, and crass disrespect for the conventions and traditions of the Armed Forces and the civilian people whom they serve.

Mr. President, ladies and gentlemen, if ever there was a case of man's ingratitude to man, you have it before you. For the evidence will show again and again, that the perpetrators of these dastardly acts, which cost other persons their lives, had taken advantage of the complete confidence placed in them by their superiors, to literally out-wit them, and stab them in the back. Their way of saying "Thank you" to those who saw it fit to promote them, and be concerned about their welfare, was to organise and implement a number one strategy of deceit, treachery and murder.

The A.G. paused for a few seconds, looked around the assembled audience, and continued confidently, "Our achievement of independence without the shedding of a single drop of blood, was a source of pride to us all, and an example to other colonial people struggling for their freedom. It is, therefore, ironic that this brilliant record should be marred by this despicable and disgraceful national act of violence, utterly purposeless and senseless.

Mr President, ladies and gentlemen, it is now time for me to give you an outline of the treacherous machinations of the angels of death and evil who wanted to plunge our dear island into bloodshed. My colleague, the Director of Public Prosecutions, will later in the proceedings be filling in the details. Suffice it for me now to give you the bare-bones of the ghastly course of events. Sir, for purely security reasons, and in consideration of the best interests of the state, it has been decided, with the professional approval of the lawyers defending those persons so far apprehended and in custody, to refer to them only by numbers, instead of their real names,. I can assure you, sir, that there is nothing sinister whatsoever about this.

What then was the course of events which if it had succeeded would have turned our country into an interminable reign of communism, bloodshed, chaos, anarchy and tyranny.

A week before the fateful day the Military Police and the Special Branch noticed something curious and unusual in the rota of the guards responsible for guarding Government House, Broadcasting House, and the armoury. The personnel had been changed. Appropriate enquiries were duly made, and the officer responsible for these duties, 001 was queried at the National Security Council meeting. He gave the plausible assurance that it was mere operational reshuffle of no special significance whatsoever. Indeed, the investigation by Military Police and Special Branch, and the military counter-insurgency unit yielded nothing strange about this reshuffle.

A couple days later following the rota reorganisation, the

whole electricity supply in Kingston suddenly went dead. Furthermore, even the stand-by generators which should have come on automatically, failed to respond to the emergency. Perhaps all these episodes, remarkable in themselves, were mere coincidences.

To cap it all, Sir, a fortnight before the fateful day, the telephone system at military headquarters, for some inexplicable reason, was in-operational for a solid hour. In all the cases mentioned no plausible explanation or reason could be adduced to account for what had happened.

At 2.30 am on 15 May, 002, the person who as the officer in charge of the RECCE regiment, should have been in the operations room as duty officer, was again for inexplicable reason absent. Well, he had a very plausible excuse. He was at the arms depot for a personal reconnoitre against possible arms-smugglers.

Somehow or another 003 who was the second in command of the platoon, whose duty was to guard the arms depot happened to have visited the spot after hearing on the walkie-talkie that some unauthorised person or persons were in the vicinity of the depot. Alas, by the time he reached the depot, the secret combination lock of the armoury had been unlocked, the soldier on duty killed, and the armoury rifled. Yet oddly enough, it took him at least half an hour before he could report such a serious incident to the operations room, as required by the regulations.

The role of 004 in all these sequential events becomes more discernible as the facts unfold themselves. 004 was the most senior signal officer on duty on the fateful day. Despite the fact that he had four personnel on duty with him at the time, despite the fact they were all experienced operators, somehow or another major orders from brigade headquarters to relevant officers to countermand the mutiny and quell it, could not get through to the intended recipients of the message. Yet there were no evidence whatsoever of any malfunction of their transmission equipment.

Finally, ample evidence, incontrovertible evidence as clear as snow will be put before you that establishes clearly that 005 was indeed in the position to nip the mutiny in the bud if he had wanted to. He had the capacity, he had the fire-power, he had the authority. The question is whether he had also the will to do his duty.

According to his statement on interrogation, 005 has stated that at about 2 am he heard on his walkie-talkie that there was some unusual military activity around the airforce base. As such, he had immediately dispatched the available soldiers on night duty at the barracks to the airforce base, which is about four miles from the main barracks. According to his statements, by the time his men reached the base, they found that nothing unusual was happening or had happened there. Yet he allowed his men to loiter round there for over an hour before returning to their guard later in the barracks.

The question before us, Sir, is whether the action of 005 was a diversionary tactic or was the work of a hoaxer, which was part and parcel of the same devious and evil plan to mutinously instigate a section of the army either as an objection itself, or as part of a grand, diabolical operation to topple the civilian, democratic government of the country.

He stopped for a couple of seconds, sipped more water,

" Shoot them, shoot them," somebody in the audience shouted.

" We want action. Fire power," others screamed.

"Order, order," a corporal on duty shouted.

"Silence, silence, order,"

The hall was quiet again, and the Attorney General resumed.

"Finally, Mr President, members of the panel, ladies and gentlemen, we come to the evil and murderous part played in the whole wretched and shocking tragedy by 007. Evidence will be led before you that should conclusively establish that he was indeed the brains, the evil genius, behind the whole operation. His hands are soaked with blood of five senior officers that he tricked into a trap, falsely informing them that they were required at an emergency counter-insurgency, secret meeting at an appointed destination. He was successful in his wicked deception because he was one of the few officers who knew the secret code for calling the five officers to such meetings. And having, got them where he wanted, he quickly shot them immediately and set their dead bodies on fire.

"My God", somebody shrieked.

An excited man of about twenty-five, sat up and shouted "Let the blood flow", before he was hustled away by one of the soldiers on duty in the hall.

The Attorney- General, wiped a few beads of sweat from his face with a white, silk handkerchief, then went on. Mr President, members of the tribunal, it is the considered view of the state that although the series of events outlined to you earlier, may, if taken in isolation, one by one, be capable of abstrusely being explained away as unfortunate accidents or coincidences, however, if these spectacular events are looked at objectively and collectively, then the inference that they together constitute a carefully engineered, treacherous scheme, designed to destabilize our army and government, would be too strong to ignore.

The essential ingredients for mutiny or attempted coup are all present in these events. The capacity of the persons before you collectively to achieve a dislocation in the army, if their diabolical plans had succeeded, is as plain as daylight. The enormous gain, financial, political and otherwise, which would have come the way of the perpetrators of the heinous crimes of 15th May, if their whole scheme had been blessed with success by providence, cannot be ignored. But providence felt otherwise. It felt that the good people of our beloved nation were not to be thrown into turmoil, bloodshed and the hands of communism, because of the wanton ambition and rapacity of a handful of misguided, left-wing, nation wreckers.

Sir, in bringing before your tribunal, only seven persons, the state has operated on the basis that although there were or must have been others, directly or indirectly connected or involved in the monstrous events already referred to, the cause of justice would be adequately served, if the brains and hands responsible for the whole de-stabilization attempt are fished out and dealt with, leaving their minions and other misguided innocents, who were obeying orders as loyal soldiers, to be dealt with later by normal procedure of military discipline and code.

In the muddy sea of treason, murder and unconstitutionality, the state, so far as the events appertaining to 15th May are concerned, is carefully fishing only for barracudas and leaving little fish alone.

In conclusion, Sir, may I remark, on behalf of the state, that your tribunal has the full support of the government and people of this country. We wish it well as it tackles its onerous task. You are assured of maximum co-operation and absolute non-interference from our side. The state pledges to abide by whatever conclusions or recommendations, which at the end of the day, you arrive at. Mr President, members of the tribunal, ladies and gentlemen, thank you".

As he resumed his seat, there was-prolonged applause and clapping from the public, and much throat clearing, with the occasional cough, here and there.

A soldier shouted "order, order", "silence, silence", boomed another. Colonel Kofi Johnson, looked at his two colleagues on the panel and appeared to be whispering something to them. They both smiled approvingly. The sort of dry indecipherable smile often seen on the faces of senior civil servants all over the world.

Next the Secretary of the enquiry, winked to the lawyers sitting on his right side, opposite the Attorney General. They were the lawyers chosen by the state to defend the men alleged primarily responsible for the events of 15th May. Each defendant had one. Leading the team of lawyers was the venerable, criminal lawyer in town, John Gordon Rocha. A man of outstanding physical andprofessional courage, 45 year-old John Rocha had built his reputation as a lawyer's lawyer , defending almost lost causes or issues and generally winning than losing. He was confident, some would say, almost arrogant, but none of his detractors could deny that he was more than a match for any person at the Attorney-General's office, including the boss himself.

He was the scourge of state prosecution lawyers, whom more

often than not, he invariably ended by pitting his enormous intellectual brilliance and legal expertise, against theirs, with the latter often coming worse off. His appearance in any case was certain to fill the court's public galleries with awe. Educated in a local Methodist Missionary School, John Rocha, had done his law degree at the famous London School of Economics, obtaining a First class with Honours. His professional training at the Middle Temple in London, had been equally brilliant. Indeed, by the time he returned home his reputation as a formidable advocate had preceded him.

He was tall, well-built, with a well-trimmed moustache. Happily married with his two daughters, he successfully warded off the clever schemes of women who wanted to know him better than he would like. It would be wrong to say that he never appreciated beauty in the scores of professional women that he dealt with, but he never, never went beyond the normal limits of civilised social intercourse. If he did, there would perhaps be a few Rochas roaming over Kingston, but there were none.

As he got up to introduce himself, as the defending lawyer for 006, somebody shouted suddenly from the public gallery.

"Hear, hear, poor man's lawyer. Great", whoever it was, was quickly silenced by one of the guards-on-duty. The other lawyers also introduced themselves and sat down.

It appeared as if the President, Colonel Jonhson was about to say something but somehow, before he had said a word, Rocha was on his feet again..

"Mr President, tribunal members, on behalf of my colleagues and myself, I wish to request an adjournment of a month, as from today, to allow us to be properly briefed by our clients and to receive appropriate instructions, Sir, since we were appointed as counsel to the persons before you we have not had adequate opportunities to consult them freely, and discuss meaningfully their plea and defence. Whilst it may not be completely justified to state that the military authorities holding our clients in custody have deliberately undermined our efforts to establish the best client-lawyer relationship between us and our clients, I think, Sir, it would be right to comment that they have allowed us so far only a few interviews with our clients in the presence of an armed soldier. This is certainly not the best climate designed to assist a client to talk freely to his lawyer. My learned friend, the Attorney-General, has just eloquently told us all of the alleged crimes of the helpless persons before you. If his allegations are even remotely true or correct, then these persons face the tribunal with their lives literally in their hands. Sir, their very lives are at stake, one would appropriately infer from my learned friend.

If it is so, then it's only fair and equitable that no stone is left unturned to ensure that the truth, the whole truth, from the side of the defence, is placed squarely and fully before you for appropriate adjudication. Sir, it is a time-honoured principle of English common law, which I should state, is our law here, that in every criminal tribunal or adjudication, the accused should be allowed free access to a lawyer or lawyers, and that no impediment or hindrance be placed in the defence's efforts to present its side of the case.

We on this side feel that an adjournment for a month, plus an assurance from you, Sir, that our clients would be given free and untrammelled access to their lawyers, alone and privately, without the presence of soldiers or guards or bugging devices in the interview room, would put us on the path of ensuring that justice is not only being done, but seen to be done. We trust, President, that you grant our well-considered request. Thank you".

Rocha resumed his seat among colleagues, with his usual self-satisfaction. The President of the Tribunal conferred for a few minutes with his colleagues, as the battery of microphones before them was turned off. Kofi Johnson talked first with his colleagues on the left, and then with the other staff. The hall momentarily was buzzing with controlled excitement, when a soldier shouted,

"Silence, Silence".

The microphones were then turned on. Kofi Johnson then began to speak as Rocha stood up.

"The Tribunal has given careful consideration to your re-

79

quest and the points which you made on behalf of your colleagues and yourself. We appreciate your concerns. On the other hand, we do not want these sittings to be prolonged unnecessarily. We have, therefore, decided that an adjournment of three weeks should be adequate for your purposes. Also, I wish on behalf of the tribunal to assure you categorically that the military authorities will be ordered by the tribunal to facilitate free, unhindered access to your clients. We trust that you find these assurances satisfactory.

"Yes, Sir. And may I express the thanks of my colleagues and myself". Rocha sat down.

Kofi Johnson whispered to the tribunal secretary sitting, before him. The secretary then announced, "The tribunal is adjourned until July 20th 10am. Please, stand".

Everybody got up, as Kofi Johnson and his colleagues walked back to the ante-room behind where they were sitting. The sad-looking, depressed, wretched accused, were led away by their guards after a brief chat individually with their lawyers.

Rocha walked to the Attorney-General, and said, "Old boy, you really went to town. It's really majestic and very professional".

Stephen Baldwin smiled, as he shook Rocha's hand. Jokingly he remarked, "John, I hope that you're not going to resort to your usual delaying tactics. Anycase, I will not be here, old boy".

They both looked at each other for a few seconds as if weighing and assessing each other. After the exchange of a few pleasantries, Stephen left in his chauffeur-driven, official, Mercedes-Benz car, accompanied by a police sergeant, with a revolver.

A few members of the public began to mill around Rocha and his colleagues, as they exchanged light conversation among themselves. The secretary of the tribunal was busy giving instructions to the typists, clerks and the vast. The spectators began to disperse some getting away by car, but the vast majority on foot. The lawyers, one by one, went into their cars, and were driven away by their drivers. Before leaving the hall where the tribunal had been sitting, the secretary went backstage to see the President and his team.

"What do you think of the day so far, Sir?", he asked the tribunal head.

"Well, you know I'm new to your country, but I must say I found both speeches most interesting. Our job is to listen, is it not so Colonel, and not to make any comments whatsoever that may indicate that we are taking sides".

The weather was getting rather hot and humid. The time was 12.30 pm, and Kofi's tummy was beginning to rumble. The three officers chatted briefly and were about to leave, when Kofi said, "I shall get in touch with you through him, so that we can meet informally a couple of times or so if necessary before we resume". Kofi said, pointing to the secretary, who like an obedient, civil servant, was not taking part in their conversation. Indeed, like all his ilk throughout the world, Daniel Newton's face never reflected his true inner feelings. He was a true and good, senior civil servant, ready and prepared to offer his best services to whoever happens to be his administrative or political boss at any particular time, in any given place.

Having seen to it that the officers' cars were ready to convey them to their houses, he politely drew their attention to this fact. And he waved to them with an air of satisfaction, as he saw off the three cars. He then supervised the shutdown of the hall, and drove his rather well-used second hand FIAT car to his office first. He spent about twenty minutes sorting out some papers and files, and then continued his journey home.

Chapter 6

On a clear morning in Kingston, the weather as would be expected for this time of the year, the tribunal to enquire into the events to the mutiny and attempted coup resumed. It had been in recess for three weeks, and judging by the looks on the state and defence lawyers, it would be right to conclude that they were ready for a long, sustained legal battle. The alleged culprits sat morosely in their allotted seats.

"Order, silence", a soldier on duty in the hall shouted as the president, and his two colleagues walked in. They sat down, and the commission's secretary, announced in dignified tones,

"The tribunal is in session now"

There was complete quiet in the hall, except for the occasional light cough and clearing of throats. The air was pregnant with much expectation.

The Director of Public Prosecutions, Frank Bell, got up and introduced himself. Sitting with him, were two colleagues, one a woman. The lawyers representing the seven alleged perpetrators of the troubles also introduced themselves. Sitting collectively in their allotted positions were their clients, who looked sad and dispirited.

Frank Bell, although only thirty-eight, had already established a firm reputation as a fiery, non-nonsense prosecution lawyer. His speciality had always been the destruction of the credibility of witnesses through intensive examination and cross-examination, heavily laid with irony and sarcasm. He was a happily married man with two teenage sons. His wife was English, but had become fully accepted by Kingston's top society. A devoted Methodist, Bell was an ambitious person, who, nevertheless had learnt to work harmoniously under his senior colleague, the Attorney-General. A man of medium size, he wore thick glasses for his myopia, the result of several years of voracious, unremitting reading. His wife, Anne, who was by training a nurse, had devoted herself entirely to looking after her family since their return from London. With a slight bow to the tribunal, Bell got up to the thunderous applause of the public gallery and other spectators.

"Frankie, the fighter", somebody among the audience shouted, before a soldier could announce loudly, "silence, silence".

The tribunal's secretary solemnly called "001, please, take your stand", as he beckoned towards the dock near the seven accused persons. 001 went into the dock, and was duly sworn in on the Bible by the secretary. The battle had now began in earnest.

Frank Bell, straightened his Inner Temple tie, looked round briefly and then began:

"Your identity, please, for the purposes of this tribunal",

"001", the poor soul replied.

"Date of birth?"

"10th December 1940, Sir"

"Place of birth"

"Kingston"

"Where were you educated?"

"Kingston Grammar School, Sir"

"And after that?"

"I joined the Army"

"Which section of the Army, please?"

"Infantry"

"How long have you been in the Army, to date?"

"Ten years"

"And how do you like it, 001?"

"Pretty good, Sir"

"Have you received any training courses during your service in the Army?"

"Yes, sir, a course at our local Military School in Management and Leadership, a course in Ballistics in U.K., and a year's Staff College Training in India".

"Fine. That sounds quiet impressive, if I may say so".

"Thank you"

"Am I right then, in stating that you're a very experienced Army Officer?"

"Well, I should think so".

There followed a rigorous examination of 001 about the events surrounding the abortive mutiny and his specific role in them. Next followed a full cross examination of the accused by his lawyer, and a final re-examination of outstanding issues following from the examination-in-chief, by the D.P.P.

One by one, day by day, week by week, the prosecution methodically went through the process of establishing beyond all reasonable doubt, that all the accused persons had committed grave acts of treason, were justifiably guilty and deserved full capital punishment. And equally, the defence throughout the period worked assiduously to establish their innocence. After about nine months of sittings, from Monday to Friday, including at least five Saturday sittings, the Commission eventually heard the final addresses of the Director of Public Prosecutions and his team, and that of Rocha and his colleagues. The President of the Tribunal thanked both teams for their co-operation and professionalism, then adjourned to write its report. This took another two months, before the final report was delivered to the country's Prime Minister. The report, finding all accused guilty, recommended the death penalty for 007, but sentences ranging from life imprisonment to fifteen years for the other accused persons. The report was given maximum publicity by the local media and official press machine. Kofi Johnson was lionised publicly.

And exactly eleven months after their arrival in Kingston, Maggie and Kofi after numerous lavish, official and unofficial farewell parties, left Kingston for home. They left with fond memories of the lovely country and its friendly people. They departed laden with numerous gifts from the Government, the Army, and civilian friends. Furthermore, Kofi had learnt a major lesson in life for himself.

"Now, I've my mind made up, by Xmas I would have done it". Colonel Johnson was talking to his closest friend and colleague, Commodore Jimmy Coker, an airforce officer, with whom he had shared many happy moments together, during their officer training course in England, eight years previously. Their friendship was based on completely shared interests. They both smoked heavily, drank heavily, had an inverterate desire for women, especially single, young women. Perhaps, the Commodore dressed better than his army friend, but only marginally. Furthermore, that Commodore Coker had an Irish wife, who was vivacious and really attractive, whilst the Colonel's wife was African and just pretty, was not a matter that affected the two officers' relationship in anyway.

Normally, anytime the two friends met during office hours or off, the conversation began and ended with their accounts of their sexual escapades and conquests. Yet this morning, the Colonel was not his usual self with his friend. Why? Pressed and pressed by his confidant, Colonel Johnson began to unburden himself. He began, rather slowly.

"Jimmy, I am worried. I am a very disturbed person, of late since my return from the West Indies I have not been sleeping well". He paused for a few moments, lit another cigarette, and then continued. "I've wanted to talk privately with you alone on a very delicate matter since my return, but I've not till now found the right time. It's frightfully important, what's on my mind".

Jimmy interjected, "Gosh, Kofi but I see you practically everyday, but why have you not told me whatever it is all the time. Why?". He looked straight into his friend's face, eyeball-to-eyeball. The room was quiet although outside the gardener could be seen busily working on the lawns. The sun, as usual, was shining brilliantly. The temperature, as frequently in the Tropics, was around the 100 mark.

Continuing his conversation, Colonel Johnson said, "As my closest friend and colleague, I have decided to inform you, and you alone, about my decision to do a coup shortly. This is a very delicate and risky operation and I have not mentioned a word of it to anyone. I trust you, Jimmy, hundred percent and I am sure that I can count on you".

"Definitely. You can rest assured that not only is your secret safe with me, but that I will do everything I can to ensure the success of the operation". The two men sat quietly for a few moments. Not a word passed between them, but somehow by body language, they felt that they were at the beginning of great things. The last time there was a military coup in the country was six years previously and since then the country had been ably managed by a group of serious-minded, professional people. They were educated, patriotic and dedicated. Indeed, the civilian government whose fate they were reflecting on, had achieved a considerable reduction in the level of public corruption, although, it would dishonest to say that bribery and corruption had ben eradicated completely.

That things had changed tremendously under the civilian regime for the good, it must be stated, was borne out by the reaction of the local prostitutes in town. They were unanimously of the view that business was bad, very bad. They generally attributed their current slump in income to "The Professor" , "The crazy professor" and by this they meant the Cambridge-educated, economics professor, who was then the country's Prime Minister. The poor soul. Little did he realise that his over-emphasis in public on the virtues of family life, and the need for the highest probity from public servants was getting on the nerves of his more randy ministerial colleagues. Furthermore, his campaign publicly to encourage a major improvement in public morality was harming badly the oldest profession on earth.

As colonel Johnson and his fellow would-be conspirator were in the process of plotting their coup, the telephone rang. The Colonel refused to take it. The phone rang and rang. Angrily, he took the receiver, and suddenly said, "Yes, Sir, PM! At your service, Sir, I will be there within ten minutes or so, Sir". He quickly replaced the receiver, sweating mildly. "Eh, Kofi, what's wrong?" enquired his friend. Kofi paused for a moment, lit a cigarette, puffed heavily on it and said "I must go now. The PM wants me immediately. But before I go, let us swear to each other our undying loyalty to the end, to be redeemed only with our blood." They both stood up at attention, shook their left hands vigorously three times, and hugged each other.

The commodore took his leave by his official car. He had by then been with his friend for exactly forty-five minutes. Alas, for sometime to come, he was never to forget this meeting. As he was driven to his office in Michel camp, he pondered again and again on the conversation with his bosom friend an hour or so previously.

Meanwhile, Colonel Kofi johnson had arrived at the Prime Minister's office at the Castle and was being ushered into the ante-room attached to the P.M's modestly-furnished office. He did not have to wait long. He was announced in by the Prime Minister's private secretary, a smooth-talking, Cambridge educated, top-rank civil servant, of impeccable credentials.

Smartly, the colonel saluted the P.M stood stiffly for a moment, till he was beckoned to a comfortable settee by the P.M. Although his heart was throbbing firmly, his army training had taught him one major thing-self control in a crisis.

The Prime Minister began the conversation, in his usual, mild academic way. "Colonel, sorry to bring you here on such short notice, but I needed to see you on a little matter". The Colonel smiled warmly, but said nothing. The boss continued, "I learn from the Director of Military Intelligence that something is going on in the Air Force base. The Director is trying to work out more details, and I felt like letting you know about this. Kofi, you know how much I personally trust you absolutely and I count on you to do more investigative work and watch the position. Since I appointed you over your three superior officers, I've heard all sorts of accusations behind my back. I've been accused of nepotism, tribalism and all sort of things, but I know that I did the right thing absolutely. With you in charge of the capital and the surrounding forces, I know our Government is in safe hands".

He stopped for a split second, and before he could resume, the Colonel, with much charm and politeness, said "Sir, you know too well my personal dedication to our Government. I've, Sir, told you many times, that I would rather die fighting , than see our Government over-thrown in a military coup d'etat. Not only do I love your government, but PM considering all that you have

87

done fore me personally, the very least I can do is to stand by you to the end, the very end. This has been my position since your election to high office, and it remains my position to my dying day".

Colonel Johnson grimaced mildy, and continued, "I live or die by your government, sir , you can count on me hundred percent". Indeed, the Colonel was, after a brief pause, about to launch into another long litany of his absolute and unshakeable loyalty, when the P.M mildly told him "Kofi, I trust you, but keep the situation under constant review. Thank you for coming. By the way, how's the family? Are the children doing well at school? Oh, your little daughter really made me laugh the other day". The Colonel, stood up, put on his cap, straightened his uniform, and said goodbye to the boss. He was about to leave, when the P.M walked to his big mahogany desk, and pulled out of one of his left drawers, a large wad of notes, in a brown envelope. He handed it to his friend, saying "This is for the children. I think it would be a good idea to buy some National Savings Certificates for them. And thank you for coming, my warmest regards to the family" .

Kofi stood at attention, saluted smartly, with a big "Thank you, Sir" and briskly walked away, to join his aide, who had been awaiting his boss in the ante-room.

On his way back to his office, in his official, chauffeur-driven, Mercedes Benz, Kofi was calm and appeared lost in thought. Unusual for him, he spoke not a word to his driver. Suddenly, he instructed the driver "The Military Hospital", "Yes Sir", the driver replied. Why he wanted to go to the hospital, when he did not, in anyway, appear ill, was a puzzle to the driver.

Arriving at the hospital, the Colonel quickly got out of his car, and briskly walked to the large ante-room attached to the surgical ward. There he grabbed the telephone, and rang his good friend, Jimmy, "Come urgently, I am at the ante-room of the surgical ward. See you soon". He calmly paced the room, and waited. Although it took his friend only a few minutes, about ten in all, it looked as if he was waiting for ages.

As Jimmy walked towards him, the Colonel smiled, and

suggested, "Let's go for some coffee". They walked to the cafeteria for officers, attached to the hospital, and over coffee, Kofi began "You know, Jim, I've just returned from a brief encounter with the "Chief", "Eh, what is it, his airforce confidant enquired anxiously. Kofi said confidently , "Calm down, old boy. It's OK. He vaguely asked about whether I knew or had heard of any simmerings of trouble at the air-force base. According to him, the Director of M.I is unhappy about what he's been hearing and the P.M wanted to check with me whether I've heard or uncovered anything".

He pursed his lips, puffed on a cigarette, and then continued "I assured him hundred-percent that nothing unusual had come my way at all, but that I would be on the look-out. You know, as he spoke, I watched him, carefully and tried to second-guess him about our operation. The more I listened to him, the more convinced I became that he had not the foggiest idea of what we have been working on. Rest assured on that", he stated.

"Are you certain, absolutely certain?"

"Yes, completely", he replied. "Furthermore as a good Apandi man, the assurance of loyalty which I gave him, Jim, was such that he could not but believe me fully. I must admit at the beginning of the interview I was rather worried, but when I found what it was all about I played the role perfectly. Looking him straight in the eye, without displaying undue emotion, I bent over backwards to assure him that his regime is safe in my hands. And we parted on the best of terms. In fact, he even gave me a fine gift of money for my children. True, the man is kind and gentle, but I'm afraid, a man has to do what he's got to do, right?" Jimmy did more listening and less talking. All sorts of ideas were going through his mind. Should he or should he not continue in the project? These were among the many questions he was trying to wrestle within his mind, when a uniformed orderly casually approached them, "Any more coffee, sir?"

"No thanks", Jimmy said, with Kofi mildly shaking his head in agreement.

Before we leave here, remember, Jimmy, nobody knows about what we've talked about today. Should anybody ask you about our two meetings today, remember to say that we were discussing promotion prospects for some of the bright lads under us, and I shall, if asked corroborate that. Please, for heaven's sake, don't fall into the M.I trap. They know nothing, but naturally it is their business to appear to know everything going on by cleverly setting traps for us, with vague, empty stories or suggestions of attempted coups, aborted coups and all that nonsense. If they're as all-knowing and clever as they claim to be how did the first coup succeed, eh?"

The two men left together for their respective cars and were driven away to their offices. It was about 5.30 pm. Back in his office, Kofi rang his wife and told her that he would be very late coming home, as he had some rather urgent report to prepare for his commanding officer. Used to her husband frequently arriving home late, Mrs Johnson, listened to it all, with the usual resignation.

With the telephone call out of the way, Colonel Kofi Johnson, Deputy Brigade Commander of the Southern Command, including the capital, Appapa, began to work out the details of his operation . First he thought of the name of the operation, and code-word, to be used to launch the fatal exercise. As he worked out various details, in his mind, his staff came and enquired whether he needed anything done before they left the office for home. He was pleasant and charming to them all, and let them go. Even his aide, he let go, as he sat there thinking and thinking. Momentarily he would pace the office methodically as if counting his footsteps. One cigarette after another were lit, as he treated himself to a few shots of gin and tonic, kept in the second drawer on the left hand side of his desk. Although the Colonel loved his drink, he never touched anything until after his office hours, and certainly not before 6 pm.

He continued to work on his plans which he had been doing in his mind for the past three months. No wonder that during that period his mistress had not been seeing as much of him, as was his usual pattern. Kofi interrupted his work and took the telephone receiver to ring his favourite mistress, Sophia, but for a few split seconds he hesitated. Then he went ahead. The phone rang for some time but without a response. He put the receiver down, relaxed in his chair for a couple of minutes, then rang again. Still there was no reply.

"Eh, what's happening? She's supposed to be there" , he whispered aloud. He rang again. This time, the third time, he was lucky. "This is 493 2311, good evening". It was the sweet mellow voice of his girl-friend, and that voice, known to him for several years, set the Colonel's mind at ease.

"Darling, what have you been doing?. I have been ringing and ringing, with no reply. I thought you were out, anyway, how are you, my angel?"

"Well, dear, nice to hear your voice. I've not seen you for ages, why?"

"You're funny. I was there only five days ago, and you call it ages, dear. Anycase, what have you been doing with yourself? I hope that you are not romping with a toy-boy or anything funny like that".

"Good Lord, what a thing to say Kofi. You've known me all these years, and its shocking to hear you talk like that. That's not funny at all".

Kofi laughed heartily, and then said, "I was only joking. Can't you take a joke, eh?"

For a few seconds Sophia laughed, then continued "In fact, I've been thinking of you very much. I had hoped that you would be coming today, so I was preparing your favourite dish, when I heard the phone ringing. Now I'm so disappointed. Well, I'll keep it for tomorrow. Will you be coming, dear?" "No, but the following day, dear. I've so much work to get through before the end of the month. Certain urgent reports have to be completed, darling. I miss you, dear". And with that the telephone conversation ended. Kofi went back to continue his planning. Sophia returned to her bedroom, where lying on her bed was the young naval officer aide of the Deputy Head of the Navy. The tall elegant, 25 year old naval officer, who looked as if butter would not melt in his mouth, had just completed a massive round of sex with Sophia, and was calmly sipping a glass of cold beer as he lay on the bed awaiting her return from the telephone. Although eight years younger than her, he had in the past few years impressed her with his sexual prowess, and acted as a fitting stand-by for the desperate days when the Colonel, for one reason or another, could not call.

"Who's it?" he asked engagingly. With a smile in her eyes, she replied "The old man. He is not coming today. As always, official business", she continued, "don't mind him"

"Well, then we will also continue our official business", he said. The second session was indeed more vigorous than the first. It was more like a marathon. To add insult to injury a la Colonel Johnson, it was his beer the young Cassanova was drinking, and it was his favourite highlife record, 'Do it till you die', which was played by Sophia for her naval toy-boy after every sexual encounter. True, sometimes a bit of Mozart was played on her hi-fi, but generally her favourites were the Colonel's favourite records, and 'Do it till you die' was never left out.

The naval officer's sexual reputation among his fellow young officers in barracks as the "giant" was well-deserved. To Sophia, he was not only the giant, but the "Supremo", the affectionate name by which he was known to her.

"You know, Akwasi, if my phone is tapped or the place is bugged then we're finished . You military people cannot be trusted a bit".

"Don't worry darling. I've often thought about this and can assure you that your phone is not tapped. Also the place is not bugged. I have checked a number of times with a close friend in M.I and he's confirmed that you are not on the list. In anycase, it would be very foolish for the old man to tap your phone or bug your place. Why? Simple. Such an action will only rebound on him, as it would plainly reveal very damaging and embarrassing info about himself. He's too worried about whether he is being tapped or bugged, instead of doing it to you. After all, he has more to lose. He is a Colonel, soon to be made, I hear a brigadier. As for me, I am nobody.

She lay there listening, as she munched on an apple, whilst trying to re-arouse the "Supremo". But even the supremo could not perform miracles. Near-miracles, yes, but no complete ones.

Try as she did, the giant's weapon would not respond. It was exhausted of ammunition. Sophia's spirit was willing, alas, the flesh of the supremo was weak. However, not weak enough for him not to be able to talk, albeit slowly and in lowly tones, "You frequently see me searching corners of your flat, and anytime you ask I say that I am searching for bugs. I don't trust the old man, not a bit. But I've not found any. I think he's shrewder than thought. So, darling relax. Don't worry".

The time was about 7.30 pm and it was pitch dark outside, as some of the street lights near-by had failed. This suited the "supremo" rather well, as he was anxious to return to his tiny flat in the barracks, and his small Volkswagen car was parked not too far from Sophia's flat.

"Are you not staying the night? After all, he's not coming. Come on", she implored. The "Giant" was beginning to entertain the idea of staying the night thus breaking a rule he had stuck to steadfastly during their two years romance. Agile as he was, his careful study of the layout of Sophia's flat had amply convinced him that in an emergency, it would be difficult, almost impossible, to get out quickly. He had, therefore, always contended himself by not sleeping at her's over-night, which action had always upset her.

"No, Sophia. No I must go. Tomorrow I've to get up early for the rehearsal of an important assignment, and also it is not in our best interest that I stay. Try and understand. I am really sorry, dear". And with these words he began to put on his clothes, although she kept on taunting him jokingly, "It's dead, what a shame. The Supremo's man is dead".

Well, even the best of things have to come to an end, at one time or another. The Supremo did not succumb to the persistent invitation to stay for dinner, or stay the night. She kissed him passionately and went inside, as he shot off into the pitch darkness. The sound of the car engine starting and speeding off, signalled that he was truly and safely gone.

Meanwhile, just about the same time that Sophia's toy-boy was speeding to the barracks, the Colonel had finished putting finishing touches to his master-plan. He was really exhausted, both mentally and physically, having revised his project a few times, frequently making alterations, here and there. At last, he was happy with himself.

He called in his driver and instructed him to get into the car his briefcase and a couple of boxes in his office. He was heading for his home at the camp, when he toyed with the idea of calling on an old girlfriend he had not seen for ages. The idea sounded attractive, but somehow, he opted for going home directly.

His car sped along. The tropical birds which chirp and sing at night were, as usual busy. The sky was dark, with the countless spots of the stars brilliantly shinning. And the moon the Tropical moon, full, bright and clear, was so clear that you could figure out the ageless moon-man. As Kofi's official car marked by its special two-star car number plate, sped along it overtook a modest Volkswagen car lumbering its way in the same direction.

"There goes the Commander", the naval officer said to him self, as the big man's car passed by. He knew the car too well, and its occupant. But for the Colonel, comfortably ensconced at the back of his car, neither the small car, they had just overtaken or its driver meant anything whatsoever.

Colonel Johnson arrived home at about 8 pm, and went straight to his wife, said "Hello, I'm back. Sorry for the delay"

"Oh, welcome home dear. Nice to see you again", she said nicely. For a mother of three children, with all the hardships that she had gone through, Maggie Johnson, looked pretty almost attractive for her age.

Dinner was served by the uniformed house-maid, a medium sized single woman of about twenty, who had been with the Johnson's for about five years. She was loyal, honest and hard working, but certainly not intelligent. Her schooling had stopped at age eleven, and from that time the local radio and regular watching of the popular, national soap opera on television called 'Doctor Padzie', constituted the bed-rock of her education Her sexual inclinations were difficult to determine. She defi nitely was not pretty, indeed was almost, but not quite ugly. She was certainly not a lesbian, but without question, did not appear to appreciate the joys of sex.

As always, she served her master and his wife dutifully, and with her work done, requested permission to retire. She was let go, and bowing, she said "Goodnight, Sir. Goodnight, Madame", and disappeared into her one room section of the servants quarters, separated from the Colonel's residence by about twenty yards.

Kofi Johnson and her wife watched television, till the 9 o'clock news. The news programme was not exciting, so the couple put off the television and put on a video film "Patton". Although the Colonel had seen it at least three times, he always enjoyed it, but it was beginning to get on the nerves of his wife. Yes, her husband was a soldier, but she, somehow, had never really fancied military life. However, for her husband's sake, she did her social rounds at the barracks dutifully, never letting out her inner-most secret that all the huge expenditure on weapons and military hardware was a colossal waste of pubic funds , especially when many people in the country had no proper drinking water , no good food to eat, and no proper housing. But she was too sensible and shrewd to tell the other army-wives, how she felt. They were all black and white, on the make, living off the ignorant, exploited masses. The going was good, why rock the boat, they felt.

Suddenly Kofi, walking towards the television set, and lowering the volume, said, "Maggie, have you heard it, I understand there has been an attempted coup against the civilian government in Liberia, and the President and all the ministers have been shot by firing squad. Hmm!. Africa, what a continent, what a place!" he remarked slowly as if speaking to himself.

"You mean the government that took office there recently after the general election has been kicked out violently. This is sheer madness!" She exclaimed.

Her husband was quiet for a brief moment, then spoke quietly, as if whispering, "let's hope that the rascals at the Air-Force base are not doing or planing anything silly. We certainly don't need another coup. All these coups have got us nowhere, we're back to square one". He paused for a second, but before he could resume, his dear wife remarked, "Kofi, dear, please, for heaven's sake, I really beg you don't have anything whatsoever to do with any of these rubbish rumours going about. We're happy as we are, especially, with your recent promotion, from Lieutenant to full Colonel, and now you are the Deputy Brigadier Commander, what more? If I hear of anything serious, I will pass it to you immediately , and would expect you Kofi, to convey it straightaway to the PM. Since your promotion, already people are saying all sorts of things, that it's because you are from the region of the PM, and that's why you were jumped over those three bastards. Of course, it's absolute rubbish, but that does not stop tongues wagging. Sometimes, I feel that such people are only praying for a coup so that we would be overthrown and disgraced, . But God forbid, it will never happen, never!".

Her husband had a final sip at his mug of beer. He looked intently, but vacantly at the mug as he held it in his right hand. He merely said, "what a funny world, dear, is it not? I am retiring now, as I've to get up very early tomorrow, to complete some report, which I've to present". So saying, he kissed his wife, and retired to the bedroom. It was about 10.30 pm, according to the electric clock on the wall.

Maggie lingered on for sometime, watching the ever-popular late-night programme, "World events". An hour or so later, she also retired to bed, to find her husband fast asleep. She got herself ready to go to bed, but returned to the kitchen to look round again, to see that everything was alright, put on the answer-phone, looked round, here and there and returned to the bed-room.

She knelt over the bed, said a rather long prayer, then put out the lights and slipped into bed. She had slept for about four hours or so, when she woke up. Her husband was not in bed. Tiptoeing into his study, she was rather surprised to see him at 4 am typing. He was also taken aback to see her.

"What the heavens are you doing, darling at this time? You've slept for only a few hours, give yourself a break. Whatever it is, is it worth-it?". Her adrenaline was flowing, and she was without blinking, looking at the typewriter. Meanwhile, her husband quickly pulled out of the typewriter what he had so far typed. In fact, he had come to the end of it by the time his dear wife came in.

He had just typed for the third time, the operational plans for the military coup which he was nursing in his mind, and about which he had broached to nobody, except his closest friend, Commodore Jimmy. He had on each occasion, after typing the piece, committed it to memory, and then destroyed the paper itself. And he was about to repeat the process when his wife came into the study.

Casually, he went on "Maggie as I told you yesterday, there's a very important report I am working on for presentation tomorrow, and I got up early to put finishing touches to it. That's all, nothing for you to worry about". As he said so, he slowly removed the type-written sheet from the typewriter, folded it, slowly, and put it in the pocket on his night-gown.

Appropriately assured that there was nothing to worry about, the good woman, went back to bed. As soon as she was out of the study, and the Colonel was sure she was ensconced in bed, he pulled the sheet from his pocket, read it over again, turned it over, and then repeated the whole thing to himself.

That piece of paper was bombshell. For it contained material, operational plans, that would profoundly affect the course of events in his country for many years to come. Satisfied completely, that his plans had been fully committed to memory, he finally wrote the whole thing by hand from memory. Then he compared the typescript with the hand-written version. It was perfect. His efforts had not been in vain. He smiled happily to himself. He was on cloud nine. "Operation Generators" had been conceived, fathered by no less a person than Colonel Kofi Johnson, the loyal, dedicated Deputy Brigade commander of the capital city, APPAPA.

He tried to pray for the success of his venture, but the prayer did not flow freely from his lips. He stopped praying, looked at his watch, then went to the bathroom. He hurriedly dressed himself, determined to leave for the office before the house-maid came in. He was so pleased to see his wife fast asleep, with her beautiful face, looking so innocent. He went quietly to the kitchen, and using an electric kettle, prepared a big cup of tea, which he had, with a piece of buttered toast. After breakfast, he pored again over the two sheets of paper, meticulously comparing them word, by word. Satisfied, he then destroyed both sheets of paper, and set off for work. Before leaving for office he wrote a brief note for his wife, "Sorry, darling, I had to leave rather early. Everything is alright. Will ring you at 9 o'clock. Love, Dad xxx".

On his way to the office, he had a change of plans. He decided to call on his good friend, at the air-force base. The Commodore liked his friend very much, almost loved him, but was still surprised to see him suddenly at his front door, so early in the morning. For it was about 6 in the morning.

Chapter 7

"Sshh, quiet", Kofi was whispering at the door to his pal. "Let's go in first", he continued, with a friendly gesture to his friend, who was rather surprised to see him call so early. The two of them walked briskly to the study of Jimmy, who then locked the door. As the Colonel was sitting there, he began, "Old boy, I've come on a very important mission. Sorry to come so early, but it is necessary, very necessary that I do so". His host kept listening, interjecting with "No problem, don't worry".

"Well, Jimmy I've completed the plans and gone over them again and again, and they are full-proof and completely kosher. What I am going to achieve, of course with your co-operation is a completely bloodless coup, without the loss of a single life. That's the twin-objective, a successful coup which is also bloodless". He looked at his friend for comment, but Jimmy said nothing, except, "Kofi go ahead. I'm with you all the way. We swim or sink together. You count on me completely".

"By the way, Jimmy, you remember when P.M called when you were at my office the other day".

"Indeed, what happened?", he enquired.

"You know, the old man asked me whether I had heard of any rumblings in the Airforce, as he was a bit concerned with reports he was getting from the Director of Military Intelligence. You bet it was not easy. At first, I thought he had, somehow guessed or got wind of our venture. But the more I calmly listened to him, the more I realised that he was just trying to probe my mind".

"So what did you say?" Jimmy asked.

"Hmm, my brother it was not at all easy, but I steeled myself and assured him absolutely that I was solidly with him, ready to crush the slightest sign of any trouble, in the Airforce or Army. I bent over backwards to assure him hundred percent.

"And did you succeed?" Jimmy asked anxiously.

"Certainly, old boy, certainly. I hate myself for having done that, but you know, all these politicians are liars, and the only language they understand is the language of liars. So I gave to him what he and his cronies often dish out to the masses-bundles and bundles of lies, except that I added a good dose of military disinformation".

Before he could continue there was a knock on the door. It was Jimmy's wife, Esi.

"I was bringing you tea, darling", she said.

"Thank you, I am rather busy now, and I will take it later, when I come out, in a few minutes", Jimmy told her firmly without a trace of emotion in his voice.

"Jimmy, briefly, I am going to fully outline to you the whole operation, on a-need-to-know basis. Namely, everything that you must know about your own role in the operation. Please, don't ask me about the role of the others, but feel free to grill me about any aspect of your own part that is not clear or needs clarification. OK"

"Yes, go on".

"I am now going to put the whole plan before you. First of all, it is going to be called ""Operation Generators"", a simple title, with maximum potential for deception, as I will explain soon. You are ready?".

"Yes, shoot ahead!"

"First, on the appointed date, at 2 am sharp, the whole telephone system in APPAPA, including all the barracks will be blacked out. Just before that, I will give you a signal for action on my walkie-talkie, "The generators are working well". As soon as you hear that you spring into action straight away.

Secondly, once you get the OK you secure the Air-force base, and get all military road-blocks put into action, with nobody being allowed in or out. Also you, Jimmy, will then alert three fighter-bombers, ready to go into action, with dud bombs, should it be necessary. That role is for purely psychological purposes, as there is no question of bombing the barracks or any civilian, government installations.

Meanwhile, stage one of "Operation Generators" would have

been brought into play with the securing of the Broadcasting House. Also the secret military transmitter at PAMA would be immobilised. "That's the vital question-capturing Broadcasting House, the nation's nerve-centre, who's to do that, Kofi?"

"Old boy, I will see to that, either by myself or by somebody else. Plans have been drawn to capture it intact and without a shot, if possible. I appreciate that 99 percent our success depends on the broadcasting centre. For past coups have shown clearly that once the centre is captured, and the news is broadcast of the overthrow of the civilian government, the rest of the officers will as always, sit tight, waiting to see how things are going, only too keen to throw in their forces on the winning side. That has always been the pattern, and will, we hope, stay so, on the D-Day. Have you ever heard of any of the troops fighting for a deposed civilian regime? Forget it". He smoked his last cigarette, then went on.

"Whilst you are on your assignment, the Chief of Staff, their deputies, the P.M., all Government Ministers and their deputies, the National Chairman of the ruling party, and his deputy, the Inspector General of police and his deputy, would all be arrested. The whole operation, starting at 2 am should, all things going well, be over by 4 am. I have allowed an extra hour, for unforeseen difficulties and problems. Thus, Jimmy, by 5 am, we should be ready to broadcast to the nation. He sighed with relief, satisfied with himself. He looked straight at his bosom friend, asked, "What do you think of it, eh?"

"Well, old boy it sounds too good to be true. So simple, it is unbelievable, but what if we meet with resistance?"

"I am expecting no resistance, no opposition. Nobody will fight for this shabby government whose hallmark is high cost of living, high inflation, and fantastic suffering. Even the prostitutes are complaining. Everybody is. Furthermore, the armoury depot will be fully secured by loyal troops, and all troops on guard duty that day, except "Company X" will be heavily drugged, and to make assurance doubly sure, they will be issued with dud ammunitions. OK?"

"Well, what can I say, it's fantastic. By the way, Kofi, why the code name "Generators"?"

"Jimmy, let me tell you this as a good friend, the essence of an exercise such as this, is its simplicity. The simpler the concept, the easier its achievement and vice versa. I chose the name "Generators", so that if by a fluke, Military Intelligence get a smell of anything fishy, I could convincingly tell them that at first I rang you to tell you that my generator was not working properly, and that I was subsequently ringing to say that it is working well. You see, in these life-and-death matters, the lie should be as close to the truth as possible, and also sound as plausible as possible. After all, the Military Intelligence chaps are not fools. They are, indeed, very clever and intelligent and any code name such as "The bird is singing" or "It is raining", or something as puerile or silly as that would rather excite their unwelcome interest in such peculiar telephone talk. See the point, Jimmy?"

"Sorry, I cannot brief you further about others' assignments. You see to yours, and others will see to theirs, right? What you should try to do, before now and D Day, is to work out a simple, I repeat a simple way of securing the Air-Force base and bloodlessly completing your assignments".

They went over the whole plan again, shook hands firmly, hugged and went out of the room calmly. The Colonel left for his office in the barracks. And his host, dressed quickly gulped his tea, which had been re-heated by his dear wife, kissed his wife and shot off, with the words, "Goodbye, darling. Sorry I was so long. Kofi, as always, came with is usual women problems! See you at lunch, love".

As her husband drove away to work, she felt rather uneasy. Not really a hunch nor the still, small voice. It appeared to the Commodore's wife that something was going on which certainly was not right. But she could not place her delicate fingers on what it was. Reflecting again and again on that rather early call by the Colonel, resulting in whispered conversation between the two men, she decided finally to ask her husband more about the visit during lunchtime.

The Colonel, meanwhile, wasted no time in completing the

details of his operation. At first he had toyed with idea of bringing the Head of Police Force into the act, but on deeper reflection, had decided against it. He smiled to himself. As if justifying before his peers his decision for not including the Police in the venture, he said, "Once they are in they will not do much, only effect the arrests of the Ministers and a few cowardly politicians, yet would demand being strongly represented in the Government. Nonsense. No way", he sad satisfyingly to himself.

With his usual efficiency and alacrity, the Colonel went through his normal, office routine, gave orders, here and there, called in his aide for instructions, then sat back thoughtfully. The eleven o'clock morning officer's meeting was soon due. But before leaving for it, Kofi Johnson made a very important telephone call.

"Good morning, oh, is that Nana Amber?", he asked,

"Yes, who's speaking", the voice asked slowly at the other end.

"Nana, it's me Colonel Johnson, you remember, we met at the durbar the other day when I had the honour of being introduced you to at AGORO. You remember, eh?", he asked.

Nana was quiet for a few seconds, then said, "Oh ye, big man, what can I do for you? How are you, anyway?"

"Very well, as well as one can hope for these days. The weather has been rather unsettled the past few days".

Before she went further, Kofi, continued, "I wanted to make an appointment to come and see you next Sunday evening. Will you be free?"

"Let me think", she paused briefly, then went on, "Not the coming Sunday, but the following Sunday will be OK".

"Good, thank you, Nana. I don't want to take too much of your time. See you next week Sunday". He replaced the telephone receiver, got up, straightened himself up, then went into the conference room, where his colleagues were beginning to gather.

Kofi was his usual self with his fellow officers, full of banter, chain-smoking, as ever, and always, friendly and polite to his friends and colleagues.

The main topics on the agenda for the meetings, apart from

routine army personnel and logistic issues, was the emergency operation known as C.C for "Counter-Coup". This was the master plan to be launched against any attempt by a military coup to remove the civilian Government of the day. The plan had originally been drawn jointly by Commander of the Tank Regiment, the Director of Military Intelligence, the Commander of the "Do or die" regiment, the Commander of the First Field Artillery Regiment, the Director of Signal Corps, and Kofi himself. The plan had been revised and fine-tuned to the point of perfection, almost. And at this meeting, chaired as before, by Kofi, the revised plan was approved, with the latest additions and modifications by the Commander of the "Do or Die" Regiment. Having gone through the agenda systematically, and with no other business on hand, Kofi wound up the meeting and his colleagues dispersed, being driven away, one by one, in their staff cars.

There was not the slightest evidence of any thing untoward going on in the armed forces.

With his daily assignments completed, Colonel Johnson went home, rather late, as he frequently did. Before reaching home, he detoured to the house of his mistress Sophia Fumey. It was about 8 pm. He had been so pre-occupied with whatever was on his mind, that he had forgotten to telephone her about his visit. He knocked twice at the door. There was no reply. He used the key he had, but the door was bolted from inside. He found this rather odd and unusual but thought nothing of it. "Perhaps", he said to himself "it's one of Sophia's odd tricks, or may be she is unwell".

Kofi was about to give up and go home, when surprise, surprise, Sophia appeared at the door, looking radiant and full of smiles.

"Sorry, darling, I was watching TV, and I must have dozed a bit. Please, forgive me, come in". The Colonel went in and as he took his cap off, he heard something like the footsteps of a man. He was not sure. So he asked, "Eh, it appears someone is walking in your garden. You hear those faint footsteps", he asked her.

Sophia feigned inattention and boredom, as if still recovering from her TV doze. She looked through the window onto the garden, and said casually, "Love, I hear nothing at all. I hope you're not imagining things, ghosts and such things".

Laughingly, she continued, "maybe it's the ghost of the old chief of the area who died sometime ago, paying us a visit". Kofi laughed, and as he did so she sighed with relief, for she could hear from a distance the sound of the Volkswagen car of her toyboy speeding away.

Relaxing over his cold beer, the Colonel remarked casually, "I am a bit tired. Have been trying to do too much, darling".

"Well, dear, I've always been telling you it's not worth it. Take it easy, man. All this up and down, meetings, reports, exercises, . . . just killing yourself, whilst the big men drink champagne and are driven about in expensive official cars, just talking, talking, doing nothing".

Lighting another cigarette, the Colonel remarked, "Dear, tonight I'm a bit tired, so just a quick one, OK?

"You mean . .", she said, turning the left hand upside down.

"Yes".

As Kofi undressed, she slipped in to the adjacent bathroom, ostensibly to wash.

"Eh, why so long? What sort of wash is it". Kofi shouted as he could wait no longer. The adrenaline and testosterone hormones were flowing smoothly and fast, and the delay was almost unwelcome. With the Colonel fully undressed, and lying completely relaxed on the bed, Sophia smelling ravishingly, walked in, locked the door, and put off the ceiling and bedside lights.

Kofi lay on the bed, rather motionless. He appeared a bit pre-occupied, but with Sophia on top of him, he did not have to exert himself much. Whether she was feigning orgasm or not, was difficult to tell, but she did make all the right noises when the Colonel ejaculated. As Kofi was lying prostrate cooling off, he fell into a deep sleep. It lasted for only a few minutes, about thirty in all, but appeared to him to be hours and hours. Meanwhile, Sophia sprightly and looking quite cool and fresh, went and had another wash, lit a cigarette and prepared herself gin and tonic.

After dressing himself, the Colonel telephoned his wife, "I've my dear, been delayed by the boss on a very important matter. Sorry, I will be home soon, just a few minutes". "I was wondering what was happening, and when I rang your office there was no reply".

"Don't worry, love, I'm on my way now!", he quickly ended the telephone conversation. As Sophia bade him good night kissing him, she felt so relieved and relaxed that a near-disaster had been averted. She went to sleep, after watching television for about half an hour. With a lovely smile on her face she slept soundly, very deeply.

However, the Colonel having arrived home, and had his supper, was in rather pensive mood. "What's wrong Kofi, what's wrong?", his wife kept asking.

"Any trouble, dear?", she continued.

"Oh, nothing to worry about", he replied vacantly. "I've just been going over a report for the P.M. That's all, darling".

"You sure, there's no trouble? No coup nonsense?. For I hear from the grapevine that something is going on in the camp, that some officers are planning a coup to overthrow the Government", she said anxiously. He looked at her calmly, and said, "What blasted nonsense is that? The usual barracks rubbish, always the same old story of 'they say, they say'. Ignore these rumours. I hear them every day, my dear. And if they ever happen to come true, we're ready for them. After all my earnest promises and loyalty oath to the P.M., and after all that he's done for me you think that I will sit there for these f......., two-pence-half penny idiots to come and walk over us?. Over my dead body! Yes, I would rather shoot myself than surrender to any buffoon, idiotic enough to mount a coup. We are ready for any eventualities", he held forth brightly.

Maggie knew her husband well after so many years of marriage. She bore his proved or unproved infidelities bravely and quietly, always hoping that one day he would change. She knew him as a drinker, but not as an inveterate liar And the brilliant performance which her husband put on that night, could have fooled any body. It was apparent to her that he was speaking from the very bottom of his heart.

"Well, Kofi, I believe you absolutely and I have full confidence in your ability to contain any situation that may arise. I feel, and feel very strongly, that irrespective of what the P.M. has done for us or not, this Government must be given a chance to run its normal five year term of office. After all, it was freely and democratically elected by our people themselves, and it simply would not be right if the Army stepped in to overthrow it. We would only be moving the country backwards and making ourselves a laughing stock before Europeans and Americans". She paused, then holding his left hand, she went on "I am only a housewife, but that's my view. The country does not need a coup".

He listened to her without a word or murmur, only adding, "I agree with you, I fully agree with you, dear", as she ended.

Unusual for the Colonel that night he skipped his usual glass of beer, and his nightcap of hot chocolate drink.

"I have to retire now, dear", he said, walking towards the bedroom, and by the time she joined him, he was fast asleep, snoring gently.

Meanwhile, at the time Kofi was listening without comment or interruption, to his wife's news on a rumoured, impending coup at the Airforce base the Commodore was ironically enough, receiving similar treatment from his wife.

"Please, darling for heaven's sake, watch the Colonel. I know he has been your friend for ages, but I don't at all feel easy and happy inside me when he comes here or rings you. It's all so mysterious, darling. For heaven's sake if he brings up any crazy, silly plan don't be a party to it. I implore you to think of the children, have nothing to do with any dastardly, obscene scheme or operation. We are happy as we are, thank God", she said.

"What are you talking about? I don't understand", he remarked.

"Well, darling it's simple. I have a strong gut feeling that this man is up to no good and will only get us in the shit, and leave us there. I don't think when he called that morning, at that unholy hour, he came to talk only about his women problems. I have no evidence, but I think there's more to the visit than his

long-standing affairs. If I am right, please, I pray to God that you
politely but firmly reject any approaches from him. I find him a
good friend of yours, but I think he's not straight. How can you
trust a man who cannot control himself to the extent that he
drinks and smokes so heavily, and cannot keep his prick off
women. All he sees in a woman is a cunt. I'm certain he's sick
upstairs. How sad!" She paused and walking towards the window, she continued, "It's amazing that he's got where he's now.
But then is it all that surprising, Eh? After all, he and the P.M.
are of the same tribe, and he is very close to the Director, I mean
the Director of Military Intelligence".

Suddenly, her husband burst out, "You women imagine all
sorts of foolish things. Who told you about a coup? Who has time
for a coup now? You are imagining all sorts of things without any
basis, whatsoever. Well, to set your mind at rest I can assure you
that nothing like that is going on. I am, darling, too shrewd at my
age to be involved in these games. And I promise you I will be
careful of him and think of what you just said".

Facing him directly, she smiled then remarked quietly "I
don't trust that bugger, darling. He has always struck me as the
sort of person that if you were engaged within any operation, he
would quickly turn round and inform the authorities, citing you
as the originator and villain of the piece, once he saw the faintest
sign of discovery or defeat. You mark it. I think I will go to bed
now. Good night". She walked away confidently, satisfied that
she had got off her chest and mind whatever was nagging her

The Commodore sat alone in the sitting-room, quiet and
motionless, looking vacantly at the wall with a number of
military mementoes, memorabilia and photographs. He was lost
in thought. Maybe he needed counselling.

A week or so after he had divulged his plans to the Commodore, Kofi called in the major under him responsible for the
disposition of officers and troops that guard the secret, military
emergency transmitter, the Broadcasting House, the seat of
Government, the official residences of the Chiefs of Staff, the
Head of Police Force, the members of the Government.

Major Yaw Tuo, who was a short, thick set infantry officer

whose thick head looked like an overblown, giant size bullet. He had risen from the ranks, was not formally educated, and always resented what he considered the snobbery of the officers who were graduates, and had, according to him 'jumped ahead from university to become officers'. In many respects he shared the Colonel's background and social class, and felt attracted to him over and above the call of duty. To him the Colonel could do no wrong.

When, therefore, he was told by the Colonel's aide that he was to see his mentor on a Tuesday morning at eleven o'clock at his office, he was overjoyed. To him, meeting his boss was an event that he very much looked forward to.

On the appointed Tuesday, at the appointed time, he walked briskly into the presence of his boss.

'Sit down, Major. So nice to see you again. How are you and the family?"

"Pretty well, Sir. Thank you, Sir".

The Colonel lit a cigarette, puffed on it then said, "Major, you know how much I love you. You mean a lot to me and I wish that I can do more about your promotion".

"Thank you, Sir. You have already done enough, Sir".

The Colonel continued, "As one that I trust completely with my own life I want to ask you to undertake a dangerous and delicate assignment for me. Will you?"

"Yes, Sir, absolutely", he remarked.

"Well, are you prepared to kill for me, if it comes to that, for nobody knows the final outcome of the venture".

"Colonel, I will go whatever you order. I am a soldier, a simple soldier, ready for your orders".

"Well, before we do anything further, Major, you have to swear a life or death allegiance. Ready?" "Sure, Sir".

So both got up and with his right hand raised, he repeated after his superior officer, "I, Major Yaw Tuo, of the "Do or Die" Regiment, do hereby swear on my life, that I will obey all orders from Colonel Kofi Johnson, in all acts before and on D-Day, divulging not a word of any part of the project to any person, whatsoever the circumstances, so help me God".

So sworn into secrecy, Yaw sat down confidently. He felt great that he was perhaps witnessing an exciting new era. "Next to consolidate your oath of loyalty, Major, there are two more things to do now. OK?" "Yes, Sir".

"Well, firstly, you will urinate into this test tube, stare into it for exactly five minutes, thinking of nothing but the venture. After that you should shake the test tube and drink your urine. OK?"

"No problem, Sir". He did exactly that. "Finally, Yaw with this small knife, I will make a small cut on my left hand, and draw a small bit of blood on this small glass slide. You will do the same and the two sets of blood will be mixed to signify our loyalty to each other until death. OK?"

"Sure, Sir". The Major dutifully obeyed the instructions, was given a piece of plaster to cover the little cut, and it was all over. Both smiled and shook hands vigorously.

The Colonel put his right index finger on his lips then opened the door for his visitor to leave. The Major was over the moon, feeling that greatness was coming his way. Returning to his office, he called for the weekly rota of the platoons that guard the specified, sensitive public buildings and certain senior top brass. He carefully studied the lists, and picked out of them a captain and other ranks, fifteen in all, very well known to him personally. Each of them, in one way or another or another, owed him a favour.

Already, he had a pretty good idea of his plans, what was to be his contribution towards his boss's venture. He figured the best way to minimise any bloodshed was to pick for D-Day officers and men that would unflinchingly obey his orders. And, it was with that thought in mind that he did his final selections of officers and men for weekly rota duty. Furthermore, he planned, with the approval of the Colonel, to hold at least one rehearsal of operational plans before the day of destiny.

However, as with all the best laid plans, there is always a snag, a fly in the ointment. In this case, it was the armoured battalion. This was the only armoured section of the army, equipped with personnel carriers, armoured cars and a handful of old tanks. Admittedly, they were rather of Second World-War vintage, but still could muster immense fire-power. Certainly, the infantry with their light machine-guns and automatic rifles, were no match to these armoured vehicles.

Colonel Johnson's dilemma was how to get the armoured corps on his side, or at least ensure that they were not against him. Yet there was another snag. The Commanding officer of this corps was a serious, professional officer, who was completely political. The Colonel at first intended to sound his colleague, but on reflection decided not to risk it. He thought of a better idea. He would rather ignore Major Baba Suleman, and concentrate on his next-in-command, Major Kwame Dampeh. The latter was also a good officer, but Kofi felt that he was more amenable to flattery and the blandishments of possible quick promotion. After all, Kofi knew that Dampeh had failed his last promotion examination, and was in a rather restless, if not outright rebellions state. Like most of the officers, the expenses at the mess, plus those at home, were making life a bit difficult to put it mildly.

Aware that Major Dampeh was a keen tennis player, he deliberately arranged to meet at the tennis court, ensuring that it appeared like a coincidence.

"You play smashing", he remarked. "One of these days we should arrange a serious match". "Colonels versus Majors".

"I am sure it would be a great hit with all the people", replied the Major.

After the game was over, the Colonel, over a glass of iced beer, lighting his cigarette, said, "If you are free tomorrow at about 8 pm, young man, can you meet me here, at this address", and as he said so he wrote on a piece of paper the address of his girlfriend, Sophia Fumey. Major Dampeh looked at the paper, smiled, and shook his head positively.

The following day, at the agreed time, he called at the agreed address. He was expecting to meet the Colonel, but surprise, surprise, was met the by the attractive Sophia.

"Colonel Johnson asked me to call, is he in, Madam?"

"No, but come in".

He hesitatingly went in, sat on a settee that was shown to him. "You're welcome, Major. I've heard such nice things about you and I am so pleased at last to have met you. Why have you been hiding in the barracks all the time? You don't go out, eh? I have gin and tonic, whisky or beer, what do you fancy?"

"Any soft drink, madam? Pineapple or orange juice or coke will do".

"What, you mean you don't drink outside the mess". A nice lad like you, how strange!"

"As a matter of fact, madam, I don't drink or smoke. I am a strict Methodist, perhaps rather old fashioned some would say ... ha...ha...ha".

"I see. Well, let me get you a soft drink with ice?"

"Yes, pineapple juice, if I may, with plenty of ice, madam".

He was slowly sipping the juice when the Colonel walked in, with an artificial goatee beard that made him look like Karl Marx, in a depressed mood.

The two gentlemen sat down. Sophia conveniently retired to the bedroom. The two officers wasted no time but went straight ahead.

"Old boy, I've invited you here for a very vital assignment. You know how well I trust you. Of late, I've been watching you immensely, and I feel the time has come for us to talk as man to man, eye-ball to eye-ball. OK?"

"Yes, Sir".

"Well, with the way things have been going of late, I felt that you would be happy to join in this venture which I plan to change the course of events in our dear country and I know that I can count on you".

"Certainly, without question, Colonel".

Kofi puffed on his cigarette, then went on. "Your role in the exercise will be vital and historic. Are you with me or not?"

"With you, Sir, all the way", he replied.

"You mean all the way to the end?", the Colonel enquired.

"Absolutely, through thick and thin".

"Good, I knew I could count on you, old boy. Hmm", he sighed. There was a brief pause. Then the Colonel led the Major to the bathroom, saying, "if so, then let's begin from the beginning"... He closed the bathroom door and they both sat on the side of the bath.

"Well, here we go. First of all, please, urinate into this basin, just a little bit, then repeat after me, OK?"

"Yes".

"I, Major Kwame Dampeh, do hereby swear on my life, that I shall, on pain of death, not leak to any person, whatsoever, under any circumstances any information about our exercise, and that from today and beyond, I will obey 100 percent, all orders from Colonel Kofi Johnson in connection with our venture, sacrificing my own life, if need be, so help me God".

After the swearing in ceremony, the Colonel then went on, "Now, Major, drink the urine. Quite harmless". He did so.

The Colonel then pulled a little knife from his right hand jacket pocket, and made a tiny snick on his left hand to draw a bit of blood. He then gave the knife to the Major and requested him to perform the same cut on his own left hand. This he did. The Colonel then mixed his blood with the Major's, saying "may the gods of BASSA bless our joint venture with complete victory. God be with us". The cuts were covered with bits of plaster from the bathroom cabinet. The two officers shook hands robustly, hugged each other and smiled. They walked back to the sitting-room and sat down.

"On D-Day as soon as you receive the signal, you are to effect the arrest of your CO, all the Chiefs of Staff and their deputies, neutralise the control room and send three armoured cars out as directed. There should be no opening of fire, under any circumstances whatsoever, unless ordered by me. Understand?"

"Yes, Sir", the Major replied, who then asked, "Am I to work out the details of these arrests myself, Colonel, or would you give specific, further orders?"

"Kwame, you are known as a resourceful officer, and I leave these details in your hands. For on the appointed day, it may not be possible to get through further instructions. Right?"

"Yes, Sir", he replied.

Deliberately, the Major asked, looking puzzled, "But what,

Sir, happens if the big guns resist arrest. Should I neutralise them?"

"Look, Kwame, this is a life and death matter, but we're trying to accomplish the objectives without bloodshed. Going by the pattern of behaviour of the big boys in previous coups, you can rest assured that they will not resist arrest. They are too shrewd for that, you see? Let me give you a tip, imagine on the day you have your best men at their residences, with the phones already cut, and the transmitter jammed, you bet they would offer no resistance when they see the stark position clearly facing them. I agree a bit of luck comes into these things, old boy. But don't worry. You get your men appropriately placed to effect the arrests at the ordered time, and I bet that by then they would be completely cut off from the rest of the word. "Sounds beautiful, Colonel, really great. It's on!"

"By the way, Major, you know some of these blokes don't sleep all the time at their official residences. Sometimes they are at camp, sometimes with their mistresses outside. And it is up to you, ingeniously, to liaise with your friend at Intelligence, so that on the night you know precisely where they are, one by one. We want to bag the whole bloody lot together, with none at all escaping, if possible. You see what I mean, Major?"

"Indeed I do. I do very clearly", he remarked smiling as he did so.

The two officers, now in a rather relaxed state, talked about social events in the camp, the latest transfers and promotions and other rather boring matters.

Finally, about two hours after their meeting in Sophia's house, the major was given permission by the Colonel to leave. "Good night, and sleep well. Ah, remember, the code is "The generator is working"'.

"Sir, how can I forget it? We are making history and I am so happy and honoured to be with you all the way, right to the very end". He saluted smartly, and slipped into the thick tropical darkness. His heart was jumping as he walked towards his car. Was this the beginning of the end, he kept asking himself. Naturally, he thought about the possible failure of the venture.

Although a brave soldier, he still could not get out of his mind the vivid spectacle of the firing squad that would certainly follow an abortive coup. On the other hand, the glory and power that would flow from success kept flashing through his mind.

"Darling, I am rather late, and also tired, so it has to be a very quick one", Kofi was telling his girlfriend, following the departure of the Major. "Ah, Kofi, what was this that went on and on and on? I thought that you were never going to stop. I was getting rather bored and lonely, lying here alone." She was undressing as she spoke. And although the Colonel only a few minutes ago was telling her that he was rather tired, he lost no time to quickly throw off his trousers, with his rather large penis ready for action.

It was not one of his best performances. As a matter of fact, it was below par, a fact well noticed by Sophia, who was not at all excited over the rather early ejaculation of the Colonel. As both lay on the bed, enjoying a smoke together, she was boiling inside. Her nerves were jangling and tinkling. She felt let down and furious, but still managed a beautiful loving smile on her face, as if she had enjoyed it enormously, every minute of it.

Knowing her man so well, Sophia was worried about the apparent diminution in his acclaimed sexual prowess.

"Eh, Kofi, what's happening? What's on your mind? Your willie seems dead!", she said as she fondled it.

Kofi just smiled but said nothing for a few seconds.

"Don't worry, dear. I'm alright. Just over-work".

"You sure?", she enquired.

"Definite, positive", he replied as he put on his clothes. He kissed her passionately, walked to his car, and sped away.

Chapter 8

It was Friday night. The rain was pouring down with the sort of viciousness that the Tropics are noticed for. As usual, it was accompanied by thunderstorms and lightning. It was the sort of night that would have kept most people at home, with their families or close friends. At 11.30 pm sharp, the heavy iron gates of the KUKU shrine at AGORO were opened by a hefty, female guard of about thirty-five years. She was about five feet seven inches in height, dressed in a completely red military-design uniform.

Her face was pretty, but not beautiful. Her hair was carefully kept, with a rather funny looking cap on it. As she opened the gates, she smiled, saluted, but said nothing. In drove Colonel Kofi Johnson, in mufti, with a grim, determined look on his face. He was keeping an appointment which, to his mind, would make or break his whole future. He drove quietly to the grassy car park of the shrine and sat in the car as he had been instructed. He sat in his car for about fifteen minutes, day-dreaming about all sorts of things - his past life, his army career, his amorous conquests and failures, his bank overdrafts and his children's education.

In the midst of his mind wandering, Kofi heard a gentle tap on the right glass door of the car, where he was sitting. He turned and looked, to find the same woman gate-keeper, standing there, completely naked. Admittedly, it was dark, pitch dark, with no lights about. Still the Colonel could see that it was the same woman that he had met at the gates in uniform, except now that she was stark naked. She requested the Colonel to follow her and they walked for about five minutes across the car park to a small hall, on whose wall were displays of various animal heads, skins, skeletons. The hall had one door, and two tiny windows. It was dimly-lit, and strangely, had an air of serenity about it.

The "KUKU Shrine" was well known in West Africa as the most powerful and most mysterious, and had had for its clientele many prominent people, including top Cabinet Ministers, the very top brass of the Armed Forces, and Police, and a few highly placed top division civil servants. It was even rumoured to have been visited by some well-known reverend ministers. For according to conventional wisdom, the Kuku Shrine could do the impossible, even turning a man into a woman and vice versa. Whether all the claims attributed to "KUKU" were true or not was not important to many of its adherents. What was important to them was that they believed in KUKU, that it could foretell the future absolutely, and stave off illness, danger, accidents and misfortune. Furthermore, the shrine was even credited with making people, after due and appropriate sacrifices, immune to bullets or poison. No wonder, there were stories going round to the effect that certain top politicians, not only from BASSA, but beyond, had made a couple of surreptitious visits to the shrine before starting their election campaigns or being sworn into office as Presidents or Prime Ministers. That all these V.I.P's also claimed to be professing Christians, publicly advocating Christian virtues, and lambasting idolatry, was nothing of surprise to all the people who knew of Kuku, or had heard of it.

Kofi sat in the hall alone, calmly thinking about his mission on this momentous night. At midnight, he suddenly heard from outside the hall, the loud beating of the well-known tom-tom drums of Tropical Africa. The rhythm was moving, and the beating of the drums sent a mild shudder down his spine. For a moment, he thought of his boyhood days in his village. He remembered being told by his grandfather, on his father's side, that long before the introduction of the telephone by the Europeans who came to Africa, the drums were a means of communicating between villages, especially in emergencies and times of trouble, such as wars. He reflected on the gradual replacement of the drums by the telephone, to the present position where they were used for funerals, for local entertainment, and for putting on public shows for Europeans or American tourists who wanted to see and hear the old Africa.

Kofi Johnson listened intently to the drumming. Suddenly it stopped. And from an adjoining room came an unmistakable voice, the distinct voice of the Kuku Shrine. It was a small, soft voice, definitely that of a woman. He could tell that it was certainly not that of the naked woman that had let him to the hall previously.

"Welcome to the Kuku Shrine", the voice began. "You're here of your own free will, and at your request, and may what you see, hear, do or say here, stay with you alone till your dying day. Kuku wants you to be absolutely sure of this and be aware of the journey which you are undertaking, as from this moment".

The voice paused, then continued, "You will be asked a number of questions to which you are to give full, direct answers. You will at the appropriate time have the chance to ask questions, if necessary. Finally, before Kuku talks to you, she wishes to assure you that whatever you ask for shall be given to you, and in return you must do for Kuku what she asks of you. I hope it's perfectly clear".

"Yes, it is".

"Before we begin the ceremony, I am ordered to ask you again, whether you are ready and prepared as from this moment to do all that you are asked, without question".

"Yes, Kuku".

"Well, what is your full name?"

"Kofi Peter Johnson".

"Age"

"42"

"Married or single?"

"Happily married", he replied.

"Kuku says, she is amused about your life profile".

"What aspect, please?" the Colonel asked.

"Sorry, Kofi, the time for questions has not come yet".

"Kuku asks whether you are happy in your present post".

"No, I am not".

"Why?"

"Hmm, although recently promoted, I feel that the Army has

118

not been fair to me. I should have got further by now. Also, I am not happy about the bribery and corruption and sexual immorality among the civilian politicians".

"Kuku asks whether all the politicians are corrupt and bad", enquired the voice.

"Yes, well, most of them anyway",

"And what can be done about this state of affairs which you obviously hate?"

"I want to change things, Kuku"

"How?"

"By mounting a successful coup"

"Kuku wishes to know whether you have the stamina and determination for such a venture"

"Yes, I am determined and I seek her blessing and support"

"Kuku states that she can bless, but not support you"

"That would be sufficient for my purpose"

"Well, so you say and so be it"

The tom-tom drums beat again for a few minutes. Some of the lights in the hall were put on and off for about a minute. Then the hall was brilliantly lit.

The voice ordered, "Kofi, take off all your clothes and put them on the little table on your left". Kofi did so quickly.

"Now, sit on the cushion on the floor, with your legs crossed yoga fashion, and look directly ahead", ordered the voice. He swiftly did as requested.

He kept on looking ahead. A young boy of about seven years wearing a pair of shorts walked slowly in front of him, holding a white dove in his left hand. He smiled, bowed briefly as he walked away.

Next walked into the hall an elderly woman of about seventy, holding a snake, a long python in her right hand. She was naked and stooped a bit, when walking. Momentarily, she held the snake before Kofi's face, so that his eyes peered directly into those of the snake.

"Don't blink, Kofi, don't blink", said the old lady.

He did not blink or flinch, and the woman with the snake went away.

119

Finally, a young woman of about thirty stood in front of Kofi, smartly dressed in a very exotic, gay dress. She was indeed beautiful, with large, lovely eyes, smallish mouth and smooth skin. She stood in front of the Colonel suddenly, then looked straight at him. Both said nothing. Kofi's heart was beating with increasing vigour and precision. The woman standing before him began to undress. The clothes came off one by one, till eventually she stood, fresh and complete before him. Her breasts were firm and not sagging, and the nipples were dark brown and luscious looking.

"I am all yours, Colonel, all yours", she said, as she coyly bent over him and began to caress him. For a brief moment, Kofi was tempted to throw all caution and prudence to the wind , and go for her. Yet, somehow, he felt that Kuku's offer was too good to be true. He felt that there was a trap somewhere. So just as he was thinking of getting up to mount a frontal attack, he felt a small, still voice inside him say, "DON'T, FOR HEAVEN'S SAKE, STAY OFF".

It was not an easy decision, especially as his penis was bobbing up and down, with his veins protruding all over his limbs. Still Kofi stood his ground.

"Well, Sir, this is your last chance. Now or never", she said, as she jumped on him, tickling his balls.

"No thanks".

She began slowly to collect her clothes, and walk away. He sighed with relief as she blithely went away.

Suddenly, Kofi was hearing, "Kuku is happy with your determination and singleness of purpose. Kuku wishes you well". All the lights were then put out. The tom-tom drums began again, accompanied by much blowing of horns. Abruptly, the drumming stopped.

"Kuku asks whether you've brought the items which you were asked to bring along".

"Yes, Kuku".

"All of them?" asked the voice,

"Yes, Kuku"

"And where are they?"

"In a box in the boot of my car".

"What items does the box contain, Colonel?"

"Kuku, as ordered, the box I brought contains the liver of a woman, the heart of a man, and the kidneys of a child. Also I brought the 3000 U.S Dollars".

"Good, good. Well done, Colonel, but Kuku wishes to know, before accepting your sacrifices that they were not obtained by bloodshed. Kuku hates bloodshed. So Colonel tell Kuku how you got the human organs. For Kuku abhors human sacrifices".

Kofi thought for a moment, and decided to come clean.

"Kuku, I got them without shedding blood:.

"How did you come by them then?"

"Kuku, my aide knew somebody who works at the military hospital mortuary, and he provided the organs from the cadavers of some unknown displaced persons. They cost 100 dollars in all, excluding the cost of the vacuum box. There was no bloodshed, whatsoever, in the procurement of the organs".

"And where is the box now, Colonel?"

"In the boot of my car, as I said earlier"

"Kofi, please get up and walk to the curtain on your right. Draw it apart".

He did so, and there sitting was the box he had brought from APPAPA, and the last time he saw it was in the boot of his car, under lock and key, properly secured.

The Colonel was beginning to wonder whether he had been drugged somehow, or had been somehow tricked or hoodwinked. He was beginning to smell a rat. Still he was determined to go ahead with the rituals to the very end.

"Kuku wishes you now to make a wish, what you really would like to be done for you, Colonel".

"I request Kuku to bless me so that my coup, which I plan succeeds. That's all I want, Kuku", he said.

"Kuku indeed blesses you and wishes you success in your venture, only on one condition. There should not be bloodshed in anyway at all. Can you do that?"

"Yes, Kuku, I can".

"You sure?" "Yes, Kuku".

121

"Kuku further states that so long as you don't shed blood in the exercise, no blood will follow you, but after the success of the coup and beyond, once you shed blood, then remember your blood will ultimately be shed also. Those who live by the sword shall indeed die by the sword. Colonel, do you understand completely?"

"Kuku, may I please ask a question now?"

"Not yet".

"Kuku wants you to get up now, and repeat the following words with your right hand raised over your head". "I Kofi Johnson do hereby swear before Kuku, the shrines of shrines, the queen of queens, the arbiter of death and life, that I will not directly or indirectly, be responsible for the shedding of human blood before, during and after the coup, and during the period of my administration of the country. So help and bless me, Kuku"

Kofi repeated the oath as ordered. After that Kofi was brought a bowl of what looked like a nasty concoction. It smelled very badly and looked awful.

"Kuku asks you to drink the liquid from the bowl. Take it from the hand of the small boy and drink it all. It is the elixir of life made from honey, human blood, goat's milk and factor x which you need not know about".

The Colonel drank it all, and sat down, as ordered. He began to feel drowsy and quickly fell asleep. By the time he woke up he had been asleep for a clear couple of hours. He quickly came out of his slumber, and was intrigued about the two missing hours. For all that he remembered was drinking from the bowl and sitting down.

"Kuku is happy with your efforts, Colonel. Now you have been fully initiated as an obedient son of Kuku, the shrine that you can rely on day and night. You may go in peace".

However, before he would leave, the small boy with the white dove, the elderly woman with the long python and the young woman who stripped naked before him, all came to say goodbye to him. One by one, each repeated, "Kuku wishes you well and may you rule for a long time". As they said their farewells, they shook hands with Kofi Johnson and bowed. The Colonel felt elated. He was over the moon and very relaxed. He felt that he had made it at last. Kuku, the shrine of shrines, had blessed him and his venture.

He drove back home a very happy man, inwardly satisfied that he was at the end of his days of obscurity, as he saw them, and that the days of greatness and honour would shortly begin. Although the whole ceremony from the time of his arrival at the car park, to his departure had taken just over three long hours, Kofi felt that it had been among the best spent three hours of his life. The visions of endless, adorable women parading before him as Head of State; with all sorts of financial, commercial and other requests; the visions of him chairing cabinet meetings, welcoming ambassadors and other Heads of State, filled his heart with immense joy and contentment.

Chapter 9

The Head of Special Branch invited Colonel Kofi Johnson to lunch on a bright Tuesday afternoon. The venue was the Chinese Restaurant at the Hilton Hotel in APPAPA,. A popular meeting place for a good number of local and foreign businessmen, the restaurant provided a relaxed, informal atmosphere for doing business, or talking politics. Indeed, many a romantic two-some had enjoyed the marvellous facilities provided by the restaurant. And equally important, the food was good, very delicious.

Over shark fin soup, sweet and sour pork, steamed yellow rice, and a hot, mouth-watering beef stew, the wily lawyer and the Colonel talked over the security situation in the country. It was one of their routine weekly meetings held in each other's office alternately. Over the months, the two men had come to trust each other absolutely, and knew each other well. As a matter of fact, even their families were on first name terms and got on extremely well. For both men were engaged in the joint cause of ensuring the survival and stability of the civilian government, by seeing to it that there was no coup to topple the two-year old democratically-elected government.

"Kofi, I am so pleased you could come", the Director began, after the usual small talk about the hot weather and other inconsequential matters.

The Colonel made a friendly gesture, of no particular significance. He lit a cigarette, puffed thrice on it, and appeared to leave it in the ash-tray burning away.

"Old boy, I felt I should let you know about one or two things, which have been brought to my serious attention".

"Don't say it is the usual coup talk, the usual rubbish, eh?"

"Well, I really don't know. My men report that they have noticed some changes in the rota of the soldiers and officers, detailed by your side to guard the usual strategic centres in town, and I wanted to sound you on these changes, old boy", he said.

Kofi listened to all this intently, not giving the slightest indication that inside him he was very, very worried. He was not sure whether his plans, somehow, had leaked. He was not sure whether his colleague was just kite-flying or bluffing.

Calmly and unemotionally, he remarked, "As a matter of fact, my staff officer and operations officer handle these rotas, and the changes are just routine, which indeed they brought to my attention only yesterday. The purpose is to ensure that none of my men get used to one spot too long. Furthermore, these sudden changes help me to keep the element of surprise and uncertainty in my own, firm hands, you see what I mean Kojo?"

"Yes, I do. I only felt that I should clear the matter with you so that if there was any special significance to the changes you would be aware and take appropriate action, old boy".

They continued with their lunch, and after quickly going over some routine security issues affecting the capital, and the provincial capitals, they settled on coffee.

Just before they got up to leave the Colonel said, "You know the rascals that were trying to foment trouble in the Second Battalion, we nipped the whole thing in the bud and they have been cashiered from the Army".

"Well-done, man, well-done. We indeed must give democracy a chance to grow in this country. These coups and abortive coups only make us a laughing stock before the whites - of course, publicly, they would not mind which regime is in control, but privately they are very amused with all these coups in Africa. It's behaviour they associate with immature adults, who have gone bonkers!!"

The Colonel laughed heartily, and said, "Man, you are dead right. Absolutely. Well, you know my views on coups against a democratically-elected, civilian government. I say no more".

"Oh, by the way, you remember the case that we discussed the other day at our meeting; you know, the rape of the fourteen year old girl by the Deputy Minister. Well, after conversations with the PM, he's adamant that the prosecution should go ahead, irrespective of any political repercussions or consequences of the case. Wished we had more of such leaders in Africa, who are not prepared, simply not prepared to countenance any serious criminal activities, although emanating from their own close political colleagues or associates".

The Colonel interjected, "The PM looks very mild and soft outside, but, I bet, he's very tough inside, as tough as a tank".

The two men shook hands, walked towards their official cars, and momentarily were gone. Returning to his office, the Director of the Special Branch, reflected for a few minutes in his chair and then made the following entry in his secret, official diary. "Discussed changes in rota with Colonel, absolutely satisfied with explanations offered. No need to worry".

For the Colonel there were very good grounds for worry. Kofi was not at all sure of what was happening. He was not certain whether any of the top secret meetings which he had been holding of late with his closest co-conspirators and confidants had leaked. He knew that the handful of intimate colleagues that he had discussed his project with, were all very loyal and dedicated to him. Still he felt uneasy. Had any of them had a change of mind? Had any of them approached the authorities, with hope and expectation of advancing their career prospects in the Army? Had anyone, inadvertently, over a drink, perhaps, loosened his tongue too much? These were some of the very numerous, intractable questions that went through his mind, as he sat in his office, following the lunch with the Director of the Special Branch.

He sat and ingeniously tried to resolve the problem. How? By quickly making innocuous telephone calls to his closest comrades, to discuss routine barracks matters, with the hope of sensing from the tone of their voices, and their general demeanour whether there was anything amiss. So the next ninety minutes found Kofi telephoning the commodore, Major Yaw Tuo, and the remaining handful in the know. Absolutely satisfied that there were no leakages whatsoever, and that things were going according to plan, the Colonel figured that it would be best to bring forward D-Day. For he was of the view that the longer the whole exercise was delayed, the greater the chance of it being scuppered, either by new, unforeseen circumstances or a possible leak or loss of nerve.

That evening a scheduled visit to Sophia, the girlfriend had to be cancelled. He spent the night, after a hurried quiet supper, making brief calls on his closest confidants. He checked a few, vital details with them, and was happy with what they told him that they had done, planned or rehearsed. He rounded off these visits with a surprise, unscheduled visit to the Broadcasting House, where, duly identified, he was given the customary respects, and waved along. All seemed to be going smoothly and as well as could be expected, or hoped for.

Colonel Kofi Johnson returned home very late, a satisfied and happy man.

"Darling, where have you been all this time. I've been so worried for you. By the way, both the PM and the Director, I mean of Special Branch, rang looking for you".

"And what did you tell them, love?"

"I told them that you had gone out to see some friends and that I would give you their message".

"So do you think I should ring now. It's rather too late".

"I think so, darling".

"Then I shall telephone them first thing tomorrow".

The two telephone calls which Kofi made to the Prime Minister and the Director of Special Branch, completely allayed any fears which he had previously entertained about anything untoward, such as a leak. Wily as he was, he took the opportunity, in both cases, to emphasise his absolute loyalty to the government. He went even further in indulging in a bit if disinformation, by telling both the PM and the Director that he was planning the following week to institute a further security system, designed to root out politically unreliable company commanders. It all sounded fine to the ears of both the PM and the Director, who, had not the slightest cause, whatsoever, to doubt the loyalty and professionalism of the Colonel.

That appearances can be deceptive, may be judged by the

fact that right to the moment of truth, neither Kofi's wife, his close colleagues, apart from those in the know, nor any of his political masters could detect anything unusual about the Colonel's demeanour, movements or activities. Nor did Sophia Fumey, his mistress, notice anything unusual about her paramour, except for his diminishing sexual appetite and prowess, which she put down to overwork and stress, an idea deliberately sowed in her head by Kofi.

Although ostensibly a devout Roman Catholic, the Colonel also firmly believed in voodoo and juju, and to boot was superstitious. Being born on a Friday, he for many reasons, felt a special attachment to Fridays. Kofi thus felt that his venture stood the best chance of success if it took place on a Friday, any Friday. Consequently, he decided, after much soul searching, on the following Friday. This gave him only six days to finalise his plans, as it was a Saturday when he firmly and finally settled on D-Day. To be sure and certain that the officers at Military Intelligence were thrown off the scent, he kept up his normal routine at the barracks, popping in at the officers' mess, off and on, and making telephone calls, here and there. He also scheduled an officer's meeting for that Friday, 11 o'clock. Kofi even put in a brief appearance at Sophia's to maintain the myth of his Casanova image.

However, the last visit to his mistress before D-Day was a complete fiasco. Despite all Sophia's enticement and encouragement, the Colonel could simply not deliver the goods. As he fondled the rotund breasts of Sophia, he thought of the good old days when the very sight of her thighs had set him going all out. He smiled to himself but said nothing. His mind was firmly honed in to the on-coming events of the following Friday.

Before leaving Sophia's home, the Colonel handed her a brown envelope. "Sophia, dear, this is for you, but not to be opened until next Saturday morning. Give me your word of honour, hand on heart, that you will not open it till Saturday morning".

"Yes, I will not open it till then", she said.

"Ah, a better idea, Sophia, put it in your small travelling box, the one I brought from the West Indies. Lock the box and give me the key, and I will send you the key on Saturday morning. Darling, it's for your own good, that you do not, I repeat, do not open this envelope till the specified time. OK?"

Sophia did as she was told, then handed over the key to him. After a warm kiss and a hug, Kofi left, with Sophia at her wit's end about what the letter contained. It was to take seven solid days before she knew the contents.

It was a brief, passionate letter.

"Darling Sophia, by the time you read this letter, I would either be great and famous, or disgraced and dead. I've my dear, decided to embark on a historic venture to rid our beloved motherland of the corrupt, greedy and dishonest politicians. Taking the decision which I have done, to do a coup to remove the regime has not been easy, especially, as the PM has recently promoted me over three other colleagues, and trusts me absolutely and implicity.

Yet the truth of the matter is that I feel very strongly that only a coup would spare our people of the high cost of living, fantastic inflation, bribery and corruption which I see all around me, and which constitute the lot of the masses. I can assure you, I am not doing this out of greed, ambition or recklessness. I am doing it out of my love for our people, and for that objective I am prepared to risk my life.

I know that if I succeed, I will be hailed by all and sundry as a great patriot, a dedicated statesman, the country's redeemer. But if I fail, I will certainly be denounced as an irresponsible, callous, over-ambitious, puffed up officer, a scoundrel, thief, rogue and even mad. I am aware of the dangers of failure - my colleagues and I will certainly face the firing squad, after a brief kangaroo trial.

Sophia, I can assure you that I am not bad or mad. All that I am doing is for the good of our nation, as I can see it, so pray for me. For as Tennyson says in his famous poem "If thou shouldst never see my face again, pray for my soul! More things are wrought by prayer than this world dreams of....." You see, darling, I am not as illiterate as my enemies think! With love and best wishes to you, now, and always".

　　Yours ever

　　K "

He drove home and wrote an identical letter to his wife, except that before signing off he added these words. "Look after the children should anything happen to me, and if you need any financial assistance, don't forget to get in touch with my uncle Bempah at Hampang. I have a share in the family farm, and my interest in it should go to you and the children. As you know, my will is with my bank, but I doubt whether any pension or gratuity payments due to me, and other entitlements, would be given to you should the unexpected happen". This letter he gave to his wife, with firm instructions that it should be opened the night of the following Saturday, about 11 pm. He fully allayed her fears about anything happening or about to happen.

"Maggie, dear, I am scheduled for a hush-hush assignment soon, the details of which I am not allowed to divulge to you or any person whatsoever. Only the PM knows about it so, please, try and understand. Keep this letter safely, and only open as instructed".

"Kofi, I'm worried. Anything wrong? Please tell me, let me know. Of late, I've not been sleeping well at all. I have had all sort of dreams of late, in which I see lots and lots of blood. I simply don't understand. I hope no disaster is on the way, Kofi".

He listened to her amusingly, and said, "Women, always worrying about their husbands, about their children, about their grandchildren, about everything and everybody, except themselves. I've told you again and again that everything is all right. Don't you believe me?"

"I do, certainly, but I need to be reassured, Kofi".

"Well, Maggie, I assure you absolutely nothing is wrong. Trust me".

The conversation ended inconsequentially, but amicably, and they retired to bed at about eleven o'clock.

Events were moving at a terrific speed, at least for Kofi and his close confidants. On the Tuesday before D-Day, which was the on-coming Friday, Kofi arranged a secret meeting at Sophia's home. The time was 10 pm and each officer involved in the planned coup arrived by taxi individually and was in mufti. They were six in all, including Kofi. Each wore a suitable disguise, such as a beard, a pair of dark glasses, a hat or moustache.

The Colonel had got his mistress out of the way by telling her that he needed the place to discuss some confidential, highly personal matters with some colleagues till one o'clock of the following morning. Sophia had been very obliging and co-operative by deciding to spend the night with her sister who she had not seen for sometime. For she had wisely learnt from her relationship with military personnel that it was always best for all concerned, particularly for her own best interest, not to ask too many questions, or want to know too much. The less one knew, she figured, the better.

At the crucial meeting, which was opened at 10 pm prompt on that sultry Tuesday evening, the coup plotters went over the operation again and again. Each analysed his role, and its inter-relation with the others. Questions were asked and answered. Anxieties were allayed, and any lingering doubts resolved satisfactorily.

"Comrades, I suggest that each of us do a final rehearsal on Thursday, for D-Day, the following day, Friday 02 GMT sharp. Naturally, as before, you would ensure that the rehearsal appears like a harmless routine exercise or manoeuvre, OK?"

There was a pregnant pause, then the leader continued, "Naturally, with an exercise of this nature, although all the indications, to date, suggest that we have a 100 percent chance of success, history has shown, again and again, that we might perhaps not achieve our objective, not for want of trying, but for circumstances beyond our control. There are some things such as the weather which we cannot control, try as we may. And for the unforeseen situation, we should make contingency plans".

"Right, right", said the rest, almost in unison.

"Against such a possible eventuality, I've obtained these". He showed his colleagues six tiny white tablets which he pulled from the left pocket of his trousers.

"They are very good, pure potassium cyanide, very effective. They work in a matter of two or three minutes at the most. However, any of you who wishes, should it be necessary, to do the decent thing in the age-old, traditional, military way, is at liberty to do so.

Giving one tablet to each colleague, he jokingly remarked, "Chaps, let's hope and pray that we don't need them next Friday or Saturday!"

A further hour was spent by the officers going over their respective assignments and roles on D-Day. Each appeared confident and happy with the prospects of greatness which they were about to achieve. And just before they dispersed, the coup leader, Colonel Kofi Johnson said "Gentlemen, please remember, no bloodshed, I repeat, no bloodshed. We would rather lose our own lives, and go down in defeat than plunge the armed forces into unnecessary loss of lives. Right?"

"Yes, Colonel", said Major Yaw Tuo.

Finally, before departing, they swore again, one by one, the oath of loyalty. They hugged each other, shook hands vigorously and left one by one. Kofi alone stayed behind for another fifteen or twenty minutes, during which time he sat pensively, looking straight at the wall in front of him. He thought of his parents, his boyhood days in his village, the struggle which his mother had made to get him education. He thought of his army career, its ups and downs, his comrades-in-arms and his enemies. He thought also of his wife and children, and what might happen to them if the operation proves a fiasco. Lastly, as if to relieve the unbearable tension, he began to count the number of women he had bedded since he became sexually active at sixteen, remembering especially how at about fifteen he had nearly been seduced by a fat, old lady of sixty five, who wanted him to be her toy-boy.

Suddenly, he shook himself from day-dreaming. It was getting rather late. Indeed it was already about half-past one in the morning, of the last Wednesday before "redemption day" as he saw it. He got up to leave, thought for a second or two, then took out of the breast pocket of his jacket the key that he had taken from Sophia.

Kofi went into the bedroom and opened the box. He took the letter out, and stared at it for a few moments. Then suddenly burst out "No fear! Man dies but once. I am going ahead, no turning back!". He replaced the letter in the little box, locked it and pocketed the key.

With his mind firmly made up, and absolutely aware of the fact that his destiny and that of others, perhaps, lay in his hands, he quietly locked the door and left. As he walked on the street nearby looking for a taxi-cab or mini-cab, he found himself humming to himself, the famous Christian hymn "Onward Christian Soldiers, marching as to war...." He was lucky with the third taxi-cab that passed by. He jumped into it and was driven home to the barracks.

It was about two in the morning when he arrived home. His wife, Maggie, had been awake and worried all the time, not knowing what was happening. There had been no telephone call, nor any message through any of his staff, or aide.

Indeed, she was about to make a telephone call to the commodore to enquire about Kofi's whereabouts, when she heard the sound of the taxi-cab stop in their compound.

"Where have you been all the time, Kofi? What's all this? You never bothered to phone or let me know where you were and I've been very worried, worried sick for you. This is unacceptable", she shouted.

"I am sorry dear. It's all my fault, please, forgive me. I was trying to sort out one or two things".

"Your usual lies. You were, I bet, sorting out your whores. That's all. Disgusting", she remarked as she furiously walked towards the bedroom, leaving her husband sitting alone morosely in the sitting room.

Chapter 10

Maggie was dreaming that somewhere in Africa, she had become Queen, surrounded by numerous courtiers and ladies-in-waiting. Curiously missing in her dream was her husband. Nor did she notice her own children. All that she could see were lots and lots of people, mostly Africans, with a few white people interspersed among them. She was suddenly woken from her dream by the sound of the telephone ringing. She remembered very vividly the day and the time. It was a Friday, and the time was half-past one in the morning. It was a thick, misty morning, with the stillness in the atmosphere peculiar to the Tropics.

As her husband had told her on the previous day, that he would be on an important assignment for the Government, from dawn of that day, and, therefore, would not be at home, she was not surprised to hear his voice on the phone.

"Hello, dear, I hope I have not disturbed you too much, how are things?"

"Hmm, everything is OK, darling and are you all right?"

"Yes, definitely, no problem".

"Should be home in a few hours' time, let's say about 4 am. Please, don't answer the telephone from this time should it ring. Bye-bye, darling, love to you and the children". Maggie, used to her husband's sometimes erratic behaviour, did not give much thought to the conversation. She went back to bed.

Immediately, after his conversation with his wife, Kofi made routine telephone calls to the officers responsible for guarding the Broadcasting House, the Telecommunication Centre, the armoury at the barracks, and the Airport. Finally, he reconfirmed his orders to the coup-plotters, given forty-eight hours earlier. To each of them it was the same message".

"The generators are working. 2 am".

With the die now cast, Colonel Kofi Johnson was calm and

collected, as he sat in his operations room an armoured personnel carrier. With him were his devoted driver, his aide, and the
radio-operator. They were all in a very excited state, except Kofi
himself. Although not privy to the details of what was happening, they were well aware that a coup was taking place. After all,
they had lived through similar experiences before, only they
were not certain on whose side their boss was.

At 2 am sharp, the telephone systems in the capital, and the
Mandalay camp barracks went dead. "Operation Generators"
had begun, instigated, led and directed by Colonel Kofi Johnson,
deputy Officer Commanding, Southern Brigade Forces, including APPAPA. Simultaneously, roadblocks were in place, across
all the six major roads, leading into and out of APPAPA.
Similarly, the roadblocks on the main roads to and from the
main barracks, and three minor army centres, went into place.
The army's own secret transmitter, not far from the capital, was
suddenly rushed by a platoon of soldiers, who quickly took it
over. And among the attackers was a young lieutenant, who had
specialised in psychological warfare during his officer-training
days in the United States.

Troop movements began about an hour following the first
signal for attack, and by three in the morning, a few truck loads
of soldiers could be seen heading towards the centre of the city.
It was the dead of night, and only a few civilians saw these
movements. Those who did, gave them little attention, for so
used were they to coups, counter-coups and abortive coups.

Kofi sat in his personnel carrier shouting out orders. Everything appeared to be going according to plan From major Yaw
Tuo, he learnt the good news that the arrests of the top brass had
all been effected, without any resistance. The poor souls, the
heads, and the deputy heads of the Army, Airforce, Navy, the
Military Intelligence stood little or no chance, whatsoever. For
they had been arrested, at gun-point by their own bodyguards,
responsible for their personal security and safety.

Miraculously, the Chairman of the Joint Chiefs of Staff had
escaped arrest, and so had his deputy. Whether it was luck or
fate at work, was a matter for conjecture. The truth of the matter

was that on the Thursday night, the chairman had not slept at his usual residence. He was soundly asleep in the home of his second wife. And where was his deputy? Well, he had on that Thursday night decided to spend the night in the small, private bedroom attached to his alternative office, in the barracks.

At about 4 am he suddenly woke up, hearing the sound of gun-fire. He felt it rather unusual, as there was no known exercise in motion to justify or explain the gun-fire. He took up the telephone receiver and tried to ring the Chairman. The line was dead. He tried the special, scrambler telephone line which was only to be used in special emergencies. That too was dead. Finally through his personal walkie-talkie, he successfully contacted the Army transmitter.

"This is Lieutenant-General Nicholas Butah, good morning".

"Yes, Sir!"

"Name, rank?"

"Lieutenant Amponsah of Signals, Sir"

"What the hell is going on?. I have been trying to get the chief and all his lines, including the Alert are not working. What's wrong?"

"Well. General, the Chief just rang me about five minutes ago, saying that some unauthorised troop movements are going on in the capital, and that whilst these reports are checked, I should relay his orders to all units that they are confined to barracks, until further orders. In fact, sir, these were his specific orders".

"Red Alert. All troops confined to barracks. No troop movements until further direct orders from General Manu".

"But I could not contact the Chief. When did you say he rang you?"

"Sir, as I said, about fifteen minutes before you contacted me".

"Any indication where he is?"

"No, Sir, not at all".

"Thank you, lieutenant. I have to come there straight away" He got himself ready, slipped out of his office in mufti and towards the gate of the barracks, suddenly heard, "Who goes there? Stop", He continued to walk towards the gate. "I say stop or I fire"". He continued to walk towards the gate. "I say stop or I fire". He stopped promptly, and was surrounded by three armed soldiers. They shone their torch-light into his face, then one of them shouted, "Ebe the deputy". The other colleagues then asked, "Deputy who?"

"Eh, the deputy chairman, himself"

"So?", asked a sergeant among them.

"Yes", replied the soldier looking directly into the general's face.

"Then put him under immediate arrest and I will inform the Colonel at once"

Kofi was listening intently to the various reports coming in, when, on his walkie-talkie he heard an interruption from Major Yaw Tuo, "Colonel, another big kill, the deputy chairman has been put under arrest".

"Hey, good-show, well-done, old boy. Keep at it. Soon we'll be celebrating. By the way, any news of the chief himself? It's vital that we neutralise him quickly, before we go on air. You would be delighted to know that all the major targets have been accomplished without any bloodshed".

"Colonel, so far I fear no news of the chief, but I've sent my scouts out, to his possible whereabouts, and I expect them soon". "Good, excellent", said the elated Colonel.

With events galloping at an incredible speed, Kofi's chain-smoking kept abreast. He instructed the driver to move along, till the vehicle came to a stop about five miles from its previous position. The driver could overhear his master saying, "Treat him as a General with respect. No undue force, except trying to escape or resist detention". He turned round, and remarked happily, to his aide "Unbelievable, the Chief himself has been apprehended. You know where, Captain, in the house of his second wife!".

Everything seemed to be going according to plan. The Colonel could not have asked or prayed for more. It looked too good to be true. Momentarily, the Colonel reflected on the physical and spiritual powers of Kuku, the goddess of AGORO. He was elated with his success. So far everything appeared to be working in his favour, including the weather. Good news followed good news. All the big fish, and their deputies, had been netted, and Kofi's plans were not only on course, but slightly ahead of schedule. He realised, that as in all previous coups, and from his study of the accounts of coups in other countries, it was paramount that the broadcasting centre of the nation be captured as quickly as possible. For, as he figured, the enormous psychological advantage which an announcement of the news of a successful coup would entail, completely out-weighed any considerations of the true course of events.

With these thoughts racing through his mind, he ordered his driver "Head for B.H., I mean broadcasting house"

"Yes, Sir"

The armoured vehicle engine was started. But before, the driver moved, the Colonel shouted "stop!".

He took the receiver of the phone in the car, and could be overheard by the driver, whispering, almost inaudibly, "Right, Good show, coming soon. Give me ten-minutes or so, but see to it that they stay in the control room, ready to broadcast. They should not be allowed to leave the room, even to shit or urinate. Right?"

He put the receiver down and told the driver to shoot ahead, all the way to broadcasting house. As they sped through the dark, night streets of APPAPA, the Colonel's heart was pumping. He looked through the small windows of his vehicle at the prostitutes busily plying their trade.

With all that was on his mind, considering that he was engaged in a life-and-death exercise, it was remarkable that Kofi could still reflect, however briefly and momentarily, on the by-gone days of his early youth when at the sight of these women, his penis would have jumped into an alert state of excitement, and he would have spent his last hard-earned dollar or pound to satisfy his sexual urge.

The vehicle was soon off the main street, and was heading towards the heavy iron gates of the broadcasting centre of the nation. As the car approached the gates, it flicked its lights thrice, putting them off and on.

"Stop, I say stop", shouted a soldier, armed with a kalashnikov rifle, as he approached the car. Momentarily, Kofi was inclined to go ahead, but thought better of it. He ordered his driver to halt. The soldier approached the car, and shining a torch-light into the car, asked, "who be you? Nobody de pass here".

"I am the D.B.C. don't you know?", the Colonel replied.

"Hey, my friend, I be tire. No sleep, I no fit for morning palaver with you, so please, please, for your own safety, stop.

I cannot order you, Mr. Minister, but in the current, unsettled situation, I strongly advise you to stay put till you see me. Please, inform your colleagues likewise, and expect me within the next fifteen or twenty minutes". Kofi was overheard by his driver talking into his walkie talkie.

The Colonel switched off his walkie-talkie. He got out of the armoured car, and walked confidently to the lieutenant in charge of the troops. Having given him the pre-arranged thumb signal when shaking his hands, he walked with him towards broadcasting house, whispering as they did so. They headed for the main studio, where the producers, announcers and technical staff were getting ready for the morning six o'clock music and news. As they came close to the door of the studio, the lieutenant smiled, and took from its upholstery his revolver. He readied it for action, as the two of them walked into the studio.

It was the lieutenant, not the Colonel, who shouted, "Hands up, don't move. Please, for your own safety don't move an inch or you are dead". The seven or so civilian staff in the studio were frozen in their tracks. They stood still and did not move. They looked on with shock and incredulity as the young officer pushed his revolver closer to their foreheads, one by one.

At the Government's emergency situation room, in the basement of Government House, to be precise in Room 505, there was much activity and excitement following the conversation with the chief, trusted military officer for the capital area that everything was under control and that yet another attempted coup against the democratically-elected civilian government of the day, had been foiled. "I told you, chaps, that we can trust and count on our man. I never had any doubts that he would never let us down. You see", so said the Advisor for National Security, with much flourish. He felt vindicated over the promotion and appointment of Colonel Kofi Johnson, which issue had divided the cabinet and indeed the National Security Council. For the colonel had to be jumped over a least three other more senior, more experienced colleagues to be installed in his current position, by which he held the fate of the civilian government in his hands. So trusted was he by the cabinet ministers, especially by the Defence Minister, that often he was invited to some of the private, tete-a-tete dinner parties of the ministers.

The self-confessed party faithful, dedicated absolutely to the survival and defence of the civilian government was indeed a darling of the ministers, who felt that if there was any officer in the army that they could count on, without a shadow of a doubt, as far as loyalty to the regime was concerned, it was Colonel Kofi Johnson.

As such, although there had been some anxious moments, after the ministers, meeting in emergency session, had spoken with the Colonel, his delay in arriving at Government House, as agreed, did not raise undue alarm. However, the minutes ticked away, and there was still no sign of the Colonel.

"Eh, chaps, what's happening?", asked the Defence Minister. "No sign of Kofi, I'm rather worried. I hope he's in no trouble", he continued. "You're a big pessimist, always worrying about this and about that", remarked the general-secretary of the party. He continued, "Patience, man, Patience".

As some of the ministers walked around the room, others peered at the ceiling, whilst a couple of them, sat intently watching the clock on the wall.

"OK, let's give him another call, to clear things. Right?", asked the National Security Advisor." "Yes", interjected a voice, whilst the rest nodded in agreement

Using a walkie-talkie, the National Security Advisor, tuned in.

"Crocodile, crocodile, can you hear me?", he intoned. He

repeated the agreed signal code, but alas, there was no response. No crocodile. Everything appeared dead, only the singing of the early morning birds could be heard from afar by the ministers. The anxiety on the face of the minister shouting into the walkie-talkie, was clear to his other colleagues, as he turned round to face them fully.

"Folks, something is gone wrong, desperately wrong. The Colonel is not answering. No response whatsoever",

"What? what do you exactly mean?. It could be a simple technical hitch. Calm down!", remarked the General -Secretary of the party in government.

"Well, I'm worried, very worried. Either he's in very big trouble or we're in complete shit! Finished!!"

"You're talking nonsense. Absolute rubbish", so said the Acting Prime Minister, who was chairing the meeting as the Prime Minister was away seriously ill, with a heart complaint.

"Look, gentlemen, I suggest that you recap, and assess the situation. Kofi appears incommunicado. He may be under arrest, seriously wounded or alive and well, and still with us, but experiencing some difficulties, which we are unaware of. We simply don't know what's happening. As such, although his delay in reaching here with the ring leaders is a matter of great concern, I think it would be wise and prudent to remain here, stay put, as he advised. Agreed his silence is inexplicable, mysterious and curious. I agree that the silence of the phones, including our own emergency stand-by, would strongly suggest that something sinister is at work, but until the position is clearer, the less dangerous position to take is to abide by the advice of the Colonel, unless colleagues have other ideas", he concluded in his usual quiet, firm, voice. The time was exactly five minutes to six in the morning, and one of the butlers attached to the Government House was serving coffee.

"Alright, let's see what is happening at B.H. whether it's all lost or not, we will soon enough know. Man dies but once, never twice. If the Colonel has let us down, his treachery would go down in history as one of the most infamous and ungrateful acts by an officer against a civilian administration. On the other hand, if it turns out that all our fears are unjustified, and that he is still loyal to us, probably mobilising his forces on our behalf, against traitors, bastards and treasonous elements, then our faith in him would have been confirmed. We do not know what the position is, let's try and see".

The General-Secretary, a short, debonair lawyer, with a first-class brain, and absolute courage to match, bristled with controlled anger as he spoke.

He walked towards the radio, and put it on. For a brief, deadly moment the place was as silent as a cemetery. Instead of the usual, expected six o'clock morning news the gathering heard military music. Indeed it was Berlioz"s "Rakoczy March".

Suddenly, the music stopped, and an unidentified male voice, full of confidence said,

"Good morning, listeners, please standby for a special announcement". The room was electrified with fear and excitement and abject madness. Ministers were nervously walking confusedly, as if expecting a mass execution. Nobody said a word. The anxieties of the ministers were due to their not being certain whether their own man, popularly known as "the Colonel" had been killed, or wounded defending the regime, arrested, or, the worst of all scenarios, betrayed them completely. Their doubts and uncertainties were soon resolved, albeit not in the way that they expected.

The radio resumed the playing of music, this time it was a piece by Mozart "Concerto in C for flute and harp", followed by popular "High Life music". Again, after a few nerve-wracking minutes, the music stopped, and was followed by word that till their dying days the ministers would never, never forget.

"Good morning, fellow citizens of BASSA, I am Colonel Kofi Johnson, Deputy Brigade Commander of the Southern Command. I am happy to inform you that the Armed Forces of BASSA, distressed about the growing economic, political and social deprivation and suffering of our people, have today overthrown the corrupt, wicked and inept Government of our dear country. In leading this historic attack on the decadent Republican Government, I have been guided by the overall best interests of our people, the suffering masses of Bassa. The corruption and the disgraceful conduct of the nation's affairs have at long last come to an end. The Republican Government is no more. The Constitution is suspended. All members of the past Government and all party office-holders at local, regional and national levels, should for their own safety, report themselves at the nearest police station or military barracks, or face being shot on sight. All these persons and their wives and children are hereby ordered not to leave the country. Their bank accounts and assets are frozen with immediate effect. Any persons attempting to assist such persons to avoid capture or arrest, or assisting in their escape from the country, will be dealt with militarily, with the utmost revolutionary zeal and thoroughness.

Whilst arrangements continue earnestly to form a new administration to redeem the country and our dear people, I wish to assure all foreigners in BASSA of their safety in the country. They should entertain no fears, whatsoever.

Furthermore, the new administration will respect and fulfil the international obligations, contracts and treaties of BASSA, and play a constructive role in the affairs of the international community, through the United Nations Organisation.

The tasks ahead of us are immense, but we are confident that with your assistance, help and goodwill, and with God's blessing, we will not fail. Please standby for further announcements. Long Live BASSA! Long Live the toiling masses of BASSA! Long Live the Armed Forces and our people. God Be with you. Thank you!".

As the national anthem began to be played following the speech the National Security Advisor put off the radio.

"Good Lord, incredible, simply unbelievable. The son of a bitch, that damned, bloody fucking, son of a whore has double-crossed us. What?".

"After all that we did for him, promoting him over other more senior and more experienced officers, wiping of his personal debts, and keeping him out of court and public knowledge, the shocking scandal of his brutal rape of a school-teacher. What a funny world. Just amazing", interjected the Defence Minister.

The Ministers, well, ex-Ministers to be exact, looked sheepishly at each other. The party general-secretary burst out,

"Well, I warned you all long, that I found his overweening loyalty too good to be true. But nobody would listen. Tribalism had so brainwashed us that we could not think straight, or see the difference between a con-man and a man of honour. You, you in particular, were most emphatic about his appointment, simply because he came from your town, and you went to school with him". As he spoke, he walked towards the ex-National Security Adviser and had to be restrained by his colleagues.

"If we get him, we will hang him by his dirty balls, and teach him a good lesson that he would carry to his grave. Such animals deserve to be treated as such. Absolutely worthless. Even dogs have a sense of loyalty, to their masters", remarked the Director of Special Branch.

"Gentlemen, gentlemen, this is a time for nerves of steel, and cool heads. I think we should calm down and think of our next move. Are the phones working now?", enquired, the Acting Prime Minister.

"No, still dead", replied the Defence Minister.

"What about our own emergency lines, also still dead?"

"Yes", remarked the Director of Special Branch.

"Then I suggest that we do not do anything rash and foolish, such as attempting to go out, armed or unarmed, to confront the unknown outside. Gentlemen, if we are to be arrested, imprisoned or, at worst, shot, let's still comport ourselves with dignity, and courage so that when the history of this dastardly day comes to be written, we would be looked upon as men who, in the country's hour of need, did not lose our personal faith, respect or dignity.

What the Colonel has done will one day produce its own appropriate repercussions, firstly on the people, I am asd to say, and secondly, on himself. He will, I assure you, live to rue this day of gross infamy and treachery".

The Acting Head of Government, paused, sipped a glass of water, and whimsically smiled to himself. He continued,

"You leave him. He is no student of history.

The same people that will soon be demonstrating wildly for him as the new "Redeemer" will be the same people who will turn against him, sooner or later. You mark it! "Vengeance is mine, said the Lord, and I shall repay". It is God, not us that will deal with him as he deserves. Meantime, I suggest that we pray to the Almighty God, in our hour of peril and need". Gun-fire could be heard outside loudly.

The dejected assembled group had almost finished praying and were reciting Psalm 23,

"The Lord is my Shepherd; I shall not want. He maketh me to lie down in green pastures: He leadeth me beside the still waters.

He restoreth my soul: He leadeth me in the paths of right-eousness for His name's sake.

Yea, though I walk through the valley of the show of death, I will fear no evit: for Thou art with me; Thy rod and Thy staff they comfort me.

Thou preparest a table before me in the presence of mine enemies. Thou anointed my head with oil; my cup runnethover.

Surely goodness and mercy shall follow me all the days of my life; and I will dwell in the house of the Lord for ever",

when they heard the screeching noise of a couple or so military jeeps. The embattled, deserted ex-ministers, trooped out of the basement, "situation room" and stood in the first floor lounge of Government House awaiting their fate. They could hear the steps of the soldiers as they raced up towards them.

"Hands up, you all. No move. Hands over your heads", ordered a young Military Police lieutenant, who led the detach-ment of about ten soldiers. Four of them carried Kalashnikov rifles, the others were armed with light machine-guns, whilst the young officer held a brand new revolver which he kept pointed to his victims all the time.

Like a set of lambs being led to the slaughter house, the past leaders of BASSA were led quietly and together to the jeeps, whose engines were kept running continuously.

On the way down, the ex-Minister of Defence, asked, "May I,

please, use the bathroom",

"No, nothing of the sort, straight to the jeeps".

"Please, be reasonable",

"No, you may shit in your pants if you want, you blood sucker", interrupted a sergeant in the officer's team. And so they walked to the jeeps, all eight of them, and were put into two of the jeeps, and driven in a convoy of three led by the officer in the leading jeep.

On the way to the notorious Kurukuru Prison, in the east end of the capital, the overthrown government ministers, could see the masses and masses of people already gathering to form huge demonstrations.

Thieves, thieves, big womanisers, you dirty rogues", some of them shouted at the jeeps, as they identified some of the fallen being driven to their new place of residence.

One of the people standing by and shouting, even came close to one of the jeeps and with his right fist shaking menacingly cried,

"Kill them all. Let their blood flow. Never again. Hang them immediately. No mercy". "No trials, Cut their big balls".

The former Acting Head of Government, looked at him and winced.

"Only last week I held a big rally at the park here, and there were thousands of people cheering us, and our government. I even remember some of the placards praising us for our excellent work. Now look at this!" He turned to one of his colleagues.

One of the soldiers accompanying them, unable to control himself made his contribution.

"I be only soldier man. No politics. You big men go for politics, so you go to jail. No more women to poke. No more bribes. No more champagne".

The ex-ministers said nothing, but kept peering at the hostile demonstrating public, through whom they passed.

"Unlike previous Cabinet Ministers who after coups, competed with each other in the condemnation of their own governments and political actions, please, gentlemen, if we are even to die by firing squad, we should not give these traitors the pleasure of seeing us humiliate ourselves like madmen", re-marked the general-secretary, with considerable aplomb.

Finally, the excruciating journey was over. The jeeps stopped at the gate of the infamous Kurukuru Prison, and as they walked into it one by one, the former Acting Head of Government was heard to state,

"Hmm. Politics in Third World countries end always the same. In prison and disgrace, if you are lucky, or in death by firing squad, or public execution, if you are not so lucky!!. Always the same old story!" And with that the calm, Pat Podo, led his colleagues into captivity of unknown duration or fate.

Chapter 11

"Name? Home address? Occupation? Date of Birth? Place of Birth?", these were the questions asked by the senior warder of the prison, one by one, to all the ex-ministers, as they stood in line, stripped to their bare pants, before him. He methodically wrote down their answers on separate sheets for each detainee. The time was exactly 9 pm, on the day of the coup, the memorable Friday, which had brought their world crashing completely round them.

"Gentlemen, I am Tinga Moses, Senior Prison Superintendent, responsible for this prison. You will be kept in the clinic wing of the prison, which we have already made for you. Whilst here, until further notice, you will be treated as prisoners. No unauthorised books or magazines. All letters from you and to you will be vetted, and you will be allowed one family visit per week, once the formalities for prison visits by your families have been established between the Prison Director and the Attorney-General. Lights out is at 10.30 pm, and the morning bell goes at 6.30 am".

He paused, looked round at the men, who were almost naked, blinked, then smiled and continued,

"We will do our best, within the rules to make your life here, comfortable. The prison food is not bad at all. After all there are some here who have lived on it for over twenty years, look very fit, and even put on weight! Indeed, some of our inmates come to like it so much here that as soon as they leave they quickly return. You see it's not all that bad and unbearable", chuckling as he said so.

"Any person, whoever he is that tries to break any of the rules will if caught, be severely punished here, and furthermore, will certainly be sent to Kankan Prison, where, I fear life is extremely difficult and unpleasant. Understood?"

"Yes, Sir", the detainees replied almost in unison.

"Any questions?"

"May we know under what law are we charged, justifying our incarceration here?", asked the former General-Secretary of the party.

"Gentlemen, please don't make my difficult work any more difficult than it already is. Try to be reasonable and co-operative and I will play my part as a professional prison officer. Right?"

"Sir, you've still not answered our question", he insisted.

"Well, Sir, if you want an answer it is simple. In case, you're not aware, there has been a military coup, your Government has been overthrown and you're being detained here, for being ministers in the ousted regime. That's all. No more, no less. OK?"

"Well, we wish to register in the strongest possible terms our protest against our illegal arrest and detention without charge and we demand immediate access to legal representation, now", the fearless ex-General Secretary continued, "Yeah, yeah", chorused his colleagues.

"Sorry, I've no orders to that effect. My instructions, as at this present moment, are to effect your detention in the clinic and assure your safety and protection".

Although it was now getting to 10 pm the detainees could clearly hear the public demonstrations outside, interrupted by gun-fire. The tiny holes of the prison, with the iron bars to prevent escape of anything but air, still made it possible to hear the baying cries of the masses.

"Kill them all. Hang them by their balls. Firing squad. Firing squad. Fornicating bastards. Criminals".

"I cannot simply believe what I am hearing. Only last Saturday, we held a superb, mammoth, public rally nearby, not so far from where we are standing. Yes, that's when the chief of the district publicly prayed that our Government should last not the usual five years, but fifty years. And look what they are saying now", remarked the former Attorney-General, whose wise counsel was always sought by colleagues, before and after the coup.

Situated near the beach, in the east end of APPAPA the prison which was to be the detainees' temporary, official residence was built by the Danes in the sixteenth century. It was among the first European buildings in Africa, and many of the items for the construction of the fort, apart from sand and water, were transported from Europe. For a number of years it was the seat of Danish administration in Africa. Subsequently, it passed through the hands of the Dutch, and eventually ended as British centre of administration.

During all that period, from its construction, till the abolition of slavery, millions of slaves passed through its dingy underground cells, on their way to South America, United States, West Indies and Europe.

The fort retains its centuries-old, sinister and evil notoriety right up to this present day. And local legend had it that between two and four in the morning everyday, those with ears to hear can still hear the agonised cries and prayers of the slaves, as they awaited their unknown fate.

At 10 pm the ex-ministers were marched in line to the clinic wing of the prison. Guarding them were two armed prison officers one in front of the line, and one behind. As soon as they reached the ward, they were allotted bunk-beds, with an aisle in the middle separating the metal beds on both sides.

At the extreme end of the ward, were four cold showers, adjacent to three toilets.

For a few moments as the new inmates stood round to familiarise themselves with their new environment, the heavy metal doors of the ward were opened by a young warder. In trooped a new batch of ex-ministers, party secretaries, chairmen and other functionaries of the ousted regime. One of them, a former Minister of Transport, had severe bruises on his face and body, which upset the rest of his colleagues.

"Jack, what happened? Why all this?", asked the former Interior Minister, as he and his colleagues gathered round him.

Jack Banya, a Chicago University Graduate in Economics, was by all accounts a good, honest man, who before the coup was popularly known as "Mr Clean", because of his strong views on bribery and corruption. In fact, at forty, he was often spoken of as the future Prime Minister or President. He was well-liked by all and sundry, although some critics considered him rather naive about the darker side of politics.

"Well, brothers, on hearing the announcement, early in the morning, I tried to mobilise popular support against the coup, by visiting some of the more reliable Army officers in the barracks. As you know the phones were all not working, so I had to go about in different taxis dressed as a woman". He was almost in tears. "At about 8 o'clock, I was stopped at the army checkpoint near the university. I was being driven as a passenger, by an old taxi-driver friend of mine. Both of us were forced out of the taxi and sent to a little hut where we were asked the usual questions, name, date of birth, occupation, address, and whether we knew the whereabouts of any ex-ministers or party officials. Having satisfactorily answered all the questions, we were let go. My heart was thumping mad!"

Even in his agony he put on a little smile, as he continued. "We were just about to enter the taxi and take off, when one of the soldiers, a corporal, shouted", "Hey, stop. Don't move. Sergeant, the second one not woman at all. Ebe man. No get breasts, bottom flat".

"I tell you, I nearly fainted. I simply did not know what to do, with the kalashnikov rifles pointing menacingly at us". He sighed and went on, " We were frog-marched to the little hut, where both of us were stripped naked".

Laughing, the sergeant remarked to the amusement of his comrades, "Corporal, you damned right. He no get cunt, what woman be this, with big penis? Silly wig you wearing. Suddenly, a slap went on my left cheek, followed by two on my right. From nowhere, a series of blows rained on me from the corporal and another soldier, whilst a third one forcibly pulled my private organs. The driver, sadly was beaten even more mercilessly and threatened with immediate execution. Hmm, it was an unforgettable experience. We were interrogated again, and I had to give my true identity. After they had roughed us to their satisfaction, we were forced to sit on a bare wooden bench. "

151

Captain, we catch one big man, former Minister of Transport, trying to escape. He ebe dressed like big woman. Yes we search him. He be man with a big penis, wearing wig. We fixed him proper, and we send him along soon, with the driver, we caught him". I could over hear the sergeant, as he talked on the phone. He finished his conversation with big laughter.

"Well, my friend, I have order send you straight from here to Kurukuru Prison. You big men all the time flying New York, Washington, London, Paris, attending big conferences, whilst we suffer plenty. You do fucking nothing, but talk, talk, talk plenty, eat plenty good food, drink champagne and fuck white women all the time. No care for the masses. Eh? You steal our money and save in London, New York, Paris and in Switzerland in secret bank accounts, Eh? Well you are going to a place of complete, rest from conference, rest from good food and champagne, and rest from fucking white women. Other abuse, comrades, passed from this man's lips, which I cannot repeat here".

He started to sob, as colleagues consoled him, with words of encouragement.

"From this ordeal, we were both driven in a military jeep to the Ridge Police Station, where my driver-friend was detained, and I was driven here. All I can say is that one day, God, God Himself will deal with the Colonel, deservedly. He will not get away with this monumental act of infamy and treachery".

He finished speaking. The former Acting Head of Government, then said, "Gentlemen, let's pray", to which they all agreed, and bowed their heads. "Lord, into thy hands, we commit ourselves this saddest of days, for our country, its people and ourselves. Forgive us our sins, O Lord, and whatever we have done wrong. Turn not thy face of mercy and compassion from us in our hour of need, and if it be thy will deliver us from this ordeal.

The God of Israel who brought the Jews out of captivity, Thou who saved Daniel from the Lion's den and also saved Noah from the belly of the shark, we pray to thee in our agony to deliver us.

We pray for the safety of our families, relations and friends that we have left behind, and may they be spared undue suffering, for thy name's sake. Amen". "Amen", responded all of them, in voices, which were firm and bold, considering that from early morning, the time of the announcement of the coup till that hour, nothing, neither water nor food had passed their lips.

Brusquely, a young prisoner entered the ward and shouted, "Gentlemen, this be it".

The detainees turned and looked round, and standing behind the prisoner was a warder, directing operations. "Sorry, we so late with your first prison chop. The fact be you not expected at all".

One by one, he called the names of the ex-ministers and party bigwigs, as the prisoner handed each of them a rectangular aluminium pan with a handle, containing pieces of hard, two-day old, boiled cassava, with a sprinkling of salt, and a tiny piece of fish, about the size of a thumb, sitting on top. Calmly and quietly, the men collected their pans.

When it reached the turn of the former Deputy Minister of Health, a fastidious eater and connoisseur of food, under more congenial circumstances, he was handed his pan containing rock-hard cassava, with the head of a herring sitting defiantly on the cassava pieces. As the ex-minister peered at the herring head, and the eyes of the herring did likewise at him, he suppressed the tears beginning to roll off his face.

"Fancy that nine hours ago, my wife's seven cats were eating freshly boiled cassava, mixed with beautiful gravy and sardines from Harrods, and here I am not even lucky enough to get that to eat. Yes, that's life".

By 11 PM the detainees had finished their first prison supper. The warder came in again, made a roll-call, and finally departed with a loud "Good night, sleep well".

It was about 11.30 PM that lights were finally put out, an extra hour grace in honour of their first night. As there were not enough beds and mattresses some of the detainees had to sleep on mats, and a few on the bare floor, all fully clothed, as they were when first arrested. Trying to sleep was obviously not easy, especially due to the frequent anguished cries of one of the

153

former ministers. "Oh, God, please help, help, it's my family I'm worried about, not myself. My children, so young, and my wife with nobody to look after them", he sobbed. He went on and on, making everybody's life hell. His crying was beginning to be infectious, so the Minister of Health after failing to console him, had to shout, "Look my friend, you're not the only one with a wife and children. What do you think? We are all in the same boat. Please, for Heaven's sake, control yourself and calm down. What is all this weeping leading to? Please, please stop. Control yourself".

The little frank speaking worked effectively, and he quietened down. The whole place became quiet, and soon some were snoring, some sleeping and others just lying awake contemplating the past, the present and the future.

At 6 o'clock in the morning the detainees had gathered round the prison radio in the ward, perched on the wall, almost nearing the ceiling, Although they were not expecting any miraculous release, they still could not rule out the possibility of a miracle happening, in answer to the numerous, prolonged prayers in the night.

"Good morning, listeners, here is the news read by Abraham Wakawa. The new administration, to be known as The People's Revolutionary Council, has been formed, under the Chairmanship of Colonel Kofi Johnson. It consists of Commanders of the Army, Navy, Air Force, Border Guards, the Police, the Chairman of the Joint Chiefs of Staff and...." The relevant names of the members of the new regime rolled off the tongue of the announcer, and then he added,

"The new Government has issued its first decree. It confiscates all the assets, both local and foreign, of all the specified persons, namely, the public office-holders, at local, regional and national levels, and their wives and children, in the ousted regime. Failure to abide by the decree will carry a mandatory twenty-five year prison sentence, upon conviction by a People's Tribunal, over which there is no appeal". He went on, "The Police have reported that last night the former Transport Minister, Mr Jack Banya, was arrested at the eastern border whilst trying to escape from the country. He was dressed as a woman, wearing a big, expensive wig.

New Regional Governors have been appointed for all the regions by the new administration, and their predecessors are currently handing over to them.

Popular, mass demonstrations continue to take place in all major cities, welcoming the advent of the new regime. Also telegrams and telex messages condemning the previous regime and welcoming the new, have been pouring into Government House, according to a military press release just published.

Now here are some of the other news items . . . .".

One of the listeners put off the radio, and an animated discussion quickly started among the detainees. "Good Lord, even the "Do or Die" Regiment did nothing. Let down by everybody. And these are supposed to be loyal troops dedicated to the defence of the regime. What price loyalty?", asked the former Interior Minister.

"What do you think has happened to the Commander of the Parachute Regiment. He was a good, reliable man, who unlike the traitor kept his loyalty to us very private. I hope that he too has not gone the same way of filthy treachery", remarked the former Defence Minister. He looked completely downcast and dispirited as he spoke. Fresh discussions took place among the detainees following the bad news from the radio.

"The masses will not stand for this. After all they elected us, in free and fair, democratic, general elections. Even U.N. experts and observers, Western correspondents and TV journalists who covered the elections all agreed that we won clearly and cleanly, by overwhelming popular support. And we are only in two years out of the five year period. Why, why did our own man do this to us?. The former Agriculture Minister paused and almost sobbing, continued,

"There was no need for all this act of treason which will certainly set the nation's progress back by at least ten years. Yes, ten years"

"Oh, no! more than ten years. I figure at least twenty years. For once the trend of military coups gets established in the nation's political structure, it becomes very, very difficult, most impossible to eradicate it. Notice what's happening in South America. You mark it and see". The normally quiet Pat Podo, former acting Prime Minister, who till then had been listening to all intently, but saying nothing, was now making his contribution to the discussions.

"I am sure that the West, especially the US, will not recognise or support this bunch of bastards and traitors, who have never understood democratic government. I am convinced I.M.F. and the World Bank will both boycott them, and put on the screws", intoned the former Finance Minister.

"I fear you're not being realistic. The West could not care a toss. So long as their own vital interests or their own citizens are not touched, they could not care less. After all, they would always argue that the coup is an internal affair of BASSA, and that by convention and under International Law, they do not interfere in the internal affairs of other states. As for the World Bank and the IMF, they are nothing but the creations of the United States, which alone contributes about twenty five percent of their upkeep.

As such, our problem should be ensuring that the West, especially the United States, hears our case sympathetically and listens. Unfortunately, for us, America has here no significant economic interest here, nor do they have vital, strategic bases here or around us. To cap it all, they are not in anyway reliant upon us at all for the almighty oil!. This is our situation, stark, simple and rather depressing", said the former Foreign Minister, as he shrugged his shoulders.

"You really think that with all their talk of democratic, participatory government, and their well-known commitment to freedom, America will leave us in the lurch, and let us rot here or be shot. I find this difficult to believe, what?", the former Head of Government, was asking expansively.

"Well, I think I must know them fairly well. Not only was I educated there, but I am married to a Wasp American, and I think I can claim a modest understanding of what makes them tick. Should I not understand them better, than let's say, some other colleagues, considering my rather long association with the West, especially America?. You mark it, and see, as soon as the dust settles, the US, to be followed by other Western nations will recognise the new regime and continue business as usual, as if nothing has happened, without butting an eye-lid".

His colleagues listened intently, as the former deputy foreign minister continued his analysis of the likely Western reaction to the forcible overthrow through a military coup, of a democratically-elected, civilian government, in a Third World nation. He went on, confidently, "After all, see it from the point of the US administration of President Woodward. If no vital US interests, economic, strategic, or human are at stake here, how could the administration justify to Congress and especially to the general public, via the media, the risking of American lives to uphold an African government, over three thousand miles away from America. What are they going to tell their people, eh?".

"I see, hmm. That's a pretty serious predicament then", said Podo.

"I fear so, Sir", commented the former deputy foreign minister.

"Furthermore, friends, we lack gravely two major public platforms in US for influencing public opinion or Congress. Firstly, unlike say the Jews, the Polish or Irish community in America, we do not have a strong, powerful immigrant voice there to put our case, and influence things in our favour. It is true that African-Americans, who form about 12 percent of the US population are rapidly building their strength in the US, but sadly, they have a very long way to go before commanding the sort of powerful influence on government, as enjoyed by the Jewish, Irish or Polish communities in America.

"The situation is really bad", interjected somebody. "Secondly, although we have a few friends among the present US administration, the fact still remains that, as we never employed a powerful lobbyist firm in the US, it means that our case cannot be put effectively before the media, Congress and the Administration. I suggest, therefore, that we begin, as quickly as possible, to find ways and means of getting letters smuggled out to the US, to friends, relatives, sympathisers, both black and white, putting the true facts before them, and begging them to mobilise the media, Congress and the Administration on our behalf. That's what we have to do now. Now!", he concluded.

Just as he finished his succinct review, the door opened, and there entered Tinga Moses, the chief Superintendent of the prison. The time was exactly ten in the morning.

"Gentlemen, please come round. I have been asked by my superiors to hand this to you, one by one. These forms and questionnaires about the assets of yourselves and your wives and children. These forms are to be filled carefully and honestly. I am instructed to emphasise to you that failure to answer all the relevant questions or to furnish all known data or information, carries, automatically, a mandatory prison sentence of twenty five years, following exposure and conviction by the military tribunals, dealing with investigations into your individual cases. I hope I've made myself crystal-clear. Any questions?" Complete silence.

"Well, I'm happy the message has got across".

Next, he called the detainees one by one as he handed them each, the 8-page forms. On each form were questions about name, address, occupation, date of birth, details of local and foreign bank accounts, sources of income since beginning of employment, right to the day of the coup, details of patterns of expenditure from the time when the person concerned began to earn, income tax details, holidays expenditure, venues and dates. Also required were details of both movable and liquid assets, both local and foreign, how acquired and when.

Each detainee took his form and looked at it gloomily.

"Sir, when should the forms be ready", asked one of them.

"You have two weeks to complete them", Tinga shot back.

"May we have access to our personal documents and papers, as without them it will be impossible to complete these forms properly", enquired the former Director of Special Branch.

"I've no instructions to that effect. You are expected to know what you have been earning and how you have been spending it during the past years, depending on how long you have been working. Sorry I cannot help you further". Tinga Moses walked away and shut the door.

"What sort of nonsense is this? How can one be expected to remember all his earnings and income and expenditure over say the past ten or twenty years. Absolute madness. Can these traitors themselves remember details of their income and expenditure in the last twelve months, straight from their bloody, thick heads?", asked the former Interior Minister. "This is all a charade. They are just preparing us for a show trial to justify their criminal, treasonous act of bloody infamy".

"You wait, one day, very soon, their turn will assuredly come. There's a big, unpleasant surprise awaiting them. They are digging their own graves, that's all", remarked the former Attorney-General.

Outside the prison walls, events were progressing at a terrific speed. New social, political and military allegiances were being rapidly formed. Senior, top civil servants who, only a few days ago, were proud to be called "loyal servants of the Administration", were vying with each other in their vitriolic condemnation of their former political leaders. Even leading academics and intellectuals, highly respected in society joined in the free-for-all campaign of vilification and abject, chameleon-like tactics, and behaviour

The new Redeemer was equally busy, flying by helicopter, visiting the various military barracks, to consolidate his support and control. Where-ever he visited, in the local towns and villages, the placards were the same. "Kill them all", "Show no mercy to the greedy, corrupt politicians", "Cut their balls out", Let the rivers of blood flow", "Firing squad, firing squad".

In his widest dreams, Colonel Johnson could not have imagined receiving such rapturous, public acclaim, as he toured the country. He commented to his aides,

"I knew all the time that the regime was like a ripe fruit ready to be plucked. Fancy how easy the operation was. The Administration fell utterly like a pack of cards, once we made our initial moves". To which his aide-de-camp, slavishly added,

"Sir, what you've done will go down in the history of Bassa, as a matchless act of patriotism, courage and devotion to national duty. Sir, if I may say so, as soon as things settle down, we must find ways and means of getting these bastards to vomit some of their ill-gotten gains in Swiss, British and American bank accounts. All we need do is threaten them with indefinite detention or even firing squad, unless they unload themselves, of a major portion of those vast amounts of money".

"Don't worry, Major, I've it in mind. As soon as the committees and commissions to investigate their assets are formed, we will parade them before those tribunals, humiliate and ridicule them, and destroy their credibility completely in public. Then we will get them whilst in prison, to issue the relevant authorities for the withdrawal of the moneys from the foreign banks. When the cash is in hand, then we will offer them limited releases on medical or humanitarian grounds. What about that?"

"Excellent. That's the right medicine for them, Sir". "In so doing, we will be transferring some of the funds from them to us, and also appear to be responding to such international organisations as Amnesty International, the UN Commission for Refugees, Red Cross and the rest, which will soon be worrying us to release the detainees or put them before the usual civilian courts. Already, the pressure is beginning to build up, especially from the United States. And as we depend so heavily on America for food, aid, loans, and the rest, we simply cannot afford to ignore their requests".

"By the way, remind me to find a place for my old friend, Colonel Sampson. In the bad, old days when things were really rough and awful he was helpful to me in so many ways. So was the former Chairman of the Joint Chiefs of Staff, and I really felt uneasy that he too had to be netted as part of the exercise".

He paused, lit a cigarette, then resumed, "I am sure that as a military man of experience he understands the predicament I was in on the great day. I had no alternative. None whatsoever. And although since his release, I've called him in specifically and apologised to him, I don't know whether he has forgiven me, or ever will".

"Chairman, why not deal militarily with the old guys on the pretext of early retirement, and the need to bring in new blood?"

"Not now. Tactically, things have to be done step by step. We must consolidate our position, using these same top brass, and when everything is OK, then we quietly and smoothly ease them out of their positions. After all, with the recall of all the politically-appointed, non-career ambassadors, there will be so many new positions to fill".

Whilst this intimate, tete-a-tete conversation was taking place in a remote town in the northern province of the country, not so far from the largest army base in the north, an urgent telephone call came in for the new Head of State. His aide took it and then gave it to the boss saying,

"It's for you, Sir, from the President of the House of Chiefs".

The Chairman's heart missed a beat, before he took the receiver. For, of all the powerful, influential Chiefs in the nation, the President of the House of Chiefs was the greatest in influence, and since the coup, he had not been too keen to throw in his weight behind the new regime. He was thus a personage to be avidly courted.

"Well, President, good afternoon, Sir, what a surprise. I am at your service, now and always. What an honour to receive this call", he said in the friendliest of tones.

"I have decided after careful consideration to throw in my full support behind you. It has not been an easy decision, I can assure you, hence the delay. For as you well know, I am fully and publicly identified with the old regime, as a strong Republican. I did so unashamedly, and with conviction. As such your action has completely upset the political apple-cart, and thrown all allegiances into the melting -pot. I am not apportioning blame for what's happened, although, personally, I would have wished you had allowed the civilian government to do at least four years out of its five year period. As it is, one day you may be open to the accusation that you did not give the civilian administration enough time and opportunity to show what it could do".

The Colonel listened intently to the Chief, who continued,

deliberately,

"In the circumstances you've put me on the spot, either to openly support you or refuse to do so, and I am under great pressure from the populace to declare my stand quickly. I cannot sit on the fence anymore. My court is split evenly, and it has not been at all easy and simple. I hope and trust that posterity does not judge me too harshly, as having let down my people in their hour of need. Well that's life. I am authorising a press release this evening at 6 PM to the effect that in the national interest, and taking everything possible into consideration, I've decided to support the new regime, and I call upon my people to do likewise.

Before I finish, Colonel, may I make the strongest plea possible for the early release of the detainees and their proper and humane treatment whilst under your care. Don't forget, you are responsible for them ultimately, not your staff or agents. Thank you and good-bye".

The Colonel putting the receiver down, shouted with joy,

"Major, we've done it. It's in the bag. The King of Kings, Victor of Victors, The Supreme Chief himself has given in, and is backing us. He's issuing a press release this evening to that effect. What a day!. Ensure that Broadcasting House, and the papers give it full, tip-top prominence and publicity. Now I can relax a bit. You've no idea how relieved I am!! Get me madam on the phone, and also Sophia at once".

"Yes, Sir".

For the next few minutes, he just sat there and smiled to himself, looking at the ceiling all the time. Even the antics of two wall lizards in the room did not appear to bother him. He was on cloud nine, and felt completely self-satisfied. That single telephone conversation had squelched all his fears of a likely violent uprising by the masses, at the instigation of the great Chief. And Johnson's fear and dread was that such public challenge to his tenuously held authority would have forced him to use troops to quell it, thus leading to a very probable loss of lives.

He remembered well what he had been told by the KUKU

Shrine, before he embarked on his adventure. It was a simple message, namely that the venture would succeed so long as there was no shedding of blood, and that the very day blood was shed under his regime, he was finished in toto. The still, small voice of KUKU kept running through his mind all the time "No bloodshed, or you are finished".

"Sir, madam on the line", said his aide.

"Hello, love. How are things at home. Sorry I've not been in touch earlier. How are the children?" He burst into laughter, as he listened to his wife recount events at the home front, plus gossip talk that had come her way. Finishing his conversation with his wife, he got on the phone to Sophia Fumey, his girl-friend of several years standing.

"Yes, OK. So you read the letter. Well, plan a special celebration when I return. I've been touring the major towns and centres mobilising support. Everywhere, it's the same good news. Fantastic public support, with some of the women putting their shawls on the ground for me to walk on as a conqueror. We've done it, Sophia, great!!. Keep your fingers crossed for me. See you soon, darling!!".

Chairman Johnson was over the moon. Reports from the capital, from both his wife and mistress, amply confirmed the military and police intelligence reports which he had been receiving since he left the capital. Everything was under control. The masses, organised and unorganised, were baying for the blood of their former political leaders. And the public adulation of him continued to gather momentum, at unstoppable speed. Things could not be better for the man who was born in obscurity, of humble parents, and received little formal education, but now had the whole country at his feet. Following the comprehensive tour of the nation, during which at a public, traditional ceremony in the second largest city in the country, he was given the hallowed title of "KATAMANTO" (The Warrior of Warriors) Chairman Kofi Johnson returned to the capital a very happy man indeed.

However, for the detainees and their wives life was not so pleasant. As their family bank accounts were frozen, the wives could only, with the Attorney-General's authority, withdraw 150 US dollars per month in the local currency for subsistence and general living expenses. Apart from the long, laborious time-wasting routine the wives had to go through to get the relevant authority from the Attorney-General's office, the money also was grossly inadequate, especially for those with large families, and without their own private homes in the capital. Furthermore, the detainees, were still on prison rations, some weeks after the coup, without any sign of improvement in their living conditions. This led to fierce debates among them about what was the best course of action to take.

"Gentlemen, we shall all refuse to fill the assets forms, challenge the legality of the regime and our arrest, and defy them to detain us indefinitely or shoot us. After all, we will die one day, anyway. These animals should be confronted, and we should not take all this lying down", remarked the former Attorney- General, on a grey Monday morning, as it rained outside.

"Let's bring their perfidy into the open by showing them that we are ready to die", he ended.

"Yes, I fully agree with you, but I feel that in our present situation challenging the legality of our arrest and detention or for that matter the legality of the coup is a futile, academic exercise. Where will that get us? Nowhere. I think we should rather fill the forms to show the public that we have nothing to hide or be ashamed of, and then use our appearance before the commissions or committees as a platform for publicly launching open attacks on our accusers, so that the public can hear our side of the story. For as it is, many of them still believe the unadulterated rubbish that all we did as ministers was flying to Washington, New York, London and Paris, drinking champagne, eating good food and screwing white women. True! They believe this nonsense. You remember the hogwash the soldiers were talking on the jeep as we were being brought here. It would have been a waste of time to have tried to reason with them, but at least before the public, military tribunals we can talk before they stop us. The TV cameras, radio recorders, journalists especially the foreign ones, will all be there".

He turned round to face the ex-Attorney-General. "This is my considered view, old boy, for what's worth. And I invite colleagues to give it strong consideration", said the former Head of the Administration.

"But the point is that by filling the forms and appearing before the committees, we are both directly and indirectly, giving de jure recognition to this illegal, criminal regime, thus boosting their image and authority, and consequentially undermining our own. Our own credibility is at stake", interjected the Attorney-General.

Somebody shouted "Don't let's be too clever by half and naive. Surely, we are here under the authority of that regime, albeit distasteful to us. So, in my view belabouring whether we are under the regime or not is really not very helpful. We are here because democracy is dead, and guns are talking. It is as simple as that, friends", remarked the former Minister of Agriculture, who in his pre-government days was a University Professor of Modern History.

A long, intense discussion next took place among the political prisoners. Eventually, the former acting Prime Minister summarised, in a deliberate voice as follows:

"Colleagues, our position is more desperate than we may imagine. We've been let down by all those we counted on. Britain, the US and the major Western creditor nations have all recognised the regime. IMF and the World Bank have even sent in experts to assess the local situation with a view to granting more economic aid and assistance. Even many of the foreign businessmen, especially the British, that we had thought of as close, reliable friends have deserted us and joined the enemy camp. To cap it all, leading British academics, I agree not all, who know BASSA well, have now joined the bandwagon of public condemnation and discrediting of us.

Our own people we now know too well, where they stand. As we are down, they don't want us anymore, only our blood, I am sad to say. In the circumstances, I advise that we all fill the forms as thoroughly and honestly as possible, and put on as brave and respectable a show as possible, when we are brought before the public, to be interrogated.

Finally, may I remind some of our colleagues, especially the lawyers, that in a previous coup, the lawyers by actively participating in the defence of previous ex-ministers appearing before the tribunals, had thus given, practical, albeit indirect, recognition of these tribunals and committees,, and the military regime that fathered them. It is, therefore, too late in the day to bring up the question of the legality of the regime now. Its legality sadly lies in its success, as evidenced by our presence here. I therefore, advise colleagues to go ahead and deal with the forms appropriately".

"Alright, let's put it to a vote", so said the Attorney-General. By a majority vote, it was decided to act as advised by the former acting Prime Minister, and the meeting dispersed.

Chapter 12

"Imagine we have been here for almost three weeks now, and apart from the warders and our prison friends downstairs, we have not set eyes on a single soul from outside. What's happening? What is the Red Cross doing? What about our Church leaders?", asked Pat Podo, in calm tones which still could not hide his anger and frustration.

The rest of his colleagues nodded. It was an hour or so after the usual breakfast of mealy porridge, with two cubes of sugar each. No milk.

The group of detainees was beginning to disperse, when the former Agriculture Minister said,

"Here we are, Protestants all apart from Mike, and since our detention none of the prominent churchmen has showed his face or raised his finger on our behalf. You remember before the coup, how they loved and cherished being invited to Government House dinner parties and other social functions. Hmm! when you're down even church leaders, the spiritual guardians of the nation, do not want to know you. What a shame!".

"Don't be ridiculous and unrealistic, my friend. With the bullets flying left and right, and with these trigger-happy soldiers let loose, roaming about, what do you expect them to do? Stick their necks out and be shot or roughed up?", asked the former Finance Minister. They were all getting ready to go down for the morning walk when Tinga Moses, walked in.

"Please, stay put, for the time being". The detainees wondered what was in store for them. They were expecting no good news from their captors, and all were worried about their families. As for themselves, they were resigned to their fate, a long, arbitrary imprisonment at best, or the firing squad at worst".

As they stood near their bunk-beds talking about their

plight, the door opened again. In walked, a white, American Catholic priest, Father Peter Murphy. He stood before them in his snow-white cassock, and dog-collar. He smiled and for a few pregnant seconds he said nothing, as the detainees gathered round him, excitedly.

After introducing him, Tinga Moses left the priest alone with the detainees and returned to his office nearby. "Father, thank you for coming. May God bless you. Thank you. We are so happy to see you", said Pat Podo, on behalf of the group.

"Father, when will we be released? Are we going to be given a proper trial? Will we be shot? What are the Chiefs and Church leaders doing on our behalf?".

These were the questions that rained on the American priest from all sides, as he stood there surrounded by persons who only yesterday were the high and mighty of BASSA.

The American priest, in a most benevolent manner, raised his right hand requesting them to calm down, so that he could speak. He was justifiably understanding of the excitement, almost pandemonium, which his visit had caused.

"Gentlemen, I am very honoured and happy to be among you this morning. I have been sent by my bishop, His Grace, Dr. Issac Antol, to bring you all the well wishes of the church, and to enquire about your conditions. You are assured that the churches are doing everything possible to effect your early release, or your quickest public trial. Please, take it from me, as a humble emissary of the church, that you are not forgotten".

He stopped for a few seconds, then went on, "It's not been easy during the past few weeks I can assure you. The bishop, assisted by his priests, is not only praying for you earnestly, but also putting maximum, considered pressure on the new authorities on your behalf. Things are not proving easy and simple, but we are doing our very best".

"But Father, what about our families?", asked the former Interior Minister. "The amounts which they are allowed to withdraw are simply inadequate to cover general expenses, school fees, transport and the rest. Please, bring this to the bishop's attention".

"I sure will do so".

"Also, we feel that as we have not been given the due process of the law, we should till we are tried and convicted, be allowed visits by our families, and food from home. Sir, the grub here is too grubby, and we plead with you and the bishop to intercede with the powers that be", remarked the former assistant Director of Special Branch, Edward Mumuni.

"Hear, hear", chorused the rest of the detainees.

"My visit is meant to be introductory and exploratory, and I hope it is the start of many visits during which we shall get to know and trust each other".

"By the way, Father, what do you think of this coup, the unjustified, unwarranted overthrow of a democratically-elected, civilian government, which has done only two years out of its five year tenure? Is this fair? What is the West doing about it?", requested the former General Secretary of the overthrown party?".

Father Murphy listened intently, then smiled in a non-committal way. "Well, as you can appreciate, as a church we cannot be involved in political or state affairs. As such, it is difficult to answer these questions of yours. The bishop has already made certain strong representations to the new regime, and it would be inappropriate for me to go into them here and now. Our duty as we see it at this moment, is to ensure that you are treated humanely and properly, that you are safe, and that the hardships on your families are reduced to the barest minimum. This, I assure you on behalf of the churches, we will continue to do. Don't worry about that".

One of the detainees raised his hand, wanting to ask a further question, but was advised by the former head of government, not to.

"Father Murphy's visit has brought solace and light into our life of darkness and gloom. We feel enormously uplifted. Already, Sir, you have gone over your allotted time by ten minutes, and we are very grateful, deeply touched. May I on behalf of all of us here, thank you and the bishop, and the Roman Catholic Church for this great act of courage, humanity and love. You've

169

not only been praying for us, but also have taken concrete, practical, risky steps and measures on our behalf, and we thank you very, very much. Finally, Father, do convey our love and best wishes to our families in these sad times", concluded Pat Dodo.

"Certainly. I sure will do so", he looked round the ward, went to the toilets and showers, tested some of the beds with his hands.

"Well, I figure I've seen and heard as much as possible within the time allowed to me by the prison authorities", said Father Murphy, with a strong Irish/American accent.

"Let's pray. Dear Father in Heaven, we pray and beseech you to look after these children of yours in this hour of need. Bless them and their abandoned families. Continue, Oh God, to strengthen their faith in you, as the only saviour and protector, through the name of thy Holy Son, Jesus Christ.

And may God the Father, The Son and the Holy Spirit be with you, now and forever. Amen".

"Amen", responded all the detainees.

Finally, Father Murphy shook hands with them all, one by one, and then left. He had been with them in all for about one hour. It was a most unforgettable experience for the fallen politicians.

No sooner had the priest left than an emotional discussion began among the detainees.

"I am hundred percent certain that he was sent by the CIA to assess our situation. I always believed, as an article of faith that the US will not let us down. They will not abandon us, at least, not completely", boomed the former Director of Special Branch.

"But how do you know he's CIA or acting on their behalf?", asked the former Foreign Minister, cynically.

"Where's the evidence?"

"Look, my friend, we are not in a court of law to be talking of evidence. These are things you feel in your bones, without being told. You ask yourself, why is it that with all the hundreds of churchmen in the country, the first, as a fact, to visit us, is a white, American, who has lived in BASSA for many, many years? It cannot be mere coincidence! You mark it !!".

Normally a quiet person, the former Education Minister, Christopher Doe, who had not been talking much, so far, interrupted,

"Whether he's from the CIA or not, the fact still remains that when the going got rough, very rough, and we were abandoned by all, only the Catholics, somehow managed to come and visit us. That we are all non-Catholics, except Mike, makes the situation so ironic and sad. You watch . . . . . .".

Before he could finish, the former Interior Minister shouted, "These Protestant Ministers are all cowards. All of them. They are not prepared to risk putting their lives or those of their families in danger. All the big talk on Sundays from the pulpits, to impress gullible congregations. At testing time, they vanish".

"Look my friend, you cannot talk such arid nonsense. Not all the Protestant Ministers are cowards. Have you not heard of Pastor Niemoller and Pastor Bonhoffer in Hitler's Germany, who at supreme sacrifice of their own lives, denounced the Nazi dictatorship. Also in South Africa, Rev. Michael Scott, Bishops Trevor Huddleston and Tutu and a number of Protestant clergy fearlessly, were in the fore-front of the anti-apartheid struggle.

In any case, how many of us were going to church regularly when we were in office, and why should the church leaders now come to our aid? Although I am not a Catholic, I don't think we should allow your denunciation to go unchallenged or uncorrected".

"But you'll agree that the Catholic record when it comes to challenging oppressive regimes, and defending the defenceless, whether in Africa or South America or China, appears generally far better than that of the non-Catholics, eh?", asked Kwame Donkoh. Grudgingly, the former Interior Minister agreed, with a long drawn out. "Well, you've got a point here". Smiling to himself as he listened, the former Foreign Minister, interrupted at this point.

"Brothers, I'm sorry to tell you certain unpalatable home truths, but in our present situation, it is essential that we assess, as accurately as possible, who are likely to bail us out.

First of all, we must dispel this idea that the American priest came from the CIA. I simply don't believe it".

"How do you know?", interrupted somebody. I've no evidence either way, it's true, but to me all the indications are that he was an emissary of his church, pure and simple, as he himself said. He has been in BASSA for many years, and has been known for the concern that he has shown each batch of political prisoners after each coup, to date, including this one.

Also, with all the major, intractable issues and problems in the Middle east, Eastern Europe and Asia, Africa, whether we like it or not, is at the bottom of the list of priorities of the US State Department. As such, from the US point of view, it is very unlikely and would be unjustifiable for the CIA to get involved in our predicament.

Finally, as BASSA does not pose a communist threat to America as would be the case of a communist oriented state or island close to its borders, BASSA going communist or not, is of no interest or relevance whatsoever to the US. After all, if Britain, which has had a long, historic association with BASSA, and has considerable economic interests here, is not intervening on our behalf, on the grounds that to do so would be interferring in the internal affairs of BASSA why should we expect the Americans who have nothing here to intervene?", he asked rhetorically.

"In short, we're on our own, then,. That's what you're really saying, and if so, then we better concentrate our minds on firstly getting improvements in our present conditions, and secondly, pleading for our release, if I understand you properly", remarked the former Agriculture Minister.

"I am afraid that's the position", replied the former Foreign Minister, nodding.

"If we could mobilise, somehow, the church leaders, especially the Catholic Church, to our side, may be some good will come out of such an exercise", commented the former Acting Head of Government.

"You mark it, our own Protestant Church leaders, I mean the Methodists, Presbyterians, Anglicans, Salvation Army, and the rest will not show their faces, with the soldiers trigger-happy, and the bullets flying left and right. But as soon as things quieten down, if we are still alive, you will see them coming here to tell us that all the time they were praying for us, and working behind the scenes for our release. You wait and see!", concluded the former Trade and Industry Deputy Minister, Jacob Yaabaa, who had been very upset about the failure of any of the Protestant Church leaders to turn up at the prison.

"This has been a major lesson for me, as a Presbyterian", he went on, "as soon as we leave this hole, I shall publicly renounce my membership of the church. I am finished with them as from today. You cannot in a crisis count on them to show any spiritual courage. All talk, big talk", said the former Education Minister, with the rest nodding in agreement.

"You see, before coming here, we often, to put it mildly, were disenchanted with the Catholics for being too straight-jacketed, and too doctrinaire and inflexible. Now look at it, it is they that are sticking their necks out for us, whilst our own church leaders lie low!", interrupted the former Finance Minister.

"Now we know who our enemies and friends are, but it's too late in the day. But should we, in the unlikely event, get another chance, we should be more discerning about how we choose our friends".

"Before we disperse, may I remind you to complete the assets forms as quickly as possible, and as thoroughly.. We will prove to the whole world that all the allegations against us that we are thieves, that we have salted away money in America, Switzerland, and the UK., and that as ministers we did nothing but fly about sleeping with white women and drinking champagne, are all untrue and a load of unadulterated rubbish.

For my part, I can assure you all that since my student days in London, I've not slept with any white women, whatsoever. Since taking office, I have never been to Switzerland or America, and only twice have I been out. The first was to Ethiopia for the Annual Conference of the Organisation of African Unity, and the second was to Israel.

I have no overseas bank accounts, secret or otherwise, and I am prepared and ready to face my accusers. Truth will come out soon, I trust". So spoke the former Acting Prime Minister, as colleagues listened to him intently, without murmur.

"Whether they are going to shoot us or not, we will let the public know that the coup was unjustified, illegal and unnecessary, and that our hands are clean", said the former Attorney-General. He went on. "No wonder they call BASSA and such countries, the "Third World" or "developing world". For can you imagine in any civilised state, such as the United States, a bizarre situation where the commander of the army around Washington D.C, marches on the Capital, arrests and detains the Chairman of the Joint Chiefs of Staff, the Chiefs of Staffs and their deputies, the National Security Adviser and furthermore militarily removes the President and his Cabinet, and other senior members of his administration, and places them in custody. What sort of nonsense and madness is this?.

Only in these backward countries can such foolishness be tolerated by the population, who in any case, supply and maintain the very army through their taxes. The army should be protecting the duly elected administration of the civilian government, and the population". He paused to control himself, but before he could resume, somebody shouted,

"The whole damned army should be abolished. The whole lot of crazy bastards should be dispersed and sent to work on the farms. That will teach them a lesson".

"But how do you abolish the army. At the least whiff of such a move, they will act first, overthrow you and probably shoot the whole government. This is the problem. That's the puzzle. It's no easy, simple matter", the Attorney-General continued.

"My friends, I think the problem is not so much with having the army as such. The problem is that you have an army, led by over-ambitious officers who simply do not believe in the democratic processes or respect them an iota. After all the U.S., U.K., France, Japan, all have massive armies, yet they are completely under political control, taking their orders from the democratically elected leaders of those nations. The idea of any hare-brained Colonel or General coming with the crazy idea of a coup

174

would be laughed out of court by his colleagues so heartily, that they would all agree to advise their high-spirited colleague to see a shrink. And if he stubbornly refuses to do so, I am sure they will carry him bodily to one promptly!".

The former Education Minister was ending his contribution, when the former Health Minister came in, "Even in the Soviet Union, China and Eastern Europe, the Armed Forces do not involve themselves in civilian politics, even though the civilian regimes in these states are not democratically elected, anyway, not by the normal western democratic methods. You see, our chaps here are bastards, would be failures in civilian life, who, enter the army, navy and air-force, as a last refuge, and taking advantage of their positions, brutally assault their pay-masters, the unarmed civilian regimes. After all what chance has an unarmed, defenceless man, whose night-watchman, paid by him, suddenly turns on him, using the same instruments provided him by his employer?", asked the former Director of Special Branch, who, had been sitting broodingly on his bed all the time.

"Education, proper education of the army, especially the officers, that's what is lacking badly. They need, to rephrase the biblical expression, be reborn in the democratic processes. They need to be taught well that their sole function is to defend the state, that is the country and its people, against an external enemy, and that it is not their business as soldiers to decide through the barrel of a gun, who should or should not govern the country. Until this fundamental education of the armed forces is undertaken vigorously and completed thoroughly, we would have on our hands coups, coups, coups all the time. That's the job at hand for future civilian governments", advised the former Education Minister.

With that conclusion, the discussion ended, and the detainees went down to the yard to walk and exercise.

Outside the prison walls life was quickly returning to normal. The new regime kept on consolidating its position, through the massive exercise of patronage. Difficult chiefs were bought off. Problematic senior officers were either retired summarily, or appointed as ambassadors to far-flung corners of the world. Top civil servants were working at immense speed in the condemnation of the old regime and in the fulsome praise of their new political masters. Leading university intellectuals did their bit, by castigating the fallen politicians and producing lucid pieces debunking all the work, good and bad, of the ousted administration.

Various national organisations, farmers, workers, students, and others, including the national association of prostitutes, all joined in the frequent jamborees of rallies and demonstrations to vilify and attack the past leaders. It was the norm for the placards which they carried to read "Down with the screwers. Down with Western Democracy. Kill them all. Firing squad the answer. Castrate them now. Bring back their stolen foreign money". Other placards were too disgusting to recount. Indeed, it was just as well that the detainees were inside prison. For with periodic firing of guns in the air, and with the masses so worked up and excited, if any of the detainees had per chance, shown their faces to the public, they would have to been beaten to death.

Such was the pattern of events that had been set in motion by the new dictators, who set out to restructure the country in their own image. Xenophobia, especially of white people, was encouraged. As the new government, delved into the massive financial reserves, goodwill and credit-worthiness, painstakingly built up by the old regime, it cocked a snoop at its Western creditors by publicly announcing that it would unilaterally repudiate certain debts.

It defied the foreign creditors to do their worst, and the latter did nothing. The growing popularity of Colonel Kofi Johnson appeared unstoppable. Leading international statesmen, for some curious reasons, were frequently in BASSA, to call on Chairman Johnson, and have photos taken with him.

As he grew more confident in position and authority, foreign businessmen, particularly from the West, grew more determined to be associated with him. They all, in most cases, joined in the campaign of vilification of their former friends, who were languishing in prison. The progress of the new administration gathered pace with time. It appeared to have friends all over the country, and no enemies anywhere.

The families of the detainees became the targets and objects of public ridicule, and were on occasions spat upon. As for abuse in public, they got it plenty, as men and women, old and young, intelligent and not-so-intelligent, all and sundry, tried to settle old scores and grievances. Some of their grievances were over their not having been given jobs or housing. Some of the complainants were men who, rejected in love by women that they adored, put their misfortunes down to the presence of a former minister or top official in the shadows, as the cause of all their amorous troubles. Some of the screaming and baying women were of the view that the ex-ministers had ignored them for white women or had slept with them and not offered them adequate compensation or remuneration. They believed that the ex-Ministers had salted away huge fortunes in secret bank accounts in Switzerland, UK and U.S.A; these being allegedly some of the monies which the ministers had gone and borrowed from the World Bank and I.M.F. for the country.

Whatever the excuse or justification, or reason, the taunting cries of the excited masses were the same, as day by day, the detainees in shabby-looking civilian clothes, were driven in Police and Army jeeps to face the military tribunals investigating the sources of their income, their patterns of expenditure, when, where, and how of each major expenditure, and those of their wives and children, since they started earning any income. Over a period of months, the detainees got used to the same old, merciless placards.

"Hang them all by their balls", "Show no mercy", "Big thieves", "Castrate them now", "No tribunal. Hang them all". Such were some of the sentiments carried on the placards as read by the detainees as they were whisked through the crowds. They were completely bereft of any friends whatsoever, except for their immediate families. Yet, stripped of all the razzmatazz and ballyhoo, engineered by the new regime, these enquiries amply showed that by and large, the ministers and other top officials had not been dishonest and corrupt, as trumpeted by the national radio. Infact, all the evidence showed that many of the ministers were in debt to their eye-balls, in their service to the nation. Admittedly, a couple or so had more property, real estate, and bank balances than could be accounted for by their salaries and other incomes. Despite claims to ancestral wealth to justify such unaccounted for wealth by the small handful of ex-public office holders, which claims led to loud shouts of "Thieves", "Switzerland", "America", "U.K.", "banks", by the public at the tribunals, it was apparent that apart from this tiny minority's dubious, financial and other activities, the state had abysmally failed, in its efforts to expose the alleged massive fraud and criminal depletion of public funds by the ex-ministers and their colleagues.

As for the wives, there was not an iota of evidence of any corruption, or wrong-doing, whatsoever, except in one isolated sad case. Infact, the wives, it transpired, were only putting up a public front of affluence and luxury, whilst in fact, they were in many cases, deeply steeped in debts of various forms and sizes

The celebrated answer by the American-born wife of the former Deputy Minister of Health, Pearl Kambu, in answer to a question by the public prosecutor, at one of the four tribunals aptly summed up the plight of most of the ex-ministers' wives

Exasperated by the frequent answers of "Nil", "None", "Cannot remember", "Nothing", to most of his questions as he interrogated her over the assets questionnaire forms that the blonde lady standing before him and the tribunal had filled in and presented, the prosecutor asked, angrily,

"So, madam, what are your assets then?"

"I have no assets in this country. My only asset here is my husband and he is in Kurukuru prison".

"Hear, hear. Good talk", somebody yelled from the back of the hall, as some of the audience began to clap their hands.

"Silence, Order", shouted one of the tribunal officials, whilst the prosecutor settled his nerves. He felt put down by the American woman, and was visibly angry. For by then he had become used, like the other prosecutors, to the fawning and slavish replies to questions, during interrogations, by the African Ministers, their wives, and the witnesses that they called to support their claims, or statements, in one form or another.

Indeed, Mrs Kambu's brave performance before the tribunal quickly became the talk of the town, as the news spread. Even in those difficult and harrowing times, her sterling qualities that had shown through in the pre-coup days were once again as clear as crystal.

No wonder, the prosecutor, contemptuously dismissing Mrs Kambu, had turned to the Chairman of the three-man military tribunal, and then remarked,

"Sir, as Mrs Kambu's only asset, according to her, is also before this tribunal, may I request her discharge, with the right to recall her if and when necessary".

"Certainly". And turning to her, the Chairman of the tribunal said "You may leave now".

"Thank you, Sir".

This is the sort of ordeal that the detainees and their wives had to go through, daily, weekly, monthly, as one by one, standing in the dock, they were rigorously and heartlessly interrogated and re-interrogated over bank statements, income tax forms, and other papers, over expenditures, matters and issues that took place ten or twenty years previously. No wonder that three ministerial wives and two former ministers, it was rumoured then, had nervous break downs that shattered their lives forever.

Fate sometimes acts very cruelly. With all the emotional and psychological stress that the detainees were going through for themselves, and those of their families outside, with all the gross humiliation of the daily car journeys to the tribunals, accompanied by armed police officers and soldiers, which the detainees had to endure, fate or providence dealt an extra deserved or undeserved, mighty blow to one of the detainees. The hapless victim of the wrath of Providence or Fate or Nature, was the former Deputy Minister of Transport and Communications, Peter Dawson.

In the pre-coup, happier days he was a highly-respected,

criminal lawyer, who had given up a flourishing practice, to serve his people. Becoming a minister was for him a considerable financial sacrifice, but he felt it was worth it, for the opportunity to assist in the development of the country, following Independence. He had an Irish wife, and three children, a boy, aged ten, and a girl of eight, and another girl of six years.

Mrs Elizabeth Dawson, was a Dublin-born, ex-nursing sister, who, during her stay in BASSA, devoted her time to looking after her children, and doing voluntary, unpaid charity work among the inmates of the only psychiatric hospital in the capital city. She was a devoted mother, a decent, respectable, housewife, who was ever so ready to help the poor and the needy. Her husband, was to the public at large a good man, who appeared to love power more than money, thus making him unique among his people.

That he was a good family man was apparent to the public, many of whom felt that his marriage across the racial barrier was an example to many others. It was precisely for this reason that the episode that over-took the poor soul, about three weeks after his political detention, caused such a stir, both in the prison among his colleagues, and also outside.

On a hot, Friday afternoon, with considerable difficulty and overcoming many odds, Elizabeth Dawson, had driven her little, Volkswagen car to the Attorney-General's office, to secure a pass to visit her husband in Kurukuru prison. To achieve her objective meant going from one civil-servant to another, about four in all, before finally reaching the desk of the Attorney-General himself. She waited patiently for about twenty-minutes with her children in the ante-room attached to that of private secretary to the Attorney-General.

"Who's it?", enquired the Chief Law-Officer, as he enquired about those wanting to see him.

"Mrs Dawson, Sir. Coming to have her prison visit form signed. Sir".

"I'm fed up. Tired", said he, as he gesticulated to his female secretary of around thirty.

"Sir, she's here with her children, and the prison closes to visitors at 4 pm. Please?"

The Attorney-General, puffing coolly on his cigarette looked at the clock on the wall of his office. It was 3 pm. With much reluctance, he remarked, "Let her in, but no more today. I've other things to do".

"Yes, Sir".

The secretary quickly returned to Elizabeth Dawson and her children, and took her, with the children, to the Attorney-General.

"Sir, please, would you kindly, sign my visitor's form. I'm sorry to bother you".

He beckoned her to sit down in front of him, then told her. "You may probably not know this but your husband was very instrumental in the arrest and harassment of my younger brother under your administration, for no explicable or known reason. I never understood why he acted as he did. And now look at the situation you are in. The wheel of fate has gone a full circle, our roles are inter-changed, and I am a good man to refuse your request, and further ensure that he rots there in that damned hole".

She listened calmly and said nothing. Her heart thumped as she saw him resume his monologue, whilst taking his pen.

"Well, I am signing this because of the children. I try to live by my Christian principles, although it's not easy these days, but we should keep trying. Goodbye and good luck and my regards to him".

He returned the form signed to her.

"Thank you, Mr Attorney-General. I am very grateful and will never forget your kindness". With that, and a modest bow, she quickly left the office with her children. As she walked away, the new Attorney-General, Joshua Dankah, looked at her and smiled to himself. "What a funny world", he mused to himself.

For Elizabeth Dawson, the next stop was the office of the Director of Prisons. She drove the three or four miles quickly, as time was against her. There again more waiting. Time flies, and was flying fast. She was told that the Director was busy and could not be disturbed. She pleaded with his private secretary for a while, and then had a brilliant idea. Her stay in the country for several years had taught her that in extremely difficult, official situations, a little bribe, here or there, could work wonders and open all doors. So she instinctively opened her bag and pulled out of it the equivalent of ten US dollars in the local currency. A broad smile suddenly appeared on the secretary's fine face. Then she got up and said, "please, wait a moment".

She walked to her boss, and was there for about five minutes, returning with a confident smile.

"May I have the form, madam?"

She took it from her and returned to the Director, and before Elizabeth Dawson, could even think of what was at all happening or going to happen, she had returned with the form signed by her boss. With a profuse "Thank you once again", Mrs Dawson, quickly dashed out of the office with her children. The time was 3.45 pm, and she had only fifteen minutes left, if she were to make it to the prison in time.

Luckily for her, the notorious prison was not all that far. Still she drove as fast as safety would allow, and was there by 3.55 pm, with her children. She had beaten the deadline by five minutes. After her identity and papers were checked by a young prison warder, a corporal on duty, she and her children were led into the ante-room, attached to the main office reception.

"Madam, you're almost late. What can I do for you?"

"I've come to visit my husband. Here's the permit. Look".

He requested her to leave the children in the ante-room, and follow him to the prison reception. This she did, as she instructed her children.

"I will be back soon darlings. Don't move anywhere".

In the office reception, the corporal opened the visitors' book and then asked,

"Madam, what's your full name?"

"Elizabeth Naomi Dawson"

"And your husband?"

"Peter Dawson, former Deputy Minister of Transport and Communications".

"I see", he said, poring over the page of the visitors' book before him.

For a couple of minutes both were silent. Then the corporal remarked,

"Madam, there must be some mistake here. I don't understand. For according to this entry, Mrs Dawson visited her husband yesterday in the morning".

"What. What do you mean?"

"Madam, I am a mere warder doing my job. According to the page before me, Mrs Dawson or somebody calling herself Mrs Dawson, came with an official, signed permit, to visit her husband. I was on duty, and clearly it is here, she was allowed half an hour with her husband, in the presence of me and one of our warders, who later initialled the visit.

"But I find this inexplicable. I am Mrs Dawson. The one and only Mrs Dawson. There must be a mistake somehow".

"Madam, if you don't believe me you look at the page yourself. Book no lie, as they say".

She quickly took the visitors' book from him, and as she did so, it dawned on her that either there had been a gross instance of mistaken identity, or that the husband she loved and had loved for several years, was guilty of an unpardonable act of gross adultery and deceit.

She was ashen in colour, as she asked the warder, "Was the woman black or white?"

"Black", he replied.

"Was she tall or short?"

"Tall", he replied calmly, but perplexed over what was upsetting the white woman sitting before him.

Next, there was a long sigh from the white Mrs Dawson. She sat as motionless as a sitting Buddha. All that she could muster was,

"I see. Now I understand".

She then called for a piece of plain paper, and then took a pen from her bag. Rapidly, and with tears rolling off her face, she wrote,

"My dearest Peter,

I've just learnt with complete horror that your wife Mrs

Dawson visited you yesterday at this prison, and was with you for about half an hour. The warder on duty has not only told me this shocking news, but confirmed it by showing me the visitors' book, with the signatures of your Mrs Dawson, yourself and the warder on duty.

The children and I had come to see you and give our moral support and love, but in the circumstances, my religion as a Catholic and my own personal principles leave me no choice but to pack and leave at once. Right away.

Now I understand your frequent, unexplained long absences from home nightly, on the standard excuse and pretext of attending long Cabinet meetings or seeing the President, or dealing with a backlog of ministerial work. I innocently believed you all along, but now I am wiser, thanks to your Mrs Dawson's visit.

Furthermore, I now do understand the mysterious disappearance of certain expensive toys and bicycles of our children, for which you even had your own younger brother thrashed, as the likely culprit. What a ghastly and inhuman thing to do!.

Well, for my part, this is it. I am going home with the children to pack and leave by coming Saturday's plane for London. It will be hypocritical and unnatural to do otherwise. I am taking not a pin from the house, but will approach the other British wives and the Irish Consul for assistance to buy air plane tickets. Subsequently, I shall call on my solicitor in Dublin to file a divorce petition.

The children send their love, and we really do wish you well in the future. Goodbye and good luck.

Your devoted wife,

Liz."

After finishing the letter, she carefully folded it and requested an envelope from the warder. She sealed the letter and handed it to the corporal, who was still perplexed by her behaviour.

She got up to go. The warder asked.

"Madam, no visit?"

She looked at him sadly, and remarked "Forget it!" And with

hat, she collected her children and drove away. She was very angry, very upset and very disappointed with herself and her life.

She drove on, heading for home, but about three miles from the prison, made a detour to a street, in a rather run-down district of the capital. At a white, three-bedroomed bungalow, with a modest garden in front, she slowed down, and stopped. And there before her very eyes was a young African boy of about six years, happily riding a child's bicycle, which her son had used, and which sometime ago had suddenly disappeared from her home.

One look was enough. She saw a rather familiar face. She noticed a tall, rather elegant African woman in perhaps her thirties, walk towards the boy. Alas, the face, at least part of what she could see, looked familiar!.

Elizabeth Dawson was as good as her word. A day after the tragic episode, she sold some of her personal belongings - hats, frocks, dresses, shoes, jewellery, and other items. Contributions were made by the British and Irish Consuls, the Foreign Wives Association and by one or two local friends. And by the next plane, the white or European Mrs Dawson, accompanied by her three children, left APPAPA airport, for London, en route for Dublin, Ireland.

For Peter Dawson, the beginning of the end was ushered in rather innocently enough. At about 8 pm of the fateful day, just after supper, (hard-boiled yam and plain watery meat-less, vegetable soup), he was called to the office of Tinga Moses, the Senior Prison Superintendent.

"I have a letter for you. Please sign here, as received".

"Thank you".

Dawson opened the letter, and started to read it, and as he went on, he kept repeating to himself, "Incredible", "Unbelievable", "Why me?"

He returned to his fellow inmates, as if he was dazed. He was absolutely speechless, and friends thought it best to leave him alone, fearing that perhaps he was bereaved.

Chapter 13

Right from the week of the military coup, in which the democratically-elected, civilian government was forcibly overthrown, the wives of the ex-ministers and senior party official got busy. They began to rally support among the church leaders for a public petition which they wished to put before the new Head of State, Chairman Kofi Johnson. Petition upon petition, some hand-written, others typed on ancient, rickety manual typewriters went to the Chairman from the distressed women. Most of them were never answered. In all the petitions, the grass widows were asking for the new regime to allow them to see their husbands, collect their laundry for cleaning, and be allowed to send them food from home.

The wives also requested, with abject humility, that their husbands be properly put on trial before the normal civilian courts, instead of hurriedly constituted People's Courts, which were really military tribunals, all but in name. They further pleaded that pending their open trial, the husbands be released and placed under house arrest, with the wives becoming sureties for their husbands. In the glow of immense success, public support and invincibility, the new military regime .scorned these requests, but the wives carried on regardless.

Under the most harrowing conditions, holding secret meeting, mostly in their homes, and at the Roman Catholic Cathedral in Appapa, the wives discussed and planned their strategy, and what to tell the Chairman, if they had the chance. The Cathedral had been made available to them by the saintly Catholic bishop, who fearlessly, right from the start stood firmly, very firmly for freedom, liberty and human rights.

The leading light, investigator and campaign chief was the American-born Mrs Pearl Kambu. A blond, medium sized woman of about five foot six inches, with a pair of pretty intelligent green eyes, set in a beautiful face, she was about thirty-two, at the time of the military coup, and had been married to her lawyer husband for about nine years at the time of the national tragedy. They had met in New York, where the would-be husband was working as a newspaper correspondent, and later as a senior diplomat. She was born in Brooklyn, of Liberal Jewish parents, who had luckily left Germany as Nazism was beginning to take root. She worked as a manager in her father's jewellery shop.

At the time she and her husband were overtaken by national events, her husband was a Deputy Minister for Health and they had two daughters, aged six and four. Funnily enough, their marriage had taken off rather unusually. For initially, her father, a successful business man, with a completely adorable wife, was opposed to the idea of their only daughter, the apple of their eye, marrying a goy. And it took sometime, in fact, a considerable time, before they relented and relaxed, and gave their approval, albeit with much misgiving.

Ironically, just as her parents were won over, trouble started from another quarter. With the future husband's father long dead from alleged poisoning by his own relatives, so that they could inherit his vast wealth in BASSA, Pearl was upset to learn that her husband's mother was also creating problems. She could not understand why her son, her eldest, the first lawyer, and later senior diplomat from their town, should ignore all the local beauties and marry a foreigner. She simply could not understand it. She felt betrayed by her son.

As such on at least a couple of occasions, her son had to fly home to explain matters, coax and cajole, persuade and mollify not only her, but also a few aunts and uncles. Finally, all problems of concern between son and mother were happily resolved, and the couple planned to marry in Washington D.C. by Jewish wedding rites. At long last the path appeared smooth and straight forward. But was it?. For just before fixing the wedding date, the future bride-groom , had written to his Foreign Minister as he was obliged to, requesting official permission to marry a foreigner. This was a straight forward request, at least as seen by George Kambu himself.

Alas it was not to be. For while awaiting the requested approval, he was attending a conference in Washington D.C. when the telephone in his hotel room rang one afternoon.

"This is the James Paxman column of the "Daily Reporter", ringing from London". The young diplomat was startled, and asked,

"Yes, can I help you, Sir?"

"Sorry to intrude, but we wanted to know whether you could comment on the refusal of the Foreign Minister of BASSA, to grant your request to marry American-born, Pearl Goldberg. Any comments, Sir?. Is it colour-bar in reverse?, the cultured, English voice went on.

George Kambu was perplexed, as he himself had not received the news, which he was expecting by the arrival of the next diplomatic bag.

Astounded, he said deliberately, "Well, Sir, I've not received the reply yet to my request, and until the arrival of the diplomatic bag, there's nothing useful that I can say at this stage. Sorry, I cannot help you further". But before he could ring off, the English voice, ended with, "Well, Sir, we are carrying the story tomorrow, which we are reliably informed is also going to be used by a leading Washington paper and the most influential Israeli paper, apart from the Times here".

And so it happened, just as the English newspaper man had said. On the following day, the "London Times", the "Washington Post" and the leading Israeli paper, "Mavrim", carried the stories in their inside papers. As such, when the diplomatic bag did arrive, and Kambu got the anxiously expected letter, reading it brought no surprises By the courtesy of the newspaper man that had telephoned him from London, he knew the contents already. Yet how the English newspaper gossip columnist and his counterparts in USA and Israel, got hold of the story before he did, was a minor mystery that occupied Kambu for sometime, and took a little time to resolve.

Being determined fighters as they were, and still are, Pearl and George, worked on this last obstacle. Following a number of letters and telephone calls by both of them to and from Washington DC., London and Appapa, Kambu eventually wrote a long petition to the President of BASSA at the time.

The petition succinctly devastated the Foreign Minister's arguments that by marrying a foreigner, George Kambu, was placing himself in a position to be potentially, a threat to state security. Citing instances of eminent British and American Ambassadors with foreign wives, Kambu rested his case on the mercy of the President, whose wife, ironically, was a foreigner anyway.

Furthermore, the fact that BASSA relied heavily on the U.S., U.K. and Israel, for economic and military aid, loans and other services, including the training of BASSA's army and security service, seemed to have escaped the Foreign Minister in his enthusiasm to do his duty, as he saw it.

To this day, Kambu vividly remembers what the President told him, when he had to go home for consultations about the expected arrival of a foreign delegation to BASSA.

With Kambu sitting in front of him, in his modestly furnished office, the President said,

"I saw the memo from the Foreign Ministry, but I did not mind them. In this world, it is the person that counts, not his or her skin colour". That finally settled the matter. After that meeting Pearl and George Kambu were happily married in a liberal Brooklyn synagogue in New York. Thus by the time of her arrival in BASSA, Pearl was a bit used to the in-fighting of Bassain society and politics. Being an avid "people watcher", devoid of much formal education, she had graduated in the "University of Life", and become very perceptive and knowledgeable of what makes people tick. She had common sense in plenty. During her stay in Bassa, she was actively involved in the social and cultural life of the people. She learnt the major local language, formed the Foreign Wives Association in Appapa, and was a well-known social worker, especially for destitute children; discharged, ex-psychiatric patients, and American and European wives married to Africans who had fallen on bad times, following the break-up of their marriages.

Twice a week she rode regularly as a paid guest, at the nearby Army stables, and her habit of frequently giving the soldiers on duty gifts of cigarettes, cans of beer, coca-cola, chocolates, and sometimes, money, made her popular among the soldiers, and ensured that she and her guests always got the best horses available.

Her strong American accent was strange and delightful to the ears of the soldiers, who always asked her to try and get them visas to go and study or work in America. They felt somehow, from the way she dressed and conducted herself, that she was not only wealthy, but had powerful connections with the U.S. embassy.

However, much as she loved Bassa and the people, the more so, as she lived in the country, Pearl could never come to terms with the customs of polygamy in the country, and why the women put up with it. She could simply not fathom it out. As for the claim of some local men to be able to sexually satisfy more than one wife, she treated the whole thing as a gigantic joke and farce. Her own pet theory, as a trained counsellor was that such men, rather made these fantastic claims of exceptional sexual prowess, to cover their sexual inadequacies and deficiencies. She was also shocked again and again, by some of the dietary habits of the people such as the husbands or "big men" being given better and more food than growing children.

Pearl was unquestionably a very good, sympathetic person, devoted mother and wife, an ideal example of the legendary "Jewish mamma". She kept a kosher kitchen, entertained frequently, to make friends and influence people in Bassa, especially for her husband. And was rather sad that the Bassains never invited her and her family back. Still she loved the people, and they in turn loved her. Perhaps the only criticism which some of the local people had of her was that she was too conservative, and inclined to be over argumentative. Also they could not understand her problem with polygamy, and what she frequently called "child abuse", which to them was "child correction".

Such was the affection felt for Pearl that when the news

broke that the Administration, in which her husband served as a Deputy Minister, had been toppled by a military coup, a number of soldiers and officers, all in mufti, except one or two, called at her home, to offer sympathy, and moral support. Some even brought her the little that they could muster; a few eggs, live chickens, yams, onions and cooking oil. These people lived in revolutionary times when it was most imprudent and unwise to visit close relations of those in trouble, but a few of Pearl's former friends who had, one way or another, benefited from her kindness, in the good old days, did not forget her.

At long last the good news arrived. After anxious weeks of waiting and suspension, the wives of the ex-ministers, collectively received a letter, addressed to the wife of the ex-Foreign Minister on behalf of the wives. It brought excellent news. The Head of State, Colonel Kofi Johnson had agreed to see a delegation of not more than twenty of the wives, on the next Thursday, at ten in the morning at his office in MANDALAY camp, in the main barracks in APPAPA. The letter was signed by the Political Adviser to the Chairman. Received on a Friday, the wives had barely a week to prepare for their historic meeting with the Head of State. Consequently, Pearl, with her usual enthusiasm for action, began to galvanise and mobilise as many of the wives as possible. Some were contacted by phone, others through personal visits, and a few through friends of friends. The situation was desperate and needed quick action.

On the Sunday following the receipt of the letter, a major meeting was held in the Roman Catholic Cathedral, after the normal morning service. Bishop Antol not only prayed for the women, but also advised them on the best approach to take at the meeting. Again and again, he emphasised the need for patience and self-control.

"Ladies, what you say or do at the meeting will determine to a considerable degree, the fate of your husbands and the Chairman's reaction to your requests. My church and my priests are with you all the way, and will continue to pray for you, as before. You may rest assured on our behalf. God be with you. Let's pray".

The Bishop led in saying the Lord's prayer, and as they all

said "AMEN", some of the women were sobbing, and some crying. His work done, Bishop Isaac Antol retired to his private quarters nearby, leaving the women to continue their deliberations.

A spirited and lively discussion took place. Some of the women wanted the delegation to adopt a defiant, hard-line. Others cautioned moderation, whilst a couple or so, were damned scared and afraid of the possibility of their being also locked up. The discussion went on and on for about three hours. Eventually, the moderates prevailed. It was agreed collectively to present a verbal petition, imploring the Head of State to immediately release their husbands and place them under house arrest, and pending that to allow the wives to send the detainees food from their homes, collect and clean their laundry, allow two or more family visits per week, each of one our duration, in the absence of prison officials, and the increase of the monthly allowance they could draw from the frozen accounts of their husbands and themselves, from 150 U.S. dollars to 400, as the first figure was grossly inadequate. For some of the wives, especially those from outside the capital, were becoming almost destitute. The women also agreed to add the request that as their husbands had not been given the due process of law and been convicted, they should be allowed books and magazines, and letters without censorship by the prison authorities.

The main points of the petition, agreed upon, it was decided to appoint a leader. The ex-Foreign Minister being the eldest was suggested by one of the women.

"Well, I am honoured to hear what you've just said, but for many good reasons, I would rather suggest that Pearl leads the delegation. I have considered the whole thing carefully, and it is not out of fear that I suggest her. After all, being the oldest here I have less years to live, and thus even less reason for fearing detention, imprisonment or death. What is at stake is more important than your life or mine. Our primary objective is to ensure the success of our mission, and the achievements of the requests that we are going to put before him. And all things considered, I think that Pearl is the right person for the occasion".

"Hear. hear. I think so too", somebody shouted from the back.

One of the ladies, the wife of the former Deputy Finance Minister got up.

"I am sure this is an excellent idea. We all know Pearl. She's one of us totally, and can deliver the goods better than any of us can do. I fully support her as leader", she concluded and sat down, as the rest burst into clapping.

Finally, the wife of the former Local Government Minister got up,

"Not only is Pearl an excellent choice, but also as she is American, they will not dare touch her. At worst, she may be deported with her children, but we might probably end up in prison, with or without our children. Such is the position in which we are. You see!".

So it was quickly agreed that Pearl was to lead the delegation on the fateful Thursday morning. She got up and smiling said,

"I will certainly do my best, friends. We are all in the same boat, and we swim or sink together. I cannot promise miracles, but I will leave no stone unturned to achieve our aim. I am confident that with your sincere co-operation and God's blessing, we shall overcome, if not, then one day. Yes, we will achieve victory, God willing. Thank you all".

There was a thunderous burst of applause and cheers, as she sat down. One of the women, emotionally walked from the rear of the meeting, kissed her on the cheek, and handed her a white handkerchief, remarking, "With this we will go together towards victory and freedom".

Before the meeting dispersed, the ex-Foreign Minister's wife, who had been chairing the meeting, suggested that it would be a good idea if they could get any one of the prominent church leaders to accompany them on their forthcoming mission. As they were all but a couple of them Protestants, it was suggested that they approach one of the eminent Protestant church leaders to go with them. They all felt that it was an excellent idea, and a shrewd move.

Then, one by one, five of the wives got up to castigate and

condemn the non-Catholic clergy for their naked cowardice and dereliction of their spiritual duties, and their failure unequivocally to condemn the coup to date. Each speaker was even more condemnatory than the previous one. As the last one sat down, Pearl Kambu got up to speak.

"Friends, I almost said, friends-in-trouble together, I've listened calmly to the previous speakers, and I have a little contribution to make, which may or may not surprise you". She paused for a second or so, with the hall very still, no whisper or throat-clearing or coughing whatsoever.

Then she went on calmly,

"Since the coup, I have personally called on five prominent , well-known leaders of the Protestant churches in Appapa, begging them to openly support our cause, and lend their great influence and prestige to our campaign to free our husbands. Wherever I went, believe me, it was the same story. "We are praying for you and working behind the scenes on your husbands' behalf, but cannot help you any further. That would be doing politics, and we are church leaders not politicians. In fact, in one instance, I was not allowed beyond the gate of a well-known church leader in Appapa, and had to shout across the gate my request to see the man concerned. When they knew what I had come about, I was not let in, period!.

All my efforts to appeal to them have so far failed miserably, but if you wish me to try again, I shall certainly do so", she ended.

"Don't bother, Pearl. It's a waste of time. Absolutely", remarked a lady behind her.

"I fear it will be the same old response, 'sorry we are praying for you, working behind the scenes, behind closed doors, cannot help any further'. What's the point in spending more time and energy on them. Because we are out, they don't want to know us anymore. That's life!", remarked the wife of the former Housing Minister.

The meeting was then brought to a close with the decision that His Grace, Dr. Isaac Antol, the saintly Roman Catholic Bishop of Appapa was to be requested by Pearl to accompany them on their rather difficult meeting with Chairman Kofi

Johnson.

Straight from the meeting, Pearl Kambu walked to the Bishop's House, and informed the Bishop's secretary that she needed urgently to see him for a few minutes. The bishop was too busy in his study, and the secretary was not very keen to disturb him, but could not resist the pleas and supplications of Pearl.

"Well, I will go and see",

A few moments later he returned, and then said, "Madam, please, follow me".

Pearl was led to the bishop's study, where he beckoned her to sit down.

"Oh, how did your meeting go? Everything alright?".

"Yes, your Grace. Thank God. Furthermore, I've been asked to come and make another request",

"So?"

"Yes, Sir. It's a very tall order, bishop. We should be most grateful if you could accompany us next Thursday, 10 am to meet the Chairman to present our petition. We really do need a religious heavy-weight like you, Sir, and as we have nobody to turn to we are coming to you. The irony of it all is that practically all our people are Protestants, but they now feel more and more that their salvation and redemption is with the Catholic Church. Sir, can you help us ?

"Pearl, don't worry, this is no problem at all. Glad to help, if I am free".

He called in his secretary and after a brief talk with him about his scheduled appointments for the following Thursday, instructed him to make appropriate alterations, leave Thursday free, but inform in time all those affected by the Thursday appointments.

On that Thursday morning, at about 9 am, the wives began to arrive at Gate 1, of Mandalay Camp. Some went by car, others by taxi, and the more financially stretched by foot. The weather was warm and humid, and soon it began to rain. Not the usual, heavy tropical downpour, but still fairly heavy enough to make it extremely uncomfortable for the persons walking in it. The women were dressed in their best clothes, local and Western.

195

They gathered together full of courage, hope and expectation.

At promptly 9.30 am, the bishop's car pulled in and at the back of it, was Dr. Antol, splendidly attired in his full church vestments, as the Bishop of Appapa, capital city of Bassa. He smiled and waved to the women, who spontaneously burst into loud "Hear, hear. The Bishop is in!". The sergeant on duty checked the vehicles, cracked a joke or two, with the wives and the Bishop, and ordered his soldiers to wave them on. Soon they were at Gate 2, where another stop and check of vehicles took place, with positive and happy results.

Eventually, they reached Gate 3, the final gate, which was about one hundred yards from the heavily guarded office of Chairman Johnson. Expecting the same stop and search of vehicles as before, without any problem, the delegation suddenly heard,

"Stop here everybody. All come down. I say come down", shouted a wild, hefty-looking sergeant, with a long moustache, which obviously had received no care for weeks.

All the vehicles stood motionless, with their occupants as silent as mutes

"You no hear me. I say down", the sergeant shouted further. Pearl got out first of her old, almost decrepit Volvo, 2-door car and went to the sergeant,

"That's the Bishop of Appapa, and we have all an appointment with the Chairman. You may check with your superior officers". With the rest of the delegation looking on, and as if to impress them all, he bellowed angrily.

"Madam, I don't care ebe cardinal or Pope himself. Order ebe order. Nobody pass here except by foot. I simple soldier man, only obey orders?."

"But sergeant, see for yourself, it's raining. Be reasonable. Please, think for yourself, for heaven's sake!"

"Look, madam, I mere soldier, I get order I act, not think! Mine not reason why. In my job, madam, you no think, you obey, simple. Either you all de foot or you stay with me. Okay? Understand?"

"Please, our appointment is ten o'clock and we have only

fifteen minutes left. You're deliberately wasting our time. Why not ring your officers for clearance?".

As she made her request, she saw the soldiers under the command of the sergeant, laughing at the bishop and the women. Indeed, one of them, a corporal remarked, to the amusement of his colleagues,

"Big men's wives, they do nothing but eat, eat, plenty good food, while we baboons suffer. Everyday diner party, every week-end dance. Sergeant fix them proper".

As Pearl was making no headway with the sergeant, nor the bishop himself having any more success, and as time was not on their side, the bishop advised them all to get down, and walk with him in the rain to their appointment. Perhaps, by divine intervention, the rain became less unpleasant, but it was still not the same as a dry day.

At about five minutes to their appointment the delegation, led by Mrs Pearl Kambu, and accompanied by Bishop Isaac Antol, Roman Catholic Bishop of Appapa, reached the headquarters of the army, and were led to a large hall. They had just enough time to spruce themselves a little bit, gather their thoughts together, before they were led to a medium -sized, empty office, in which seats for about forty people had been arranged. Facing the seats, on a raised platform was a shiny mahogany executive table, with chairs for seven, three on each side. The middle chair, an expensive, eminent-looking one, was obviously for the Chairman himself.

At promptly one minute past ten, a door opened, and a military orderly, announced,

"Ladies and gentlemen, the Chairman of the People's Revolutionary Council". And in walked, Chairman Kofi Johnson, followed by six colleagues in his government. They were all in resplendent military uniforms. Two senior naval officers, two from the Airforce, and two from the Army. Unsmilingly, they sat down after the Chairman had taken his seat. As an afterthought, a chair was brought in quickly for the Attorney-General.

Behind the panel, stood the Chairman's A.D.C., the Press

Secretary, and two armed captains of the parachute regiment. Also standing in the room were four other soldiers, with automatic, light machine-guns, one in each corner of the room. A couple of secretaries, seated near the Chairman's table completed the whole ensemble. The room was quiet, and even the fall of a feather could be heard.

First to speak was the Chairman.

"Good morning, ladies and gentlemen. Pleased to see you all. Happy you could come along". He stopped momentarily and looked on his right, and as he was about to resume, he saw the hand of the bishop raised,

"I see, the Bishop himself is here, so as a good Catholic, I've to be very careful", said he, half-serious and half-joking.

"Well, your Grace, how nice to see you, can I help?"

"Mr Chairman, I am really delighted and honoured to be here. I should not strictly be here today, but I could not resist the invitation of the Ministers' wives, I mean, ex-ministers' wives, to accompany them on this august occasion , as their spiritual adviser and comforter. I hope you've no objection, Sir!".

"Not at all. After all, don't forget I am a Catholic, although perhaps a lapsed one, by your standards".

The Bishop smiled in a non-committal manner, then said, "Thank you, Mr Chairman", and sat down.

"Well, over to you ladies. I notice from your correspondence that your leader is Mrs Yaw, wife of our former Foreign Minister. Good".

As he spoke, Mrs Grace Yaw, got up. "Mr Chairman, after much deliberation and discussion, we have decided that Mrs Pearl Kambu should act as leader and spokes-person for our delegation. We trust that you don't object. Sir".

"Not a bit. No problem".

Pearl Kambu, dressed in a most impressive, light green suit, with a few diamantes in front, got up to speak. The room was hushed. And with the Chairman looking intently and benignly at her, Pearl began.

"Mr Chairman, I wish on behalf of all of us, and myself to thank you very much for finding the time, despite your busy

schedule, to receive us. We are deeply touched and very grateful".

"That's alright. You're welcome", remarked the Chairman
smiling. Before Pearl could continue, the Head of State went on,
"I remember you very well. When five years ago your husband,
who was then editor of the Times, and you, stayed at my
residence, during his official tour of the Western Province, you
kindly gave my children lots of chocolates. That's right. Yes?"

"True, Sir, but if I may say so, it's a period of my life that I
would rather wish to forget".

"Oh", remarked the Chairman, as he winced. "Anyway,
please continue".

"Sir, since the coup, the wives of the ex-ministers and other
detainees have suffered immense hardships, which, due to lack
of time, I cannot go into now. We are being thrown, on very short
notice, from our previous government houses, and this has
brought untold hardship for all of us, especially those who come
from outside Appapa. Indeed, some at this moment are destitute, with nowhere to stay with their children.

Secondly, the monthly allowance we are allowed to draw
from our frozen bank accounts is simply not enough, especially
for those with large families. Sir, can you imagine having to live
on 150 U.S. dollars or its equivalent, a month, to pay for food,
rent, essential bills and expenses, transport and other items. As
you know, Sir, all our vehicles have been confiscated since the
coup, and sometimes even the taxis don't want to take us". There
was a little giggle among the Chairman's colleagues, but he
himself did not laugh.

"The high cost of living, Sir, you said was one of the reasons
for the coup, and , here we are, Mr Chairman expected to live on
150 dollars. Our children, the future citizens of this great
country are suffering needlessly. Their schooling has been badly
interrupted with possibly irretrievable results. And we have all
become the butt of national mockery and jokes.

Thirdly, we plead with you as the father of the nation, and
the fount of justice and fairness, to allow us to send food daily to
our husbands in prison, collect their laundry, and send and

receive uncensored letters from them. Also, as educated people, their lives are blighted without books, magazines and newspapers to read.

Fourthly, we implore you, Mr Chairman to allow us daily visits to our husbands, each visit of one hour duration, without the presence of warders or prison officials, or without the place being bugged".

The Attorney-General, ever so keen to please his new mentor, butted in, "We don't bug the prisons".

"So you say, Sir". Everybody in the room either smiled or laughed lightly.

"May I continue, Mr Chairman?"

"Certainly, we are listening very well, Mrs Kambu".

"Well, Sir, you would be relieved to hear that I am almost done. I now come to the last, and certainly the most crucial aspect of our humble petition. We beg you, sir, as Head of State, and leader of the nation, to release our husbands and place them under house arrest. We the wives shall then be held accountable for their guaranteed stay in the country and their appearance before the tribunals. Mr Chairman, immense pain and suffering are being caused to all the families by the detention of our husbands. Our children are crying, and we appeal to you, in the name of Almighty God, and as a father yourself, to think of what the wives and children are going through.

Meanwhile, Sir, pending release of our husbands, hopefully expected very soon, kindly authorise that the issue of prison visit permits is expedited. As it is, often we spend a whole morning or afternoon, or sometimes a whole day, going from here to there, from the Attorney-General's office, next to the Director of Prisons, to get just one single permit,. This, sir, is our life since your revolution, and we are indeed suffering harshly. We are at your mercy, father of the nation, Sir, we humbly appeal to you. Thank you, Sir".

As Pearl sat down, her friends burst into applause and clapping with one lady shouting "Hear, hear. Well done. Pearl". A junior officer standing in a corner, yelled, "Silence! Order! This is not a theatre. Don't you see the Head of State here?"

The room became quiet and still again.

All eyes in the room were trained on the Chairman as he held brief, whispered conversation with his friends on the panel. It took not more than ten minutes. Everybody in the room, certainly the wives and the bishop, if not the soldiers, were all excited and expectant.

Suddenly, the Chairman winked to the Attorney-General, who then remarked,

"The Chairman is ready to deal with your requests. Order". He sat down, with an air of importance.

"Ladies, my colleagues and I have carefully listened to your petition, and given it much thought, and will at this juncture say that we are now in a revolution, which demands revolutionary action. Taking your requests one by one, I wish, on behalf of myself and colleagues of the People's Revolutionary Council, to respond as follows. Don't forget that we are also human, and are mindful of your suffering, especially the children. In the circumstances, the best we can do at the moment is this.

One, on the question of housing, I am instructing the Attorney-General to allow those of you without your own private homes in Appapa, to stay for an extra three months, whilst you find alternative accommodation. But you will be staying as tenants of the Government, and will have to pay fair rents, to be appropriately determined by the Housing Department.

Two, the monthly allowance will be raised from 150 to 300 dollars, per month, as from the first of next month. Special approval will be needed to be granted by the A.G's office for funds to be drawn for children's fees. Also, each family will get, with immediate effect, one car released from its confiscated cars. The Attorney-General will see to that.

Three, you will be allowed, as from next Monday to take one meal a day, to your husbands but the meals will be opened and examined by prison staff to ensure that some of you don't try to poison your husbands, and put the blame on us!. Also, laundry can be taken in or out, but will be examined for bombs or grenades. However, no uncensored letters, magazines, books or papers will be allowed. There are plenty of Bibles and old, approved journals and magazines in the prisons to occupy them fully", he said with a smile.

Four, the visits will stay at one a week per detainee, I fear in the presence of the warders, for obvious security reasons. Each visit shall last one hour. Also I am instructing that the permits be issued quickly and that you don't have to wait at either the A.G.'s office or at the Prison Director's for more than fifteen minutes. I don't see the point, myself, quite frankly.

Finally, your most important plea, the question of your husbands' release. Sorry, we cannot agree to that at all. These men are bomb-throwers, dangerous, and also leaders and they will only cause chaos, confusion and havoc, if released. They are dangerous. They are crafty leaders and we cannot afford to release them now".

Suddenly, Pearl Kambu got up and angrily asked, "Sir, but you cannot punish them for being leaders. Most of them have never seen or handled a grenade, certainly not my husband. And as for being leaders, Sir, even ants have leaders. You have overthrown a civilian government, and now you blame them for being leaders of their people". She was sitting down, when the A.D.C. to the Chairman, shouted,

"Sit down and don't be insolent. How dare you? What do you think of yourself and where do you think you are, in one of the southern United States, where you treat some African-Americans as second class citizens. You idiot".

A captain from the "Do or Die Regiment", standing in a corner, fuming walked towards her, and remarked vigorously,

"This is Bassa not America. If you know what's good for you madam, you'll apologise and shut up, you hear, madam?" The whole confrontation took place in a few split minutes, as the Chairman and his colleagues looked on with shock and amazement.

"Silence, Order", were being shouted from various corners of the room. The Chairman sat there with his hands supporting his head. Briefly he lit a cigarette and then smiled, as he turned to his colleagues on his left, murmuring something.

"Well, I think we better adjourn for a few minutes for things to settle down". As he got up to walk away to his office, adjacent to the room, followed by his six colleagues, and the Attorney-General, a military police captain, walked to Pearl and ordered her to follow him.

"For what? And to where? I am an American citizen and you have no warrant, whatsoever, for my arrest. Who ordered my arrest?".

"I say follow me, madam. I don't care whether you are U.S. citizen or not Obey".

The bishop, trying to intervene was completely ignored, and nearly pushed aside. Some of the wives were crying, whilst others implored Pearl to follow the man, and terminate proceedings. Pearl sat tight and refused to move, till the bishop asked her, promising to protest strongly and openly to the Chairman when proceedings resumed.

For half an hour Colonel Johnson was closeted in his office with his colleagues, the Attorney-General, and a couple of advisers.

"You know, I really like Mrs Kambu. I remember her kindness and generosity to my children when she and her husband stayed with us for about a week, when I was Military Governor in the West. I did not see much of her husband, who was visiting the various Times correspondents in the area, but I saw or heard much about her. She took my children often to the beach, gave them plenty of chocolates and other gifts, swimming suits, and the rest. And my children were always pestering me - 'Daddy, we want to go to the chocolate lady. She is very kind', they kept saying",

He puffed on his cigarette and went on,

"When my wife and I were leaving for Jamaica, we planned to call on her. Unfortunately, I could not go, but my dear wife did. And you know what, the lady gave her a beautiful handbag and other gifts for my children. What a shame that the only time that I've seen her since she stayed with us, should be under such dreadful circumstances".

He appeared really uneasy about the altercation which had caused the intermission.

"Well, Chief, I fear, we must use her as an example to the rest", intoned the Attorney-General. "If we let her get away, the rest and others who come to hear the story, would say, that it was because she was white , and American that's why she got off scot-free. Her behaviour was unpardonable, and she could be charged, and successfully prosecuted before any of the normal civilian courts, not to talk of the People's Courts. After all Article 8, Section 2, of the Public Order Act, passed under their own regime, makes it a felony to insult, abuse, or bring into public ridicule, the Head of State, the Prime Minister, and other categories of Senior Public Office-holders".

"Yes, we must teach her a lesson, and let her know crystal clear that this is Bassa, not Alabama or Mississippi, Right?", enquired one of the Chairman's colleagues.

"Hmm! Apart from my regard for the woman, there's also this factor. You know how heavily we rely on the Americans for economic aid, loans, food, and other services. Touch one of their citizens and you get their ambassador here coming in with long protests, the State Department badgering our man in Washington DC, and all the media in the U.S. opening an orchestrated campaign against us. And without U.S. aid we are finished. That's the trouble".

"Still, I think she should be dealt with militarily, and to hell with the consequences. We shall not starve", remarked an air commodore colleague of the Chairman.

"Old boy, it's easier said than done. If we don't handle this simple, little matter properly, and it gets out of hand, the Americans can easily cut off our economic lines, and using their influence at the I.M.F., the World Bank, and U.N., and elsewhere, cause major economic chaos and food shortages in our country. The people will then start demonstrating and rioting, and we would be hanged by our balls, or face the firing squad".

"Alright, Chairman, as a compromise, when we resume, give her a strong, public reprimand and warning", suggested one of his colleagues.

"That's too mild. Let's add a brief detention", interrupted the Attorney-General.

"How long?", the Chairman enquired.

"Sir, I think two weeks will be adequate".

"What? Are you crazy? Without charge or trial, whatsoever? Certainly not. I cannot be party to this", remarked the Chairman.

After a few more minutes discussion, it was agreed to reprimand her and give her two days detention in a guardroom, not too far from the Chairman's office. As such, about half an hour following the adjournment, the Chairman and his team returned to the meeting.

All seated, he looked round and could not see Mrs Pearl Kambu.

"Well, ladies and gentlemen, shall I say, we are resuming where we broke off, hoping that tempers have cooled now. But where is Mrs Kambu? I don't see her here".

The military-police captain who had incarcerated her quickly shot in. Sir, I've put her in the guardroom to cool off".

"Who ordered you?", the Chairman asked angrily.

"Nobody, Sir".

"What, you did it on your own authority?".

"Yes, Sir!"

"Bring her back at once".

Within minutes the captain returned to his boss with Pearl Kambu. The room was tense as the women looked pitifully at Pearl.

"Sit down, Mrs Kambu".

The chairman briefly whispered to his colleagues on the left and right, then angrily said,

"Captain, you had no orders or authority to do what you did. None whatsoever, and no justification. We are running a disciplined army not a bunch of irresponsible, trigger-happy soldiers. This simply will not do. You're given a week's guardroom detention, with hard labour, with immediate effect. Take him away!", he ordered. His A.D.C., with much alacrity, took away the military police captain to the very guard-room, where he had only an hour or so earlier, put Pearl Kambu.

There was much clapping and excitement in the room, which lasted for a couple of minutes, before being terminated by the Attorney-General.

"Ladies and gentlemen, we shall continue now. Mrs Kambu, you may resume your petition , if you have anything more to add".

Pearl got up and said, "Mr Chairman, I am very sorry for losing my temper, and perhaps saying some things that I should not have said. Probably, it was the way I said it. I apologise , unreservedly, on behalf of myself and my friends".

"Thank you, Mrs Kambu", interjected the Chairman.

"All that I wish to add, Sir, is that the wives and children of the political detainees, appeal to you once again as father of the nation, to order the immediate release of our husbands. We are suffering enormously, Sir. We indeed are. Thank you. Sir".

She sat down, as her friends began to cheer and clap, whilst the Chairman and the panel looked on. A young officer shouted "Order, Order". This brought silence back to the room.

"My colleagues and I, during the break have reviewed your petition again in considerable detail. We are indeed anxious to help you all, but the nation's overall security must take priority. We are not conducting a personal vendetta against the detainees, I assure you. In view of your pleas and verbal appeals, we have decided that in addition to what we offered you before the break, we will further undertake a quick review of the detentions, and start a phased release, probably in three months from now depending on the security situation. Madam, that's as far as we can go at this moment. We hope that you appreciate our position".

He paused and looked at the Attorney-General briefly, then went on, "As for your unfortunate outburst, after consultations with A.G. we have decided to give you a two-day detention. However, taking into account your family situation, and your own unwarranted detention by military police, brief as it was, we reduce your detention as from now to ten hours". And as he said so he looked at his watch, and his colleagues nodded in agreement, whilst the A.G. put on a sheepish, fawning smile.

"Thank you all for coming. Thank you bishop", with that the Chairman concluded the session, and led his colleagues out of the room. Meanwhile Pearl Kambu was led politely to another guardroom nearby. "Somebody, please inform my Embassy about your detention", she shouted. And as she walked away, she could not resist turning to look at the military- police captain, avidly looking through the small, barred window, in the very room that an hour ago or so was the residence of Pearl.

The women were beginning to disperse. They were morose, depressed, but half-contented, that at least some of their requests, thanks to Pearl had been granted, but the bishop was far from happy. As the Chairman's team was leaving, he quickly went to one of the senior orderlies.

"Please, tell the A.D.C that I want to see the Chairman urgently for just a couple of minutes, not more than ten at most, if he can spare a moment".

The orderly relayed the request to the A.D.C. who, in trepidation, told his boss, carefully choosing his time, when the boss appeared a bit more relaxed and vulnerable. At first the Chairman was reluctant to see the bishop. For he had been very unhappy about the reports he had been receiving from the Military Intelligence and the Special Branch that the bishop had allowed the Cathedral to be used by the women for meetings and that he was giving them spiritual advice and material comfort. He was torn between his duty as a revolutionary and as a Roman Catholic. After a few moments deliberation, he puffed at his cigarette continuously, smiled, and sat quiet, looking vacantly in the air.

"Okay, let him in".

"Thank you, Chairman, for sparing the time to see me. I know how busy you are and I will be very brief. I see it's getting to one, and I'm sure you will be going for lunch, so I'm going straight to the point quickly".

"Take your time, bishop, and go ahead".

"I've come, Sir, to beg you in the name of God, the Almighty Himself, that you seriously consider the ten-hour detention of Mrs Kambu. This is too serious a matter for me to go away without the strongest protest personally to you, not only as Head of State, but also as a member of my flock, although of late I've not seen much of you.

Chairman, please, think, think and think again. Detaining an innocent, harmless mother of two small children, with her husband already in prison, without a charge or trial. Is this fair? Is it Christian? How would you feel if this is done to your own wife, Chairman? My spiritual duty and responsibility require that I speak to you frankly, without fear of favour, hoping and trusting that you will listen, reflect, and take the right decision. I hope I am not boring you, Sir, but may I state that this little matter is bound to be heard by the U.S. Embassy, the foreign press, the British and Israeli Embassies, and it will be blown out of all proportion. And should that happen it will be you, you alone, that will be held responsible, not your colleagues, not the A.G. but you, Kofi Johnson, alone".

The Bishop wiped off the sweat on his face with a white handkerchief, and stopped for a moment.

"I am listening", remarked the Chairman.

"Meanwhile, Sir, what happens to her children during the detention. Who is to look after them? And should anything happen to them, on whose head shall the blame lie? I am afraid, Sir it will be on the head of not the A.G., or the P.R.C, but on yours.

Finally, Sir, may I remind you, if you did not know already that Mrs Kambu is Jewish. Many of her relatives suffered unimaginably in the Holocaust. Her parents, from what I hear, are prominent, wealthy supporters of the Republican Party in New York. And once it gets through the Jewish grapevine what you've done, you would be wise to expect that sooner or later, the Jews will exact appropriate retribution. You mark it, Sir. For as a result of their heinous extermination during the Holocaust, the Jews have an unwritten oath never to allow a single one of them to be touched, innocently. Thus by taking her on, you are taking on not only Israel, but the Jews in the U. S., U.K, France, and elsewhere. Is it all worth it, Kofi? You simply cannot, cannot win, or expect to escape unscathed. So for Heaven's sake, and the sake of your own, think, think, and think again".

As he paused, the Chairman, asked, "And so what do you want me to do, bishop?"

"Simple, order her immediate release. You can do it, if you want to, Chairman".

"But it was a collective decision."

"Kofi, don't make me laugh! You know very well that whatever you say they will agree slavishly, with vigorous nodding and smiling.

"Wouldn't I lose face if I give in so easily, and be laughed at by colleagues behind my back that the Colonel had been beaten by a civilian housewife?"

"Nonsense, forget about what they will say behind your back and do the right thing as a Catholic. Don't forget, Chairman, that the same people who are today shouting "Hosanna, Hosanna" will be the very same people who will be yelling "Crucify him, crucify him". I hope that you've got the message, Chairman. I pray so". The Chairman smiled and then looking askance at the bishop said,

"Well, as a compromise bishop let's say five hours, that's about four hours from now. After all, I've to have something to tell my colleagues, so that it does not appear as a total capitulation. Try and see my problem too".

"Okay, let's agree on four hours", remarked the bishop. "The extra hour is a special request from your own church, the Romam Catholic Church. Right?".

Reluctantly, the Chairman agreed.

"Good. You've won. Four hours then. Let's go for lunch, bishop. I'll be honoured.

"Thank you Chairman. Very kind of you, but I am staying in the corridor, without lunch, or water, like Mrs Kambu, until she is freed, and I have returned her to her home and children."

"Bishop, you're difficult. Very tough", remarked the Chairman, as he called in his A.D.C. "Instruct the sergeant that Mrs Kambu is to be released three hours from now, and handed over personally to the bishop. Understood?"

"Yes, Sir?".

Bishop Antol left the Chairman's office and sat in the corridor on a hard seat. He spent the next three or so hours reading a small-sized pocket Bible and counting his rosary beads. The Chairman left for lunch by a back-door, so as to avoid the bishop. Meanwhile through the tiny, barred window of the cell, Pearl Kambu could see prominent citizens of Bassa, many of whom she knew as close associates of the defunct regime, walking past her to shamelessly renew their allegiances with the new military regime.

About an hour before she was released, a young tall colonel in mufti, opened her cell door and went, in, saying, "Madam, I am sure we've never met, but my wife tells me that when she was a student in New York, and your husband was an envoy there, you were very generous and kind to her in many ways. My name is not necessary. Sorry, I cannot help you much, or, release you, but I brought you this from my wife".

He then pulled a can of iced coca-cola from his pocket, gave it to her, and left the room. In the 3 ft. x 3 ft. cell, with very low ceiling, and a tiny window, with the temperature almost 100, and very humid, Pearl Kambu sipped the drink slowly, savouring every drop. And it somehow tasted more delicious and soothing than any other drink she had ever had in New York or elsewhere. She spent her time praying, thinking and humming the "Battle Cry of the Republic".

At precisely 5.30 pm, Pearl was released and handed over to the bishop as agreed. The bishop accompanied her to her home, where her children had been collected from school by an English neighbour, a school-mistress, who had been looking after them. On the way she stopped at a sweet shop and bought her children some sweets and fruits.

"Mummy, mummy, where have you been? We miss you mummy!" As the children ran to her lovingly, she tried to suppress the tears welling in her eyes.

"Hello, little darlings, sorry to be so late. I went to get you some lovely sweets and fruits. Sorry I was away for so long, my dearest".

Pearl and her children had a lovely evening, well, as lovely an evening as could be in the circumstances. They went to bed early, without any change in the routine of the children, despite the major drama unfolding all around them, both at home and outside.

Just after breakfast, the following morning, Pearl was getting ready to take the children to school when a military jeep drove into the front yard of her house. And out stepped an African woman of about forty, in civilian dress and a woman soldier looking about thirty-five.

"Good morning, madam, are you Mrs Kambu?", asked the woman soldier, with her companion looking on.

"Yes, I am, and what can I do for you?"

"Well, we have been ordered by the A.D.C. to the Chairman to take you and your children straight away to the Chairman".

"But the children are ready for school now. Why should they come along?"

"Madam, we are merely obeying our orders. I am sure there's nothing to worry about".

"Can't I drop them at school and go with you?"

"No".

"I see. Can I ring the U.S. Embassy before we leave. Only a couple of minutes".

"No. Look, madam, we're wasting time".

Pearl hurriedly closed her kitchen and a few other doors, and then mounted the military vehicle with her children. As she was about to be driven away she shouted at her maid, "We are being taken by force to the Mandalay Camp to see the Chairman. Tell the American Embassy".

Silently they drove away and were soon at the office of the A.D.C. to the Chairman, who was waiting for them.

"Oh, madam you are in. Good morning and nice to see your children. Always beautifully turned out. Great. The Chairman will see you shortly. Just a couple of minutes or so", said the A.D.C.

He spoke briefly on his intercom in a language that did not appear familiar to Pearl. Then he turned round to her, and remarked, in a friendly manner, "Let's go".

Mother and daughters followed the A.D.C. to the Chairman's office, where they were welcomed by their host, in a most relaxed way, as if the events of the previous twenty-four hours had simply not taken place.

"Really nice to see you, Mrs Kambu. I am so pleased you could come with your children. And I am sorry for the inconvenience that I've caused you".

"That's all right, Sir".

"I simply had to see you at the earliest possible opportunity", said the Chairman.

Pearl and her children looked on.

"Believe me, I am deeply sorry about what happened yesterday. And I wanted to apologise to you personally, for my role in it. It was nothing personal. After all, I've not forgotten your kindness to my children when you stayed with us, and also the lovely gifts you gave my wife and children when they came to say good bye to you, before our departure for Jamaica. How can one forget these things? And it is such a shame that our second meeting should be under such awful circumstances. I am upset and sorry".

"Well, Chairman, I understand. These are sad and difficult times for all of us, and I am equally sorry for losing my temper and saying what I should not have said, or, let's say, the way in which I said it. Please, accept my heart-felt apologies".

"You see, you lost your temper and I lost mine in public. That was not good. Now that I've apologised and you have done so, kindly accept this little present from me as a sign that we are friends again".

He pulled out of his wallet hundred US dollars in ten-dollar bills, and was handing them over to Pearl when she said,

"Chairman, I am a married woman and my religion and personal principles do not allow me to accept such a present. Thank you, anyway, Sir".

"So, you've really not forgiven me, eh?"

"I have Sir, but I simply cannot accept money from men, apart form my husband, parents or close relatives. It's nothing personal, Sir, against you. Believe me".

"I see. If you insist, then I give it to my two little friends here". And as he spoke, he gave each of Pearl's daughters fifty dollars, remarking, "Go and buy some lovely sweets and toys with it".

"Thank you sir, but please don't forget the plight of the detainees. Good Bye, Chairman".

The children curtseyed to the Chairman, who was looking at them appreciatively. Pearl also thanked him, and shaking her hands the Chairman said, "Good bye and good luck. Hope to see you soon". They were quickly led out of the Chairman's office by his A.D.C. who handed them back to the jeep-driver, and his companion, with instructions to drive Pearl and her children straight to the International School, and then to drop Pearl at her house.

The next day, Pearl was scheduled to visit her husband in prison. As always she was accompanied by her two children. Coup or no coup, they were always immaculately dressed, although Pearl herself had, since the coup taken to wearing only black, as a protest, till the release of her husband. Whilst the usual family conversation between her and her husband was taking place, in the presence of a prison officer, who was taking notes, the children piped in.

"Daddy, Colonel Johnson gave us fifty dollars each yesterday. He said we could buy sweets or toys with it".

George Kambu laughed, but was intrigued about the generosity of the Chairman to his children, until Pearl narrated to him the whole story. The prison officer looked aghast, and could only muster a little mummer, "You Americans are great", as the interview ended.

Through the grape-vine, by the bush telegraph, and by coded language, the news of the dramatic confrontation of Pearl Kambu and the Chairman, had quickly spread within the circles of the political detainees and their families. And as with such stories, it gathered more and more momentum and greater sensation, as it went from person to person. Indeed, one version even had it that an American woman, trying to slap the Head of State during the meeting, had been shot dead".

Well, the real true story was to come not from George Kambu, but from one of the detainees in Kurukuru prison, who had heard it even before George did.

The Deputy Minister of Civil Aviation, excitedly returned from the toilet, and was telling friends whilst Pearl and George were having their allotted one hour interview.

"Here we are calling ourselves big-men, minister of this and that. Brave men. Yet what Mrs Kambu has done, none of us could ever do, or dream of doing. We are all a bunch of cowards, that's what we are. Cowards, I say bloody cowards, we all".

"Calm down, old boy. Calm down. What is it?"

The excited deputy minister, walking about the ward, eventually settled down. Carefully and methodically, detail by detail, he narrated the story of the historic meeting between Pearl and the Chairman, and her subsequent arrest, detention and release. The ex-ministers were beginning to disperse back to their beds when one of them remarked morosely, "You can count on the Americans. If they come out to help they go all out. This is what I call proper marriage, not the type that begins to shake or break when you are in big trouble!"

That night, after the usual discussions and prayer, the ex-ministers and their colleagues went to bed in a very sombre and deflated mood. For they all agreed that indeed what Pearl Kambu had said and done, none of them, could ever contemplate doing. Indeed, they kept talking among themselves for so long, that it was only at about one in the morning that the place became quiet and peaceful.

Suddenly, at about 3.30 in the morning, pandemonium could be heard by the detainees from the quarters of the convicted criminals. There were incoherent shouts, here and there, but strongly could be discerned, in the local language,

"He's f . . . . . . my bottom. Please help. He is poking me. Hard".

The lights in the cells of the criminals all went on. The emergency alarm went on, and so did the lights in the section of the political detainees. As the ex-ministers were locked in, they could not get out to learn the truth of what was happening. This added to their puzzlement. It was only at about 8 am, that the

214

warder on duty in the section of the political detainees came in and told them of the story of what had happened.

Apparently, one of the prisoners, a man of about thirty, who was serving a seven-year sentence for rape, had viciously attacked an inmate, without going through the unwritten, prison ritual of wooing his intended partner with gifts of cigarettes, sardines, corned-beef or money. As such, his sexual overtures had been strongly repulsed by his companion, who had shouted asking for help to desist the unwarranted sexual attack. That the attacker was the senior verger of the prison church, a man looked upon by his co-prisoners as very upright in many ways, was an aspect of the story that tickled the warder enormously.

He concluded his story by informing the detainees that following a quick internal adjudication, the attacker had been given a year's extra imprisonment and the victim, a month for creating a public nuisance and noise. The warder himself was hilarious about both the attacker and the victim. He felt that the victim should have laid back quietly and enjoyed it, and then complained later officially, instead of disturbing the whole prison!

He left to resume his duties, as the detainees broke into a lively discussion about the history and causes of homosexual activity, whether it was hereditary, genetic, or self-acquired, and whether it is natural or unnatural.

Chapter 14

Six months after the military coup that had propelled Colonel Kofi Johnson, from the position of Deputy Commander of the Southern Brigade, to that of Chairman of the People's Revolutionary Council, and Head of State, everything appeared to be going at his behest. The weather was good, rain was plenty, the harvest bountiful. Food, machinery and vehicle parts, and other essential items such as medicines, fertilisers and building materials, ordered by the previous civilian, Republican administration, were all arriving at the airports and ports on schedule.

At home, Kofi Johnson was looked on as the Father of the Nation, the fount of all privilege, honour, patronage, and largess. Wherever he wet, waving his white handkerchief, as he drove in his official Rolls-Royce, he was hailed rapturously as king, president, prime minister, and much else rolled into one. Decent-minded, highly educated men, pillars of society, competed with each other in their public acclaim of the Chairman. Most of the businessmen that did so, felt they had to ensure that the large, juicy Government contracts and orders came their way.

The intellectuals were convinced that nothing short of public self-flagellation and kowtowing would ensure the safety of the public and other offices which they held. As for the media people perhaps they had no choice, as the radio and press were owned and run by the state, of whose employees they were.

Some women, were only to keen to give their all to the Head of State, or those close to them, to obtain financial favours for themselves or their close relatives or friends. Ironically, with all his pre-coup notoriety in the camp as a rabid womaniser, Kofi Johnson, with all the women at his disposal, flaunting themselves at him, was at last finding sexual relations more trouble than they are worth. Perhaps, the spirit was still willing, but certainly the flesh was weak, and getting weaker all the tome.

The army was completely loyal and the other ranks were proud of the fact that one of them, their own man, so to speak, was now in full control of the country. Their enthusiasm for his regime was particularly enhanced when their salaries were doubled overnight, and some of the perks which had been taken away by the ousted civilian regime were reinstated. There was simply no question of their assisting the return of the defunct Republican administration, or their revolting against the military junta. The least signs of trouble brewing were neutralised or if necessary, crushed vigorously.

Internationally, the Head of State's prestige soared, especially among European and American business-men that traded or did business with BASSA. They all agreed, with the local Asian and Lebanese business communities that Chairman Kofi Johnson was the best thing that happened to BASSA, since its Independence. Whether it was a result of the efficiency and drive of the press officers, diplomats and intelligence officers, attached to the various embassies of BASSA in Europe and America, and Asia, the fact still remained that Kofi Johnson, somehow, had achieved a respectability and honour abroad, especially in the foreign media, that never went the way of his civilian predecessors.

Only the university students, off and on, mounted some mild demonstrations on campus, but these were ineffectual. They were not reported by the local media. Foreign correspondents based in APPAPA generally ignored hem, and the local police ensured that the demonstrations were quickly dispersed, and the ring-leaders photographed secretly, either individually or collectively. Furthermore, the existence of paid informers within the student body, some of whom were the most vociferous among the student activists, saw to it that the plans and purposes of these innocuous demonstrations and protests were known to the authorities, right from the moment of their inception to the point of their execution.

No wonder Colonel Kofi Johnson, Chairman of the People's Revolutionary Council, and Head of State of Bassa, felt that indeed he was monarch of all that he surveyed. With some American and European officials calling on him, he felt a deep, inward self-satisfaction that he had beaten Idi Amin of Uganda, who considered it the apogee of his public career as Head of State that a British Foreign Secretary had had to crawl before him. Indeed, Chairman Johnson felt convinced that Amin's earlier achievement of having himself carried in a palanquin, openly and in public by whitemen, was no feat at all, compared with his own position.

It was in this happy, contented frame of mind and spirit, that Colonel Johnson decided to make his master move. On a Friday afternoon, during the one o'clock news broadcast there was a sensational news item.

"It is officially announced from the Chairman's office that the Chairman of the Joint Chiefs of Staff, the Commander of the Army, Navy and Air-Force, Heads of the Police, and the Border Guards, and their deputies, are retired with immediate effect. Also retired are the commanders of the Northern and Southern Brigades. Their future assignments, if any, will be announced later". The whole nation was stunned by this unexpected news. For many people had grown accustomed to the persons summarily retired, as some of the pillars of the military establishment. They had acted as a link with the civilian past, thus adding an element of continuity in the administration of public affairs, as seen and understood by many citizens. As no reasons or explanations were given for their abrupt and brusque treatment, the citizens of BASSA were puzzled and mystified.

However, the Colonel was keeping a secret promise which he had made in the early days of the coup to one of his close aides. The top-brass would be kept on to give an air of respectability, continuity and legitimacy to his junta, but as soon as they had served their collective purpose they would be dropped as hot bricks. This was what had happened, with his own new appointees, replacing the retired or sacked officers

Some of these men were sent out as ambassadors to far-flung ends of the world. Some were granted hefty commercial loans, at very low interest, to go into farming or business if they so wished. Some took no further appointments and preferred to stay at home and rest.

At the same time, the Chairman gave lucrative, prestigious public appointments to his old cronies. Sophia Fumey, was made Commissioner of Women's Affairs, and her toy-boy, through her constant persistence and persuasion, was appointed a senior adjutant in the navy, thus jumping over three other colleagues. Boozing and womanising old pals of the Chairman were not forgotten by him. They all got more than they deserved. Nor did he fail to remember the important persons in his past life; his former money-lender and the head of the Kuku shrine. The money-lender was appointed as special finance consultant to the Ministry of Finance, at a huge salary, and the priestess was given the accolade of "Spiritual adviser to the Chairman", on a mind-boggling salary.

Kofi Johnson's recipe for making friends and influencing people, by buying them off with attractive public offices, patronage or cash, seemed to have produced excellent results. The march of Kofi on the path of greatness and success was quite literally unstoppable. With all the incredible public adulation and praise from leading church men, traditional leaders and chiefs, the intellectuals and businessmen and women, not to talk of the masses, who went almost beserk anytime they saw him drive in public, the Chairman seriously felt that if his regime could not claim to last a 1000 years as Hitler claimed for his Third Reich, his would last at least a hundred years!

Yet curiously enough at the very moment when the Colonel felt completely invincible, was the time that Pearl decided to act. She had prayed, she had fasted, she had written pleading letters to eminent local chiefs, churchmen and intellectuals, begging them to intervene with the Chairman on behalf of the detainees including her husband. She wrote also to her own ambassador, and to the ambassadors of other Western countries. The theme was the same. Never despairing, she had also sent letters to the President of the United States, the Vice-President, the Secretary of State, the Assistant Secretary of State for African Affairs, the mayors of New York, and Washington DC and the governor of New York State. She wrote to her synagogue in New York, her parents and a few friends she remembered. All these overseas letters were smuggled out by sympathetic friends.

The local letters elicited no response whatsoever, except from the Roman Catholic Bishop of APPAPA. No one was prepared to stick his or her neck out for that "Silly American woman", as some called her. With power coming from the barrel of a gun, genuine local friends were very thin on the ground. They appeared to have vanished into the thin tropical air.

Most of the overseas pleas got no replies either. A few did, but apart from abundant expressions of sympathy, their general response was similar. "That they could not, in any way, interfere in the internal affairs of BASSA, but hoped that the detainees would be accorded their human rights under international law and convention".

Some friends and relations sent gifts of children's toys, clothes and money. Judiciously dividing her time between looking after her two children, taking them to school, appearing before the military assets tribunals, and going round fetching the pass for prison visits, and shopping, Pearl Kambu, still found time to relentlessly pursue the cause of her husband and his friends. Finding that her long, laboriously hand-written letters were yielding no positive results, she decided to alter her strategy. She arranged a series of informal meetings individually with the wives of the ambassadors of the United States, Britain, France, Germany and Italy.

At each meeting, she was politely received, given the best of tea or coffee and cakes, plenty of sympathy. Her request was the same all the time - begging the wives to request their husbands to intervene vigorously with the Chairman for the early release of the prisoners. To impress on the wives the seriousness of her plight, Pearl often went to the envoys' wives with her children. These diplomatic visits eventually led to a meeting being arranged for Pearl with the American Ambassador, John McGovern a tall Texan, Yale-educated, lawyer.

That Tuesday morning was momentous to Pearl, for she had pinned all her hopes on that meeting. She was of the view rightly or wrongly, that the U.S. Ambassador could solve all her problems. As she was led into the smartly-furnished office of the U.S. Ambassador, on that bright Tuesday morning, Pearl was rather nervous.

"Sit down, Mrs Kambu, welcome and nice to see you again. Have some coffee. How are the children?"

"Pretty well, Sir and thank you for agreeing to meet with me, despite your tight schedule. I appreciate it very much. Sir".

"Well, that's what we are here for", remarked the Ambassador.

"Mr. Ambassador, I've come to appeal to you personally to use your good offices to intervene with the Chairman of the People's Revolutionary Council for the release of the detainees. We are indeed suffering as a result of the detention of our husbands, and I thought that certainly a direct protest from you will help", she continued.

"Mrs Kambu, as you may well know since the coup my embassy has done its damnedest to bring to the attention of the new regime the plight of the detainees and their families. To both the State Department and to the regime, we have made our position clear, but you would appreciate that there's a limit to how far we can go. We cannot, and will not interfere in the internal affairs of BASSA, and any requests that we have made to date are purely on humanitarian grounds". He paused briefly, then resumed, "after all, Mrs Kambu, you, as an American citizen are safe, and none of our citizens have been touched. Our legal standing in this matter of detainees is thus a very tricky one, and we have to tread warily".

"But surely, Ambassador, considering that they have overthrown by force a freely elected, democratic government, which was anti communist, you could do more to persuade the State Department to intervene on behalf of these innocent people".

"As I said earlier, Mrs Kambu, this mission is doing all that it can to assist, believe me. You appreciate, I'm sure, that as Ambassador my duty is to inform, advise, and carry out the relevant policy sent to me here. We merely execute it. That's the position".

In between sipping her coffee, Pearl asked, "But surely, whatever policy is decided in Washington, is moulded on the advice of their man on the spot, in this case, you, Sir. And it appears to me that because the people in trouble are Africans nobody cares much. I'm sure if they were Poles, Germans or Jews, somehow, a formula would have been found or worked out to save them, or at least get them released and put under house arrest, Sir? What about the C.I.A. can't they help at all?"

"I can assure you that my position has nothing to do with colour, race or nationality. I'm duty-bound to report as faithfully and accurately as possible the current situation, and advise accordingly. What the final policy is decided on has really not much to do with us here. Sorry I cannot be more helpful. As for the C.I.A. they cannot be involved in such situations, not at all, especially following Watergate. However, as I told Betty to inform you, as a U.S. citizen, our doors and services are open to you and your children anytime. You can count on the consul, myself and the rest of the mission. We'll continue to do what we can". As he spoke, he began to get up, signalling by body-language that the interview was over.

"Well, I'm really disappointed that my meeting with you could not offer me more support and assistance. Still, Mr Ambassador, thank you, all the same for granting me this interview. Good-bye". She started to walk towards the door. The Ambassador shook her hands, and with a friendly. "Thank you for coming, Good-bye", he shut the door.

As soon as Pearl left his office, he called for the file on Mrs Kambu. His private secretary brought it in, and he began to leaf through the copies of the petitions to the President, Vice-President, Secretary of State, and others in New York and Washington that had been sent along to him. He sighed to himself, and reflected on his inability to do more to help his fellow citizen.

Pearl's efforts to elicit more positive help from the British, French and Dutch Ambassadors met with no success either. In each case, it was all politeness, respect and friendliness, but no further direct help in securing the release of the ex-politicians, than they had done already. In fact, it was beginning to appear to Pearl that all the Western ambassadors seemed to be acting somehow in unison. Ultimately, exactly a week after her unsuccessful meeting with the US Ambassador, she got an interview with the Israeli Ambassador, Daniel Levy, a retired Colonel in the Israeli Defence Force. Pearl was determined to grasp at this opportunity with both hands, and make the best out of it. She felt that it was high time she played the Jewish card.

With his usual politeness and friendly manner, Ambassador Levy welcomed Pearl into his office on a Tuesday afternoon, following her meeting with the US Ambassador.

"Hello, Pearl, Shalom, and so nice to see you. I hope you are alright. Do sit down, please".

He gestured her to a chair opposite his desk, then said, "You know Pearl, anything that I can do, I'm doing, but sadly, we are leaving".

"What, you mean leaving BASSA?"

"Yes, I fear so. Have you not heard it already? We've been asked to close the mission, following the break of diplomatic relations with Israel yesterday, and I have only a fortnight to pack up and leave. All of us".

"Good Lord, what's this? Just the time that I needed you so badly. What a shame. I have come to plead with you to request your Government to do more for the release of my husband and his colleagues. They are in a dreadful state, Ambassador". He listened carefully, with a sympathetic face.

"These people have committed treason, and other state crimes, and they should not be allowed to get away with it. Pardon my language, Daniel, but they are complete bastards, and should be punished for what they've done".

The Ambassador smiled, and said "I fully understand how you feel, Pearl, but there is very little that we can do. Our hands are tied by International Law, conventions, U.N. resolutions, and so many other restrictions. Furthermore, with diplomatic relations broken between our two countries, our influence here is reduced to zero".

"You mean, there's nothing that you can do here at all?"

"Yes, Pearl. That's the position. Nothing whatsoever".

"But what about something outside, Ambassador?"

"What exactly do you mean? I don't understand?"

"Well, to be frank, I mean assisting positively in the immediate removal of this bunch. Nobody will shed a tear for their demise, I assure you, if it's successful".

The Ambassador winced, and speaking slowly said,

"Pearl, you are seriously asking me or Israel to facilitate the removal of this regime. What a thought?. My Government will not countenance such an idea at all. It will be horrified, although it has broken diplomatic relations with BASSA. It simply cannot be done. Out of the question. Sorry, very sorry".

"But we did intervene in Uganda, by mounting that first class and almost impossible rescue mission of our captured people in Entebbe".

"Ah, Pearl, that was different. The very lives of our people were at stake, and as you know, since the Holocaust we vowed never again to sit back and meekly allow our people to be massacred. In Bassa now there's no such situation. You see there is a big difference. I am afraid we cannot intervene or help in anyway whatsoever. Sorry".

"What a shame. These animals are going to get away with it and perhaps stay in power for years and years. For if nobody from outside comes to help them, the people here cannot do much. They are mostly cowards".

"Well, I don't know about their being cowards, but if it is any consolation, may I remind you that the Third Reich which was planned and expected to last a thousand years, survived only twelve, blasted years. Twelve, horrific years impressed on the individual and collective memories of all Jews, and practically all, decent-minded God-fearing people, wherever they may be. That is life. Sometimes the impossible becomes possible".

"I understand", remarked Pearl dejectedly.

"By the way, don't forget, when we are no longer here and you have any urgent, life-threatening problem to contact her. Shalom and Good luck". He smiled as he said so, assuredly, and with that the interview came to an end. Pearl left Ambassador Levy's office confident that although she had achieved nothing, absolutely nothing, at least she had got a lot off her chest, and that she had banded about one or two ideas that perhaps might bear fruit, hopefully one day.

That Tuesday afternoon was to become a very memorable one in the life of Pearl, and for that matter in the lives of the African detainees languishing in various prisons right across Bassa, as involuntary official guests of the communist oriented, military regime of Colonel Johnson. For at the very time that Pearl's interview was going on with the Israeli Ambassador, unknown to her, three thousand five hundred miles away in New York city, her father Abraham Goldberg, after many secret negotiations, wheeling and dealing and lobbying, had been able to get the support of four very close New York friends of his, who, with him, had been able to raise ten million dollars. The money was the comfortable minimum needed to recruit a group of American and Israeli ex-officers, soldiers and intelligence personnel, needed to mount a successful military overthrow of the Johnson regime in APPAPA, release the detainees, and restore the ousted, legitimate administration. The road to that Tuesday meeting in New York had not been at all easy. Meetings and negotiations had to be conducted in the utmost secrecy. Indeed, apart from Abraham Goldberg himself, nobody knew the identities of the four other wealthy men who were bank-rolling the operation. The four preferred to remain completely anonymous, known only to Abraham.

The crucial meeting at which the nuts and bolts of the delicate operation were fully discussed was held not at Abraham's lovely house in Brooklyn, but in a modest hotel room in Manhattan, hired specifically for that purpose, by Abraham Goldberg, under an alias. All other meetings were to be held there.

At the initial meeting between Abraham and the three persons that he and then recruited, the urgency, seriousness and riskiness of the operation were laid bare. Of these persons, who formed the core hands and brains of the operation, one was ex-C.I.A, another was a retired Marines Colonel, and the other an ex-Major of the Israeli Defence Force. Their search and recruitment had not been easy, but ultimately had been achieved.

They were all tall, well-built men, exuding the air of confidence typical of the mature, successful American male. Although all were Jews, there was nothing, by physical appearance or accent which would associate them with the Jewish people. The meeting they were having in the hotel room that Tuesday was the first time the three persons had ever come together, although individually they had previously met with Abraham on a couple of times for briefing.

"Oh, it's so good, you all could make it dead on time", said Abraham as he opened the meeting. The time was about 6.30 pm.

"As I've informed each of you before, the assignment which you are undertaking is very exciting, high-risk and important. Upon its success depends your own lives and the lives of literally hundreds of others. This is an important, but worthwhile mission, against a dictatorial regime, which if not checked quickly, can cause a great deal of havoc and suffering. As such, you are engaged in a noble cause you can be proud of.

Everything possible will be done to make the operation a complete success, as you would see. It depends very much upon you. For purposes of this exercise you will go as representatives of a well-known US arms manufacturer to Bassa, its capital APPAPA. You are the core of the whole operation, and you are going there next month to establish a sound bridge-head for the on-coming contingent of soldiers, who after training will join you there.

"Any questions so far?"

"None", they replied together. "Also as you know too well, apart from your contract fees, suitable, very generous insurance policies have been taken up on your behalf, for the benefit of your next of kin individually. You will be referred to for all communications as Triple 5, Triple 4, and Triple 3, and you, Colonel will be the team's leader, that's Triple 5, and Major you will be Triple 4, and Jim as Triple 3. Right?"

"Yes, Sir"

"Suitable arrangements have been made with the Defence Supplies Inc. which will act as your cover 'employer'. Should any persons check your credentials or bona-fides, the company will supply appropriate information establishing your names and identities as respectable employees of theirs", Abraham went on.

"I think, Sir, that in view of the communist nature of the regime, perhaps, the CIA. may be interested in assisting, if we cautiously approach them", said Triple 5.

""Well, as ex-CIA. operator myself I would not advise it. First of all, they are very likely to refuse our request, especially so, since Watergate, and in so-doing we will unduly expose ourselves and gain nothing out of the operation.

Secondly, Africa is so low in the order of priorities of CIA. that I doubt very much whether what goes on in an obscure, little African state like Bassa would interest them very much.

Thirdly, when you think of the activities of Kim Philby of the British Secret Service, even if the CIA. decides to help, how do we know whether an inside mole may leak the whole or part of the operation to the Bassa Government, for ideological or financial considerations. How can you tell, gentlemen?."

His colleagues listened intently. Abraham looked round them and then said,

"I think Triple 3 is right. Absolutely right. These days one cannot be too cautious, and I am inclined to agree with him that we keep the CIA out".

"I suppose the same could be said for Mossad", said Triple 4.

"Yes", piped Abraham.

"Well, then, we do our own thing and stay out of their way", said Triple 5.

"If I may finish this collective briefing. You will be given generous entertainment and living expenses. Should stay in the best hotel in Appapa and entertain the military top-brass lavishly. No expense spared. You, especially Triple 5, should do everything possible to become a confidant of Colonel Johnson, of course, by a carefully worked out, stage-by-stage strategy. Work yourself into a position where he cannot do without you, move without consulting you or piss without seeking your advice". They all chuckled momentarily.

"If even this means licking his boots or sitting in the African sun naked, you should be ready to do so flawlessly and with aplomb.

Gentlemen, what's at stake is more important than the personal dignity or comfort of any of us. No stone should be left unturned to ensure the complete success of your mission, and your own safe return to your families. Right?".

"Yes", replied Triple 5.

"You should judge each situation and adjust accordingly. If a conversation sounds anti-American, then you join the chorus. If even necessary, Colonel you should manufacture a big quarrel with triple 4, and if you are in the confidence of Chairman Johnson, invite him to settle your quarrel. He would love playing the role of the big mediator.

You, gentlemen, are in the fore-front of a major operation, whose success will certainly create history. And towards that end, you're to play your roles perfectly as arms salesmen. And if this means, eating what you don't want to eat, drinking what you loathe, and dancing in public with your pants down, then so be it. One wrong move, and you've blown the whole thing. Right?".

"But what if sexual favours are placed before us, let's say, as a mark of the chairman's friendship and personal affection for us?", asked Triple 3.

"Of course, you should take them up, with both hands. Don't be a fool. Only you should, for your own protection and safety, wear a condom. After all, the sex act, by itself is nothing really. Like a crime, the act is only complete if the physical side, namely the sexual intercourse, is accompanied by the relevant emotional and psychological state of mind. And in your case, the latter would be missing, thus negating the whole thing. OK?, asked Abraham Goldberg.

"That sounds perfect and sensible", remarked Triple 4. After all, they would begin to suspect something odd or fishy, if they gave us lovely, attractive women and we behaved as if they were

1ot good for us", continued Triple 4.

"Ah, yes, on the question of your fees, as I informed you ndividually in our previous briefings, all the payments will be nade through your lawyers. Also the agreed insurance policies 1ave been effected, and copies deposited with you lawyers.

The problem of what happens in the unlikely event of a ailure. What would happen to you? This is a legitimate concern vhich we have seriously considered and gone over carefully. 5hould the unforeseen happen, and you are apprehended, you nay use the tiny cyanide tablets, which you would be given one each. If you find the torture or suffering unbearable and impos- ;ible, then you may consider using them. Otherwise, we have vorked out an elaborate scheme with some friends in the media, .o draw national and international support for you. We shall "aise hell and secure your release through the UN., Red Cross, ind our own contacts with the CIA. and other security organisa- .ions. Don't worry, we have friends in very high places, and will :ome to your immediate rescue. You can count fully on our "escue mission should anything untoward happen. Rest as- ;ured!", said Abraham.

"Good. Sounds all right. But you did mention the recruit- nent of the rest. Also their training".

"That's so. Whilst you are beavering away in BASSA, the "ecruitment and training of thirty colleagues of yours will take)lace here. Their final training sessions will be fine-tuned to fit n with your programmes and operational plans from BASSA, vorked out by you as the men on the spot. That's why your ;uccess in fulfilling your own roles is so vital to the success of the vhole operation. May I emphasise that this is a matter of life and leath. And hundred percent success is when you all return home ilive to your families and friends. If there is to be any death, let t be that of the black Hitler in BASSA and his evil cronies. Right?.

Finally, remember in all these Third World countries, the appropriate present, be it money or equivalent opens all doors. I mean all doors! So, although you are to keep strict record of expenses, as required by contract, remember, always to buy your way through. Don't spare any funds to save your lives". Abraham stopped for a while "I think we shall break for today", he said, when he resumed.

"Sure, real good", said Triple 5.

"You'll be informed of the date and time of your final briefing before departure. Meanwhile, get cracking on your visas for BASSA. I understand their consul here in New York, is a very friendly chap", remarked Abraham. They got up as he did, and after shaking hands, left one by one.

The next few days the three gentlemen spent studying their operational plans, and reading as much about their work as arms dealers. They also found time to learn a few local words and phrases of the major language in BASSA, which happened to be the one spoken by the Chairman of BASSA.

After an introductory visit to the Bassain consul in New York, followed by a grand lunch at a very expensive restaurant in Manhattan, the visas, valid for three months, were quickly secured. Furthermore, the arms manufacturers, armed with their glossy, expensive looking catalogues, so impressed the consul, that he gave them a very commendatory letter of introduction to the Bassain Military Attache in Washington, DC. The lunch, plus a modest gift had produced wonderful results.

Next stop was Washington DC. where the arms dealers, punctually kept their appointment on the next Wednesday afternoon, 2.30 p.m. with the military attache. The consul's letter did the trick. The military attache, in view of the importance of the trio's mission to BASSA, invited them to a lovely lunch at a famous restaurant in Georgetown. The Americans as a token of friendship, gave him a good, expensive watch. This was after the coffee had been served, when the military attache promised to give them a letter of introduction to the Chairman of the Joint Chiefs of Staff. This letter was particularly significant. Furthermore, the attache undertook to coax or persuade the Ambassador also to give an introductory letter to Chairman Johnson, as Defence Secretary.

The trio thus returned to New York City having achieved a personal introduction to the Ambassador, with a letter from him to the Chairman and one from the military attache to the Chairman of the Joint Chiefs of Staff. It was a remarkable achievement in a very short time, by soldiers who were making their first tentative moves in the diplomatic arena. Not bad at all. They were learning fast. And although, rather happy with their initial forays into deception, disinformation, and covert operations, they knew only too well that the test was yet to come. And the venue would not be New York, but in BASSA, in tropical Africa.

Returning to New York, they quickly went through the obligatory inoculations for travel to the tropics. After that they had a final briefing with Goldberg, at their usual venue. Everything was checked. Their appearances fitted their respective roles. They all looked typical American WASPs - tall, slim or well-built, blonde and immaculately dressed in blue or dark business suits. Triple 4 had a respectable-looking moustache. None wore a beard. They looked as good goys straight from the pages of the advertising magazines. Their knowledge of weapons and security systems was up to date. Standing and holding their expensive, leather brief cases, they oozed with the air of self confidence and money, associated world-wide with American businessmen.

Following a last farewell dinner on the Friday before their departure, at which all present, the trio plus Abraham, made the best out of the occasion, the date of departure was fixed for the following Tuesday. The flight was PANAM 001, to London, from J.F.K. Airport at 18.00 hours. At the airport, all were relaxed and looked as they should. They carried no letters, apart from the official letters of introduction. Except for their passports and health papers, credit cards and a few identification items, they carried no other tell-tale material. They chose expensive clothes and underwear suitable for the tropics. Their brief cases were bulging with US. dollars in various denominations. They also carried a variety of presents, expensive pens, watches, jewellery, and other items. They were ready to go.

Just before their departure, having kissed their wives Goodbye, Abraham told Triple 5,

231

"Please, find a way to call on her and give her my love. And assure her that everything is being done to solve her problem soon, so she should not worry at all. Do you remember her address?"

"Yes",

"In any case, why not accidentally bump into her at her favourite shopping centre, which I learn, is near the central post office. Right? Goodluck".

After their last flight call, the trio, the vanguard of the dicey, gigantic operation to remove Chairman Johnson of Bassa, disappeared into the departure lounge and were soon airborne. Arriving at London Heathrow, after six and a quarter hours flight, they took a taxi to London, and went to the Cromwell Hotel, in Kensington, where they had booked three adjoining rooms. A couple of days were spent in London getting over the jet lag, going over their plans and doing a bit of sightseeing. They took in the usual tourist attractions, Buckingham Palace, the changing of the Guards, St. Paul's cathedral, Tower of London, the US Embassy in Grosvenor Square, Mayfair, and Harrods. They also bought UK Government premium bonds to the value of £3000, £1000 for each of the three children of Chairman Johnson. Suitably armed with the Premium Bonds, presents and lots and lots of money, they left for APPAPA, the next Thursday, by the national airline of BASSA.

Arriving at the APPAPA international airport, they were met, surprisingly, by a young lieutenant from the army. He ensured that they were quickly whisked through Customs and Immigration, and driven by him to their hotel.

"Thank you, officer. This is a good introduction to your beautiful country. I'm sure we are going to enjoy our stay here."

"You're welcome, Sir. We received a telex from our military attache in Washington DC to look after you well. Don't hesitate to let me know if I can be of any help. This is my number", he said with a smile.

"Well, nothing special, tonight, just tired. We all need a good rest. Ah, we have a letter for the Chairman of the Joint Chiefs of Staff, so please, arrange for us to deliver it personally at the earliest possible time. Thank you".

"No problem. You're welcome, Sir".

"Goodnight, and once again our thanks".

"Goodnight, Sir". The young lieutenant then left the hotel and drove to his modest flat in the barracks.

At eleven in the morning after their arrival, fortified with a good, English breakfast of cereals, sausage and eggs and toast, watered down with black coffee, the American defence experts were led into the huge office of the Chairman of the Joint Chiefs of Staff of BASSA. General Paul Manu, was a tall, hefty officer, whose stiff bearing belied a kind and good heart. Forgetting the humiliations of the coup day, several months ago, he carried on with his duties professionally as if the coup had never taken place.

"Oh, what a pleasure to welcome you to Bassa. Do sit down, and feel at home", he gestured to them, as he showed them where to sit.

"Our military attache has already sent us a telex about your coming, and I hope that you will find your stay here useful and worthwhile".

As they sat down, he jokingly said, "You Americans are spoiled. You have everything in abundance - food, money, oil. Everything. No wonder you call it God's own country".

Triple 5 introduced himself first,

"General, we're honoured and delighted to be here and are touched that you could see us at such short notice. You are very kind. My name is Jamie Lynch, although most of my friends call me Jamie. My other two colleagues are Peter Sinclair, and John Branson. Sir, as you may probably know already, our company is one of the largest arms manufacturers in the US, especially in the fields of ballistics, counter insurgency and aerial warfare". He paused for a moment, and was delighted with the smile on the General's face.

"Sir, our catalogue says it all and we are here to offer the services of our firm, assess your needs, if you find us worth doing business with, and work with you. General, we firmly believe, unlike other arms manufacturers in co-operating actively with our clients to study their true needs and then satisfy them, in as cost effective a way as possible".

"That sounds very good", said the General as he listened. He momentarily looked at the glossy brochure that he had been handed.

"We are certain that this letter from your man in Washington DC speaks for itself. General, you have a first-class chap in DC. Very sound".

"Pleased to hear that. I recommended him for that post, and I am very pleased with his performance so far".

Jamie continued, "Sir, we wish to assure you right from the beginning that your request is our command, and we will be pleased at all times to be of service to you in anyway. Each of us is a specialist in his own field, but collectively we work together to produce a solid, coherent objective, to the satisfaction of our clients. Later, Sir, in confidence I shall give you some names of our clients."

As Jamie spoke his two colleagues looked on politely.

"Don't bother, Jamie, if I may call you so. Our DC man has provided us with the relevant vetting reports on your company and your positions in them and we welcome you to Bassa as friends. Naturally, you need a couple of days of acclimatisation it's too hot here. Hotter than Florida or the Nevada Desert, think. By the way, how long are you planning to stay?"

"As long as you want us, General".

"Well, the General chuckled. The Americans smiled politely but said nothing.

"My own view is that as you cover such various important aspects of the defence industry, it would be best to introduce you to the Defence Secretary himself. I mean the Chairman himself. Meanwhile, I will set up a small ad hoc group of senior officers to study your proposals and suggestions. What about that?"

"Sounds, fine by us, Sir", remarked Jamie. "I think my friends agree with me".

"Sure. Sounds great and businesslike. So I suggest, if I may that you return to your hotel, and start your local adjustment process. As soon as the Chairman is free to see you, we'll give you a call. Meanwhile, if there's any problem or request, don't hesitate to contact my ADC."

"Sir, before we leave, we've brought you a little gift from the US, as traditional African custom demands. We are merely going by protocol, and we trust that you'll find our modest present acceptable."

As he spoke, Jamie pulled out of his jacket breast-pocket, a beautiful, little box containing an expensive ROLEX wrist watch.

The General, opening the box, exclaimed in a very satisfied tone,

"Good Lord, what a marvellous thing. Terrific. The sort of gift to be treasured, and kept as a family heirloom, passed on from generation to generation. I really do appreciate it very much. You are so kind!"

General Manu hugged Jamie then shook his hands vigorously.

"See you all soon", he said as he said Goodbye to the trio. His ADC ordered one of the staff cars to take the visitors to their hotel. When they were gone the General sat back in his heavy chair, and smiling, weighed the gold watch in his hands for a few seconds.

"Get me the Chief, quickly", he ordered one of his secretaries.

"Sir, the Chief is on the line".

"Good afternoon, Sir. Sorry to bother you, but I need to introduce to you three American defence experts, who have just called on me. Chief, they are terrific, and I think we can do business with them. Their leader is bringing a letter to you from our man in Washington DC, and they have been highly recommended by one man in DC, Sir", remarked the General gladly.

"OK, I would love to see them. Certainly, but General, are you sure hat they are not CIA operators, under cover as businessmen. The CIA is very ingenious and resourceful, you know."

"Chief, they are kosher. Our military attache in Washington did a discreet vetting of their company and the chaps before clearing them. Their brochure and catalogue are a piece of art, out of this world. You just look at them."

"OK, General, let them come tomorrow at 4 p.m., sharp. You know Americans are sticklers for punctuality. By the way, General, how was the meeting yesterday?"

"Went very smoothly, Sir. Very good, will be reporting to you fully soon."

"Cheers then, General. See you tomorrow and thank you for calling."

No sooner had the General finished talking to his boss, than he ordered his aide to book the appointment with the Head of State's office, and arrange the necessary security clearance. He also instructed him to inform the Americans that they were scheduled to meet the Chairman, Kofi Johnson, the Head of State, the following day, and should be ready to be collected at 3.30 p.m. at the foyer of their hotel.

At ten minutes to four the military staff car conveying the three Americans had been cleared through all three security gates. And at one minute to four, the three gentlemen were announced in by the ADC to the Head of State. Standing next to Chairman Johnson was the General, beaming with a friendly smile.

"Well, Chief, these are our American visitors. That's Mr Jamie Lynch, he team leader and his colleagues Mr John Branson, and Mr Peter Sinclair."

"You are welcome to BASSA. How do you like it so far?"

"Pretty good, Sir, excellent. A bit like home."

"I hope you enjoy your stay", said Chairman Johnson, who then signalled to his aide to leave the room.

"The General has told me quite a bit about your visit and I really look forward to some useful work between you and him. It all depends on him", he said, as he turned to the General.

As they sat down, the General said, "Chief, they brought you a letter from our man in Washington. I don't know whether you want to read it now, Sir."

"Sure", remarked Chairman Kofi, as he took the letter from Jamie.

"How's the land of plenty?", he asked, "America should help us more. We need help, we're a small, tiny country", intoned the

Head of State as he gestured with his fingers to demonstrate the smallness of BASSA.

"Good. Very good letter. Welcome once again. Although I'm the Defence Secretary, the real work is done by the General and his staff, so if you pass muster by him, then it's okay with me. He's my right-hand man, and in these matters I go by what he advises. He's a first-class officer. The General is my mentor in more ways than one", the Head of State went on. The Americans listened intently and politely,

"Let's have some tea, gentlemen", remarked the Head of State.

"That's a very good idea, sir. Very kind of you. That's the traditional Bassain hospitality that we've heard so much about. So kind", said the visitors

Appropriate instructions were sent out, and shortly a large silver tray, with the best bone china, and solid, silver cutlery, both bearing the coat of arms of the Head of State, was brought. A variety of cakes and biscuits were also brought in by white uniformed household staff.

Over tea the Chairman and his right hand man discussed some of the proposals and ideas of the visitors, with much of the talking being done by the businessmen. A few questions were asked here and there by the Chairman. The tea and the meeting were brought to a close by the Head of State when he said, "I am reasonably happy with what I've heard and seen so far. However, a lot of work remains to be done before we can conclude anything positive. So, please liaise with the General and keep me in touch. "As he said so and began to rise, the visitors and the General got up with speed, bowed and took their leave.

However, just as they were about to walk away from the presence of the Head of State, Jamie said, "Your Excellency, Mr Chairman, may I request humbly a brief talk with you alone, of not more than a couple of minutes."

"Sure, but not too long."

"Well, Chief, if you don't need me still, then I had better rush to see to some backlog, Sir. I request permission to leave."

"Granted, but ring me tomorrow morning after the meeting,

237

Right?"

"Yes, Sir", said the General. He saluted smartly and left. The two Americans calmly waited in the private office of the ADC.

"Mr Chairman, I felt that although we are a team, there are certain things which I prefer to do alone, without my good friends being present. I trust them absolutely but certain situations are best dealt with on a person-to-person basis."

"Sit down, Mr Lynch."

"Mr Chairman, I brought these little gifts from home as African custom demands. There's this gentleman's gold watch, for you, Sir, and this jewellery for madam". Taking them from Jamie, Chairman Kofi Johnson glowed with pleasure and delight.

Jamie went on, "Sir, I even did not forget your children. In London I bought these Premium Bonds, sold by the UK government. I bought £1000 each for each child of yours, and let's hope that one of the numbers wins any of the weekly prizes which range from £250,000 (half a million dollars) to £50 (100 dollars).

The beauty of it all is that the holder of the bonds can get his money back at any Post Office, if he wins or does not win. He cannot lose.

"Go on, Mr Lynch, how can this be? Who has heard of a lottery draw in which you can get your money back when you don't win. That's impossible. Come on."

"Sir, it's true. The lottery has been run by the UK Government for several years, but not many people know about it. The prizes are derived from the interest which you would have normally have accumulated on the moneys used to purchase the bonds, if the moneys were in a bank. That's how, Mr Chairman."

"Fancy that. I've diplomats in London, and one intelligence officer there, yet I don't hear about such things. I doubt whether they even know about it themselves. Completely useless. Just eating and drinking champagne and running after white women. That's my diplomat's contribution to BASSA."

"Mr Chairman, I don't think you should be too hard on them, with all their problems, duties and the rest. Still I am so happy and delighted that you like it. Let's hope your children win prizes, weekly and monthly. Who knows the jack-pot may be waiting for them."

"That would be nice. As a matter of fact I would like to buy some for myself, my wife and a friend or two."

"Sir, it's very simple. You just fill in the relevant form and sign it. Each person can buy a maximum of 30,000 US dollars, that is, £20,000. Incidentally, we took from a London post Office, some of the application forms, and they are in our hotel. I can, Sir, send them straightaway, or as you instruct. No problem. I hope that when the Chairman wins the jack-pot, again ad again, he will not forget me, Sir."

"Certainly not. Why should I? Well, I think your friends must be wondering what is happening, so you better be going now." He pressed a small electric bell near his desk, and in shot one of his aides.

"I trust you and the General get on well, and produce some useful proposals for us. Nice meeting you, Jamie. Goodbye", said Chairman Johnson, as he shook the hands of Jamie Lynch.

Three days after their arrival in Appapa, Jamie and his team were summoned to the office of the Chairman of the Joint Chiefs of Staff, General Manu. It was a rather cold morning, by tropical standards. The General welcomed the team in his usual affable way. As he introduced his team of four officers, he said,

"These are the guys you would be working with. Brilliant staff officers, they will need from you quality specifications, prices, details of spare parts, training programmes, and the rest. I expect a thorough exchange of ideas and views, so that the final report which we put before the Chairman is really solid and acceptable. Right?"

"Yes, Sir", replied Jamie.

"And I think two or three weeks at most, including visits to relevant arms depots to assess what is at present available, et-ce-tera, and what are the minimum and maximum needs, considering the financial position of our nation."

"Sir, I suggest a month at least, given the amount of travelling that will be involved. I don't think it would be advisable to rush things, Sir", suggested the most senior among the Bassain officers, detailed to work with Jamie's group.

"Hmm. If we delay too long, the boss will soon be breathing down our necks, Furthermore, he may need your report urgently, in order to compare with another one which he got from a Swiss team a few weeks ago. You see the problem, chaps?", asked the General.

Over coffee the American and Bassain teams began to get acquainted with each other, and they got on very well. Even at this initial meeting the Bassain officers were so impressed not only at the glossy, expensive-looking brochures of the Americans, but also by the knowledge, expertise and smooth talk of the Americans. Their informality and easy-going manner struck a very friendly chord in the hearts of the Bassains. The Americans returned to their hotel completely satisfied with the progress so far made.

At precisely 2 p.m., following their meeting with General Manu, Jamie's telephone at the hotel rang.

"Good afternoon, Sir. This is the Chairman's M.S., I mean Military Secretary. You are requested to report at the Chairman's office at 3 p.m. today. An official car will come to pick you up, at 2.45 p.m.. Sir. Thank you, Sir."

"I sure will be ready at the foyer", said Jamie.

He quickly spruced himself up, armed himself with one or two brochures, catalogues, and premium bond forms. He also took along photos of his wife and children, and his US passport. As always he had a few one-dollar, and five-dollar bills with him for emergency tips to the guards, gatemen, and ushers, for goodwill.

"Folks, I've just had a call from the Chairman's office. He wishes to see me at 3 p.m. today. I don't know what it is about, you just keep your fingers crossed for me, and hope that everything goes well."

"This is good news, Jamie. Everything seems to be going smoothly. I'm sure that the boss has taken to you, and wants to put some big business in our way. I am certain of it. Meanwhile, Good luck", remarked Peter Sinclair, as his other friend looked on.

Arriving at Chairman Johnson's office, Jamie was quickly led to his small, private office, attached to his main office, where a few days before Jamie and his two colleagues had been welcomed. The Chairman welcomed him profusely.

"How are you doing Jamie? Hope you are not finding the weather too hot. It takes some time to get used to it, and I would advise you and your friends to take it easy. Sit here my friend. Sit down."

"Thank you, Sir", Jamie said, as he sat down. "By the way, Chairman, here are the Premium Bond forms which I promised you. Also I thought you may be interested in these photographs of my wife and children."

"What a lovely family. Well done. Good family man, That's the type I want around me. They are more responsible than single men. Don't you think so?"

"I agree with you entirely, Sir. You are absolutely right."

"Jamie, I called you here on a very important matter. I've been thinking very much about you and the possible services you could render me personally." He puffed on his cigarette, then continued, "Do you believe in Fate? Well, I do and I believe your coming to me is the answer to my prayers to God. I need somebody honest and hundred percent reliable, and I've been looking round for one for many weeks. I want someone absolutely reliable and discreet that I can trust implicitly. All I've round me are people who pay lip-service to me, but who are damned treacherous and would stick the knife in my back if they got the chance", he kept looking at Jamie as he spoke.

"Sir, I am at your complete service, with the utmost discretion. My team and I are here to service you and work with you, to your satisfaction. We've no interest here but to do a job, as demanded or instructed by you, and then with our work completed, quietly leave Bassa."

"That's the spirit, the type I want, who has no direct personal interest or involvement with BASSA. Just here to work and leave", said the Chairman.

"Before I instruct you on what I want you to do, Jamie, I fear you must first swear an oath of allegiance to me."

241

"No problem, Chairman."

"Well, you are to strip naked, completely naked, and repeat the following words after me, with your left hand on my ceremonial sword, and your right raised above your head."

Jamie did as he was told, and then repeated the words, "I, Jamie Lynch, a US citizen, do swear by the Kuku Shrine to execute all the orders from Chairman Johnson, with absolute faith and honesty, divulging no information whatsoever to any person. So help me God."

Duly sworn in, the Chairman then pulled out a small paper cup from his drawer, and ordered Jamie to urinate in it. This he did. "Now drink it. It's quite harmless. Indeed in parts of India it is used as medicine. Go ahead, Jamie."

Without wincing or exposing his inner feelings, he drank his own urine.

"Now you are fully initiated we can talk. Now and for the future my prestige and life are going to be in your hands, and I shall trust you absolutely above all others. My life is in your hands completely. Don't forget that if you try anything funny or disloyal, this is BASSA, and it will not be too difficult to arrange a convenient car accident or heart attack for you. This is a matter of life and death for both of us. You understand?"

"Yes, Sir",

"Jamie, I want you to leave all this defence survey and review to your two friends, and undertake some secret assignments for me. Forget about your work with the General and the rest, and devote all your energy and attention to my work."

"Certainly. Will do as instructed, Sir."

"I want you to go to Switzerland, open an account for me, and deposit there some money, gold and diamonds. You know that as Head of State, I cannot easily go there, it would look too suspicious. Also my bodyguards and secret servicemen would get to know of it. Furthermore, no sooner have I travelled out of the country, than some idiot would be trying to overthrow me. You see my problem, Jamie."

"I do, Sir and I do sympathise fully with you."

"You will be provided with a diplomatic passport tomorrow,

242

a first-class air ticket to Geneva, and back, with an ample expense account. Can you do it, Jamie, can you leave in the next couple of days."

"No problem, Sir. Can leave tomorrow, if you wish, Sir."

"You should travel all alone, and don't get in touch with the Bassain embassy in Geneva."

"Sir, may I suggest Zurich, so that we cut out completely Geneva, where your embassy is."

"Good. Bright chap. You may need to do three or four trips in all, as the moneys to be carried over are rather a lot. You know, once you are in a position like me in the Third World, you would be foolish not to think of a future safe-haven abroad, in case of the usual expected emergency. You see what I mean, Jamie ?"

"I do, Sir."

The Chairman next led him to a small ante room where there were five diplomatic bags and four wooden boxes. As he pointed them out to Jamie, the Chairman said,

"They contain, five million US dollar bills, gold bars and diamonds to the value of twenty million dollars. And you would deposit them in Switzerland. OK",

"Absolutely."

The next few minutes were spent on general family chatter, in a most relaxed and friendly atmosphere. The two men got on famously, like brothers.

"By the way, Sir, may I make two requests?"

"Sure, shoot ahead."

"First of all, I was asked by a friend of a family friend in New York to give his love personally to his daughter here. One Mrs Pearl Kambu, and I don't know how to contact her at all. Will it be asking too much for one of your aides to direct me to her house?"

"That's very easy. I shall order the driver to take you there on your way back. She's a good, honest woman, but mind you, she is Jewish and does not like me very much. Still, do give my warmest regards to her and her children."

Secondly, sir, please, ensure through the General that my two colleagues do as much work as possible, visiting the relevant depots and centres. We want our work here to impress you and our folks back home, Sir."

"Don't worry about that. You fulfil your Swiss assignments well, and you can rest assured about the contracts for your company back home. That should be the least of your worries. Here I decide. Right? You're just the type of person I've been looking and praying for. A non-Bassain, close adviser and defence expert, who will be 100 per cent loyal to me. And your reward for that will be my absolute trust and your elevation to the position of my chief adviser on everything-defence, foreign affairs, local affairs, security and all the rest. I think that's a fair bargain."

"Yes, Sir. Absolutely."

The two men continued their informal talk for a few more minutes. Then the Chairman got up, and with a hearty "Good-bye, Jamie", called in one of his aides to get Jamie to Mrs Kambu's house, on his way to the hotel. Both men thus broke off, completely satisfied and delighted with the outcome of their meeting.

It was a pleasant surprise that late afternoon when Pearl Kambu saw a white man come out of his car and walk towards her door. For since the coup, her friends and visitors, both black and white, male or female, had become fewer and fewer. The occasional American or British diplomat dropped in, that was all.

"Good afternoon, Mrs Kambu. I am Jamie Lynch, from New York, with a message from your daddy."

"Do come in and sit down, what a pleasant surprise. Really fantastic. How's mum? And my dad?"

"Both are very well; in the pink of health."

"And the shop?"

"Doing great, I was told by your dad. Well, Mrs Kambu, I ..."

"Oh, call me Pearl."

"Well, Pearl. I am on a very important mission and have to be brief. Your dad wants me to assure you that all your letters have been received with thanks and that everything is being done soon to change the situation. You understand. Towards that end two friends and myself are here as representatives of a US arms manufacturing company. We shall be here for a while, and would be working closely with the Government. Don't breathe a word of this to anyone, on pain of death. If we need to contact you, we shall do so appropriately. You continue life as usual. There is no need to be writing further to your parents. Everything is under control, Pearl."

"It is vital for the operation and your possible future role in it, if any, that you keep up with your present routine and way of life, as if nothing is happening or is expected. Right?"

"Yes, Jamie. Sure."

"How are the children doing?

"Pretty well, thank you. Would you want to see them now?"

"Pearl, another time. There'll be plenty of time for that. Give my love to them both. But don't forget, when ever you see me in public, or elsewhere please ignore me. If I need to talk with you or any of my two colleagues we will do so, but otherwise always ignore us, if we ignore you. OK? And no more letters to New York. OK?"

"Yes, Jamie. And thank you very much for coming. Love to dad and mum. Goodbye. Shalom!"

"Shalom, and bye-bye", and shaking her hand firmly, Jamie left to join his car back to the hotel. Dropped at his hotel, his five-dollar bill tip to the driver made a good impression on him.

Jamie quickly called a meeting of his two friends at his own room, where he narrated to them, word for word, detail by detail, what had transpired at the office of the Chairman, and at Pearl's house. The excitement of his two colleagues was apparent to Jamie, who concluded his report by stating calmly,

"Gentlemen for the next two days or week it's vital that you pursue your work with the military team assiduously. Use every opportunity they give you to study the location and layout of the broadcasting centre, the Kurukuru prison, Government House, the Airport and the ammo depots, all in the course of duty. Ignore me completely. Indeed occasionally you should complain jokingly to your Bassain counter-parts or the General that you now see less and less of me, and that you are both doing the donkey work, whilst I sip champagne with the Chairman. You see what I mean, a similar joking criticism against me. Also occasional mischief such as inviting some of them to dinner for a tete-a-tete conversation, without me, will all help to consolidate their confidence in you, and assist in my own relations with the Chairman. Any questions?", asked Jamie.

"As we appear to be progressing so well, so fast Jamie, should we start exploiting possibilities of building a sound contact in the Bassain top brass. What about it?", enquired Peter.

"Not yet, Peter not yet. We have to go gingerly. Indeed err on the side of being too slow. Time is on our side, folks."

He stopped momentarily, then resumed, "By the way, I shall be travelling to London soon, possibly a few more such journeys. Don't be at all worried. It's all part of my role in the scheme of things. You carry on with your work, making friends and influencing people. No letters or telephones back home, only the occasional post card to your families, if necessary. Whilst abroad I will telephone Abraham and brief him fully and appropriately on your behalf and my own also", Jamie concluded.

They retired to Peter's room, where they ordered dinner by room service and had a thoroughly enjoyable, celebratory meal.

Meanwhile in New York, Abraham Goldberg, had begun the recruitment of the main assault team. It consisted of ten Israeli Jews, all ex-Mossad, and ex-Israeli Defence Force Paras, and twenty ex-Marines and Green Berets from the United States. Again they were all American Jews, with the fitness, strength and dedication vital for the assignment ahead. As with Jamie's team, their fees, insurance and other details were appropriately worked out with their lawyers in New York, to the complete satisfaction of the men concerned and their lawyers. All that was left to be done, from Goldberg's point of view, was a word from Jamie advising them on the next phase to be implemented, namely the training of the thirty men for their tropical assignment.

The recruitment of the ten Israeli Jews had not been at all easy. However, through contacts established by a friend of a friend of Abraham in Jerusalem, the problem was eventually olved. And the ten first-class, dedicated soldiers were flown to Brooklyn in New York. With the recruitment of the American Jews, once the men were told of the anti-Semitic, anti-American, anti-democratic, pro-Communist nature and flavour of the Bassain military regime, they were very understanding. Their financial interest in the venture then began to assume a significant ideological commitment and dimension.

A week after Jamie and his team had arrived in Bassa, and had settled into the daily routine of meeting their local counter-parts studying the defence needs of Bassa, their costs and other problems, Jamie was called by Chairman Johnson's ADC, on a Wednesday morning, before he left the hotel.

"The Chief wants to see you at 5 p.m. today at his office, Sir. A car will come and collect you at 4.30 p.m. Is that all right, Sir?"

"No problem. I'm honoured and will be in the hotel foyer at 4.30 p.m. Thank you. Cheers."

At 4.30 p.m., one of the military staff cars attached to the Chairman's office, collected Jamie and whisked him to the office of the Head of State.

"Sorry, to have brought you here on rather short notice, Jamie, but I knew that I could count on you", said Chairman Johnson, dressed in a nice, grey suit, as he welcomed him.

"How are you, anyway?"

"Great. Feeling wonderful in your marvellous country. Your people, Sir, are so friendly and so courteous".

"Nice to hear that, Jamie. I fear you are to go on your first assignment tomorrow. This will be your trial run, and we see how things go. Right?"

"Yes, Sir".

"When you return to your hotel, please, give one or two passport photos in a sealed envelope to be returned immediately to me personally. Your diplomatic passport is ready for you, bar the photo and your signature. A first-class return ticket to London, for departure in the morning by British Airways is ready. Here's something for travel to Switzerland and back to London, plus ample hotel and spending money. Do enjoy your-self. As the saying goes, all work and no play makes Jack a dull boy. OK?" He puffed on his cigarette, then said,

'Ah, I nearly forgot, try and avoid my diplomats in London and Switzerland. They can be such a nuisance. I hope that everything goes well, and in an extreme emergency, you may ring me on this secret number. Also when you've successfully completed your mission, you should immediately send me directly a telex from London stating simply "My directors have fully accepted your business proposals. Boston".

Opening a side door that led to his main office, Chairman Johnson, pointing to some boxes said,

"You're to go with boxes one and two, and the diplomatic bag. You get ready tomorrow morning about ten in the morning, and a private car, carrying this cargo, will come and collect you and your personal effects straight to the plane. There will be no Security, Customs and other checks. Everything has been seen to, OK?"

"Oh, you're so kind, Sir. Just the sort of military perfection Sir, which has brought you where you are now. Terrific, Chairman. Sir, may I suggest that you give a tinkle to the General to ensure that my team's work goes ahead whilst I'm away. I don't, Sir, want the mice to play whilst the cat is away".

"Jamie, don't worry about that. Let them carry on at their own pace. After all, this is the Tropics, not America. You worry about your assignment, and let them do their own thing. You see what I mean?"

"Yes, Sir".

"So, if I don't see you again, goodbye and goodluck for tomorrow. By the way, don't forget to send the photos today by the driver, and the car coming to collect you will bring along your passport, requiring only your signature to complete it. Cheers my good friend. Good luck. See you soon".

"Goodbye, Sir, shall get in touch with you as soon as possible Sir. Once again my heart-felt thanks to you for your confidence in me. It will never be misplaced or abused. Goodbye, Sir".

The Chairman shook Jamie's hand firmly, and hugged him then showing him the door, said, "See you soon".

The following morning, at about ten, Jamie was quickly

whisked through the V.I.P section of the International Airport of APPAPA, with all the local officials showing due respect, by saluting and nodding approvingly. After a non-stop uneventful flight of six and a quarter hours, Jamie landed at Heathrow Airport, where he passed through the "Nothing-to-declare" section without any problem. He immediately hailed a taxi and drove to the Mayfair Hotel in London's West-End, where he secured a room for an overnight stay. After a refreshing cup of tea, and cookies, he settled down to telephone Goldberg in New York. It was about 18.30 GMT, that's 13.30 hours in New York, and Abie was completing his lunch of salad, salami and bread when his telephone rang.

"This is Triple 5, Abraham. How are you doing? I am in London, on my way to Switzerland to deposit a fortune there on behalf of your friend. Oh Abraham, we've almost made it so far. Peter and John are working on the defence needs with access to the airports, armouries, Broadcasting House, Government House and all the major sensitive centres of government.

"Fantastic and unbelievable. You lucky lads. Well done".

"And I'm already initiated by a weird voodoo custom as your friend's right-hand man. His life is almost in my hands. Everything is going well, very well. Too good to be true. To cap it all, he's become so enamoured with us, especially with me, that we have been provided with official, chauffeur-driven cars, and the hotel expenses waived by Presidential order. And for this present assignment, he's given me enough to hold a celebration on, when we return. How's phase two going?"

"Well, I've completed the recruitment, and begun the initial training, waiting for your go-ahead to begin the intensive training. So we can go ahead now, Jamie?"

"Certainly. Sure. We may have to push forward our plans by a few weeks. It's a case of striking while the iron is hot, Abraham. Tomorrow morning, I leave for Zurich and after my assignment there I shall give you a ring. Cheers for now. Shalom".

"Shalom to you. Shalom again. Goodbye", remarked Abraham before he put his phone down, a happy and delighted man.

The following morning Jamie, using his diplomatic passport, caught the ten o'clock Swiss Air plane to Zurich, and was there by two hours. He dashed, by taxi, to the Swiss Corporation Bank in Martin Luther Street, where he duly opened a secret account in the name of Kofi Johnson of P.O. Box 8285, APPAPA, BASSA. He gave in the diplomatic bag and the two boxes, whose contents were evaluated, counted and checked. The 100 dollar bills came to three million, and the gold and diamonds were valued at five million dollars.

Jamie gave in a piece of paper with Johnson's signature on it, and also a small letter, which read briefly, "The undersigned, Colonel Kofi Johnson, of P.O. Box 8285, Appapa, Bassa, do hereby authorise only Colonel Jamie Lynch of P.O. Box 8285, Appapa, Bassa, to operate this account on my behalf", signed Kofi Johnson".

The dour Swissbank Manager, with a bland, expressionless face, read the letter and took it. With the formalities completed, he gave a receipt to Jamie, stating the total amount, and also a round copper disc with the number 6350 0783 on one side. With his delicate job fully discharged, Jamie took a taxi to the airport and three hours later was back in a London hotel, a very happy man indeed. He immediately telexed his mentor in Appapa.

In Appapa, Chairman Johnson was going through some memos from the Defence Department, when an aide brought in a sheaf of telex messages in a dark-green folder. Among them was a message from London, stating "My directors have fully accepted your business proposals. Boston". The Chairman sighed with relief and smiled as he held the telex in his hand.

True to his word, Jamie immediately telephoned his New York mentor.

"This is Triple 5 again, Mission completed. I've just deposited eight million in your friend's newly opened account in Zurich. Cracky! I've just informed him by telex, and he must be over the moon. The personal identification number disc is with me now."

"Marvellous. Terrific. I think we should go ahead straightaway. Don't you think?", asked Abraham.

"Absolutely. Proceed with the training. I am sending you today by air courier a large envelope with all the relevant details, photos and internal diagrams of the strategic objectives, operational plans, and the rest. I was thinking of popping to you myself with these materials, but I thought it would look too suspicious if he got to know of my sudden visit to New York. What do you think?"

"Oh, no, don't come here yet. Continue your good work as before. Perhaps, on another European visit you may find the excuse to dash here to see your ailing mother or report your progress personally to your company. "Please, keep copies of the info and data, securely in a London bank, as a standby".

"As a matter of fact, I've done so already. You cannot be too cautious when dealing with these Bassains, Abraham".

"Well, well, well, what can I say? Just keep our fingers crossed and pray. Keep at it, Colonel, and my warmest regards to your pals. Chao".

"Goodbye and Shalom", ended Jamie.

After a day's rest in London, sightseeing and watching the British television, Jamie returned to Appapa. Welcoming him back to his office, Chairman Johnson hugged him and remarked happily, Jamie, you're great. A perfect example of an American gentleman. Thank you very much. Well done. Jamie you're a full blown Bassain, as from today".

"Thank you, Sir, most kind of you".

"You know what?, Your successful mission deserves special celebration by the two of us alone. I will fix a date soon. Meanwhile, you know what? I am going to have a special celebration myself alone, well not entirely alone, tonight. Next time, Jamie, you will learn more about what I mean. Goodbye for now and keep up your good work. You're now my right hand man. Cheers". As the Chairman said so, he embraced Jamie, shook his hand and led him to the door.

"Thank you, Sir, and Goodbye", intoned Jamie in a most friendly and respectful manner.

With Jamie gone, the Chairman got Sophia on the phone at once.

"I will be in tonight at 7 pm, darling. How are you, dear?"

"Very well, darling, very well. Always thinking of you"

"Well, prepare for a special celebration tonight. It may be till day-break so get ready. See you soon, darling. Bye-bye", ended Chairman Johnson.

Chapter 15

Jamie Lynch resumed his defence review program with his colleagues, who in his absence had been working flat out. Furthermore, they had struck a close friendship with Brigadier Kojo Pandi, the officer commanding the Southern Forces, including those responsible for Appapa, the capital

"Well, this guy, Brigadier Pandi, seems to get on well with us, and we have been trying to sound him out gingerly to see whether he would be interested", said John Branson, during a major report on their work to Jamie.

"Of course, as with all such approaches one has to be very careful, and always leave an escape route out", said Jamie.

"I find the man sound, and I think we can do business with him."

"Well, I want to study him for a few more days, perhaps over lunch or dinner. I want to be absolutely certain that he's kosher before I recruit him", remarked Jamie.

"Well, I shall arrange a luncheon date with him next week, in the officers' mess and you can bump into us, by accident. Right?", said John Branson. "That sounds pretty good", replied Jamie.

So a week or two later, whilst Brigadier Kojo Pandi and the two Americans were lunching at the officers' mess, Jamie bumped into them, was invited to join, which he heartily did.

"Well, what are you guys feasting on?", asked Jamie.

"Please join us, we have just finished the first course and are on the main course of peanut, beef stew, yams, okra and tomatoes", said John.

"That sounds mouth-watering", said Jamie.

"Brigadier, this is our boss, Jamie. Now we see less and less of him, as he dines and wines with the Chairman himself. He's forgetting us already", remarked Peter.

"Not at all. Only the past few days I've been very busy on one or two important jobs. That's all."

As they ate, the brigadier did not say much. He appeared uneasy in Jamie's presence. And the talk was rather inconsequential and boring. "Thank you for inviting me. Next time it will be on me. Many thanks. I've got to rush", and so saying, Jamie got up, and shook hands with them all and left.

"Brigadier, what do you think of our boss? Great. Very sound man, with sterling qualities", asked John. "I cannot assess him yet, but he appears a man of outstanding courage and conviction. You think he's reliable? He's so close to the Chairman!", said the brigadier.

"I suppose we have to work on him further, Brigadier. Leave that to me", said Peter.

Lunch over, the three dispersed, and Peter and John went to their hotel rooms to work on certain reports about their work.

Over a period of five weeks a few more innocuous looking meetings took place between the two Americans and the brigadier. They were openly held at the tennis court, at the beach, or over dinner, in the presence of all and sundry. Once or twice they were joined by Jamie, coincidentally. Also John a few times met the brigadier alone. Eventually, the American team became convinced that the brigadier was reliable and meant business. A full meeting was, therefore, arranged between him and Jamie at the brigadier's office one Wednesday morning.

Jamie's closeness with Chairman Johnson, and the fact that he had become virtually the Chairman's chief adviser on defence, finance, agriculture, foreign affairs, health and welfare matters, ensured that his meeting with the brigadier was seen by fellow officers as nothing unusual.

"Thank you for your time, brigadier. I think we can at this stage be frank with each other. My two colleagues have given me a full situation report on you and I think we can do business. Let's get it straight from the beginning. We've the same objective, and we must work together. You see what I mean."

"Well, I think so. But how do I know that you will not get me into trouble and leave me in shit, Jamie?"

"Nonsense, I should rather ask whether you will not let me down and report to the boss. In any case, nobody will believe you if you did. And you the bearer of that bad news will go, before I do. Right?"

"Go on. I'm listening."

"Simply put, brigadier it is like this. It is essential that loyal, democratic officers like you forestall a major national catastrophe by restoring the ousted, civilian regime straightaway. We will do all the donkey work, and leave the honour to you personally."

"How?, and also how do I know that you're not setting a trap for me?"

"It's nothing of the sort. Already, we've committed each other to the point that if any of us divulge anything we will hang together. I am serious. Trust me, as I trust you and we will both survive and win".

"OK, what are your proposals?", asked the brigadier.

"Very simple, Kojo. On D-day, between 2 am and 4 am, the Chairman will be neutralised and handed over to you, the broadcasting centre will be captured and the members of the former Government released from Kurukuru prison. As soon as these three vital objectives have been achieved, we will give you the role to announce the successful counter coup on behalf of democracy and freedom, led by you."

"Is that all my role?", asked Pandi

"Not really."

"I shall ensure that all troops are dispersed for a 48-hour period before D-day, and you should have only at your disposal a small group of loyal, armed soldiers to join you in completing the take-over. You and your fellow officers will be the heroes and we will quietly return to the US, our job done.

"To minimise bloodshed, you're to move your forces only when we signal to you that the three objectives have been achieved, completely and successfully."

"How, Jamie? assuming the phones and other means of communication are not working on that day?"

"Don't worry, brigadier. Leave that to us. We shall long

before that date give you a tiny transmitter-receiver, and as soon as you hear a voice say "The three sparrows are dead", then you spring into action, put your men in strategic positions and head for broadcasting centre. Right?"

"Who else knows of this plan, Jamie?"

"Nobody, apart from my two colleagues. Certainly no Bassain person, military or civilian, apart from you. Brigadier you are the lynch pin in the whole exercise. Its success depends on you. Whether democracy is revived in Bassa lies heavily on your shoulders. Are you ready for the historic call of duty and destiny?"

"I am. Yes!"

"Brigadier, this is a serious matter of life and death for me, for you, and for many others. Let this remain a secret between us. Right?"

"And you let this be a top secret between the two of us, Jamie?"

"By the way, if Intelligence dare question you about our meeting, they would not dare, but in case they do, we both keep to the same story, that I came to discuss with you possible transfers, re-structuring of high command and other troop movements that the Chairman is interested in. In fact, as soon as I return to the boss's office, I shall talk with him about such restructuring and such troop movements, and that I've had an interesting talk with you about them.

"But, Jamie, what if we are bugged. We're finished", said the brigadier anxiously.

"Hey man, what do you take me for, a damn nit-wit? Before coming I had checked and found that your place is clean, and that's why I came and felt free to talk so frankly. Kojo, remember from now to continue your normal routine as if nothing has happened. Keep working with my colleagues in your usual course of duty, and ignore me completely. If I need to get in touch with you I will find ways and means of doing so. OK?"

"Yes, understand", remarked the brigadier.

The two men got up shook hands vigorously and said Good-bye to each other.

Peter and John continued their work with their Bassain counterparts. With each meeting the Bassain requests for various up to date surveillance equipment, helicopters, and assault rifles changed and grew. It appeared to Peter and John that the sky was the limit as far as funds available to the Bassain officers were concerned. The Americans' work involved detailed study of the Broadcasting Centre, Government House, the central armoury, the secret military transmitter and other sensitive installations. Indeed, they were so overwhelmed with the requests to visit this and that military location or centre, that sometimes they had to feign a polite disinterest in some of the assignments.

Step by step, by sheer hard work and devotion, Jamie had made himself indispensable to the Head of State. Chairman Johnson sought his views on everything, from defence to education, from sex to religion. To him Jamie could do no wrong. He spent more time with the Chairman, than with his own American colleagues, and indeed had been given an impressive office next to Johnson's, so that he would be always available to the Chairman.

Behind his back, Jamie was jokingly referred to as "the vice-president". His favoured position was beginning to generate envy and resentment among certain local, senior military officers and some ambitious civilians. This was, through the grapevine, beginning to reach the ears of Chairman Johnson. He was not angry at these rumours but privately delighted that he had as his most trusted right-hand man, a non-Bassain that his enemies could not buy or bribe.

It was in this state of mind, that Chairman Johnson received on a Thursday morning and envelope marked "Top Secret. For Chairman only" from the Director of Military Intelligence. It was a brief letter, but potentially most devastating. As he read the letter, he grew more and more furious.

"Dear Chairman,

RE: US. Citizen Jamie Lynch

I should be most grateful if, in spite of your onerous duties and responsibilities you would spare a few moments to give this matter your urgent attention. Reports reaching me from very reliable sources strongly suggest that Jamie Lynch, a US. citizen, leader of the team of American defence experts, is most probably a CIA. operative, with the cover of a businessman. Although positively vetted by our man in Washington DC. before his arrival here, with his two comrades, I have good reason to believe that he is against your regime and is a spy.

His close association, therefore, with your Excellency, the Head of State of Bassa, Chairman of the People's Revolutionary Council, Leader of our Nation, is a matter of grave concern to the Military Intelligence. Why as leader of his team, he should appear to neglect his group, and engage in local governmental activities, more often at your side than at the side of his comrades, gives much food for thought.

Furthermore, a few weeks ago, he flew to London on a Bassain diplomatic passport, and my strong suspicion is that he is probably also engaged in drug trafficking. My men were able to tail him up to London's Heathrow airport, but beyond that, with all the confusion at the airport, they lost him.

Sir, whilst the evidence against this American is not conclusive, I feel duty bound to bring these matters to your urgent attention, so that you may advise yourself accordingly and as you deem fit.

Long Live the Revolution! Long Live our valiant Leader. Long Live Bassa!

Your most obedient servant,
Col. Charles J Poku, Director,
Military Intelligence."

Trying to control his temper, he called his ADC to get him Jamie immediately. The poor soul was in conference with his colleagues at the hotel, when he was summoned by the phone to go to see the Chairman immediately. As he entered the Chairman's office, Johnson burst out, "Jamie read this. Read this rubbish. I'll get the bloody fucking idiot removed at once. See, see this". He handed the letter to Jamie, who read it standing. He read it slowly, and then looking at Johnson, eye-ball to eye-ball stated, "I knew it was coming, sooner or later. Natural envy and resentment. Perfectly understandable, though inexcusable, Sir."

"I'm a goodman to get him shot. The cheek of him following you. What does he think of himself. I shall retire him with immediate effect. That will teach the dirty buffoon a lesson. What do you think, Jamie?"

"Chairman, if I may say so, this is a time for calm nerves. I know you are upset, but you should try and see things from his point of view. Here they are all trying to be as close as possible to you for their own selfish reasons, and next comes this American who comes between them and you, and is seen as the right hand man of the boss. Naturally, they will hate it and do everything possible to get rid of me.

You notice they left Peter and John out, because they are harmless, from their point of view. It is me that they are after. And after getting rid of me, Sir, they have you in their sights. That's their game."

"That's so Jamie. They are damned treacherous."

"Sir, you be cleverer than they are. Don't remove him now. Ring and thank him for his marvellous letter, and say you are thinking seriously about it. And continue to treat him with your usual kindness and courtesy, then at the next army re-organisation, you give him a kick in the arse. After all, Chairman, you are a great man. You single-handedly master-mined a perfect, bloodless coup. You are a man of destiny and these rogues don't come anywhere near you as an officer and a gentleman. Wait, Sir, we will teach them a lesson, but at the right time, Sir."

The Chairman calmed down a bit, then said, "Look, Jamie. You know what? I am going to give the bugger a call on the lines you suggest. Listen in through this extension."

Chairman Johnson picked up his special, red emergency telephone, and asked the operator to get him the Director of Military Intelligence on the phone at once. "Sir, that's the DMI on the line, Chairman", said the operator.

"Oh, Joe, how do you do? How are things. You know, I was just thinking of you, when I received your letter an hour or so ago. Very important letter. I've read it carefully and I think I'll act on it appropriately at the right time. Thank you so much, old boy. Regards to all the lads. Cheers."

"Thank you, Sir, and I shall be supplying you with more info and intelligence reports, as they become available. I am delighted you appreciate the work of my boys and me. Thank you, Chairman", responded the Director of Military Intelligence, rather elated and proud with himself.

After the telephone call, the Chairman and Jamie, laughing to each other, with absolute self-satisfaction, resumed their conversation.

"You know, Jamie, I've a brilliant idea. The idiot states confidently that he's had you followed. Well, it's simple. I am ordering the Director of Special Branch to put a 24-hour hard surveillance on him, until further notice. Consequently, when we come to giving him the kick in the pants, we'll have enough evidence on him to hang him, or at least to make my removal of him eminently justifiable. What do you think, Jamie?"

"Excellent idea. Brilliant, and as with all your strategies, Chairman, so simple, in design and execution."

"Jamie, I would like you to go on another Swiss visit next week, if you have no objection, and don't consider the notice too short."

"Not at all, Sir. Your wish is my command, Chairman, as I've always stated. Any time."

"It is then next Wednesday, please same procedure, route, and feed-back signal, OK?"

"Yes, Sir. Chairman, may I make a request, a very humble one."

"Sure, go ahead"

"After my assignment, on my return can I pop to New York to see my company to brief my bosses directly about our progress in Bassa so far, and to assure them that everything is going well and that a big contract is on the way, and that they should not worry. You see, although one may send telex and other reports, Sir, it's not the same, as a personal briefing. I will be in New York for not more than a couple of days."

"Jamie, I need you here, and if I agree to your New York visit, t's on one condition. Simple. Whilst there, find time to visit one or two real estate agents, and choose for me provisionally three, desirable residential properties, in the best part of New York City. Nothing more than let's say 2 million dollars, with four or five bedrooms, sitting rooms, study and swimming pool, if possible. After examining three of such properties, would you bring along their photos, designs, and advise me on the one to settle on."

"That should not be too much problem, Sir."

"With all these coups and counter-coups in the Third World, and seeing what has happened to others in positions similar to mine, would it not be rather foolish and naive on my part, not to think of a couple of safe havens outside Bassa, in case of emergency?"

"Sure, you are being very foresighted and wise, as always, Sir. Don't leave anything to chance, Chairman."

"You're a man after my own heart, Jamie, you understand me better than my own brother or wife."

"Thank you, Sir, I am happy you appreciate my modest efforts."

"It's settled then? Wednesday morning the car, with the cargo in it, will come to pick you up at the hotel, and the rest is as before, Right?"

"Yes, Sir"

"Goodbye, then. Regards to your pals", said the chairman, as he saw his American friend to the door.

Returning to his hotel, Jamie called a quick, emergency meeting of his colleagues. He briefed them thoroughly on the latest position, his last meeting with the Head of State, and the urgent need for them to continue faultlessly with their work, entertain generously and make friends. Receiving from them all the material and intelligence reports which they had acquired in the course of their work and socialising, Jamie, had a long, detailed discussion of the operation with them. Finally, as head of the team, he summarised the position in the following way.

"Well, things appear to be moving very well and fast, and whilst in New York, I shall present to the boss, the final plans, subject to last-minute fine tuning, if necessary. Agreed?"

"Yes, Jamie", replied Peter, with John nodding.

"Till D-day, I shall ensure that whatever changes, the brigadier stays in his position. It is vital. Having recruited and groomed him to this position, it would be disaster if we were to lose him, and start grooming his successor. It will be my job that this does not happen", remarked Jamie.

"John, did you check on the transmitter and those details?"

"Yes, Peter. Everything is fine. The wave lengths are clean and good."

"The operational plans then will be split into two phases. Phase 1, will launch the operation at 2 am of D-day. This is the most important and most sensitive aspect of the whole exercise and will be undertaken by us.

First, our thirty chaps will come by two military helicopters, plus a stand-by helicopter. They would be armed with A47 assault rifles, or light machine-guns. Each of them will carry water and rations for 48 hours. A trained medical orderly will be attached to each team.

The first team, under John will be responsible for attacking Broadcasting House, overcoming the guards and capturing it. You will be allowed one to two hours for that. The second team, led by Peter, will be detailed to make a surprise descent on the infamous Kurukuru prison, overpower the guards and warders and release the political prisoners. This team will then rush the Acting head of Government, plus a few of the ex-ministers to the Broadcasting House, which should be then in our hands. And the third team, led by me, will effect the arrest and capture of the boss, wherever he may be, and his handing over to the brigadier. He will certainly that night be with his mistress, Sophia Fumey, and I intend to arrest them both and hand them over to the other side. You know, just as the Italian partisans did to Mussolini, and his mistress, towards the end of the Second World War. That's a touch of history for you!.

All three teams will operate simultaneously, having arrived at the designated spot by the two helicopters, already mentioned. All operations will be by our own code names, using our own transmission system, as already discussed and agreed on.

The brigadier is responsible for phase two of the operation. He would, upon receipt of an agreed signal from me, following the launching of phase one, neutralise the emergency communication system, both civil and military, in the capital. Simultaneously, he would effect appropriate road blocks as necessary. With the major three targets under phase 1 captured, and with the brigadier's select troops ready to neutralise any untoward military action, a radio and television broadcast of the counter-coup would be made by the brigadier and the released members of the previous government. We shall try to avoid, as much as possible, any physical, military action, unless unavoidable or forced upon us. In any case, I shall ensure that the Chairman, issues a red-alert order, stopping all troop movements for 48 hours as from D-day except by his own personal authority. Also for the same 48- hour period, no officers or men, shall be with live ammunitions, except of course, the few, selected loyal men of the brigadier.

"What about the landing pad? Is it reliable?", enquired John.

"Solid, absolutely perfect", replied Peter.

Before Jamie could continue with his comprehensive briefing, Peter remarked "I'm rather still worried about last minute changes in the army which might lead to the brigadier being replaced. Should that happen all our efforts would have been in vain."

"Indeed that's a matter for concern", quipped Jamie. "But I'll see to it that whatever happens, the brigadier stays put. I agree completely with you that it would be a disaster if we were ultimately to lose him", remarked Jamie. "To recap, I wish to state that unless something really awful happens, there's no reason why the whole operation should not be completed within two hours at most, bloodlessly. As a matter of fact, our chaps coming in can by themselves alone achieve the purpose of the whole operation. The trouble is keeping the spoils of war intact, in our hands, and that's why the brigadier's intervention is so essential."

After a little more discussion, during which the triumvirate went over their individual roles, the meeting ended, and the three together went to the hotel dining hall for dinner.

His second Swiss mission successfully completed, Jamie, as previously agreed with Chairman Johnson, returned to New York via London. Welcoming him back in New York, Abraham Goldberg, remarked jokingly, "Jamie, Vice-president of Bassa, welcome to the Big Apple. Your success has, oh boy, been phenomenal. Well done."

"Well, it was a pleasure to serve. We have won the battle, but have yet to bring to you complete victory, and sure, we are going to do it soon, very soon", said Jamie confidently.

The two men carefully went over the operational plans, with a fine tooth-comb. Every possible eventuality foreseeable was noted, and analysed.

"I suggest that the training of our chaps be quickened, in case, we need them earlier than planned."

"Well, so far they are not doing too badly. We got them acclimatised to tropical conditions by doing their training in a rented farm in Florida. Ah, I should say, the sketches and photographs have been of fantastic use and value. We were able to build dummy copies of the prison, the broadcasting centre and the house of the Chairman's mistress. They have gone over these very well, and they have been very good students."

"What about transport, Abraham? It's going to be rather difficult?", said Jamie.

"Not at all. We are arranging for our chaps to travel as tourists to a neighbouring, friendly country, and from an arranged spot, they will be picked by the choppers to your side in Bassa. Then they are in your capable hands. There will be two choppers, as we discussed, plus a back-up one, for emergency."

"The timing is important. I've in mind, let's say a couple of months from now. It would be the bastard's official birthday. It will be celebrated on a grand scale, with huge military parades, and a public holiday."

"And what do you intend to do clever Dick?"

"Abraham it's very simple. Our men will be split into three groups, one led by each of us. Simultaneously, one group will attack and capture the broadcasting centre, the other, the notorious prison and release the former government ministers, whilst my group carries the privilege and honour of arresting the boss himself. For only probably I will know where he's spending the night on the day of action, and therefore, should be in the best position to sort him out."

"What about armed resistance, Jamie?"

"I've considered that. I shall get the Chairman to issue a red alert order withdrawing all live ammunitions from all units, officers included, and also banning all troop movements for a 48-hour period. Namely 24- hours before the hour of destiny and 24-hours after. As such, only a few, selected troops loyal to the brigadier will carry live ammunitions."

"I see."

"We expect no armed resistance, but even if there were any, it would be a hollow, ineffectual one."

"Jamie, you're a genius. Fantastic. By the way, we're getting you the best communication system available. Very powerful and sleek."

"Good. Very good, Abraham. I knew I could rely on you absolutely", Let us not forget, our man wants me to look round the city for a two million-dollar hide-away, in case of an emergency. An expert in the art of treachery himself, he's expecting to be stabbed in the back anytime, at any moment, by his people. He's damned scared, and would you believe it, sleeps at a different house or location, every night. What a life!

Further more to guard against a possible coup whilst he's away, he's decided never to leave the country. Rather childish, as if these measures would help him in anyway when the day of reckoning does come."

"Well, Jamie, let him indulge a bit in his fanciful ideas and schemes. Keep on faithfully saving the fortune in Switzerland for him. Keep on abiding by his whims and fancies. Try and get him the best million-dollar pad in Manhattan. Whether he'll live to enjoy all these attributes of wealth and power, is another matter. I do indeed pity the poor soul."

"Oh, Abraham, I nearly forgot to tell you about the ridiculous, mumbo-jumbo,, voodoo swearing-in ceremony that I had to go through. He made me strip naked, and place my left-hand on his ceremonial sword, and with my right-hand raised had to swear to him an oath of loyalty, which may be broken at my own peril.

Jokingly, he warned that a convenient heart attack or car accident could easily be arranged, should I show a whiff of disloyalty."

"Good God. You mean you had to go through all that nonsense?"

"You bet, but that's not all, I had to drink urine."

"What? His or yours?"

"Mine"

"Thank God. Dreadful and disgusting, but certainly not life threatening. I assure you."

"I know. So I am now his right hand man, and advisor on everything, including his sexual activity. What a cheek?"

"I suppose, it's part of the programme of restoring freedom, democracy and sanity in a benighted country, and this is part of the price we have to pay", remarked Abraham.

"By the way, Abraham, don't forget to ensure that the chaps, apart from their medical inoculations, also take their anti-malaria tablets. They should begin doing so, at least a week before departure. We'll be too occupied to afford cases of malaria fever on our hands", said Jamie.

The next couple of days, Jamie spent with his own family; taking a few hours off to fly to the Florida camp of the soldiers to familiarise himself with them, and give them a pep talk on their mission. In New York City, he collected brochures on four houses and apartments, within the two million-dollars range, and looked perfunctorily at three of them. He then flew to London, en route to Bassa, his mission for the Chairman dutifully accomplished.

Exactly a week after his return to Bassa, there was an attempted coup. It was organised by a group of sergeants and master-sergeants. Although it did not succeed, ten soldiers loyal to the regime were injured. Chairman Johnson was shaken by the incident and came to rely even more on Jamie, whose views were sought avidly and acted on always. On the advice of Jamie, Chairman Johnson ordered the Director of Military Intelligence to thoroughly investigate the incident and flush out the perpetrators. Depressed and disappointed that he had not been able to forestall the abortive coup, and anxious to consolidate his position with the boss, the director was carried away by over enthusiasm. He ordered a rigorous interrogation of fifty persons who had been arrested as suspects. Ten of these were civilians, including the younger brother of the National General Secretary of the ousted civilian administration. The poor soul had just been released from detention, when he was quite wrongly implicated in the coup. Tortured mercilessly and brutally by the D(Death) Section of Military Intelligence, he collapsed in a pool of blood and died. The director, felt that the incident deserved to be reported to the Chairman himself.

The day after the incident he went to see his boss and narrated to him what had happened.

"You bloody fool. Are you mad? You were to interrogate them not kill anyone. See what you have done, Director? You've put me in a untenable position."

"Sir, my men were not instructed to go so far, but must have been carried away by the circumstances."

"What circumstances? The fact is you've caused the first murder under my regime for which I am directly accountable. See the immense trouble that you have brought on my head?", he stopped for a second or two, and then went on "You've soiled my hands with innocent blood, and I did a coup without any bloodshed whatsoever. I am asking Jamie to conduct an immediate inquiry into the incident and your role in it. Meanwhile you are retired from the armed forces with immediate effect. Goodbye."

The director quickly disappeared from the scene. Jamie was called in.

"Oh boy, I am devastated by the incident. The death of this innocent civilian. Those stupid guys are so clumsy and inefficient that they arrested the younger brother of the person they wanted, all because he had the same surname. What sheer nonsense. And the poor chap is dead."

"So sorry to hear all this, Chairman. Can I help in anyway, Sir?"

"Perhaps. Yes, you see, Jamie, my spiritual adviser, the tall woman that comes here off and on, is the oracle of a shrine at AGORO. Before the coup I consulted her and she told me that I would succeed and rule for a long time, so long as there was no bloodshed, whatsoever. As you know, my coup was completely bloodless, and now these buffoons have put my whole future in jeopardy, by what's happened."

"You mean, Sir, that there is a spell on you, following this incident?"

"Yes, I fear so, Jamie. I am finished. There is blood on my head."

"Sir, I have a suggestion. A couple of years ago, I knew of a spiritualist in Arizona, who had an established nation-wide reputation for seeing into the future, with perfect accuracy. Presidents, pillars of industry, eminent men and women, of both races consulted her. Have I your permission, Sir, to contact her."

"Do so, Jamie. Pronto. Money is no problem."

"You sure, Sir. Her fees are rather high."

"That's alight. Please get her here at once, like a good friend."

So Jamie set in motion the whole process of getting the American spiritualist into Bassa. Forty-eight hours following Jamie's request the blonde, thirty-five year old American medium and woman guru, was ushered into the presence of Chairman Johnson. After the relevant introductions and discussions between Jamie, the woman and the Chairman, she picked the following day, a Friday to hold a seance in the Chairman's private office.

The time was about 8 PM when the seance began. Jamie was in the ante-room, and only the American woman and the Chairman were in the office. The Chairman was naked and sat yoga-fashion on the floor. The guru recited a long string of mumbo-jumbo and abracadabra, as she looked into the crystal ball. Then she suddenly stopped, and fell into a trance, or so it appeared to the Chairman. Then she spoke out, "I see a lot of bloodshed, Sir, but it's the blood of your enemies. I see you smiling with your mother, as she congratulates you on the long successful administration of your country. I see hundreds of happy children waving to you, wanting to touch you. And I hear consistently a voice saying, "There goes Chairman Kofi Johnson, a man after my own heart."

"Sir, don't worry. You've many, many glorious and happy years ahead of you."

As the ritual ended, she gave a gold-plated bracelet to the Chairman. He was to wear it at all times on his left wrist for luck and to fend off evil spirits. Kofi was now a relaxed, delighted man. A couple more sessions were held. Then a V.I.P 3-day tour of the capital city was arranged for her before her departure. Before she left for the United States, the Chairman called her in, and in presence of Jamie, gave her 25,000 US. dollars in 100 dollar bills, and an impressive diamond ring. And with that the spiritualist disappeared from the scene and from the Chairman's life.

A fortnight after this incident, Jamie, on the pretext of visiting a fellow American, called on Pearl Kambu. The day was Wednesday, and it was a rather hot afternoon.

"Pearl, I bring you love and greetings from your dad and mum. They are both well and send their love to you and the children. Everything is fixed now,, and you have a major role in it. You know June 15th is the Chairman's birthday, and it will be a public holiday, with major parades in the city. Right?"

"Sure."

"On that day, you're to drive your car, or any car, and be at this address by 2 in the morning. In front of the house, stop your car, and open the bonnet, as if the engine is giving you trouble. You will be approached by two soldiers. Then tell them that you are going to call on someone that is seriously ill and has just called you and the car is bothering you. As they come to your aid, they will be arrested by our men, and the rest is our business. If when you stop, the soldiers don't come out, walk towards the house calmly. They appear armed, but they carry no ammunitions.

As you see them arrested you shoot out of the scene, and return to your bed. OK?"

"Yes. What about my children?"

"You may leave them at home, or with a trusted friend. Don't worry. Everything is under control. Can you handle this delicate mission, Pearl?"

"Certainly. It sounds exciting, Jamie."

"I assure you that by about five o'clock that morning, we will be celebrating. It's as kosher as you can get. Every potential problem has been studied and dealt with. Keep your fingers crossed and pray. It may be worth your while to familiarise yourself, in the daytime, with the area and the address and make a couple of trial runs. Right?"

"That's a good idea."

There followed a little chat on the family, and minor matters of interest. Then Jamie left, but before doing so, said, "The day before that, I shall ring you and tell you not to forget to visit some of the US citizens in difficulties. OK?"

"Yes. Thank you very much and goodbye."

On June 4th, Jamie, with the Chairman's permission and approval visited AKASA, the capital of Bassa's neighbouring state. There he finalised arrangements for the arrival by air of the thirty ex-US and Israeli soldiers, posing as tourists. Heavy bribes to ensure that their huge luggage and other personal items were not searched by Customs were paid by Jamie. Furthermore, arrangements to effect their transportation into Bassa, by the three military helicopters were put into place.

Enjoying his freedom out of the clutches of Chairman Johnson, Jamie rang Goldberg and requested that the men be ready to arrive by air at AKASA, as he had arranged. By the time of this call, Abraham had only ten days or so to make the final arrangements. Frantically he mobilised the forces. They were twenty strong, dare-devil, battle seasoned Americans, and ten Israelis of equal calibre. Apart from their equipment, weapons, routines, they were set to go, not as mercenaries, but as people with a mission. They knew that although from their briefings and training, the risks were minimal, they still existed. They felt

God was on their side.

The last meeting of the group of thirty, before their departure for Bassa was a most memorable one. At about 7 p.m. on their last Saturday night in the United States, they gathered at the hotel room, where they usually met. Following drinks and general chat, they went to a private room in the well-known, east-side PLAZA hotel. There they celebrated the Sabbath meal, presided over by Abraham Goldberg at one end of the table, and his local synagogue's rabbi at the other end.

"You go with the blessing of Yaweh, the God of Israel, who brought our ancestors from captivity against insuperable odds. For over two thousand years, despite all efforts and attempts to annihilate us, as Jews, we have survived and succeeded, by our faith in God. May this God, who protects those without a protector, who makes the impossible possible, safely bring you back home, after the successful completion of your mission. Shalom!"

The prayers ended with the rabbi leading the group with the words from Psalm 53. Prayers over they were all relaxed, and talked in a friendly, cordial way. They were Jews of Lithuanian, Russian, German, Polish, French, Italian, Latvian, and Irish ancestry. Although they had not known each other long, they had already developed a strong feeling of brotherhood and comradeship, which bound them together.

A couple of days after their last pre-assignment Sabbath meal in New York, the team of thirty, fully equipped, with their luggage carrying all their essentials, arrived by air in AKASA. They had only a couple of days in the city of AKASA, as businessmen from the United States. The little respite was a good break and also essential for final acclimatisation with the tropical conditions, before D-Day.

Meanwhile in Bassa, events were moving with a terrific speed. The whole nation was agog with excitement, as preparations were made for the birthday of the Head of State. School children were rehearsed in parades upon parades. The armed forces were drilled in the processions and marches that were to be held in the capital city, and the chief provincial cities. There were buntings everywhere and the festive air was palpable. Everything was going according to plan. The Chairman was looking forward very much to his birthday celebrations.

On the very day that the group of thirty soldiers arrived in AKASA, Jamie had two very important meetings in Appapa. One was with the Head of State and the other with the Commander of the Southern Brigade.

"Chairman, I need to discuss this matter with you urgently, Sir"

"Shoot ahead, Jamie. Remember that you've another assignment lined up after the celebrations."

Sure, but Chairman I think I should bring this to your immediate attention. It's a matter I've given considerable thought to and my conclusion is firm. To prevent any officers taking advantage of the parades, to stage any untoward action against your person, I request that you issue immediately a 48-hour red alert order, banning the carrying of live ammunitions by any soldiers or officers. This would mean that for 24-hours covering the official functions, no soldiers would be carrying live ammunitions. As such, as you take the salute on the day or ride through the city, waving to your beloved people, no officer or soldier can carry out any dirty tricks. Sir, I hope you appreciate my deep concern."

"Indeed, I do, Jamie, I do. You're really a genius and I shall never forget this until my dying day. I know what I will add to this safety precaution, an order banning all troop movements without my express, personal authorisation. What about that?"

"That's brilliant, as always, Sir."

"In any case, most of the time, the men guarding broadcasting centre, the prisons and here, are unarmed as a precaution against coups. For I consider it a greater danger that they are armed than unarmed. Don't you think so, Jamie?"

"Sir, that's the perfect recipe against coups. In your exalted position, Sir, one cannot be too cautious and careful. You cannot and must not trust these bastards. Please, Chairman, your nation needs you for many, more years".

"Thank you, my good friend. It all depends on you. I indeed

owe you a lot".

"You're welcome, Sir. And it's a pleasure and honour to serve you".

After some little friendly chat, the relevant orders were drafted and signed by the Chairman. He then called in his military secretary to send them by telex to all the commands, and the Chairman of the Joint Chiefs of Staff. That done, the Chairman had to leave for a meeting of the National Women's Organisations. As soon as he left., Jamie called in the Commander of the Southern Brigade for a little chat at his office. He elaborated to him the Chairman's latest orders, and also took the opportunity to inform him that D-day was the on-coming Thursday 2 am prompt. As it was already Monday, late in the afternoon, it meant that the brigadier had only a matter of a few hours to be hundred percent ready to play his part. He was in an excellent, combative and confident mood. He smelt victory in his nostrils and was raving to go!.

On his way to the hotel, from his office next to that of the Chairman, Jamie called on Pearl Kambu. Over a matter of a few minutes, they went over her assignment on the coming Thursday 2 am. She was in a calm collected frame of mind, and determined to discharge her duties accordingly.

Finally, Jamie checked and re-checked on the sleeping arrangements of the Chairman, and had it confirmed that he would be sleeping at Sophia's on the Wednesday night. He also held further meetings with his two colleagues. Information and data and other details were gone through to the utter satisfaction of all three. Everything seemed to be going according to plan. The Monday evening and night passed off uneventfully.

The following day, Tuesday, Jamie made unscheduled visits to the Broadcasting centre, Kukukuru prison, the Central Police Station and the headquarters of the Special Branch. They were all ostensibly courtesy calls meant to bring Jamie up to date about their state of readiness for the Chairman's birthday celebrations the following Thursday.

At long last, the die was cast. On Wednesday night, the twenty American and ten Israeli soldiers, with their ammunitions, weapons, rations and medical kits left their hotel. They gathered by rented cars, at a local car park, not far from the local football stadium. The time was exactly 11.30 pm. From there they were whisked by two large Apache helicopters to a pre-arranged spot, well within the borders of Bassa. Accompanying the two helicopters was an empty standby one.

They were welcomed by 003 and 004 who divided the thirty teams into their pre-arranged teams. 003 was responsible for team three, 004 for team 4 and 005, who had stayed behind for team 5. After they had transferred from the helicopters, they applied their camouflage black face creams, and put on their Bassain military uniforms and boots. They had become to all intents and purposes, Bassain soldiers, bar their accents.

Jamie, as the leader of the whole operation, was sitting in a car, not far from his hotel, directing operations by the smuggled transmitter sent in from New York by Abraham Goldberg. At one o'clock dawn of Thursday, Jamie completely satisfied that the Chairman was ensconced in the bed of his mistress, gave the order for the launch of Operation Big Apple. Three Bassain military trucks, procured by special request by Jamie, for the Chairman's security purposes, conveyed the three teams over the sixty mile journey to Appapa. Jamie joined his group at 2.15 am, about two miles from his hotel, whilst the other teams, headed for their due destinations.

Meanwhile, at about 2.00 am, Pearl slipped out of her bed, and wearing a nurse's uniform set out for her rendezvous. Before leaving, she wrote a little note for her children.. "Little darlings, sorry I've got to go out urgently. Will be back soon, but if I am not in and you need anything urgent, ring Auntie Nevenka. Love, see you soon".

She was at her spot at 2.25 am, stopped and opened the bonnet of her car. Immediately, two armed soldiers walked towards her and shouted, "Hey, Madam, what you want?"

"Sorry, officers. I was going to see a sick woman who rang me and my little car is giving me trouble. Please, can you help? I beg you, Sirs".

"Madam, this be Chairman private residence. No car stop

here, but as ebe you, we help. How be you madam?"

The two soldiers had begun to peer into the car's engine with their large torch-light, when suddenly, in a flash, Jamie's military vehicle arrived on the scene.

"Hands up you all. Don't move, or you are dead, dead as a dodo. Understand?"

The two Bassain soldiers were quickly disarmed, gagged and handcuffed. They were then blind-folded and their legs put in leg irons. Then they were swiftly bundled into the military vehicle. Pearl had time only to watch momentarily the disarming of the soldiers. She next closed the bonnet of her car, and sped back to her house and was comfortably in bed by 2.45 am.

Meanwhile, as the soldiers were being neutralised, Jamie, leading a team of three Americans and one Israeli walked to Sophia's house. After positioning two soldiers he suddenly broke into Sophia's bedroom. It was all over within a matter of a few split seconds.

The Chairman was completely naked. Sophia had a long, expensive cotton nightdress on.

"Chairman, it's all over now. You are under arrest. Hands up, both of you. One move and you are dead. Completely dead".

The soldiers accompanying Jamie had their automatic rifles trained on Chairman Johnson's head. As a military man, and master of treachery, he understood very well what game was at foot. He offered no resistance, as he was gagged, blindfolded and handcuffed. His ear holes were appropriately plugged.

"Madam, quickly, quickly, put on something decent. You may need it awhile", said one of Jamie's companions.

She quickly put on a tight-fitting dress, then was also blindfolded, gagged and handcuffed. The lights were put out and the pair led to the military vehicle, where they were thrown in.

The vehicle, under Jamie's direction, drove to his command post near his hotel.

Meanwhile, the team heading for the prison, had reached there at 2.40 am. One of the soldiers under the command of 003 threw tear gas near the six sleepy Bassain soldiers guarding the prison. Before they were aware of what had hit them, there were shouts of "Surrender, hands up. Don't move". They all raised their hands in surrender. They were disarmed swiftly, hand-cuffed and blindfolded and given the heave-ho into the military vehicle. 003 accompanied by four of his men, broke into the prison, headed for the clinic wing. When he reached there it was about 3 am.

"You're free. Free at last. Get up all of you. We are taking you to broadcast to the nation. Hurry, Hurry", shouted 003. As he did so, the former Acting Prime Minister and his colleagues, jumped from their bunk-beds with alacrity and partly dressed were rushed to the military vehicle.

In all, 003 and his men took with them about ten ministers and the party General Secretary, saying,

"The rest of you should find your way home or to broadcast-ing house. There's no time to waste. We must leave now. Cheers", remarked 003's next in command.

The liberated men were driven to Jamie's command post, and as they were going, former Acting Prime Minister Pat Podo, remarked "It's unbelievable. It's just like a dream come true. God's name be blessed. Long Live America. Long Live the United States". As he mumbled again and again to himself, some of his colleagues were crying with joy, whilst others just sat there speechless.

As soon as 003's team reached Jamie with their trophies, Jamie contacted 004 at broadcasting centre. The news was not good. 004's team had run into fierce resistance and already two Americans had been injured, albeit not seriously.. For somehow, by a fluke, the captain in command of the soldiers at the broadcasting centre, had managed, despite the Chairman's orders against the carrying of live ammunitions, to load his revolver. On hearing this news, Jamie, accompanied by his own vehicle and men, plus cargo, and 003's team and captured soldiers and liberated politicians, headed for the broadcasting centre.

They reached there at about 3.30 am. The forlorn resistance was still continuing, but the Bassain soldiers, although armed with rifles and light machine guns, were without any ammunitions.

As such, their resistance was ineffectual and hopeless. Only the captain kept on shouting "I'll die for the Chairman. Long Live the communist revolution. Long Live the Chairman".

"I think we'd better neutralise him", whispered Jamie. He ordered the boisterous captain to be shot in the right foot and left hand which was quickly done. As the captain was being disarmed, Jamie noticed a shining gold Star of David round his neck.

Surprised, Jamie asked, "Are you Jewish?"

"No, Sir, my mother was".

"Then you are Jewish. Shalom".

The disarming of the captain and his band of soldiers signalled the end of their resistance and the complete achievement of the three objectives of the coup. Jamie's work was done. As agreed previously, he immediately signalled the Brigadier of the Southern Forces. The brigadier got his message at 4 am. Immediately, set into motion his part of the programme. Platoons of armed soldiers were detailed to effect the capture of the Chairman's headquarters, the Chiefs of the Army, Navy, Air Force, Special Branch and the Director of Military Intelligence also the Chairman of the Joint Chiefs of Staff. Also arrested were their deputies, and members of the military junta. As in each case, the arrests were made by their own body guards, these procedures did not take too much time.

Road blocks were put in position, as ordered by the Brigadier, as he rushed in an armoured car to meet with Jamie at Broadcasting house, as agreed. By 4.30 am he was with Jamie and his people.

"Well, Brigadier. It's been a nice day. Thank you very much for neutralising the communication system and the lights at 2 am sharp as agreed. It was spot on, perfect timing. Now it's all over, and your trophies are here, alive and ready for you", said Jamie as his two colleagues listened.

"Friends, without you, this fantastic success would have been impossible. We owe you a great deal. Bassa will be eternally grateful to you. We thank you from the very bottom of our hearts for your sacrifice in bringing about a return to sanity, freedom and liberty in our dear country", said the brigadier.

"I suppose, it's now up to us to hand them over to you. The rest is entirely in your hands. Also we should settle the question of the announcement. May I suggest that you leave us out entirely and claim all the glory for the loyal, freedom-loving officers and men of Bassa. The victory alone is our reward. I think you should first announce the demise of the old regime and introduce the new, liberated members of the past, civilian government that we have with us. What about that? And for good measure, you should add that John, Peter and I, for being closely associated with the defunct regime, have been deported with immediate effect and left the country".

"Yes, that's good. Very good, but I feel very strongly that I should make a little mention of your supreme sacrifice and that of Mrs Kambu".

"Well, it's up to you, but honestly, try to minimise our role".

"However, it's important that the new administration be introduced to the nation at once, before we depart", said Jamie. And as the bridagier did so, the American and Israeli soldiers prepared to return to the military vehicles that had brought them to Appapa, whilst medical treatment was given to their colleagues injured in the counter coup.

Meanwhile, the newly liberated ex-ministers, having calmed down, began to compose their first victory statement to the nation. As they did so, the captured soldiers from the broadcasting house, Kurukuru prison and from Sophia's house were handed over. By 5 am the brigadier was ready to broadcast to the nation.

However, before doing so, he ordered the captured soldiers to be given water and then locked in one of the rooms in the broadcasting house used for storing old, derelict equipment. Next, he convened a court martial in studio 5, to which were brought the Chairman, and his mistress, and nine other members of the military junta of Chairman Johnson. Three hooded officers sat in front of a desk and called, one by one, for the names of the arrested members of the overthrown regime standing before them. They were stripped all to their pants. The trial was simple, very brief, very perfunctory and quick.

The hooded officer asked, "Your name?"

"Colonel Kofi Johnson".

"Say Mr not Colonel, you've disgraced the Army!".

"Mr Kofi Johnson", he replied quietly, almost in a whisper.

"Occupation?"

"Chairman, People's Revolutionary Council".

"Firing squad: Next? Name?"

"Major Mumuni Brimach".

"Mr Brimach, you mean?"

"Yes, Sir".

"Occupation?"

"Vice Chairman, P.R.C".

"Firing Squad. Next?"

Thus, one by one, all the members of the overthrown regime, who already had been captured were dealt with.

One of the hooded officers asked,

"What about that damned prostitute?"

"Ah, we nearly forgot her", replied a colleague.

"Bring her along", said the hooded officer who appeared to be the most senior of the three hooded persons.

Standing before the trio, absolutely petrified, she was asked, "Name?"

"Sophia Fumey, Sir".

"Are you Mrs Johnson?"

"No, Sir".

"Firing squad. Take her away".

All of the condemned men and Sophia Fumey were taken to the courtyard of the broadcasting house, blindfolded and tied to trees and shot immediately. A note was given to the brigadier as he readied himself to begin his broadcast. It said, "Chairman, plus mistress, and colleagues, sent to democracy school". The brigadier smiled as he quickly glanced at it. As he began his broadcast, the bodies, all naked had been bundled into military vehicles and were being rushed to the Green Star Square, the public precinct of the capital which had witnessed many military parades, with the salute being taken by Chairman Johnson.

Quickly, two posts were installed, by some soldiers, and the body of Chairman Johnson completely naked, was hanged upside down on one of them. His mistress, still wearing her nightdress, was also hanged upside down. The other bodies were set in a circle round the two posts.

Whilst this was going on, the brigadier had begun his broadcast, preceded by military music, interspersed with pieces of Mozart, Handel and Bach. The brigadier, after being introduced by a young captain from the Information Section of the Army, said in confident tones,

"Fellow citizens of Bassa, Good Morning. I am very happy to inform you that loyal, decent-minded, officers and men of the Bassain Armed Forces, have today overthrown the illegal, illegitimate, usurper regime of the traitor Kofi Johnson. His government is no more, and the democratically elected government which was unjustly and illegally overthrown has been restored to office with immediate effect. Johnson and his friends have been captured, have been dealt with military precision and certainty. Evidence of this is available at Green Star Square.

I wish to take this chance to thank very much the invaluable and indispensable contribution which certain American and Israeli comrades made to the great success of today. Bassa owes these unsung heroes an enormous amount of gratitude. Whilst you rejoice, please, keep calm and leave it to the Army to do any sorting out of bad, unwholesome elements within itself. Here's the former Acting Prime Minister, thank you".

Pat Podo began nervously "Ladies and Gentlemen, this is a historic day in the lives of all of us. This is the day when infamy and treachery got their due rewards. We do not have enough words to thank the loyal officers and men of the Armed Forces of Bassa who have made this day possible, and have brought back decency, the rule of law and democratic government back to our country. Our heartfelt thanks go to them and to their few dedicated Americans and Israelis, who were prepared to lay down their lives for Bassa.

As we resume office, we invite you all to celebrate this great joyous day, but please, please avoid unnecessary recriminations and acts of vengeance. We shall set in motion the due process of law to deal with all those responsible for plunging Bassa into this nightmare. For our part, we shall continue to do our very best to uphold our constitution, the rule of law and observe all the human rights of our citizens. We shall indeed learn from our past experiences, and mistress.

Finally, following the death of our dear President four months ago, our first order following our release and restoration to office is to appoint Mrs Pearl Kambu as President, for all the dedication and immense, super-human contribution which she made personally to bring this day about.

She is American, she is white, but in her heart of hearts, and in her actions she is more Bassain than many, many of us. Ladies and Gentlemen, Pearl is our new President, for the duration of our term of office. We want to built Bassa into a land where Jews and Gentiles, whites and blacks, men and women, whatever their races, colour or religious persuasion, live in harmony and tolerance, working for the same purpose, the upliftment of humanity and the reduction, if not the eradication, of human suffering and ill-will. Thank you all, and may the Almighty God bless you all".

As he finished his speech, the mass demonstrations had already started in Appapa. The same old placards saying "Hang them all", "No Mercy", "Firing Squad", "No trials", "Hang them by their big balls', "Let the blood flow", were all back in motion. It looked exactly like the good or bad old days. Jamie and his brave men were airborne in their helicopters, en route to New York. Their mission had been accomplished hundred percent, with sadly a bit of bloodshed, but certainly no loss of life.